# Secrets
## *at the*
# Dover Café

Ginny Bell went to school in Dover, never realising at the time what a fascinating and crucial role the town played in World War Two. She is an editor with The Novelry where she works with new writers. *The Dover Café at War* was her first novel and there are now six books in the Dover Café series.

**Also by Ginny Bell:**
*The Dover Café at War*
*The Dover Café on the Front Line*
*The Dover Café Under Fire*
*Return to the Dover Café*
*The Dover Café on Trial*

# Secrets
## at the
# Dover Café
## Ginny Bell

ZAFFRE

First published in the UK in 2026 by
ZAFFRE
An imprint of Bonnier Books UK
5th Floor, HYLO, 105 Bunhill Row,
London, EC1Y 8LZ



A CIP catalogue record for this book is available from the British Library.

Paperback ISBN: 978-1-78512-910-0

*Also available as an ebook and an audiobook*

1 3 5 7 9 10 8 6 4 2

Design and Typeset by IDSUK (Data Connection) Ltd
Printed and bound in Great Britain by CPI (UK) Ltd, Croydon CR0 4YY

The authorised representative in the EEA is Bonnier Books UK (Ireland) Limited.
Registered office address:
Block B, The Crescent Building
Northwood, Santry
Dublin 9, D09 C6X8
Ireland
compliance@bonnierbooks.ie
www.bonnierbooks.co.uk

*To Ali. The very best sister anyone could wish for.
I would be lost without you.*

# Cast of Characters

**The Market Square**

**Castle Family**
*Nellie Castle* – Opinionated matriarch of Castle's Cafe
*Donald Castle* (died in 1927) – Nellie's husband

    **Nellie's children & Grandchildren:**
*Rodney* (32) – Officer in the navy
*Marianne* (30) – Best cook in Dover, lives and works at Castle's Café
    *Donny* (11) – Marianne's son
    *Teddy* – Marianne's baby son
*Jimmy* (25) – Currently fighting for the French Resistance
*Bert* (23) – Corporal in the army, away on a mission
*Edie* (21) – Works as a mechanic at Pearson's Garage, married to Bill Penfold
    *Vivien* – Edie's baby daughter
*Lily* (19) – A trainee nurse at the Casualty Hospital

**Castle's Café**
*Jasper Cane* – Donald Castle's best friend, surrogate father to the Castle children
*Cissy Ford* – Nellie's cousin, lives at the café
*Elodie* – French orphan, rescued by Colin, now living and working at the café
*Alfie Lomax* – Marianne's husband. Corporal in the 5th Buffs. Recently left Dover
*Gladys* – Worked at Castle's Café. Murdered by Susan Blake, 1941

**Abbots Cliff House**
*Marge Atkinson* – Good friend of Marianne, Reenie and Edie. Officer in Wrens
*Maria Longhorn* – Marge's colleague
*Emily White* – Marge's colleague
*Becky Purviss* – Marge's colleague
*Captain Thomas Bennett* – Marge's commanding officer
*Mrs Benson* – Housekeeper

**Casualty Hospital**
*Nurse Dot Calloway* – Lily's friend
*Colonel Jeremy Mason* – Patient. Obsessed with Lily

## Turners' Grocery

*Ethel Turner* – Good friend of Nellie's
*Brian Turner* – Ethel's husband
*Reenie Turner* – Their niece and Marianne's friend, left Dover to become a land girl
*Louis* – French orphan rescued by Colin, now living and working at the shop

## Perkins' Fish

*Phyllis Perkins* – Good friend of Nellie's
*Reg Perkins* – Phyllis's husband
*Wilf Perkins* – Their son
*Freddie* – Wilf's son and Donny's best friend

## Bakery – the Guthries

*Mary and Jack*
*Colin* – Mary and Jack's son. Currently fighting in France with Jimmy Castle
*Susan Blake* – Mary's niece, in prison for murder

## The Royal Oak

*Mavis Woodbridge*
*Derek* – Mavis's husband
*Stan* – Mavis and Derek's son
*Daisy* – Wife of Stan, was a good friend of Marianne, Reenie and Marge. Died 1940

## Pearson's Garage (Where Edie works)

*Clive Pearson* – Edie's boss
*Bill Penfold* – Mr Pearson's nephew and pilot with the RAF. Married to *Edie Castle*

## The Fanshawes

*Henry Fanshawe* – Donny's father, currently in an asylum
*Elspeth Fanshawe* – Henry's wife. In prison for spying
*Jeremy Fanshawe* – Henry's brother, runs Fanshawe's Brewery

## Other Characters

*Katy Atkinson* – Marge's sister. Missing for sixteen years
*Muriel Palmer* – Runs the WVS
*Dr Palmer* – Muriel's husband
*Lou Carter* – Runs whelk stall in market square. Local gossip and secretly runs black market business
*Terence Carter* – Lou's son. Wheeler dealer on the black market
*Mr Wainwright* – Local solicitor, in love with Cissy Ford
*Adelaide Frost* – Member of market square community
*Mr Arthur Gallagher* – Runs the newsstand
*Tom Burton* – Cobbler
*Ron Hames* – Journalist at *Dover Express*
*Bertha Bancroft* – Spiritual medium
*Captain Gilbert Roberts* – Head of Western Approaches Tactical Unit
*Peter Holmes* – SIS agent

# A Brief Background About The Game

On 1 January 1942, Captain Gilbert Roberts was charged with setting up the Western Approaches Tactical Unit. The Allies were suffering heavy losses in the Atlantic, thanks to the very effective U-boat hunting packs, and the threat of starvation to Britain was horrifyingly real.

Arriving at Western Approaches in Liverpool, Roberts recruited a group of Wrens to help him devise war games to teach naval captains new manoeuvres that would help them avoid U-boat attacks.

To do this, Roberts and his team studied battle reports from convoy escorts and recreated the battles in war games to try to work out how the U-boats were operating. Once they'd done that, they then devised manoeuvres and tactics by which the escorts could evade and/or defeat the U-boats.

These games were played out on the top floor of Western Approaches, with chalk grids and counters. The first game they created was called Raspberry – not after the fruit, but because one of the women suggested they were blowing raspberries at Hitler. Later games were named Pineapple and Banana.

The team ran weekly six-day courses from 1942 to 1945 and despite early scepticism, the results spoke for themselves, as gradually the tide began to turn in the Battle of the Atlantic, and the German U-boat fleet shrank.

After the war, although Captain Roberts was recognised for his contribution, the women who worked alongside him were largely forgotten.

That has changed in recent years, however, and the Wrens' role in helping to beat the deadly U-boat packs has been recognised in various ways. Simon Parkin's book *A Game of Birds and Wolves* provides a fascinating insight not only into the background to the games and their effectiveness, but also into the lives of the Wrens and Captain Roberts – the scene in my book where Marge is launched along the table like a torpedo was inspired by a similar party described in his book. The men and women of Western Approaches worked hard, but they certainly knew how to party!

In 2022, a TV docudrama called *U-boat Wargamers* was made – and is available to watch for anyone who's interested. I confess, I haven't watched it, because I only discovered it after I wrote the book, and I was scared to know how much I got wrong!

But I'm glad that after so many years, the women who helped Roberts become the German Navy's most feared enemy, have now been recognised.

I first read about The Game when I was researching one of my earlier Dover books, and I immediately decided that I would have to include it at some point. Luckily, I already had a character ready and waiting to be selected by Captain Roberts to help him. And so I waited patiently until I finally reached a point in the war where Marge could step up. She strikes me as someone who would have been a perfect fit for Roberts' elite group of Wrens.

I've taken a few liberties with history in my own story. The game was in its very early stages in January 1942, so I doubt they were running courses yet – but it suited the timing of my book to change this slightly.

Plus, although Roberts set up a couple of satellite centres to teach the game, none were on the south-east coast. But Wrens were stationed at Abbots Cliff House during the war to listen in on German shipping communications. At the time, according to one of the Wrens who lived and worked there, it was a rattly, damp house, but they made the most of their time by hosting parties and, from the sound of it, having a lot of fun! So, I decided it seemed like a good place to station Marge and her friends.

Now, Abbots Cliff House is completely restored and very beautiful. It's available to rent as a holiday let, if any of you fancy spending a couple of weeks high on the cliffs in Capel-le-Ferne. The views really are spectacular! And, of course, the sound mirror is just a short walk away. It might look like an ugly lump of concrete, but I found it so fascinating, I just had to include it!

# Prologue

*November 1941*

Ellen walked slowly along the platform at Dover Priory Station as people streamed past her, some tutting impatiently at her dawdling. The salty tang in the air mixed with steam from the train brought memories she'd shut away for years flooding into her mind.

She stepped through the exit and looked around, taking in the damaged, smoke-stained buildings, the evidence of war everywhere. Everything looked the same, but different. Much like her.

Gripping the cardboard suitcase that contained some spare underwear, a pair of stockings and her prized silk dressing gown with the dragon embroidered on the back, Ellen walked down towards the High Street, limping slightly in her too-big shoes – they had been all the WVS had. They'd also given her a brown pleated skirt, a white blouse, a navy blue jersey and a musty-smelling black wool coat. For the first time in years, she looked like a woman of thirty-one, as opposed to the twenty-one she had been trying so hard to maintain. In fact, if she were being brutally honest, she looked more like forty-one, but beggars couldn't be choosers. And she was definitely a beggar now.

Gritting her teeth, she walked on. It was time to face her past.

# Chapter 1



*Castle's Café, Dover, January 1942*

Nellie Castle glanced at the clock for the umpteenth time; never had the day felt so long, and yet it *still* wasn't five o'clock. In the kitchen, her eldest daughter Marianne was kneading dough, while Elodie, the French orphan they'd taken in the previous year, was preparing one of her famous stews for the following day. Her cousin Cissy was in the pantry singing an old music hall tune that Nellie hadn't heard since the last war. 'Algernon, oh, Algernon, I'm fairly gone on you.' She'd always hated that song. For a woman who had made her living playing the violin, Cissy really couldn't hold a tune. At least she sounded cheerful, which was more than could be said for Nellie. But that was nothing new. She didn't think she'd felt cheerful since before the war.

The café was only half full, a few soldiers and, of course, Adelaide Frost, who'd been lurking here most of the day with her blasted knitting, her long nose twitching as she listened in to the conversations around her. Her grey hair was pulled into such a tight bun that her eyebrows were raised, making her look perpetually shocked – which she generally was. Still, the eavesdropping kept her from quoting the Bible, so small mercies and all that. Opposite Adelaide, Muriel Palmer was expounding self-importantly about her volunteer work at the new community restaurant.

Nellie ground her teeth. She would never begrudge any poor blighter a cheap meal, but they could have set up somewhere else. Instead, the Ministry of Food had opened it in St Mary's church hall, barely three minutes' walk from the café. If it was so great, why didn't the two of them stay there, she thought sourly.

'Oh, Mrs Castle,' Muriel called over. 'I've been trying to persuade young Elodie to help us out with some cooking at the restaurant. And bless her, the girl seemed not to understand what I was saying. But it would be *so* beneficial for *the people* if they could sample some of her Potofer.'

Nellie frowned. '*Potofer?* I ain't got the foggiest what you're talkin' about. And Elodie's got enough to do here without you stealin' her off me.'

'"One person gives freely yet gains even more; another withholds unduly but comes to poverty,"' Adelaide intoned, her eyes never leaving her clacking needles.

Nellie's cheeks heated. 'I've already come to poverty! And I can't spare the girl. End of.'

Muriel dabbed at her lips with a napkin. 'Come, come, Mrs Castle! We need all hands on deck at a time like this. And I wouldn't dream of asking Marianne. She's got her hands full enough, what with the baby and all.'

'Such a sweet child. I was there, you know, when he was born.' Adelaide's expression softened. 'I like to think it was our encouragement that brought little Teddy forth just a tiny bit quicker.'

Nellie rolled her eyes. The story of her grandson's birth during a shell attack the previous May had become Dover folklore. She wished she'd been here, rather than at the Old Bailey in London, where she was giving evidence at Susan Blake's trial. She shuddered, glancing instinctively over at the window, as though expecting to see her friend Gladys collapsing outside, a bullet in her stomach, and Susan Blake holding a gun. It was almost a year since Gladys had died protecting her youngest son, Bert, but she saw the scene frequently in her nightmares, the shock and horror as fresh as if it had happened yesterday.

Just as she relived those moments in the witness box when she'd stood in the highest court in the land and lied, placing the blame for Susan's horrific act on Bert and her daughter Edie.

The familiar anger and remorse rose in her throat, almost choking her. Why had she listened to Rodney? It was her eldest son who'd insisted she betray them. But she couldn't blame him entirely. After all, she was the one who'd set this sorry chain of events into motion fourteen years ago when her husband Donald had died.

She'd betrayed her children to protect herself, and she'd been paying the price ever since because neither Bert nor Edie were speaking to her. And who could blame them?

Since that awful day, Edie had barely left the garage at the top of Castle Hill where she lived and worked. It was a mere twenty minutes' walk away – but she could have been living in Timbuktu as far as Nellie was concerned. She'd not even been allowed to visit when Edie's daughter Vivien had been born.

As for Bert, he'd left Dover and married Dot, a nurse at the hospital, without saying a word about it to her. Dot had returned to Dover months ago, but Bert had apparently disappeared off the face of the earth. If her daughter-in-law knew where he was, she was keeping it to herself.

Then there was Jasper . . . Her heart ached a little at the thought of the man she loved. He'd been disgusted with her, and though he was one of the few people who understood why she'd lied in court, their relationship had changed. He still came to the café, but his previous warmth had disappeared. She'd taken his love for granted for years, and now it was gone, the colour had leached out of her life.

Every time she saw him, she could sense the weight of the question hanging between them. He was waiting for her to confess her deepest secrets to him, but he was expecting too much. No matter that her heart was breaking, some things were better left unsaid.

She glanced at the clock again. At last!

She clapped her hands. 'Right, everyone, that's your lot. Time to leave.'

'Give us a chance to finish our tea, woman!'

She turned a hard gaze on Mr Gallacher, who spent far too much time here, when he should be manning his newspaper stand. 'Don't you woman me! Out!' She pointed to the door. 'And when you return, bring your manners with you.' She bustled out from behind the long, dark-wood counter and went to stand over him, watching beadily as he drank the last of his tea.

'There now, that weren't so hard. Up you get.' She went to open the door, but someone shoved it from the other side with such violence, she stumbled back, as a tall man wearing a black trilby low over his brow, a long camel-hair coat and a scarf pulled over his mouth walked in.

'We're shut!' she snapped, recovering her balance.

He pulled the scarf down and looked at her. 'Not to me you ain't,' he said in a voice like gravel.

Nellie shivered at the coldness in his brown eyes, but she refused to back down. Folding her arms, she widened her stance. 'To the whole bloody world 'cept Churchill and the King.'

Ignoring her, the man shouldered past and sat down at one of the tables. He gestured to the customers. 'Might be better if this lot go, though.'

'How rude!' Adelaide tutted, her eyes gleaming with curiosity as she examined the man.

He exuded menace, and Nellie was suddenly overcome with misgiving. Whoever he was and whatever he wanted, she sensed she'd better do what he said.

'Come on, you lot. Out!' She opened the door and went to stand outside, shivering as the cold wind gusted up her skirt.

'Psst, Nellie.'

Nellie jumped and looked to her left. In the darkness she could just make out the figure of a large woman wearing a long dark coat and hat.

'Is that you, Lou?' Suddenly the man's presence made sense. She should have bloody known it!

Lou Carter represented yet another mistake she'd made. In a weak moment after the trial, she'd agreed to let the woman store some of her black-market goods in her basement in return for her ensuring that Nellie's testimony never made it into the local press. Apparently, Lou had dirt on the journalist, and to be fair, it never had been printed in the *Dover Express*.

But Dover was a small town, and since the war had started there weren't that many locals left, so the fact that she'd told everyone at the Old Bailey that Edie was spiteful and vengeful, and Bert was a heartless seducer of innocents had gone round the town in a flash. But a promise was a promise, and Nellie wasn't one to welch on a deal.

Recently, though people had started to mutter about the suspicious-looking men who periodically turned up at the café, so she'd put her foot down. Not hard enough, though, if the spiv who'd walked in as though he owned the place was anything to go by.

'Lou?' she repeated. 'Is that bloke one of your mates?' she snapped.

'I . . . I'm sorry, Nell, but . . .'

Nellie could almost feel the tension vibrating off the other woman, and it made her anxious. Lou had more front than Blackpool, and she'd never heard her sound scared before.

'Good evening, Nellie,' Adelaide Frost called, her tone dripping with curiosity.

She looked over her shoulder. 'Bye, Adelaide, Muriel.' She listened as their footsteps walked away, then turned back. 'Well?' she hissed. 'I told you that the deal was off. I did my bit, but I can't risk it anymore. So if your mate wants to use my basement, he's out of luck.'

Lou reached out and grasped Nellie's arm. 'You better do what 'e says, Nell. Seriously, this bloke ain't your run-of-the mill spiv.' Then she turned and walked away, leaving her words to settle like lead in Nellie's stomach.

Shivering, she went back into the café. Doing her best to ignore the man, she took a mental note of where everyone was. Marianne, Elodie and Cissy in the kitchen, Teddy was upstairs with Donny, who was earning money babysitting his brother for a few hours each day while his mother worked. They should be safe there, at least. No matter what Lou said, she had no intention of doing what this man wanted.

She cast a sidelong glance at him. He'd unbuttoned his coat, and the left side hung low, the inside pocket revealed. Poking out of the top, she could see the handle of a gun.

A sliver of fear uncoiled in her belly as it occurred to her that this wasn't about stashing a box of tea and some petrol in her basement. This was something much more dangerous.

# Chapter 2



*Western Approaches, Liverpool, January 1942*

'Gotcha!' Marge Atkinson jumped up from the floor and threw a small counter into the air. She'd removed her uniform jacket, and her navy-blue skirt was smudged with chalk dust. Her bright red hair was pulled off her face and pinned in a victory roll. It took ages each morning, but Marge was a firm believer that if you looked good, you felt good. It didn't always work, but it definitely helped.

The floor was marked out in a large grid; the chalk lines spaced exactly ten inches apart, some with a black or white counter sitting within the box. The four other women who'd been playing the game with her, stood up and clapped. To the untrained eye the room looked like the scene of a children's game, and sometimes that's exactly how Marge felt when she played. It was wonderful to be allowed to let her competitive streak show without feeling judged.

Her colleague Becky Purviss came out from behind one of the canvas screens that had been set up around the room. She'd been sending orders to her teammate, Emily White, who'd singularly failed to avoid the torpedo from Marge's U-boat. 'You've just sunk a ship full of food,' she said. 'Not sure you should be celebrating quite so hard.'

'The point is, Purviss, that you failed to give the correct order to your ship to avoid the attack,' said a small, thin man wearing naval uniform with four gold bands at the cuffs of his jacket. His hair was slicked back with Brylcreem, ears sticking out prominently, giving him a boyish appearance that was not matched by his grave expression.

Becky scowled. 'I used the same manoeuvre the *Memnon* used, as instructed.'

Marge smirked. Her friend hated to lose as much as she did. Earlier that day, Becky had successfully dropped a depth charge on her U-boat, and Marge had had a job holding on to her temper.

The other women emerged from behind the screens. Sixteen Wrens, each carefully selected to take part in Captain Roberts' top-secret project, which so far consisted of learning naval manoeuvres and moving counters around the floor.

'Just so!' The captain leapt forward, his face alight with excitement. 'And this was exactly the result we expected. And *this* is why we're here.' He swept his hand around the cavernous room that took up the top floor of the Royal Navy headquarters in Liverpool. 'And you know what they say, don't you? If you always do what you've always done, then you'll always get what you've always got!' He pointed triumphantly at Marge, who raised the counter in a gesture of victory. 'This is what's been happening ever since the war started. And that's why we're here, ladies – to teach our naval officers new tactics and new methods. Because if something doesn't change soon' – he looked around at each of them, his expression deadly serious – 'this country will not only lose the war, but we will starve.'

Marge dropped the counter onto the linoleum floor, and in the shocked silence that followed his statement, the sound echoed around the room.

'In recent months the merchant navy has lost scores of ships, each one full of equipment and food. Food destined for this small island that is trying its darndest to survive against the odds. So, this might look like a game' – he gestured towards the floor – 'but make no mistake, this is deadly serious and could help save this country.'

Marge stared around her. This looked nothing like the head-quarters of a top-secret project. There were no filing cabinets, no typewriters, no papers or plotting boards on the wall.

'You don't believe me, ladies? Well, the results will speak for themselves.' He put his arms behind his back and began to pace in front of them, his head bent forward slightly, as if he was walking against a headwind. 'But there is still much to do before we can prove our worth. More tactics to learn, more manoeuvres, and more games. We can't play Raspberry for-ever, because once it's used at sea, the enemy will soon work it out. We must keep moving forward at all times!' He pointed towards the ceiling, and for some reason they all looked up.

Then they glanced round at each other and giggled. They might be doing important war work, but honestly, after the jobs they'd been doing – mostly plotting room work or typing – this one was by far the best. Challenging, of course – you needed a good memory and good maths to be able to plot the ships' courses – but compared to the back-breaking hours she used to spend hunched over a plotting table in the tunnels beneath Dover Castle, this felt more like a holiday.

Captain Roberts clapped his hands. 'Right, then! Back we go. Positions everybody. Atkinson, I want you to be the captain this time – take a seat behind the canvas, please.'

Obediently, she went to sit behind a white canvas screen. A hole had been cut into it, giving her a restricted view of the floor, designed to imitate the field of vision a ship's captain would have in an actual battle. And the game began again. This time she got to give the orders and so, keeping an eagle eye on the shipping positions, she passed continual orders to her runner. On the floor, Becky was now in charge of her merchant ship, while behind another screen Emily was passing orders for the U-boats.

The game was swift and tense, and by the end, Marge had successfully sunk Emily's submarine. This time she didn't leap up. She'd always known this was a serious project, but after what Captain Roberts had just told them, she had truly begun to understand that this was far more than a game. This could be life or death for the officers they would teach. From now on she would focus and learn until she knew every manoeuvre possible to help their ships avoid the hunting packs of U-boats that had been laying waste to allied shipping in the Atlantic.

After another couple of games, with the captain constantly making minute adjustments to the tactics and manoeuvres, they were all exhausted.

'Good work today, ladies,' Captain Roberts said. 'I understand there's a bit of a party on tonight. Go and enjoy. You all deserve it.

'Why don't you join us, sir?' Marge asked hopefully. She'd grown to like the Roberts. He was a hard taskmaster, but he was unfailingly polite and respectful, and he never patronised them. Quite the opposite: he expected a high level of numeracy and intelligence, and if they couldn't grasp the game quickly, then they were transferred.

'My party days are over, Atkinson. But I believe a few big ships have just docked. No doubt, there'll be plenty of young men eager for some winsome company.'

Marge laughed. At thirty, she was the oldest of the group, and her winsome days were well and truly behind her.

There was a knock at the door and another Wren came in with some messages. 'From the plotting room, sir.' She handed them to Captain Roberts. These were the day's shipping movements that he would pore over for the rest of the night.

'And something for you.' The girl handed a slip of paper to Marge, winked, then turned and left.

Marge glanced at the message and smiled, recognising her old friend from Dover, Jeanie's, writing. She'd transferred at the same time as Marge, and it had been wonderful to have a friend here.

*Aeneus* docked today! All crew returned safely.

She caught her breath. Rodney was back! Rodney Castle had left Dover to return to active duty shortly after she had transferred to Liverpool. And ever since, there had been a constant thrum of anxiety in the back of her mind. Playing this game had made the worry even more acute as she now fully understood the dangers of an Atlantic crossing. Despite the fact that they'd parted on bad terms, he was the last thing she thought about as she went to sleep and the first thing she thought about in the morning. She'd never considered herself to be one of those women who clung to the memory of a man when they'd made it clear they didn't want her. Yet it seemed she was.

Becky was looking at her curiously. 'Not bad news, is it?'

'Nope. Just news about someone I used to know.' She screwed up the paper and threw it in the bin.

# Chapter 3

*Castle's Café*

Nellie practically ran into the kitchen; she needed to get everyone out of there.

'Who's that, Mum?' Marianne was standing by the large oak table in the middle of the kitchen, kneading dough for tomorrow's bread.

Nellie ignored the question. 'I'll finish that, love. You get upstairs and see to Teddy.'

Cissy came out of the pantry, a tea towel over her shoulder, hands dripping soapy water onto the tiled floor. 'Did I hear you say you'd finish the kneadin'?' she asked, her sparse auburn eyebrows raised.

'That's what I said. You can finish the washing up later. You too, Elodie, love. Up you go. I'll 'elp you sort it all out later.'

'Quick, mark this down!' Cissy cackled. 'January twelfth, 1942, Nellie Castle offered to knead the dough and 'elp with the washin' up.'

'Just go, will you,' Nellie said, glancing anxiously over her shoulder.

Curious, Cissy looked through the kitchen door and her smile dropped. She shook her head. 'I thought this were all

over, Nell,' she said quietly. 'You promised you'd 'ave nothin'
more to do with that woman's contacts.'

'This is nothin' to do with Lou,' she said sharply. 'It's a private
meetin' with a new supplier, so go upstairs an' I'll explain later.'

Elodie and Marianne each glanced through the door as they
went to the stairs that led up to their flat.

'He doesn't look like a butcher or baker,' Marianne hissed
suspiciously as she went past.

Nellie tried to give her a reassuring smile. 'What, they all
look the same, do they? Go on, get on with you.'

Marianne didn't look convinced, but she did as she was told.

Cissy, however, proved more difficult. 'I ain't leavin' you
alone with him. I'll stay right 'ere.'

'Don't be so dramatic, Ciss. Get upstairs and start the dinner if you want to be useful.'

Cissy narrowed her eyes. 'If that's just a new supplier, then
no reason I can't sit in, is there?'

'Please, Ciss.'

Cissy sighed in defeat. 'Shout if you need me, love. But after
this, you an' me will be havin' words.'

Once they'd disappeared, Nellie took a deep breath and
stalked back into the café, determined not to show her fear. The
man looked relaxed, leaning back in the chair, his long legs,
clad in smart wool trousers, sprawled in front of him. But no
matter how well-groomed he was, the man radiated menace.

'Make yerself at home, why don't ya?' she said sarcastically.

He chuckled and removed his hat, revealing dark hair, shiny
with oil. 'Pleasure to meet you, Mrs Castle.'

Nellie pursed her lips and stared back at him. Without his
hat she was able to see him more clearly. He was a mountain of
a man, with wide shoulders, enormous hands and a broad face

with sly brown eyes, thick lips and a nose that seemed to have been spread across his face. He was smiling, but his eyes held a cold, watchful expression.

'Who are you and why are you here?'

'Johnny Fox at your service,' he said mockingly. 'Heard tell that you 'ad a useful little basement down there.'

'What of it?'

'I got a few things needin' storage and a friend recommended this place.' He grinned, and she noticed that his two front teeth crossed over each other.

'Well, your friend were misinformed. I ain't in the business of doin' favours for spivs.'

The man wagged a finger as thick as a cigar at Nellie. 'That's all right then, cos I'm not askin' for a favour. I'm tellin' yer. We need your space for a bit. An' you will let us have it. Now, my associate's waitin' in your yard, so go open the door for 'im, there's a good girl.'

Nellie snorted. 'Don't you "good girl" me. My basement's for shelter only. And it's not as if there's a shortage of secret spaces round 'ere, is it? There's caves and shelters all over. Not to mention any number of abandoned buildings.'

'And risk any old Tom, Dick an' Harry wanderin' in? I prefer my hidin' places to come with built-in security. Now, I won't ask you again. Get the door.'

Nellie swallowed nervously at the unmistakable threat in his voice, and went to open the back door, where a figure loomed out of the darkness. Pushing through the blackout curtain, he walked along the narrow passage to the kitchen, where he dumped a couple of cardboard boxes on the table right next to the dough, causing a cloud of flour to rise into the air.

'Oy! Put that on the floor!'

Ignoring her, he went outside and brought another three boxes in, which he dropped on the floor next to the table. Each one was tied with thick string in a complicated knot, over which was a wax seal, and from the thump they made as he dropped them, they seemed quite heavy. With a nod at Johnny Fox, he left.

'All we ask is you store these boxes. Once in a while, someone'll collect one of 'em, and we'll be droppin' more off as and when. No need fer you to do a thing, love. So long as you keep yer trap shut, and the boxes safe, you an' me'll be golden.'

Nellie stared at the boxes suspiciously. Aside from the string and the wax, they looked innocuous, and not at all difficult to hide, so she couldn't understand why he'd brought them here. 'What's in 'em?'

'That ain't your business. Now let's get these downstairs. That the way to the basement?' He gestured to the short corridor that led to the back door. When she nodded, he picked up a couple of the boxes and waited expectantly for Nellie to lead the way.

Nellie had no choice but to concede. The man was armed and dangerous, so she'd have to do what he said for now and figure out how to get out of this situation later.

She led him downstairs and into the basement. It was a large space, which they'd made as comfortable as they could, with colourful cushions around the wall, and some old café chairs set around a rickety table. Towards the back on the right, the ceiling sloped down, and it was here she'd created a space to hide things, back in the days when she used to buy a little extra from Lou's son Terence to help people who'd lost everything. Until she'd run out of money, she'd managed to feed a lot of people with that stuff.

These days she still gave as much as she could, but it was nothing like the elaborate food parcels she used to dish out. Instead, she tried to budget more carefully, saving up the flour and sugar so they could still make food to take to the caves, where so many people were forced to spend their nights – and even their days. Poor old Mr Evans who'd been so terrified of the shells he'd moved in, had died of pneumonia just a few months ago, as much a casualty of war as any who'd been killed by bombs or shells. But he would go unrecorded; just an old man dying a natural death. But what was natural about living in a cave?

She pulled the curtain aside, wishing she knew what she was dealing with. Those boxes might look harmless, but Johnny Fox wouldn't go to this much trouble if they weren't valuable.

'Nice little set-up you got here. Just a shame you use it as a shelter. Imagine how much you could put down here if it were shut. Any chance of closin' it off?'

'Sure, why not? Dunno why we hide from the shells anyway,' Nellie said sarcastically.

He shrugged. 'Just a thought, love. Stash that lot, will ya, Frank.'

The young man had followed them down and obediently crawled to the back of the space, pushing a box in front of him.

'Just a few more, Mrs Castle, then we'll be out of your hair,' Johnny Fox said as Frank crawled back out and went upstairs.

'Cover 'em with this.' Nellie grabbed an old picnic blanket from a crate by the wall and threw it at him. And I'm warnin' ya, if whatever that is gets found, I ain't keepin' me mouth shut about who left it.'

'Oh, I think you'll keep your mouth shut, Mrs C.' Johnny Fox smiled nastily. 'And if one of them seals gets broke, I'll know you've been peekin'.' He lowered his voice. 'And we really, really don't want that.'

Nellie turned away to hide her fear, and a thick silence fell, broken only when Frank returned with more boxes.

'That's the lot, guv,' he said.

Johnny nodded approvingly. 'Good job, mate. Get back to the motor and I'll join in a few.'

Once the boy had left, Johnny turned to her, malice gleaming in his eyes. 'By the way, you got a couple of smashin' little grandsons. An' then there's that little darlin' up at the garage. Me an' her mum 'ad a lovely chat while she were fixin' the motor. Now, what was her name . . .' He paused, his eyes never leaving Nellie's face, then he clicked his fingers. 'That's it, Vivien. Five months old an' pretty as a picture. Ain't you lucky to 'ave all your grandkids close.'

He put his hat back on, winked at her and strolled to the stairs.

Nellie stood stock-still, unable to even breathe. It was only when she heard the back door close that she drew in a long, shaky breath. Going over to the table, she dropped into a chair and put her head in her hands. The message had been received loud and clear. *Keep your mouth shut. Or the babies would pay the price.*

# Chapter 4

*Western Approaches*

It was getting late and the party was in full swing in the ward-room, the air thick with cigarette smoke, and a gramophone played 'Ain't Misbehavin'' at full volume. The furniture had been pushed to the sides, and a long table was littered with bottles, ashtrays and glasses. Naval officers and Wrens chattered over each other, while a few attempted to dance in the cramped space. Marge poured herself a small measure of rum and turned to look out over the scene. Her head was spinning and she knew she should call it a night, but leaving a party early went against the grain. She knocked back the rest of the drink and poured herself another.

Someone banged into her and the drink sloshed onto the table. Cursing, she turned to see Emily being twirled around by her partner.

A man's voice suddenly rose above the cacophony. 'Who wants to be the torpedo?'

Marge grinned wickedly. 'Emily'll do it!' Her eyes slid to the slim blonde. Small and dainty with brown eyes, Emily was nineteen but could have passed for fifteen. She was also one of the cleverest women she'd ever met.

Although she didn't look very clever right now. Her hair was falling round her face and her lipstick was smudged. She was clearly drunk, but not so drunk that she couldn't level a death stare at Marge.

'Oh no, I think Marge would be much better suited. She's the right size after all.'

Marge glowered at her. But then her lips twitched. 'I prefer statuesque,' she responded. She'd always been the tallest of any of her friends, and the most curvaceous. Although since rationing, she was slimmer than she'd been since she was fourteen.

Emily grinned back. 'Touché.'

Around them, chants of 'Marge, Marge, Marge!' started up.

Marge took a large gulp of her rum and slammed the glass down on the table. 'All right, I'll do it!'

Tucking her shirt more securely into her skirt, she patted down her hair and marched over to a couple of officers, who were positioning two tables down the centre of the room.

Becky approached her. 'Are you sure about this?'

'Why wouldn't I be? Just make sure the cushions are ready.'

Whoops and cheers rang out as Marge lay down on her stomach on the table. Four men stood on either side of her, and at her nod, two grasped an ankle each, while the others held her beneath her shoulders.

'Ready . . .' They picked her up. 'Aim.' They swung her back. 'Fire!' They launched her down the table, and Marge slid along it so fast that she flew off the end and crashed into a man who was standing too close. His drink went flying and instinctively he put his arms around her as they both fell to the floor, his breath leaving him with an audible 'Oof' as Marge landed on top of him.

There was a moment's shocked silence, then the room erupted into laughter and cheers as Marge, red-faced, stared down into the man's face.

'God, sorry, Martin,' she muttered. 'You all right?'

He tightened his arms around her. 'Oh, yes. Haven't felt this good in years.' Then lifting his head his lips latched on to hers.

Just for a moment, Marge allowed him to kiss her, before pulling away, leaping to her feet and executing a wobbly curtsey.

It was only as she straightened, blowing her hair out of her face, that she noticed the figures in the doorway and her heart stopped.

Standing at the front of the group was Rodney Castle. For a moment their eyes locked, and she had an overwhelming desire to run into his arms.

But then she noticed his expression: cold and contemptuous. Anger washed through her. How *dare* he look at her like that! The man had no idea how to have fun. Well, she'd show him that she didn't miss him. Tossing her head, she held out a hand. 'What does a girl have to do to get a drink round here?'

As soon as a glass was pushed into her hand, she threw back the contents, her eyes never leaving Rodney's face.

He shook his head, his lips twisted in a slight sneer, then he turned on his heel and left.

Despite her anger, Marge had to resist the urge to go after him. Her days of chasing after Rodney Castle had ended the minute he'd told her he didn't love her.

She just wished she felt the same . . .

# Chapter 5

*Castle's Café*

Nellie wasn't sure how long she sat there, fear weighing down on her. But eventually, as the cold and damp started to seep into her bones, she stood and went over to the curtain. Pulling it back with shaking hands, she dragged off the picnic blanket and stared at the ten neatly stacked boxes, the white wax seals gleaming in the light. There was nothing to give a hint of what was inside. They were just plain cardboard boxes; the sort you might use to send a parcel in the post. And yet, they were so important that Johnny Fox had threatened her grandchildren.

Despite what he'd said, she was tempted to have a look. At least if she knew what she was dealing with she might be able to come up with a plan to get herself out of this mess. But she didn't dare. The man scared the living daylights out of her; even his name seemed threatening – a creature that hunts at night, taking whatever it wants and leaving a trail of destruction in its wake. No doubt he'd made it up for just that purpose.

Crawling into the space, she lifted one of the boxes and shook it. It was heavy and solid, but there was no rattle. So not ammunition then. But if it wasn't food, petrol or guns, what the hell was it?

Footsteps on the cellar steps made her back out of the small space and flip the curtain back into place.

'What you got yerself mixed up with this time?' Cissy stood in the doorway, eyes narrowed.

'Shouldn't you be clearin' up?' Nellie snapped.

Cissy flushed. 'Thought you was gonna do it. "I'll 'elp sort it out later,"' she parroted Nellie's words from earlier. 'I'm no fool, Nell, and that man . . .' She shook her head. 'He looked dangerous. You're out of your depth.'

'Oh, calm down, will ya. I'm just doin' him a favour.'

'You've never laid eyes on the bloke in your life,' she squeaked. As always when she was riled, Cissy's voice rose a few octaves. 'It were bad enough when you hid that stuff for Lou . . .' She paused. 'Oh, I get it. This is Lou's doing, ain't it?'

'Leave it, Ciss. It's nothin' for you to get your knickers in a twist about.'

'The only person I can think of who'd know a bloke like that is Lou bloody Carter,' Cissy continued, as if Nellie hadn't spoken. 'He looks like one of them gangsters from a film.' She shook her head. 'If you think Adelaide and Muriel'll keep schtum about this visitor, you're more stupid than I thought. But knowin' you, you won't listen to me. You always do just as you please.'

Nellie bristled. 'As I please? You've got no idea what I 'ave to do to keep this family safe!'

Cissy raised her eyebrows. 'You think lettin' a load of spivs use the basement – which the whole bloomin' market square tramps in and out of most days – is keepin' this family safe? If anythin', you're puttin' the family in danger. And I'm not goin' to sit around and watch you do it.'

Nellie let out a bitter laugh. 'What you gonna do? Call the police? Report me?'

'I'm gonna talk to Jasper, and me and him are gonna get rid of whatever they've left here! And yes, I'll call the coppers if I 'ave to!'

Panic fluttered in Nellie's stomach at the thought of the police or Jasper knowing about this. Not till she knew what all this was about. 'Don't you bloody dare! This 'as nothin' to do with you or Jasper. This is *my* house, *my* café, an' if you don't like what's goin' on, then you can bloody well leave!' It was the fear talking, and she regretted the words almost as soon as they were out of her mouth.

Cissy gasped. 'What the hell's got into you? Are you really puttin' Lou Carter and her mates ahead of me?' Her voice trembled and Nellie looked away, guilt eating at her. Her cousin had always stood loyally by her side. They'd been estranged for over thirty years until last year, and that had been all Nellie's doing. Throughout that time, Cissy had written to her every month, but Nellie had thrown the letters away unopened.

Her cousin drove her mad sometimes, with her high, piping voice and her screeching violin, yet no one had a better heart than Cissy. But Johnny Fox had cast a menacing shadow over her, and she couldn't let anyone else get involved. She was on her own with this one.

Cissy's stance softened. 'Just tell me what's goin' on, love,' she said, holding out her hand. 'Am I right? Is this Lou's doin'?'

Nellie didn't reply, but Cissy knew her too well, and her silence spoke volumes.

'You and her . . . I've never understood why you rate her so much.'

'Look, Ciss, just cos you're me cousin, it don't give you the right to tell me how to live me life! You left, remember? Me an' Lou 'ave a longer history than me an' you, so don't go passin' judgement on me.'

Cissy's eyes filled with tears. 'You an' me are connected by *blood*, Nell! An' that stands for a lot more than servin' that woman tea for the past thirty years.' She strode across the room and before Nellie could stop her, she'd whipped the curtain aside.

'I said leave it, Ciss!'

'Do you even know what's in them?' she said, staring at the boxes.

Again, Nellie didn't answer, and Cissy nodded knowingly. 'So, they could be bombs for all you know. One small spark and the café could go up.' She pointed a finger at Nell. 'Did you even think of that?'

Nellie winced as Cissy's voice rose even further, but at least she could reassure her on that. 'It's not bombs or guns,' she muttered.

'Oh, so you've examined them closely, 'ave you?'

'It don't feel like ammunition,' Nellie responded, pursing her lips.

'Lovely. Nellie Castle, who's never fired a gun in 'er life, knows there's no guns and bombs in the basement just from feelin' the box.'

Nellie shivered and wrapped her arms around herself as in her mind her ears rang with the sound of a gun firing, her hand tingling from the recoil . . . 'You don't know everythin' about me, Cissy. Trust me, there ain't no guns.'

Cissy dropped the curtain and turned to her, examining her face carefully. 'Oh, love. You're scared witless. You can't deal with this alone. You gotta trust someone, so if you don't want my help, then at least talk to Jasper. I know you an' him've been a bit distant since the kerfuffle at the trial – an' I can't say as I blame him – but you know he'll help if you need it. And so will I.'

Edie, apparently, had given Cissy a full account of what had happened at the trial and exactly what Nellie had said about her. The two had grown close over the past months. When Edie had given birth, it had been Cissy by her side, while Nellie sat at home waiting for news, her heart aching. Edie should have given birth here with her mother by her side, not in that poky little flat above Pearson's Garage, where the smell of oil seemed to have seeped into the carpet and walls.

The old anger started to bubble up, a welcome relief from the fear. It didn't matter that Edie had every right to hate her, it didn't matter that she'd brought this on herself; she wanted to see her granddaughter. Even Johnny Fox had seen her! But every time she'd gone up to the garage, Mr Pearson had gently turned her away. It was humiliating and heartbreaking, and her resentment at Cissy playing grandmother was like a lump of burning coal in her chest.

'I don't want you runnin' to Jasper. He's no more business than you interferin'.' She stalked towards the door.

Cissy sighed. 'You're a stubborn, stupid old woman! That man 'as every right! He's been by your side through thick and thin. He loved you when we was girls, an' he loves you still. An' you love him too, Nell. I saw you kissin' that night at the pub. So swallow your pride and do whatever you 'ave to to get him back. It's been months since the trial. Edie an' Bert might not ever forgive you, but Jasper will.'

Nellie looked away. If only it was that simple. Jasper understood exactly why she'd said what she had. For years, as far as Nellie was concerned, everyone believed Donald Castle had committed suicide. But on the day she'd died, Gladys had accused her of murdering him. She'd been first on the scene after Donald had shot himself and seen her standing over him with a gun.

At the time, Nellie had told her she'd just picked it up and Gladys had seemed to accept that. But apparently, she hadn't. She'd kept quiet because Donald's violent outbursts and abuse had threatened them all – especially the kids. She could still recall the row they'd had on the day Gladys died. The awful irony of their reconciliation by Donald's grave as they dug in the cold earth to plant some flowers, still made her want to weep.

What Gladys hadn't told her, though, was that she'd written about her suspicions in her diary. It was Sod's Law that the person who'd found that diary had been Susan Blake's aunt, Mary Guthrie.

So when she'd threatened to tell the court what was in the diary unless Nellie backed up Susan's defence of provocation, the fear of exposure and Rodney's insistence, had driven her to go along with it.

Jasper knew all of this and didn't blame her for Donald's death either. He'd watched as her husband had become increasingly unstable and threatening. No, that wasn't why he was keeping his distance. He wanted to know if Gladys was right. He wanted her confession . . .

Cissy shook her head sadly. 'What happened, Nell? You 'ad it all. Kids, grandkids, a man what loves you, a great business. Now two of yer kids won't speak to you an' Jasper's cold as an iceberg. An' you're risking it all to 'elp some gangster you don't know from Adam.'

'Just leave it,' Nellie snapped. If Cissy said one more word, she might say something she regretted, and she didn't want to alienate her cousin as well. She needed her now more than ever.

Cissy sighed. 'Sometimes, Nell, I don't think I know you at all. But one thing I do know is that you need to sort this out, or you're gonna end up in real trouble.' She brushed past her and went up the stairs, slamming the door behind her.

Nellie sat down and stared at the ceiling. Sometimes she didn't think she knew herself very well either. Since the war had started, her life had unravelled. Bert and Edie hated her; Jimmy, her middle son, had run off to France with his lover – Mary Guthrie's son Colin of all people! He'd run out of his wedding reception, leaving poor Reenie Turner heartbroken, and giving Mary another reason to hate her. And then Rodney had left his nice, safe desk job up at the castle and gone to sea. Only Marianne and her youngest daughter Lily were still with her. And, of course, her beautiful grandsons.

As for Jasper . . . hell would freeze over before he got what he wanted from her.

But what did it matter anyway? As he'd said on the night she'd told him as much about Donald's death as she could bear: sometimes love just isn't enough.

# Chapter 6

*Pearson's Garage, Dover*

Edie Castle paced the small sitting room, her tiny daughter screaming against her shoulder, which was wet with a combination of dribble and snot. She patted her little girl's back helplessly. 'Please, darling, please shh.'

Mr Pearson's bedroom door cracked open. 'Need a hand, love?'

'She just won't settle.' Edie was close to tears herself. During the day, her daughter was the perfect baby: sleeping, smiling and gurgling, while she and Mr P worked on the cars. With her fluffy white-blonde hair, her large, forget-me-not blue eyes and her ready smile, she charmed everyone. But at night she was a devil. It was as if she had two babies. Only Mr P knew how it was, and he was as exhausted as she was.

Her boss shuffled into the room, shrugging on a brown dressing gown over his blue striped pyjamas. 'You look done in, love. Go and rest, I'll see to the little 'un.'

Edie shook her head. 'You look done in yourself, Mr P Go back to bed.' Even before Vivien had been born, he'd looked thin and tired. He'd never fully recovered from being in prison the previous year after he'd been wrongly accused of spying.

The experience had taken its toll, and he'd recently developed a persistent cough.

Thinking about those fraught days made her realise that it had been just over a year since she'd married Bill. He'd come home on leave from the RAF to visit his uncle, only to find her running around frantically trying to find out where Mr P was being held. Between them, they'd managed to get him released and fallen in love in the process. And even though she'd been pregnant with another man's child, he'd still wanted to marry her.

They'd spent just one night together, and then he'd left. Sometimes she had to take out her marriage certificate, just to reassure herself that it hadn't all been a dream. So much had happened since then, and now she had a baby. What would he think of Vivvy?

It was so easy for him to *say* he'd accept another man's child, and his letters were always warm and loving, but the reality of sleepless nights, an exhausted wife and a messy home might change his mind. She looked around the sitting room. Old newspapers were piled in the corner, and a basket of ironing sat against one wall. Dirty cloths were slung across the cushions of the old brown sofa, and some wooden building bricks – carved by Jasper – were scattered across the blue carpet. He'd take one look at this chaos and run straight back to Lincolnshire. Flying bombing missions over Germany would seem like heaven compared to this.

'Come on, give her to me.' Mr Pearson reached over and took Vivien from her, settling her into the crook of his arm. Almost immediately the little monster quieted, gazing up at him with huge, tear-drenched eyes, her little rosebud mouth drooping open.

'There now, lovey. Things ain't so bad, eh?' he murmured, rocking her gently.

'I don't know how you do it.' Edie couldn't help feeling jealous. Did her daughter not love her? Was this how it would always be? It felt reminiscent of her relationship with her own mother; they'd always clashed, even before Edie had discovered that her mother had been instrumental in her father's death by drugging him with poppy head tea. Tea that Edie used to give him every day. She'd thought it was their special time. But in reality, the tea had driven him further into madness until finally he'd shot himself.

She shuddered, pushing away the image of her father's blood splattered across the wall, his face blown away. She'd been five at the time, and the memories had been buried deep in her psyche. But she'd always known something terrible had happened. The memories had resurfaced at the same time she'd met Bill, and sometimes she wished they'd stayed buried.

As if that wasn't enough, her mother had stood in court and declared that she was 'spiteful'! So spiteful and jealous, in fact, that she had driven a woman to murder. The familiar anger rose again, making her stomach fizz and her cheeks burn. She would never forgive her! Never! And she would do everything in her power to ensure that Vivvy was never exposed to that woman's lies.

'You need to let it go, Edie,' Mr Pearson said placidly. 'That or forgive your mum.'

She blinked at him. 'Are you a mind-reader as well as a baby charmer?'

'You've never been able to hide what you're thinkin', love. And your face goes all red and pinched when your mum comes to mind.'

Edie laughed slightly and sat down on the arm of the sofa beside Mr Pearson to ruffle her daughter's hair. 'I can't just forget. She lied to me all my life and then she told the world what a cow I am.'

Mr P sighed. 'I can't say as I blame you fer bein' so cross. But it don't do you no good to hold on to the anger. Babies pick up on that sort of thing.'

'You're blaming me for Vivvy not sleeping?' Edie snapped.

Mr Pearson smiled. 'You're a brilliant mum, love. I'm proud of you, an' Bill will be too, so don't have no worries on that score. Now, I heard Marianne offerin' to take her for the night the other day, so why don't you let her. She should be growin' up with her cousins. Specially little Teddy. They're practically twins.'

'Vivvy will set foot in that café over my dead body,' she gritted. 'If Marianne wants to have her for the night, she'll need to move.'

'It seems a shame.' Mr P looked down at Vivvy, who was still staring at him, her fist in her mouth. 'Cos your Auntie Marianne loves you, don't she?' He looked up at Edie. 'Not that I'm complainin', mind. I ain't been this well fed since before the war.'

Edie smiled. Ever since Vivvy had been born, the sight of her eldest sister pushing Teddy in his pram across the forecourt, a basket underneath containing some treat or other, had become a regular occurrence. She couldn't put her finger on it, but something about her sister's almost obsessive interest in Vivvy made Edie uneasy. She just had to hope that she paid more attention to her son when they were at home. Because when she was here, Teddy was left to sit in his pram while Marianne sat with Vivvy on her lap singing the nursery rhymes she should have been singing to her own boy. Edie tried to make up for it by showering Teddy with love and kisses and tickling his little fat tummy. But nothing could make up for the lack of a mother's love – and she knew that better than most.

'Looks like she's dropped off,' Mr P whispered.

Edie focused on her daughter again. 'You've got a magic touch. I don't know what I'd do without you.' She stroked her daughter's soft cheek with her finger. 'Do you think Bill will like her?'

'Bill's gonna fall in love with her same as everyone what claps eyes on 'er. She's special is our Vivvy.' He bent and kissed the little girl's fluffy head. When he looked up at her, his eyes were moist. 'You know me and the missus always wanted little 'uns. 'Ow I wish she could've met 'er. She'd've loved this baby somethin' fierce. Vivvy might not be my blood, but she lives right in the centre of me heart. She always will. An' it'll be the same for Bill. This one will 'ave him wrapped round her tiny finger in the blink of an eye.'

Edie smiled tremulously. 'I just hope he gets the chance to meet her.'

Mr P nodded, not bothering to offer empty platitudes; he knew as well as she did that the likelihood of Bill surviving the war was slim. The papers were full of the number of casualties the RAF continued to suffer. But she didn't need to read about it to believe it. She'd witnessed the brutal reality of air battles herself during the summer of 1940. And she saw it still: planes falling into the sea, or stuttering overhead, smoke trailing from their engines as they limped towards Hawkinge airfield.

The rumble of engines overhead just as she thought this almost made her chuckle. But then the air-raid siren started, and Vivvy's eyes flew open. For a moment she looked dazed, then she let out an ear-splitting yell.

Mr P winced. 'If we ain't careful, she'll be guidin' the entire Luftwaffe to the garage,' he grumbled as they made their way outside to the Anderson shelter.

Edie paused outside the shelter and looked up at the sky. Perched above her on the hill, the castle was lit by searchlights. And somewhere, way above them, young men with mothers, wives and children waiting at home carried out their orders, not knowing whether this might be their last night on earth.

'Come home to me soon, my love,' she whispered.

# Chapter 7

*Castle's Café*

'Mum, it's over.'

A hand shaking her shoulder startled Nellie out of a fitful sleep. She was sitting at the table in the basement, her head cradled on her arms. She winced as she sat up and stretched her neck. The long, high-pitched wail of the all-clear was echoing around the basement, and the slight throb that had been pulsing between her eyes since Johnny Fox's visit became an insistent hammer blow.

'What time is it?' she croaked. She'd barely got to bed last night before the siren had gone off, and once again the family had spent the night underground.

'Five thirty. No point going back to bed now.'

Somehow, even though Lily had returned from a fourteen-hour shift at the hospital just before the siren had gone off, she looked as fresh and lovely as though she'd had eight hours of uninterrupted sleep in a feather bed. Her blonde hair was gleaming and her blue eyes clear and bright. The resilience of youth, Nellie thought wryly. Still, at least she'd had time to put her curlers in before the siren had gone off, so she'd look halfway decent when they opened up.

'You look like death warmed up,' Cissy remarked as she folded the blankets and placed them back in an old trunk.

Or maybe she wouldn't.

'That's because she was sitting like a sentry at the table most of the night,' Lily responded. 'Honestly, Mum, you'll end up with a dodgy back if you're not careful.'

'You'd think she was keepin' watch or something,' Cissy remarked pointedly.

'What are you keepin' watch over, Gran?' her grandson Donny asked. His brown hair lay flat on one side of his head and stuck out on the other. At twelve, his voice had just started to deepen, and it always took her aback.

'I were lookin' out for you, of course,' she replied. 'And little Teddy. That's me job.'

'Come on, Don.' Marianne had Teddy slung over one shoulder. 'You can help get the café ready before breakfast. There's no point going back to bed now.'

Don groaned. 'Can't I look after Teddy instead?'

At the mention of his name, Teddy kicked his legs and squealed happily.

Marianne tutted. 'All right.' She put Teddy into his arms. 'He needs a change and a wash. Then I thought I might pop up to the garage quickly. I made too much food for Ted yesterday, and it'll only go to waste, so I thought Vivvy could have some.'

'You're goin' now?' Cissy squeaked.

'Just a quick visit before breakfast,' Marianne responded breezily. 'I'll be too tired after work. And I promised I'd bring her some of Elodie's stew.'

Cissy exchanged a concerned glance with Nellie.

'It's five thirty in the mornin'! Edie'll hardly be wantin' a horde of visitors. And who's gonna see to the café and start the breakfasts? What about you, Elodie? You hoppin' up to the garage too?' Nellie looked over at the young girl. She'd been with them ten months now, and she was still quiet as a little mouse. But by God, she could cook. And now she'd filled out a little, she'd turned into an absolute beauty. The young men were always peeking through the hatch at her. Maybe she should put a curtain up there as well, she mused.

'Don't worry, Mrs Castle. I will do breakfast,' Elodie said with a smile.

'It's too cold for Teddy to go out just yet. Anyway, he'll need a nap soon cos he didn't sleep well,' Donny said.

Bless him. It wasn't just his voice that was changing. Since his arrest a few months before, he'd become serious and careful. She wasn't sure whether it was the terror of being in custody, the threat of having to live with his father's family or his fierce love for his brother – or a combination of all three – that had done it. But the wild, naughty child he used to be had disappeared. And so had the cheeky lad who used to make her laugh. Where his eyes used to dance with mischief, they were now anxious. And though Nellie was relieved he'd stopped getting into trouble, how she missed that naughty, wayward little boy.

'I wasn't planning on taking Ted!' Marianne snapped. 'He always fusses when I leave him in the pram, and I don't get a chance to talk to Edie. Anyway, he much prefers being with you, Don, so why don't you give him his porridge and put him down for a nap.'

Nellie frowned. There was a worrying indifference in Marianne's attitude towards her younger son, and she had no idea how to make things better. When he'd been born, Marianne had made no secret of her disappointment that he wasn't a girl. She'd had her heart set on naming the baby after her friend Daisy, who'd been killed in a shell attack. Her husband Alfie had man-aged to talk her round. He was so clearly besotted with Teddy, and Marianne hated to upset her husband. But then two things had happened: first, Alfie's regiment had been posted away from Dover; and secondly, Edie had given birth to a blonde, blue-eyed child, who looked so like Daisy it was uncanny.

Ever since, Marianne had begun to visit the garage more fre-quently, and her feelings for her own son seemed ambivalent. Nellie was utterly baffled how any mother could be indifferent to their baby, especially as Teddy was such a cheerful little thing.

'Mum, I don't think Auntie Edie would like a visit this early. But maybe when you go next, Gran should go with you,' Donny said. 'I keep tellin' Auntie Edie that Gran'd love to see her, but she just pretends she don't hear me. I don't understand grown-ups. You tell us kids not to argue, but it's all any of you seem to do.' Holding Teddy close, he swept from the room.

'All right, all right! I won't go,' Marianne muttered. 'Happy now?' She threw her mother a filthy look, then followed her son out of the room.

Lily raised an eyebrow. 'That boy is too grown up for his own good. But he's right about the arguing bit. I wish I could put you, Edie and Bert in a room together so you could thrash it all out.'

Cissy snorted. 'I wouldn't fancy your mum's chances, love. Maybe you should ask her why she sat in that chair all night.' She glanced meaningfully over at the curtained alcove.

Lily frowned and walked to the back of the room and swept the curtain aside. 'For God's sake! What are these?'

'Leave them!' Nellie leapt up and hurried over. 'It's just a few boxes. Hadn't you better get ready for work?'

'Are these Lou's? Does Dad know about this?' she asked.

It still shocked Nellie to hear Lily call Jasper 'Dad'. The fact he was her father was just one of the many secrets that had bubbled to the surface since the war started. Somehow, though, Lily had forgiven her for lying to her all her life.

'No, of course not. He wouldn't be interested anyway.' Nellie folded her arms mutinously.

Lily sighed. 'I'm sick to the back teeth of being stuck in the middle between the two of you.'

'Quite right, love,' Cissy chimed in. 'Lettin' a man like Jasper slip through yer fingers is just plain carelessness.' She gave Nellie a narrow-eyed glare. 'As for all those' – she waved her hand at the boxes – 'maybe you can talk some sense into your mother's thick skull.' She picked up the tray and stomped out of the room.

Lily came over and sat down beside her. 'I wish I knew what caused the distance between you and Dad. I know it's not cos of what you said in court because he told me you had your reasons for that, though for the life of me I can't think what they could be. But if he believes it, then I believe him. And that's the only reason I haven't been hard on you about the whole thing.'

*The whole thing.* It made the trial sound like a minor problem, rather than a grenade that had detonated in the centre of their lives. And it had all been for nothing. Mary Guthrie had destroyed her family in the vain hope of saving her niece from a life sentence for murder. But Susan had been sentenced to life anyway.

'I've been thinking.'

Lily's voice brought her back from her gloomy thoughts.

'It's Dad's birthday in a couple of weeks, so what do you think about having a surprise party for him?'

Nellie stared at her aghast. 'I'm not exactly in the mood for celebratin',' she growled.

'It's not about you, though, Mum. It's for Jasper. And then maybe you and he could, you know, be close like before.'

Nellie pondered the thought. 'I'm not sure he'd like that.'

'He wouldn't have a choice. It'd be a surprise! I can pretend I'm going to take him out for lunch, and you and whoever else you want to invite, you know, the usual gang – Mavis, Ethel, Phyllis and some of Dad's friends too – will be here waiting to surprise him. Come on, Mum! We need a bit of fun. Please.' She clutched her hands under her chin and put her head to one side.

Despite everything, Nellie smiled. When Lily wanted something, there was very little that could stand in her way. 'Do I 'ave a choice?'

Lily giggled. 'No! And I promise it'll be brilliant! We just need to get everyone to bring a bit of food or drink, and Cissy can play her violin—'

Nellie winced.

'Come on, Mum, she's really good!' Her face turned serious. 'But I think you need to get rid of this stuff before then. Maybe Dad can help.'

Nellie's nerves drew tight again. 'Maybe,' she said vaguely. 'Don't suppose Dot's had any news of Bert?' she asked. She needed to change the subject, if only for her own sanity.

Lily's smile faded. 'Dot doesn't seem to know any more than we do. She's not heard from him in ages.'

Nellie knew that Lily had also been hurt by Dot and Bert's sudden marriage. It had been Jasper who'd told her, and he only knew because he'd bumped into them on their way to the station.

'All I know is that he stayed in Derbyshire with her parents until his shoulder healed. After that, though . . .' She shrugged.

'He stayed there after she returned?' she squeaked. 'Why didn't you tell me?' Even though she deserved it, the thought of Dot's mother nursing her son back to health was agonising. He'd found another mother, it seemed, and he might never need her again.

'Come on, Mum, you must have known that. Anyway, what did you expect?'

Nellie's shoulders sagged. It was true, she had no right to expect anything from Bert.

Lily took hold of her hand. 'You could always ask her yourself, you know.'

Nellie huffed. 'She won't talk to me.'

'Well, I'm sure we'll hear something soon enough. He can't have just disappeared into thin air. But there's something else I want to talk to you about. What are we going to do about Marianne? Teddy's eight months now and she still doesn't seem to have taken to him. Donny's more of a mother to him than Marianne is.'

Nellie sighed heavily. 'I know, love. Perhaps you could talk to her?' she said hopefully. 'Or maybe we should give it a bit longer. It's not as if Teddy don't get love from the rest of us, is it?'

'No, I can't talk to her. That's what mothers are for and you can't just sweep this under the carpet! You need to face things. And that includes getting rid of those boxes. Marianne said you made them all clear out of the kitchen last night when that man came in. She said he was sinister looking.'

Nellie could feel the panic building in her chest. The problems were piling up and she had no idea what to do. 'Honestly, all these dramatics! I'm just storin' a couple of boxes for someone. When they've got themselves sorted, they'll come get them. End of story.'

She walked heavily up the stairs, wishing that was the truth. But she would never reveal what had transpired between her and Johnny Fox, and she certainly wouldn't tell anyone that he'd threatened the babies. That was a burden she'd need to shoulder alone.

# Chapter 8

*Falmouth, January 1942*

Huddled in his army great coat, hat pulled low over his ears, Bert Castle wrapped his khaki scarf more firmly around his mouth. He sniffed it, hoping to catch a whiff of Dot's perfume, but all he smelt was damp wool. The thought of his wife warmed him. She'd made the scarf during their honeymoon in the spring – a week in a small hillside cottage on her parents' farm in Derbyshire. The weather had been glorious, and he'd teased her for knitting him a scarf when they were spending their days in shorts. But she'd been adamant it would come in handy, and, as he was coming to realise, Dot was usually right.

He stared glumly out at the passing countryside through the back of the truck. It was as bleak as his mood: leafless trees and spindly hedgerows that scratched at the truck as they passed. What did the future hold for him? Did he even *have* a future? He shivered. Everything had happened so fast. One moment he was waiting to be court-martialled and steeling himself to spend a long time in a gloomy cell. The next, he'd been offered a way out: join the Commandos for this secret mission and the charges against him would be dropped. He hadn't thought twice before accepting. And now here he was, on his way to God knew where to do God knew what.

They'd been driving all night, and though there were no road signs to give him a clue where they were going, from the direction the sun was rising, he knew they were driving south-west, and he'd become aware of the familiar scent of brine in the air, so they were near the sea. Was he about to be shipped off somewhere? He just hoped it was somewhere warm.

The track became more rutted and Bert's bruised backside was punished further as the truck bounced over the potholes.

Finally, they came to a stop, and he got stiffly to his feet and rolled his shoulders before gratefully leaping to the ground. Turning back, he grabbed his kitbag and looked around. He'd been deposited in front of a long, low dark-green hut with a tin roof. He could hear the roar of the ocean, which confirmed they were somewhere near the coast. The south-west coast could mean Devon, Cornwall, Wales? There were many places along this corner of the country, he supposed. No doubt, he'd find out soon enough.

The driver leant out of the window, a cigarette clamped between his lips. 'Good luck, mate. You're gonna need it.' And with that dispiriting statement, he turned the truck around and drove off.

Before he'd gone to Derbyshire with Dot, the extent of Bert's travels had been restricted to Kent, London and France with the expeditionary force early in the war – and what a bloody nightmare that had been. He shuddered. Knowing his luck, he was about to be sent straight back there. Still, at least he wasn't sitting in a damp cell eating gristly meat and mouldy bread. Plus, he had a rather smart beret, which, if he did say so him-self, made him look rather dashing.

He'd also been given various other items: woollen khaki trousers and jacket, with numerous pockets and ties. Boots, socks, and a thick jumper, which had been a godsend on the drive.

He took off his woolly hat and pulled the beret out of his pocket. He'd practised the exact angle in the truck, but without a mirror he wasn't sure he'd got it quite right. Dot would love it, though. He patted it in place, smiling slightly at the thought of her response to it. But the happy thought was replaced with a more sombre one: this lot had a reputation for danger, and he didn't fancy his chances of surviving long enough to ever see his wife again. The thought made a sharp ache start up in his chest. He deserved whatever was coming, he'd accepted that, but the thought of Dot's grief if anything should happen to him was worse than the thought of his own death ... He felt a burning at the back of his throat and glanced up at the sky. 'Whatever it takes, love, wherever I go, I will come back to you. That's my promise to you.'

'Corporal Castle?'

Blinking rapidly, Bert looked across to the hut where a tall, good-looking blond man wearing identical clothing to his had appeared.

He saluted smartly. 'Yes, sir.'

The man waved his hand. 'No need for that, Castle. Name's Newman. Lieutenant Colonel Newman. I'll be your commanding officer for this mission.' He gestured for him to come inside. 'I hear you've been recruited from the Glasshouse. We get a lot or recruits from there – blokes desperate to get out of a sentence make good Commandos. Less likely to run off. And when you find out more about this mission, running off might seem like the lesser of two evils.'

At Bert's alarmed expression, the commander chuckled and slapped his back. 'Joke, Castle. Just a joke . . .'

Bert managed a weak smile. That definitely hadn't been a joke, but even so, the informality and humour of his new commanding officer gave him a tiny glimmer of hope that things wouldn't be so bad.

'Come on, let's meet the others. Full briefing's in an hour. This is a joint navy and army operation so myself and Lieutenant Commander Stephens have been getting the troops fighting fit and battle ready, so you'll have a bit of catching up to do.'

Bert gulped nervously as he followed Newman into the hut, which consisted of one large room, furnished with plain wooden chairs and tables. Several men in khaki lounged around them, smoking and chatting. The room was warmed by a stove at one end, next to which stood a blackboard. At the other end, a hot water urn stood on a table with cups and saucers, and a jug of milk.

Newman ordered someone to get him a cup of tea and introduced Bert, who nervously took a seat and looked around. They were a motley bunch – some very rough around the edges, others more reserved. But there was an air of febrile energy around them that he found intimidating. More than one had a glint of madness in their eyes, and he doubted he had anything much in common with them. He bet none of them ducked every time a car backfired or woke in the night screaming; they'd hate him for his cowardice. Still, he needed to get them onside. His two skills, as far as he was concerned, were banter and talking girls into bed. The latter was a thing of the past, obviously, but banter he could do.

Plastering on a smile, he looked around at the assembled men. 'You lot look like the definition of "You don't have to be mad to work here but it helps."'

His comment was greeted with cheers and slaps on the shoulder. And just like that he was in. Men were simple creatures. Feed their ego, and they'd treat you like their best friend. Maybe everything was going to be all right.

Two hours later, the stove had gone out, and he sat in the freezing hut surrounded by a group of silent men as Commander Stephens and Lieutenant Newman finished their briefing for the mission.

'Any questions?' Newman asked.

*Just one*, Bert thought, looking round and seeing the same question in the eyes of each of the men. *How the hell were any of them going to get out of this alive?*

# Chapter 9

*Western Approaches*

A loud knock at her bedroom door reverberated through Marge's head. Groaning she buried her face in the pillow.

'You up, Marge?'

'Go away, Becky,' she croaked. She cracked her eyes open and glanced at her alarm clock. Seven thirty. Bolting upright, she pushed her tangled hair out of her face.

'You better hurry up!' Becky opened the door and peered into the tiny room that contained just a small single bed, a rickety chest of drawers and a bedside table. 'Ugh, it smells like a gin factory in here. And you look like you've been dug up.'

For a woman who'd been partying last night, Becky looked insultingly fresh, with her brown hair coiled in a neat bun, her cheeks glowing and her uniform crisp, the shirt starched to perfection.

'I feel like I've been dug up,' Marge muttered, dropping her head into her hands. How much had she had to drink last night? The hours after she'd seen Rodney were a blur, but judging by the persistent thump behind her eyes and a mouth as dry as the Sahara, she'd done a good job of drowning her sorrows.

Becky regarded her seriously. 'What got into you last night? Even for you, you went a bit far.'

Marge winced. 'Don't remind me.' She ached all over and her hip throbbed, probably a result of landing on that man. Oh God. Had she really allowed herself to be launched along the table like a torpedo? She didn't blame Rodney for looking disgusted.

'Come on, stop wallowing. Get washed and I'll see you up there.'

When Becky had gone, Marge swung her feet to the floor and took a few deep breaths. Then she grabbed her towel and went along the corridor to the washroom. It was a large room, painted battleship grey, with a line of sinks against one wall and a row of baths against the other. She and the other girls had given up all pretence at modesty, so she wasn't surprised to see her colleague Maria crouching in an inch of water rubbing a flannel over herself.

Maria smirked at her. 'You look about as good as you deserve.'

Marge ignored her and looked in the mirror, horrified at her pallor and the dark circles under her bloodshot eyes.

'Hey, you'll never guess who I saw sneaking off with Archie Brooks last night.'

Marge raised her eyebrows. Archie Brooks was good-looking, but he was stand-offish. Some of the girls had laid bets on who could get a kiss off him first.

'Emily!' Maria giggled. 'She's made five shillings.'

'It was only a matter of time before she won.' Marge squeezed some toothpaste onto her brush. 'What about you and Andrew? I saw you canoodling in the corner.'

'Ugh, don't remind me. It was like being kissed by a slug.'

Marge laughed, splattering the sink with toothpaste, and turned to stare at her friend, who was now standing at the sink next to hers, a towel wrapped around her.

'It's not funny. The spit was running down my chin.' Maria leant towards the mirror, examining her face. 'Look, it's chapped!'

'Stop! I feel sick enough already!' Marge stuck the toothbrush back in her mouth; in truth Maria's chin did look a little red.

'You know, I think I'm gonna swear off men,' Maria continued, rubbing cream into her chin. 'Unless Clark Gable saunters into Western Approaches, then I am shutting up shop.'

'I swore off men months ago,' Marge responded.

'Martin didn't seem to think so last night,' Maria said archly.

'I didn't ask for that!' Rodney's disgusted expression came into her mind. Sod them both. Martin for kissing her without asking, Rodney for being his usual handsome, stuck-up self.

Oh, but she missed him. She hated to admit it, but it was the truth. She'd left Dover to get away from him, but he'd travelled with her in her heart, damn him. Even though he'd told her to her face he didn't love her.

Just a few short months ago, she'd thought they might finally have a chance. But it was hopeless. Since the start of the war, it seemed there was always some crisis or other with his family, and Rodney took far too much responsibility for them all. It had started on Marianne's wedding day back in September 1940, when their beautiful friend Daisy had died in a shell attack. Daisy's death had hit them all hard, but perhaps Marianne most of all, Marge mused, remembering how Marianne had cried when Teddy had been born. It was ridiculous, but it seemed she'd thought the new baby would be a reincarnation of Daisy – who had been a tiny little blonde fairy of a woman. But everyone knew you could never replace someone.

This had been followed by Gladys's murder. Her death had been utterly shocking, but Marge had never dreamt then that the repercussions would be so wide-reaching.

And amidst the very public destruction of the Castles' famous unity, of Bert and Edie's reputations, of Jasper and Nellie's relationship, there had been her heart. Crushed beneath Rodney's paranoia and the weight of his childhood spent bearing the brunt of his father's madness. Marge wasn't sure she'd ever recover enough to fall in love again.

Anyway, what did it matter? She and Rodney were chalk and cheese. Last night was a perfect illustration of that. Rodney was always in control and perfect. Whereas she . . . was not. But even for her, she'd been loud and reckless last night, and she needed to rein it in. No one liked a loudmouthed lush.

'Oy, Marge!' Maria tapped her on the shoulder. 'Are you still with me? If we don't get our skates on, we'll be late.'

With another quick splash of water on her face, Marge pushed all thoughts of the Castles and her broken heart to the back of her mind and raced out of the bathroom.

When they entered the large room on the top floor of Western Approaches, Captain Roberts looked preoccupied.

'Before we start, ladies, I have some announcements to make. Gather round, gather round.' He ushered them forward, and the women obediently formed a semicircle around him.

The captain paced in front of them in his familiar pose – hands behind his back, leaning forward. He was a short, thin man but he carried an air of authority that few could dismiss. And because he was so engaging and so clever, they worked harder for him than they might otherwise. She was looking forward to the next few months when they would start to train naval officers; the thought of being able to order the men around gave her a thrill. If she was lucky, she'd get to order Rodney around at some point, and she'd take great delight in showing him up in front of his colleagues.

Finally, Roberts stopped in front of them, his back ramrod straight, his gold buttons gleaming under the electric light.

'As you know, things have changed drastically since the attack on Pearl Harbor. The Americans have mobilised quickly. And you know what that means?' He looked at each woman in turn.

Marge wasn't sure whether they were expected to answer, but she raised her hand anyway. 'More men to train, sir?' she said tentatively.

He grinned and pointed at her. 'Exactly, Third Officer Atkinson! Exactly! Our services are more crucial than ever. No doubt, the U-boats will be redoubling their efforts and, as a consequence, we shall have to treble ours; expand our operations, recruit more people. There is no time to lose!'

The captain's face had gone red, and Marge felt slightly alarmed. She admired his passion, but his health was fragile, and he looked like he was about to have an apoplexy.

'It has always been my intention to open satellite stations where we can teach the officers who can't come to Liverpool. But now those plans need to be moved forward. *You* are this country's best hope of avoiding starvation. Do you understand?'

This was the second time he'd mentioned how bad things were. Were they really so close to the brink? Or was he exaggerating to motivate them to work harder? She really hoped it was the latter.

'And for that reason, we are setting up two new stations. One in Belfast, one near Dover.'

Marge started. *Please don't send me back there*, she thought desperately. *I've only just escaped.*

'Third Officer Atkinson,' Captain Roberts bellowed. 'You are a native of Dover, and given your exemplary grasp of the game, and your capacity for leadership, I am appointing you to be in charge of the Wrens at HMS *Lynx* based in Abbots Cliff House. Lovely place, right on the cliffs in Capel-le-Fern. Do you know it?' He rocked back on his heels and gazed up at the ceiling.

Marge stared at him in astonishment. She didn't know the house, but of course she knew Capel. And it was far too close to Dover for her liking. 'B-b-but, do you think I'm ready, sir?'

'Absolutely! Just a couple more days training, and you will be able to teach those old sea dogs a lesson or two.' He smiled slightly. 'And I have a feeling you'll relish it.'

Marge's lips twitched. He wasn't wrong about that, but even so . . . She hadn't long completed her officer's training, and she wasn't convinced she was ready to take charge of anyone.

As though reading her mind, the captain continued. 'Of course, you won't be going alone! Emily White, Rebecca Purviss and Maria Longhorn will be joining you. And you will be working under the command of Captain Thomas Bennett who will need to be brought up to speed on what we do here – that will be your first job. So you will go down there a day earlier to show him the ropes.'

Marge's mouth dropped open. Captain Thomas Bennett? Surely it couldn't be the same man . . .

'Do you know him?' Captain Robert's eyebrows rose.

She cleared her throat. 'The name rings a bell, sir.' Her voice came out faintly, and the sick feeling in her stomach had nothing to do with the hangover. A picture flashed into her mind: a dark night, a tall man bending close to a girl with flaming red hair . . . She swallowed down the bile.

Captain Roberts smiled. 'I believe he was stationed in Folkestone back in the twenties, so you never know. He's been brought out of retirement to head up operations down at *Lynx*.'

Marge was too stunned to answer for a moment. If he had been stationed in Folkestone in the twenties, then it must be the same man.

'You look troubled, Atkinson. Do you not feel up to it? Is my faith in you misplaced?'

Gathering herself, she saluted smartly. 'No, sir! Thank you for having faith in me.' But her mind was filled with the memories of a time she'd tried hard to forget. A time that had destroyed her family forever.

# Chapter 10

*Casualty Hospital, Dover*

Lily Castle sat down at the canteen table, her tea sloshing onto the saucer.

Dot was already there, waiting for their usual catch-up before their shift began.

'Everything all right?' Dot asked.

Lily yawned. 'Aside from sleeping in the basement and a long heart-to-heart with Mum this morning, everything's great.' She rolled her eyes.

'How is your mother?' There was a distinct frostiness to Dot's voice; she'd not forgiven Nellie for what she'd said about Bert at the trial, and despite Lily's best efforts she'd refused point blank to visit since she'd returned from Derbyshire a few months before.

'She's ... I don't know, Dot. Something strange is going on. She had a visit from some bloke last night – according to Marianne he looked like a gangster – and all of a sudden, she's storing a load of boxes for him. I've got a bad feeling about it to be honest.'

Dot merely raised her eyebrows. Lily knew what she was thinking: there was always something with Nellie Castle. And she supposed she had a point; her mum was usually in the eye of one storm or another.

'But on a more cheerful note, I've persuaded her to have a birthday party for Jasper. I'm hoping it will bring them back together. Will you come?'

Dot sighed. 'No, Lily. I'm sorry, but I just can't. I love Jasper, but your mum is another matter.'

Lily decided to let the matter rest for now and changed the subject. 'Mum was asking about Bert this morning.'

Dot paled and Lily looked at her friend critically. She'd lost weight in the last few months, and her dark curly hair had lost some of its lustre. It was clear she was worried about something. Lily had been trying to gently tease information about Bert from her for ages, but whatever had happened, Dot wasn't telling her.

'What did you tell her?' Dot put down her teacup carefully, as though trying to control her movements.

'I told her the truth. I don't know and she should ask you – you are his wife, after all.' She tried to keep the bitterness from her voice. Aside from the fact that they hadn't bothered to tell her they were getting married, she'd hoped Bert might at least write to her. The thought had crossed her mind that maybe Bert had run off with another woman and Dot was too embarrassed to tell her. Her sister-in-law was so different to her glamorously handsome brother, and the complete opposite of the sort of women he used to go out with. She'd always believed they'd be perfect for each other, but maybe she'd been wrong and he was up to his old tricks. If he was, then she'd be first in line to strangle him.

'What's really happened, love?' she asked, reaching across the table to take Dot's small, rough hand.

Dot shook her head. 'I promised him I wouldn't say . . .' She looked on the verge of tears, and Lily wasn't sure whether to push her or not.

But she was so tired of not knowing. Her three brothers were scattered to the winds, and she hadn't had a letter from her fiancé Charlie for months. She put a hand to her chest, stroking her fingers over the engagement ring that hung on a chain around her neck. Charlie had given it to her the night before he left Dover just over a year ago, and in that time, she'd had a total of three letters from him. They'd only known each other for a few months before he left, and she was starting to wonder whether he'd changed his mind. She swallowed back the pain this thought caused and turned her attention back to her sister-in-law.

'Dot, if something's happened to him, you can't not tell us!'

'He's fine, as far as I know . . .' She hesitated.

Sensing an advantage, Lily persisted. 'Tell me what's going on then. Otherwise I'll worry myself to death. Please.' She squeezed Dot's hand.

Dot sat deep in thought for a moment, then seemed to come to a decision. 'If I tell you, you can't tell your mother – you can't tell anyone!' She lowered her gaze, picking up the teaspoon and idly stirring her tea, even though there was no sugar to spare, and very little tea in the cup.

Lily's tension mounted. Something was very, very wrong.

'I need you to promise,' Dot hissed fiercely, thin fingers grasping Lily's wrist.

'I promise. You know you can trust me with anything.'

Dot nodded and took a deep breath. 'He's in prison awaiting court martial.' The words came out in such a rush that Lily wasn't sure she'd heard right. But the worry and heartbreak in her friend's eyes told her that she'd heard exactly right.

'Are you serious?'

'You think I'd lie about something like this? It's all my fault. I—'

'For God's sake! What the hell did he do that was so bad? And why is this *your* fault.'

Dot looked away. 'Because I told him to confess,' she muttered.

'You what?' Lily pulled away from Dot's grasp.

'After Gladys died, Bert went off the rails . . .'

Lily nodded. They all knew this.

'Well, he did some things . . . Really bad things. And when he told me about it, I—' Tears flooded her eyes, and she put her hand over her mouth. 'I told him he needed to go to the authorities and tell the truth.'

Lily stared at her aghast. 'You did what? Did you know he'd get arrested?'

Dot shrugged, her gaze fixed on the table. 'We both knew it was a possibility.'

'Christ, Dot!' Lily sat back in her chair. 'I thought you loved him!'

Dot's head remained bowed, her shoulders shaking.

Lily softened slightly. Of course, Dot loved him. She'd loved him from the moment she'd set eyes on him. 'I'm all for doing the right thing, but for God's sake! What the hell could he have done that was so bad it would get him arrested?'

'That's Bert's story, and I can't tell you. I'm sorry.'

Lily shoved her chair back from the table. She had never been angry with Dot before, but now she had an overwhelming urge to pummel the truth out of her. 'I hope to God it was worth it!'

She stormed out of the canteen, her mind whirling with the news. Surely her big brother couldn't have done anything so bad it would lead to imprisonment. And if he had, why couldn't he have just kept quiet! Bert had been through enough without his bloody *wife* making him feel so guilty that he offered himself up as some sort of . . . of . . . what? Sacrifice? Scapegoat? She pictured her funny, handsome big brother sitting in a dingy cell, head in his hands. How could he ever be the same after this?

She glanced behind her. Dot was sitting absolutely still, watching her. Briefly, she held her hand out to her, as though begging forgiveness. Shaking her head, Lily turned and left. Despite Bert's brash confidence, didn't Dot realise how easily hurt he was? After the traumas he'd been through over the last few months – the horror of Dunkirk, Gladys dying in front of him, being shot by a Messerschmidt, the trial – she wasn't sure he'd cope with being in prison as well.

She'd thought Dot had pulled him back from the brink, but the opposite was true. Her mother always said that Bert was like his father, and she hoped to God she meant just in his looks. Because Donald Castle had been so damaged by the last war that he'd killed himself in the end. She just had to hope that Bert believed he had enough to live for. Otherwise she dreaded to think what he might do.

Dot's vision was blurred as she watched her best friend walk away. She didn't blame Lily for her anger. Months ago, before she knew Bert loved her, before she'd agreed to spend the rest of her life with him, she'd thought it would be for the best. He'd blackmailed his quartermaster – who was having an affair with a fellow officer – into stealing supplies, so he could use the goods to pay off his gambling debts. And then the officer had been arrested along with his lover, not only for stealing but for having improper relations. Bert, on the other hand, had got off scot-free.

She'd been disgusted with him at the time, and it had all seemed so black and white. Now, though, after basking in the joy of married life with the man of her dreams – a flawed man, but perfect in her eyes – she wished she'd kept her mouth shut.

But Bert was determined to do the right thing, to prove to her that he'd changed. She put her head in her hands. He'd never had to prove anything to her. All she wanted was to have him by her side. Or if she couldn't have that, to know that he was with his mates in the regiment. Instead, he was locked up somewhere and she wasn't even allowed to visit him. On the plus side, at least he was safe – after losing her brother Benji, she couldn't bear to lose Bert too. But maybe she'd already lost him. Maybe being shut up in a cell day after day had made him realise he'd made a terrible mistake marrying a woman who demanded he give up his freedom in the name of doing the right thing.

# Chapter 11

*Castle's Café*

Nellie couldn't concentrate. It wasn't just the exhaustion after a sleepless night in the basement – she was used to that. But now, aside from the usual low-level fear of living in a frontline town, the terror that Johnny Fox had brought into the café had stolen what little peace of mind she'd had.

At seven thirty on the dot, she crossed to the window and opened the blackout curtains. In the dim morning light, the market square was coming to life, and people wrapped in coats and scarves were scurrying along the pavement. Nellie barely noticed them; she had her gaze fixed on the ruined Market Hall to the left of the square, because any minute now, Lou Carter would be setting up her whelk stall.

Someone tapped her on the shoulder and she whirled round in shock.

'You gone deaf?' Cissy's usually cheery expression was stony. 'I've been shoutin' to you for ages to get this lot.'

She slammed down a couple of plates of bacon and eggs, giving Nellie a pointed look. 'Apologies, loves, Mrs C seems to 'ave lost her mind this mornin'.'

Nellie scowled and went back to the counter. As she passed one of the tables, someone muttered, 'Cheer up, love, it might never 'appen.'

Nellie turned her head sharply and glared at a young corporal. 'Do I know you?'

The young man's pimply face went red, and he shook his head.

'Then I don't see as you 'ave any business tellin' me what to do. If you want to be welcome in my café, then keep your thoughts to yerself.' She knew she was overreacting, but lack of sleep and taut nerves could do that to a woman.

'I'm just . . . I just . . .' His eyes slid towards the kitchen door and he flushed. Elodie was standing there, one of Nellie's colourful pinnies almost smothering her slender form.

Nellie suppressed a sigh. Another one. They'd have to keep an eye out for poor Elodie. She had the softest heart and couldn't bear to disappoint anyone. If Nellie allowed it, the girl would be walking out with a dozen men a week.

'Elodie's busy.' She eyed the man – boy, really. Not a chance in hell, she thought. 'So eat up and mind yer own business.'

Seated at the table behind the young soldier, Adelaide Frost had also witnessed the exchange. 'You're going to have to keep a close eye on that girl, Nellie. Who knows what sort of shenanigans she might get up to. You never can tell with those foreign ones.' Her knitting needles clacked disapprovingly.

Nellie bristled. 'What's that supposed to mean?'

'It means that you should be more careful who you allow to live and work here.'

'I reckon I should be more careful about who I allow to eat here,' Nellie growled.

'I heartily concur. But if you barred everyone you didn't like, the place would be empty,' Adelaide tittered.

There was no arguing with that logic, and unable to think of a suitable retort, Nellie pursed her lips and went to stand behind the counter.

'Ain't that the truth,' Cissy said through clenched teeth as she squeezed past Nellie to fill the teapot from the large urn that stood on the far end of the counter, where Polly used to sit. She never thought she'd say it, but Nellie missed that damn bird.

'Mrs Castle.' Elodie's soft whisper drew her attention. The girl looked nervous and a little uncertain.

'There is a man to see you.'

Nellie's heart sank. Already? And in the middle of break-fast? With a quick glance at Adelaide, whose eyes were fixed on the kitchen door, Nellie hurried through to where a tall man wearing a raincoat with a hat pulled low over his eyes, and a scarf wrapped around the lower half of his face hovered in the narrow corridor.

'I believe you have something for me,' he said. 'If you could just show me where the . . . um . . . merchandise is, I'll get out of your hair.'

Nellie frowned. His accent was like cut glass, not at all the sort of voice she'd have expected from an associate of Johnny Fox.

She gestured to the basement door, and he turned and opened it.

'Apologies for the inconvenience, madam,' he said, over his shoulder.

How could this man with his fancy accent be involved with the terrifying thug who'd threatened her yesterday? Well, posh voice or not, he could not be trusted, and she didn't intend to let him out of her sight.

In the basement the man had stacked two of the boxes and was grunting as he picked one of them up. She might not be able to see his face, but that was the grunt of an older man, and she'd noticed the way his left foot dragged slightly.

'I don't suppose you could help me?' he puffed.

Nellie arched an eyebrow at him. 'I don't suppose I could,' she responded crisply.

Suddenly the polite facade disappeared. 'Then you better find someone who can,' he said threateningly.

She knew it! For all his posh accent this man was no better than Johnny Fox.

'I can help, Gran,' Donny scampered into the basement and Nellie suppressed a groan. She didn't want her grandson anywhere near this man or these boxes.

'Now that's more like it. There'll be a shilling in it for you. Between us, we'll have this done in a jiffy.' He deposited a box into Donny's waiting arms. 'My car's parked outside the back gate.'

'Do you have a name?' Nellie asked, once Donny had disappeared up the stairs.

'Naturally. But I'm not inclined to tell you. But considering we'll be seeing each other regularly over the next few weeks, you can call me Francis.'

'What do you mean, seeing you regularly?'

Francis picked up one of the remaining boxes. 'Didn't Mr Fox tell you? Every so often I'll pop in to pick up a box or two for, er … distribution. The supply will also be replenished periodically.'

Supply of what? She couldn't fathom what on earth these men were playing at.

'And don't worry, I'm sure you'll be rewarded for your help.'

'Rewarded with threats, you mean?' Nellie snapped. 'This basement is a public shelter. That's not my idea of discreet.'

'Which is exactly why it is,' he responded.

Donny returned, his face eager. 'I like your car. Can I have a ride in it?'

The man chuckled. 'Not today. But you never know, one of these days you just might.'

He looked at Nellie as he said this and she shuddered. Was that another warning? Somehow, she had to ensure Donny and Francis never crossed paths again.

'Now take this one, and I'll give you that coin.' He put another box into Donny's waiting arms and followed him out of the basement.

In the kitchen, Cissy's mouth was in a thin, tight line, disapproval radiating from every pore. Nellie ignored her and went back to the café. Adelaide Frost was staring avidly into the kitchen; no doubt she'd be telling everyone about it the minute she left.

Nellie went to stand in the doorway, blocking her view. 'Seen anythin' you like?'

Adelaide shook her head. 'I don't like anything I've seen, Nellie. Something's going on here, and from the looks of it, it's nothing good. You might think we've all forgotten that you once had a spy living with you, but I can assure you, we haven't.'

The bell above the door rang before Nellie could answer and Jasper's tall frame filled the doorway. He was dressed in his blue ARP overalls, a black helmet with a white 'W' painted on the front perched on his bushy white hair. Nellie wanted to scream. He was the last person she wanted here right now.

Adelaide wasn't finished. 'It might be a cliché, but everyone knows there's no smoke without fire.' She looked at Jasper. 'Wouldn't you agree, Jasper?'

There was a tense pause as Nellie tried to think of a suitably dismissive rejoinder, but before she could, a thump behind her made her turn.

Elodie and Marianne were silently watching as Donny picked up the box he'd dropped.

'Sorry, mister,' Donny gasped. 'It just slipped.'

'Quite all right, boy. Take your time.' Francis kept his head lowered, the brim of his hat hiding his face.

'Need a hand there?' Jasper came to stand behind her.

The man didn't look up. 'No need.' He walked hurriedly out of the back door, Donny close behind him.

'What's that all about?' Jasper asked.

'You might well ask.' Cissy sniffed.

Jasper's bushy brows lowered. 'Don't tell me you're helpin' Lou again.' When Nellie didn't answer, Jasper put his hands on her shoulders and turned her to face him. 'Nellie? Who is that man? And why's Donny involved?'

'Just doin' a favour for a friend.' Nellie couldn't quite meet his eyes. 'Nothin' to get excited about.' She cast a filthy look at Cissy.

Jasper shook his head. 'Adelaide's right about smoke and fire. What's goin' on, love?'

*Love?* Now, he was calling her love again! 'Nothin' for you to concern yourself about.'

'Oh, stop bein' such a stubborn old fool, Nell! Go upstairs an' talk to Jasper. I'll hold the fort for a bit.' Cissy pushed the two of them towards the stairs.

Don came back in beaming. 'A shilling! Mum, Ted's sleepin', so is it all right if me and Fred go out?' Freddie Perkins was Donny's best friend and lived above the fishmonger's across the square with his grandparents.

''Course you can, love,' Nellie said before Marianne could answer. 'I'll keep an ear out for Ted.' She looked at her daughter. 'Or maybe your mum might.'

Marianne frowned. 'If you want these cheese and onion pies to be ready for lunch, then you'll have to do it,' she said shortly.

'I won't be long. Promise!' Donny planted a kiss on his mother's cheek and flew out of the back door.

'Come on then, Jasper. If you wanna talk, let's talk.' Nellie walked up the stairs, very conscious of his large, warm presence behind her. It had been too many months since he'd been up here. Despite his obvious disapproval, and the tricky conversation to come, it felt wonderful to have him so close again.

In the sitting room, Nellie went to sit in her usual chair by the fireplace and gestured to the other.

'Been a while since you've been 'ere,' she said acidly.

Jasper lowered himself into the chair, his knees creaking. 'Our last chat up here weren't so pleasant, Nell,' he said.

Talk about an understatement. He'd demanded she give up her deepest and darkest secrets, and when she'd refused, he'd left, saying that unless she told him the truth he'd be staying away. 'Sometimes love isn't enough,' were his exact words. And recently, the more she'd thought about it the more angry it had made her. At the time she'd been consumed with guilt about what she'd said at the trial. Now, though, she'd had just about enough of his sanctimonious attitude.

'You 'ad any more thoughts about that?' he asked mildly.

She looked at him sharply. 'I 'ave, as it happens. I've had a lot of time to think about that night, and the truth is, you've got a nerve. Throwin' your accusations around, tryin' to make me talk to you about the worst night of me life, and when I do, telling me I'm lyin' and walkin' out on me. If you really cared, you'd respect my wishes.'

He opened his mouth to protest, but Nellie had the bit between her teeth and held her hand up.

'You know nothing about what I've been through! And you've got no right to force me to talk about it and hold your love over me like a sword! That ain't love, Jasper. That's control, and you should know by now that no one controls me! I 'ad my fill of that with Donald.'

Jasper looked flabbergasted at her accusation. 'I never meant to—'

'I don't think you did. And I say that cos over all these years, you've been my loyal friend. But you don't have a right to all of me. I belong to me alone. My mistakes, my successes. All mine!' She thumped her chest. 'Just like my conscience is *mine*. It ain't somethin' you can have access to unless *I* choose to share it. Do you understand?'

Nellie held her breath waiting for his response. She felt lighter for saying what had been on her mind for a while now. She loved this man, but he expected too much of her.

Jasper sat silently, rubbing his hand down his whiskery cheeks. Finally, he looked up. 'You know what I think, Nellie? I think you're deflectin' from what's just happened. I ain't here to ask about Donald. I'm here cos Cissy thinks you're in trouble, and after what I just seen, I agree.'

'Do I look like I'm in trouble?' she snapped back. She should have known Cissy wouldn't keep her mouth shut. The traitor. How had she got to him so quickly?

'You look scared, Nell. And you don't scare easy.'

She'd thought that about herself too, once. But ever since the war had begun, she was terrified every day. And now she had Johnny Fox to worry about too. A man who deliberately displayed the gun in his pocket, who made threats towards innocent babies … His appearance was terrifying, but she could have dealt with that. It was the thought of Teddy and Vivvy, utterly helpless and dependent, grasped in those massive hands. She was certain he could crush their tiny skulls with one squeeze of his fat fingers. She swallowed back the bile at the thought.

She might be angry with Jasper, but she longed for his help. Throughout the years, his solid presence had bolstered her more than she would ever admit, but after her little outburst, she couldn't bring herself to confide in him. Not yet.

'So you should know that I'm not scared now. I'll tell you what I am though. I'm bloody furious at the way you spoke to me just now in front of everyone. You just added fuel to Adelaide's fire, an' no doubt she'll be blabbin' about it all over town.'

'You only need to worry if there's somethin' to blab about, love. And you know I'll help if you need it.'

She laughed shortly. 'Will you, really, Jasper?'

Jasper sighed and shook his head. 'I'll always be 'ere when you need me. That will never change.' They held each other's gaze for a moment, then he stood and walked out, leaving Nellie fuming. This distance between them was all his doing, so how dare he imply *she* was the one keeping them apart. Had he listened to a word she just said?

But even if she did confide in Jasper, what could he do against someone like Johnny Fox? No, what she needed was to be able to protect *herself*. She thought of the metal box Jasper had made for her to keep Donald's old service gun in. The box she'd opened only once in her life . . . She had no idea what had happened to that gun, and she'd never wanted to see it again. Now, though, she wished she had it still.

Standing, she went to the window and drew the curtains. At bloody last! Lou Carter was walking towards the Market Hall where she kept her stall locked overnight. After the trouble she'd brought to her door, the woman owed her. And she was going to make sure she paid in full.

# Chapter 12

*Western Approaches*

Rodney sat silently while his colleagues chatted around him, replaying the sight of Marge kissing another man over and over again, her face alive with laughter, her glorious red hair like fire gleaming under the lights. God, he'd missed her. He wasn't surprised that some other lucky man had snapped her up; she was a woman in a million, and he could hardly expect her to wait for him after the things he'd said to her. But even so, his heart seethed with jealousy and regret.

It was his own fault. He'd let her go. Those last months in Dover, with the trial and the memories of his father's madness at the forefront of his mind, he'd convinced himself his blood was tainted, and that this war would destroy him, just as the last war had destroyed his father. He'd told himself that he could never put Marge through the trauma his mother had faced.

But sailing in a convoy across the Atlantic had made him question his beliefs. It had been a terrible voyage. Two of the ships in their convoy had been sunk and he'd spent hours in a small lifeboat searching for survivors, having to push dead bodies away with an oar. Then, on the last stormy leg, his own ship had been hit, killing three men. And through it all, his sanity had remained intact. Perhaps he was stronger than he thought. Perhaps his father had been wrong when he'd told him he was a snivelling coward.

And as the crew struggled to sail the ship back, each day bringing a new danger and a new challenge, he'd realised he should never have let her go, and he'd vowed to win her back, no matter what it took.

It had all seemed so simple. Until he'd seen her in another man's arms. What a fool he'd been to think she might still want him. She would never forgive or forget the cruel words he'd flung at her – *I don't feel anything for you except desire.* How could he have lied to her like that? How could he have broken her heart?

He'd been feeling guilty for months about how he'd treated her, but clearly there'd been no need. Marge had done what she always did: moved on. He admired and hated that quality in equal measure.

'What do you think, Castle?' A man with a head as bald as an egg, nudged his arm. He was sitting with a few of his crewmates from the *Aeneus* in the NAAFI, and the talk was all about the Americans joining the war. The news had reached them while they were in the middle of the Atlantic, but the full implications hadn't really sunk in until this morning, when they'd received a comprehensive briefing. Ordinarily, Rodney would have been as eager to talk about it as his colleagues, but not today.

'Smithy thinks the war's as good as over, but I don't see Hitler throwing in the towel just cos Roosevelt's finally got his act together. What is it with the Yanks, anyway? Always bloody late to the party.'

'My point is, Larson,' said Smithy – a tall, thin man with sandy hair whose bony wrists poked out from his too-short jacket, 'last time, the war was over in eighteen months once they got involved. So, come mid-'43 maybe we can all get our lives back.'

'No way!' Larson leant forward. 'The U-boats won't stop attacking cos the Americans have joined. It's just more ships to sink for them. They'll be in seventh heaven! Unless the Yanks have some magic tracking equipment we don't know about.'

Larson had lost one of his closest friends while they'd been at sea. Almost everyone on active duty had lost multiple comrades – and he was one of them now.

'Well?' Larson looked at Rodney expectantly.

'I agree with you. But I like your optimism, Smithy. We need to find a way to destroy their U-boat fleet or we're scuppered.' He blew out a breath. 'How do they just appear?' he murmured. 'They're like ghosts.'

'Steady on, Castle! They're not magicians. Don't worry, we'll get 'em in the end.' Smithy again.

*What must it be like to have such a rosy view of even the direst events?*

There was a flurry of activity near the door, and the men looked over. 'Aye aye!' Larson said. 'The Wrens are here . . .'

Rodney kept his eyes trained on the table. If Marge was there, what should he do? Would she even acknowledge him? Should he go and talk to her? His heart thudded heavily in his chest. He owed it to himself to at least give it a go. He wasn't the type to just roll over and accept defeat . . .

'I bags the Rita Hayworth lookalike,' Smithy said. 'Nice and tall, just how I like 'em.'

Rodney's head jerked up and his breath caught as he saw her standing with a group of other women, though he barely saw them. When Marge was in the room, he never noticed anyone else.

'I prefer the petite blonde myself,' Larson said.

Rodney didn't respond; he was transfixed. She looked as regal and sexy as she always did. At least a head taller than the other women, her red hair like a beacon. He imagined what it might be like to go over to her. He closed his eyes and could almost smell her Yardley perfume mixed with cigarettes. Only Marge could make cigarettes smell alluring.

He opened his eyes again and watched as she said something to her friends and went to sit at a table, where she lit a cigarette. Then, as though sensing someone's eyes on her, she looked over at him. She went still, her cigarette halfway to her mouth.

Rodney held his breath. If she acknowledged him, he'd go and speak to her.

But after a long look, Marge took a drag of her cigarette, blew a smoke ring up to the ceiling. Then very pointedly turned her head away.

Dammit. He had to talk to her. He started to stand, but Smithy put a hand on his arm. 'Leave it, mate. She don't seem interested.'

Rodney looked over at her again. One of the other women had joined her and they were whispering to each other. Then they both looked over at him and smirked.

Heat rose in his cheeks and he shook Smithy's hand off. 'She's hardly my type. I just fancied a bit of air.'

He put his cap on and walked stiff-backed to the door.

# Chapter 13

*Castle's Café*

Nellie ran down the stairs and threaded her way through the tables, ignoring Cissy's indignant calls as she pulled open the door. She hurried across the square, barely pausing to look as she crossed the road and made a beeline for Lou, who was arranging bowls of whelks on a wooden shelf at the front of her stall.

'I want a word with you,' Nellie growled.

Lou looked up, a hand at her throat. 'Bleedin' heck, Nell! You nearly gave me a heart attack!'

'I'll be givin' you somethin' a sight worse if you don't tell me what's goin' on! I *told* you I didn't want no more of your stuff. So why did you send Johnny Fox in my direction? Who is he an' what the hell 'as he stashed in my basement?'

Lou looked away. 'Word is, it'll all be picked up eventually. So you shouldn't worry too much.'

'Shouldn't worry?!' Nellie stamped her foot. 'You seemed to be worried last night! And they're gonna be hoppin' in and out like fleas by the sounds of it. Some bloke arrived this mornin' and said there'll probably be more stuff comin'. You told me last night to do what he says, you was scared. So I wanna know exactly what I'm dealin' with!' Nellie folded her arms tightly around herself; she'd come out without a coat, but the cold breeze wasn't the only thing making her shiver.

Lou shuffled her feet. She might pretend to be unconcerned, but Nellie could tell it was an act. 'Look, all I know is that man don't mess about, so just do what he says, and you'll be fine.'

'Fine? You say he don't mess about, an' then you say I'll be fine? He bloody threatened my grandkids, Lou!'

Lou leant towards her. 'Pipe down, will ya!'

Nellie looked around and noticed a few people eyeing them curiously. 'Seriously, Lou,' she hissed. 'He 'ad a gun. An' this mornin' some posh bloke turns up an' threatens me again! You need to tell 'em to leave me alone or I won't be responsible for me actions.'

Lou's mouth was a thin slash in her face, her cheeks pale, and Nellie felt her anxiety rise. If there was one thing she could always count on it was Lou's brash self-confidence. She seemed oblivious to what people thought of her and never showed fear. But she was showing it now.

Lou tilted her head towards the ruined Market Hall. Nellie followed her to stand in the shelter of a doorway, above them a battered, blackened sign read 'Town Porters' Left Luggage Office'. Fat chance, Nellie thought wryly. Any luggage left there would be long gone. Plenty of luggage being left at the café though.

Lou reached out to grasp Nellie's wrist and leant towards her. 'I'm sorry I dropped you in it, but I 'ad no choice. An' if you don't do what Johnny says, then you an' me will be up shit creek.'

'But why?' Nellie squeaked.

Lou hesitated a moment, then let out a deep breath. 'Truth is, Nell, this is all my fault. I met Johnny up London, back when we was at the Old Bailey, remember?'

*As if I could ever forget*, Nellie thought bitterly.

'We 'ad a good chat, an' I agreed to 'elp 'im out. 'E were lookin' to expand down 'ere, you see. An' what with the south coast bein' so heavily guarded, 'e needed a local contact.' Lou's expression was shifty and Nellie had a horrible sinking feeling.

'So that's what you wanted my basement for? It was for Johnny Fox all along.'

'I mean, it were in the back of me mind, but he was goin' on about stuff he'd got from bombed-out factories and how he needed to set up operations, an' that if I helped him, I'd get a generous cut. Seemed to think whatever he were goin' to do would get him enough money to retire an' get a nice big house with servants, the lot . . . To be honest, I wanted a piece of that action, and 'e seemed all right, you know? We got on, 'ad a great night up Soho. But I swear to ya, Nell, I never would've done it if I'd known what sort of a bloke he really is. My mate warned me 'e were dangerous, but I didn't listen. Thought me an' 'im had a bit of a spark . . .'

Nellie raised her eyebrows at the thought of Lou Carter and Johnny Fox together. She was hardly anyone's idea of a gangster's moll. If things had been different, she'd have laughed.

'So I thought 'e'd turn a blind eye when I . . .' Lou flushed and looked away.

'What did you do?'

'Well, he suggested I help him with one of 'is little sidelines. Dirty postcards, playin' cards an' mags, that sort of stuff – just a bit of fun. So 'e gave me a load to sell an' offered me commission. But I . . . well, I maybe didn't declare all the money, an' he found out. I didn't realise it'd be so profitable, but blokes round here can't get enough of the stuff – horny little buggers. I figured he'd never know. An' I forgot all about the other stuff – the factory goods an' the new operation.'

'So you cheated him, and he found out.' Nellie's fury was rising. 'Why aren't I surprised! What I can't understand is what this has to do with me?' She thought for a moment. 'Hang on, are you tellin' me that I've been stashing piles of dirty mags for you?'

Lou looked sheepish. 'That and other stuff. But I figured what you didn't know wouldn't hurt you. I never realised 'e had somethin' else in mind. An' now it's too late. I'm in his clutches. So when he asked me for a good hidin' place where 'e could set up 'is distribution centre, I . . . Well, I sent 'im in your direction.'

'Distribution centre? Are you mad? It's a café, not a warehouse. And those men stand out like bleedin' barrage balloons, and believe me, they've been noticed. It's been one day, Lou, and Adelaide's already on to them. What is this venture anyway? What's so valuable that they 'ave to threaten my grandkids to make sure I do what they say?'

Lou chewed at her fingernails. 'I don't rightly know. I'm still sellin' the mags so it's not them. And I'm not allowed to keep a penny cos I'm still workin' off the debt. He's a tough bastard, Nell, so take my advice: do what he says an' keep yer trap shut. Cos what Johnny Fox wants, Johnny Fox gets. An' right now, he wants your basement an' he don't care who he has to hurt to get it.'

'I'll never forgive you for this, Lou,' Nell gritted. 'You an' me've had plenty of water under the bridge, but I reckon this might be it for us.'

Lou opened her mouth to say something, but Nellie shook her head. 'I don't trust yer, an' I don't want you in the café no more.'

Lou stumbled back. 'You don't mean that!'

Nellie was surprised at how upset Lou looked, but she was past caring. 'The only way I'll let you back in is if you get this man off my back! That and . . .' Nellie felt sick; was she really going to do this? She glanced over to the café. She could make out some blurred shapes sitting by the plastic window. A couple in naval uniform were walking arm in arm down the pavement, laughing as they pushed the door open. It was too noisy with traffic to be able to hear the bell, but it tinkled in her mind. It was the sound of home. This strange, mock-Tudor building had been at the centre of her life for decades, and now it was under threat from more than just shells and bombs.

She heard a familiar laugh and looked around. Donny and his friend Freddie were running across the square. She watched until they'd disappeared into the café, no doubt in search of food. Her heart swelled with love for him. She'd happily die to protect her grandchildren – and that included Vivvy, who she might never have seen, but she loved her all the same.

She turned back to Lou. 'The only way I'll let you back into the café is if you get me a gun.'

Lou's eyes widened. 'No, Nellie. I'm tellin' yer, don't mess with Johnny.'

'I ain't gonna be threatened in me own home! Life's bad enough without that. A gun, Lou. Or you ain't welcome.'

Not waiting for a reply, she marched back across the square. She and Lou had sparred together their whole lives; sometimes seriously, sometimes in jest. She was spitting mad with her right now, and she wasn't sure she could ever forgive her. But one thing she knew for sure: Lou would find her a gun, because in her own way she was a loyal friend. And somehow, Nellie would get rid of Johnny Fox for good. If that meant she had to commit murder to protect her family then so be it.

After all, it wouldn't be the first time.

# Chapter 14

*Western Approaches*

The following morning, Marge watched the dawn creeping over the horizon through the window. She should get up, but weariness kept her lying stiffly in her narrow bed. If she'd slept at all last night, she wasn't aware of it. Since Captain Roberts had mentioned Thomas Bennett, she'd been unable to think of anything else. Even seeing Rodney in the NAAFI had barely impacted. If she'd been in her right mind, she would have had plenty to say to him. But hearing that name had thrown her back to one of the worst times of her life, and talking to Rodney was the last thing she wanted to do.

Where was Katy now? Was she alive? Was she happy? Why had she never come home? Marge had asked these questions over and over after her sister had left, until finally she'd had to accept that she may never know.

But Tom Bennett's name had brought the memories racing back to the surface, and she'd been able to think of nothing else. No one, not even her best friends Reenie and Marianne, knew what had happened all those years ago. As far as the world was concerned, Katy had moved away to stay with relatives. After a couple of years, her parents had told everyone she was married and living in Ireland.

By the time her parents died, the lies were so entrenched that she almost believed them herself. Almost.

Groaning, she rolled over and punched the pillow, wishing it was Tom Bennett's face. Wishing she'd been older and wiser the last time she'd seen him. Wishing she could have done something – anything – to stop her sister from leaving. But she'd been fourteen, and even though Katy had been only a year older, she was not the type to listen to her little sister.

'What happened to you, Katy?' she whispered. She'd not said that name aloud in so long it felt alien in her mouth. As though she were speaking a foreign language. And yet once she'd known Katy as well as she'd known herself. She'd thought it would always be like that. Sisters were meant to be for life, weren't they?

But everything had changed when Katy had turned fourteen and her father had got her a weekend job waitressing at the naval officers' mess.

Marge sniffed back the tears as the memories cascaded through her mind. Messy, loud and rebellious, Katy had seemed so much more mature when it came to the ways of the world. And so much younger when it came to everything else. She'd relied on Marge to help with her homework, do her chores and cover up for her when she got into trouble at school. And Marge hadn't minded at all, because there was no one in the world as funny and loving as her sister. No one lit up a room like Katy, even her hair seemed brighter than Marge's, her laugh more infectious. People were drawn to her like moths to a lamp. And that had been her downfall in the end.

The change had started a couple of months into her job. The chest of drawers in their room became littered with pots of makeup and tubes of lipstick, their wardrobe full of new dresses and high-heeled shoes, which Marge knew she couldn't have afforded on her part-time wages. And when she wasn't working in the evenings, she would sneak out of their bedroom window, returning in the small hours smelling of booze and cigarettes.

But what Marge remembered most from those days was how happy her sister had been. She'd practically glowed with it, her lips in a permanent smile, her cheeks flushed, her blue eyes sparkling.

She'd been so jealous. Katy no longer needed her, and she'd felt pushed out and abandoned. Her sister had become a grown-up, while she still felt like a gauche child. When they weren't at school, her sister wore stockings, while Marge was still wearing knee socks. Where Katy's nails were painted a deep red, Marge's fingers were ink stained. But it was Katy's superior attitude that was the hardest to bear.

Was that why she'd followed her that night? To regain some power in their relationship? Or had she just wanted to join in Katy's fun? Whatever her reasons, that night marked the beginning of the end of her family.

She shouldn't blame herself; she'd been a child. But she wasn't a child anymore. Tom Bennett wouldn't remember her, but would he remember Katy's name if she mentioned it? Or had he forgotten the young girl he'd seduced and discarded as easily as a pair of old shoes? She suspected the latter. The question was, what could she do about it? Now she was older, she understood exactly what sort of a man Tom Bennett was. But what evidence did she have?

As her superior officer, the balance of power would lie with him, but one way or another, she'd find a way to get back at him.

The first thing she would do when she got to Dover was visit Mr Wainwright. She'd been working as the lawyer's secretary when her parents had died, and he'd given her a place to stay until she'd saved enough to rent a small room in a boarding house. He'd also taken it upon himself to look for Katy. He was one of the best and cleverest men she knew, and if anyone could advise her what to do, it would be him.

Her alarm clock rang, and Marge forced herself to get up. Once washed and dressed, she stood in front of the mirror and stared at herself. She'd been a child when Katy had left, but she wasn't a child anymore. She was a naval officer. She was clever. She was strong. She raised her chin and smiled grimly. Oh yes, Captain Thomas Bennett was long overdue a reckoning, and she intended to be the person to deliver it.

# Chapter 15

A week later, Marge sat on a train to Dover. It had been a long wearying journey, requiring a night at the YMCA on The Strand.

She'd boarded the first train out of Charing Cross that morning, and now, three hours into a journey that took only two hours in peacetime, the train juddered to a halt just outside Tonbridge Station. Rain was beating against the window and the fields looked as bleak and grey as her spirits.

She sighed heavily and reached into her pocket for a cigarette. The soldier sitting opposite eagerly leant forward and flicked his lighter. He'd been trying to catch her eye since they'd left London, but she didn't feel up to flirting. But she needed a distraction from her thoughts, so she dipped her head to the flame and took a deep drag, sitting back and closing her eyes as the smoke filled her lungs. Usually she loved the sensation, but she'd been smoking too much recently and her throat felt scratchy and dry, her chest tight. Maybe she should think about giving up? Or at least cutting down.

'You goin' all the way to Dover?' the soldier asked eagerly, his cheeks red.

She suppressed a sigh. Why were some men so easy to read, while others twisted your heart into knots? She wished she

could fall in love with a sweet boy like this, instead of a complicated bugger like Rodney. 'I am. Are you?'

'Yup. I've been out injured,' he said. 'Landmine on Shake-
speare Beach. There was four of us. Only three now.' He looked
down at his hands, which were fiddling with his lighter.

Marge felt a flicker of guilt. There was more to the boy than
met the eye. 'I'm sorry,' she said. 'Really I am.'

The soldier shrugged. 'Lost a few mates at Dunkirk as well.'

Marge looked at him properly. With his smooth cheeks
and unlined skin, he surely couldn't be more than twenty. But
the expression in his eyes was one of utter weariness. She'd
seen that same expression countless times since the war had
started. Rodney's eyes held the same look: it was as though
all hope had been extinguished. But then, even when he was
young, Rodney had always had that expression – as though
he'd been fighting a war his whole life. And he had, she supposed. His childhood had been a constant battle against his
father's madness and abuse.

She shook her head. She would not feel sorry for him! She'd
given him her love, her compassion, her support. And he'd
thrown it back in her face. More than that, he'd made her feel
weak and foolish. The last man who'd made her feel like that
was Tom Bennett. Naval officers were the worst, clearly.

'Sorry,' the young soldier said. 'Didn't mean to upset you.'

Marge smiled at him. 'I'm the one who should be sorry.
Sounds like you've had a bad time of it.'

'Ain't we all. Me sister's been bombed out, and me brother's
a prisoner. War's not what I expected.' He lit his own cigarette.
'Wouldn't care if we was stuck on this train forever, to be honest.'

'I know what you mean,' she murmured, turning to watch
the raindrops chase each other down the glass.

'You stationed in Dover?'

'Yup. I've lived there all my life, though, so it's nothing new.'

'Lucky you. You're going home.'

'I suppose.' It didn't feel like it, though. Home was meant to be a comforting place, and even after Katy had left, she'd still felt secure there with her friends and all the familiar places. But her parents were dead, and Dover wasn't the town it had been. Landmarks were gone, homes shattered – God knew whether her parents' house was still standing. She'd never gone back after they'd died. And now with Tom Bennett's shadow looming over her, her old home felt little more than a place of heartbreak and death.

The train jerked forward again, and as it picked up speed, the clickety-clack of the wheels seemed to take up the refrain: *heartbreak and death, heartbreak and death.* Her sister had left and could be dead for all she knew, her parents had died, Daisy had died, and then there was Rodney . . .

It was nearly a year since they'd stumbled on the truth of how his father had died. A year since he'd kissed her and told her he wanted her with him forever. All lies, of course. Because just a few months later, he'd changed his mind.

Impatiently, she shrugged off the thought and looked at the young soldier. He was still staring at her hopefully, a faint blush along his cheekbones.

'I don't suppose . . .' He cleared his throat nervously. 'I don't suppose you fancy a tot of whisky.' He held a flask out to her. 'This train's damn cold and it'll warm you up.'

She regarded him speculatively. He was probably closer in age to Marianne's son Donny than he was to her, but sod it. What was the point of moping about Rodney when there were plenty more fish in the sea.

'How old are you?'

'I'm twenty-five.' He puffed his chest out.

She raised a sceptical eyebrow.

'Well, I will be one day.' He grinned bashfully.

She laughed. She really shouldn't encourage him, but he was very sweet. And it was good to remind herself that some men still found her attractive. 'Go on then.' She took the proffered flask, tipped it to her lips and choked as the whisky burned its way down her throat.

She handed it back and smiled flirtatiously. 'So, why don't you tell me a little bit about yourself.'

# Chapter 16

Having only just made the train at Charing Cross, Rodney was the last one to leave the train. As he walked through the ticket office of Dover Priory Station, he spotted a familiar figure silhouetted in the entrance. Tall and elegant with wisps of red hair escaping from beneath her cap.

His breath hitched. He hadn't seen Marge since that morning in the NAAFI. In fact, during the past tedious week of debriefings and meetings, he'd been very careful *not* to see her. Her obvious disinterest that day had stung, and he had no desire to watch her flirting and laughing with everyone but him.

But here she was again, haunting his reality as surely as she haunted his dreams. A young soldier, at least a couple of inches shorter than her and probably more than a couple of years younger, had his arm around her waist and was looking up at her hungrily, while she smiled down at him. God, how he'd missed that smile.

There was no way he could get past without her noticing, so he called her name.

She turned and stared at him in surprise. He felt a moment's satisfaction as the young whippersnapper's face fell. *That's right, mate, hop along now. She's mine.*

Clearly sensing the challenge, the soldier said a hasty good-bye to Marge and left.

'What are you doing here?' he asked. Marge looked pale and tired, the freckles she tried so hard to hide standing out on her nose and cheeks. He had an overwhelming urge to kiss each one.

'I could ask you the same,' she said coldly. 'I thought you'd be back off to sea by now.'

'Things to do, people to see,' he said lightly. 'You going to the café?'

She shrugged. 'Nope, I have other plans . See you around, Rodders.'

Without a backward glance, she walked away from him, her back straight, her suitcase banging awkwardly against her leg. He opened his mouth to call after her but then shut it again. She'd made her feelings more than clear.

He waited until she turned left onto Folkestone Road, then slowly trailed after her. The rain dripped from the brim of his cap and his heartbeat felt heavy against his chest. If he'd known she was on that damned interminable train, he would have forced her to talk to him. He needed her to know that all the reasons he'd had for driving her away were gone; that he wanted her back. That he couldn't imagine his life without her.

But even if he'd been able to say all that, would she have cared? From what he'd seen recently, she had no shortage of admirers, which was only to be expected. Marge was gorgeous, but it was more than that: it was as if there was a permanent glow around her. He could still remember the first time he'd seen her. It had been in assembly at school. They'd been singing 'All Things Bright and Beautiful' and his eyes had wandered round the room, looking for Marianne. She'd just started, and he'd promised his mum he'd keep an eye on her. There'd been no need to worry, though. Marge had taken her under her wing, and they were standing close together, sharing a hymn book, Marge a head taller than Marianne. A ray of sunlight was shining through the windows, and her hair was ablaze.

She must have sensed his gaze because she'd glanced over at him, crossed her eyes and stuck out her tongue, making him feel foolish; she'd been having the same effect on him ever since. And, it seemed, on every other man who came into contact with her.

But she'd loved him not so long ago. Surely he could make her love him again. He just needed to think of a way to win her back.

First, though, he needed to earn her forgiveness – which was easier said than done. Marge wasn't the type to forgive and forget. Luckily, he wasn't the sort to give up at the first hurdle. He'd find a way or die trying. This time he wasn't going to let her go. He'd have to be quick about it though; he was going back out to sea soon. But he loved a deadline – and so far, he'd never missed a single one.

With that settled, his thoughts turned to the course, which was apparently meant to help them evade U-boats in the Atlantic. He couldn't begin to imagine how sitting in a dusty room being lectured to would help them in the heat of battle, but orders were orders. It was a shame there wasn't a course to help him manage his fractious family.

He sighed. He'd not told his mother he was coming, which she'd no doubt be furious about. But then everything he did seemed to irritate her. She still blamed him for the disastrous trial. It was he, after all, who'd persuaded her to give in to Mary Guthrie's threats. Frankly, he hadn't forgiven himself for that, either. He'd destroyed so much last year, but now it was time to try to put things right.

He glanced across the road, realising that he was opposite the Guthries' bakery. He hesitated as the events of last spring came back to him. He could almost feel Mary Guthrie's thin, spindly fingers grasping his arm as she threatened to tell the world that his mother had killed his father. He'd been a fool to listen to her, but he'd been scared – for his mother, for his family, for himself . . . He'd burnt Gladys's diary now, so there was nothing she could say or do that would convince people. If she tried, they'd dismiss it as the ramblings of a madwoman.

The door of the bakery opened, and a customer came out clutching a loaf. On impulse he crossed the road and went inside.

Jack Guthrie stood behind the counter. He'd once been a jolly man, who used to give them bags of broken biscuits when they were young. Now, though, he looked careworn, his scalp pink through his thinning grey hair, and his forehead deeply furrowed.

He stiffened when he saw Rodney. 'What do you want?' he asked bluntly. Then his expression changed. 'Is it Colin?'

To persuade Mary to keep quiet about the diary, he'd promised the Guthries that he would try to get news of their son. In truth, he would have done this anyway, because wherever Colin was, his brother Jimmy would be right by his side. But they'd disappeared into thin air. Which was to be expected considering they were working for the French Resistance.

Rodney shook his head. 'I've been at sea, so there's not been much chance of finding out anything. I'm sorry. I wish I could put your mind at rest.'

'Thank you. It's more than we can expect after everything that's happened.'

'How's Mrs Guthrie?' he asked. She might have turned all their lives upside down, but he couldn't help feeling sorry for her.

The man's shoulders drooped. 'Not good. Susan's sentence 'as finished her. I'm not sure she'll ever recover. So, if you're worried she'll say anything, then don't be. No one would believe a word she says anyway.'

At Rodney's surprised expression, he nodded. 'She told me all of it. Not sure I believe it either, to be honest, so I won't be openin' that can of worms – we've all suffered enough. You best leave. She'll go mad if she knows you've set so much as a toe in 'ere. Give my regards to your mum.'

Rodney left, feeling a little lighter. At least that was one less thing to worry about. Now all he had to do was survive this week with his family and win back Marge. Surely he could manage that?

# Chapter 17

Marge lowered her head and battled her way down Folkestone Road towards the High Street. She wasn't being picked up until early evening, so it gave her plenty of time to talk to Mr Wainwright.

She'd missed her old boss. He'd been a godsend to her after her parents had died in a car crash, helping her with all the admin that came with death and giving her a place to live. But more than that, he'd listened when she'd told him about Katy, and he'd promised to try and find her. But over ten years on, he'd still not managed to find a trace of her.

By the time she arrived outside Mr Wainwright's tall Georgian house on Victoria Crescent, she was soaked through, and the water had seeped through her cap and into her hair. Every part of her felt as if it was encased in ice. She'd thrown her macintosh over her uniform, but it did little to keep the cold wind at bay. She rapped on the door, her teeth chattering as she jiggled from foot to foot.

The door was opened by Mrs Frobisher. Marge had spent an afternoon showing the woman the ropes the day before she'd left to start her naval training, and her overriding memory was that she was a miserable old boot. Now the woman looked down her long nose at her, eyes widening as she realised who it was.

'Miss Atkinson?'

Marge smiled. 'How many times have I told you to call me Marge! Can I come in?'

Mrs Frobisher stepped aside. The woman still looked like she was living in 1908, with a long black skirt, high-necked blouse and her grey hair scraped into a bun.

'Is it urgent? Mr Wainwright is currently dining with a friend and has asked not to be disturbed.' She sniffed disapprovingly, which made Marge curious. *Who was this* friend? *Was it possible it was a* lady *friend?*

'Is it anyone I know?' she asked.

The woman's lips tightened. 'That woman from the café. You may as well wait in the kitchen. You can make yourself a cup of tea.' She disappeared into her small office and shut the door with a firm click.

Marge was too surprised at the news that Nellie and Mr Wainwright were having a private lunch together to care about the woman's rudeness. She couldn't imagine a more unlikely couple! And what about Jasper?

A squeal of high-pitched laughter floated out from behind the dining room door, and Marge grinned. Cissy! She'd had no idea those two were close, but it made sense: Mr Wainwright loved his music, and Cissy was a violinist, so they had a shared interest.

Glancing over her shoulder to ensure Mrs Frobisher hadn't re-emerged, she turned the handle and opened the door a crack. Like the rest of his house, Mr Wainwright's dining room was old-fashioned. A dark mahogany table stood in the centre of the room, surrounded by six high-backed chairs upholstered in red velvet. And there at the end of the table, Mr Wainwright sat with his bald head bent towards Cissy's orange one.

She needn't have worried about being noticed; the two were so intent on each other that she doubted they'd notice if a shell fell through the roof.

Well, good for them. As far as she knew, Mr Wainwright had been single for his entire life, and she knew Cissy was recently widowed. It was wonderful that these two might have found love late in life. Would she have to wait that long?

After closing the door gently, she went into the kitchen, sighing with relief at finding a fire burning in the grate. Ringing out her hair, she put the kettle on, then sat down in the armchair by the fire to wait. The warmth of the room, her exhaustion from the journey and the whisky meant that she was soon asleep.

'Marge?! Is it really you?'

She jerked awake to find Mr Wainwright standing in front of her. His plump cheeks were flushed and there was a splash of gravy on his tie.

Surging to her feet, she put her arms around him and rested her chin on his head – she'd always towered over him.

'Deary me, Mrs Frobisher should have come to get me!' He put his arms around her and gave her a squeeze.

Marge stepped away and grinned. 'She didn't want to disturb you.'

Mr Wainwright's cheeks reddened further, and he cleared his throat, rocking back on his heels.

'Just lunch with a friend. Mrs Ford was asking for advice on her will.'

'Of course she was.' Marge nodded sagely. 'You are the best in the business after all.'

'Poppycock. Now, are you going to tell me what you're doing here. How long will you be staying? *Where* will you be staying?'

Marge laughed. 'One question at a time, Mr W. I'm just here for the afternoon, waiting for transport to my new job. And I can't tell you where I'll be staying.' She tapped her finger on her nose. 'It's all very hush-hush. But I needed to see you.'

He frowned. 'Is something wrong, dear? You seem troubled.'

She gestured to the kettle. 'Let's have a cup of tea, and I'll tell you all about it.'

Once the tea was made, they sat opposite each other at the kitchen table. Marge fiddled with her cup, unsure where to begin.

Finally, she looked up at him. 'It's about Katy. Or more precisely about the man she was having an affair with.'

Mr Wainwright's eyes widened. 'What do you mean?'

'Apparently my new commanding officer is Captain Thomas Bennett.' Mr Wainwright's eyebrows rose at this. 'And I just don't know what to do. Should I ask him if he knows where Katy is? Or should I pretend we've never met? I mean, I know wherever she went, he didn't go with her, but even so, they might have stayed in touch?' She pulled at her hair. 'God, what am I thinking! Of course he won't know. Especially as I know for a fact he didn't leave with her. I'm so confused and angry. Just hearing his name dredged the whole nightmare up again.'

Mr Wainwright took off his spectacles, pulled a handkerchief from his breast pocket and began polishing them vigorously. It was something she'd seen him do countless times when he was dealing with a tricky client or problem.

'What is it?' she asked sharply.

Slowly and deliberately, he put his glasses back on his nose and sighed. 'I believe I may have found her.'

For a moment, Marge was too stunned to answer. 'Oh my God! Why didn't you tell me sooner? When did you find her? Where is she?'

Mr Wainwright held up his hand, his expression pained.

Marge felt her heart sink. 'It's bad news, isn't it?' she asked, her voice shaking.

He took his glasses off again, polishing them on his sleeve this time. 'I'm afraid I found her too late.'

Her excitement drained away. 'What do you mean? Did she disappear again?'

He reached across the table and took her hands. 'I'm so sorry, my dear. It seems that she died in an air raid in London last year.'

For a moment, Marge wasn't sure she'd heard him right. After all this time, she was getting answers, but it was too late. The news reverberated through her heart, making her entire body shake. 'Are you quite sure?' she asked.

Mr Wainwright nodded. 'She was living in a … ah … boarding house. And the only reason she was listed as a casualty is because they found a metal safe containing papers with her name on.'

'But there's been no body to identify?' she asked.

'I'm afraid the house took a direct hit and burnt to the ground.'

The implication was clear: there had been nothing left to identify.

'Then how can you be sure? Just because there were papers, doesn't mean she was there too.' Marge knew she was clutching at straws, but it was too cruel to have her sister snatched away from her again.

He sighed. 'I suppose we can't. But for your own sake, Marge, I think you need to accept that she probably really is gone this time.'

Marge nodded, her throat tight. 'Why didn't you tell me as soon as you knew?'

He regarded her gravely. 'I wanted to do it face to face. I know this is a very private grief, and I didn't want you to be alone with it. I'm so sorry I couldn't give you better news.'

Marge kept her gaze on the tea in her cup. It was weak and unappetising, but even if it had been the finest champagne, she wouldn't have been able to swallow it. Over the years she'd imagined what Katy's life might be like so many times; hoping against hope that she was happy. A beautiful house, children, a kind husband . . . She reached into her pocket and pulled out a hankie. But her eyes were still dry, so she merely twisted it round her fingers.

'And you will be working with this man you say she was having an affair with before she left?'

Marge nodded, eyes focused on the wobbly 'MA' stitched into the corner, sewn by her mother years ago. She'd never had the heart to get rid of it. She glanced up at Mr Wainwright's plump, shiny face. The flush was gone now, leaving it pasty, and she felt guilty for ruining his happy mood.

'I don't like the thought of you working with this captain,' he said. 'He clearly has a taste for young women – very young women – and I imagine he won't like you knowing his secrets.'

She laughed humourlessly. 'I think *he's* the one who should worry,' she said fiercely. 'Because I'll be watching him, and if he puts so much as one toe out of line, he'll regret it. Anyway, you shouldn't worry. I'm far too old for his tastes, and I doubt he'll remember me.'

Mr Wainwright sighed. 'Promise me that you won't do anything foolish?'

Marge didn't reply. She couldn't make that promise. Captain Tom Bennett would regret what he'd done to her sister, and she didn't care what the consequences for herself might be. 'I promise that I'll try not to,' she said with a wry smile. 'You know me, Mr W. When my dander's up, there's not a lot anyone can do about it.'

# Chapter 18

Nellie picked up the plates Elodie had deposited on the hatch and inhaled with appreciation. 'Tell you what, love, your stew's givin' Marianne's a run for its money.'

'I heard that!' Marianne called from across the kitchen. Then, seeing Elodie's anxious look, she smiled. 'I'd say it's a million times better than mine.'

Balancing a plate on each arm and one in each hand, Nellie frowned. 'Where's Cissy? She's been gone hours. And I'm meant to be havin' an hour off to 'ave lunch with the girls so we can plan this party Lily's so set on. It's not long till the big day.' In truth, she was having second thoughts about the whole idea. Especially as Jasper hadn't been in since their conversation when she'd given him a piece of her mind.

Elodie coloured and shrugged, while Marianne just looked knowing. They clearly knew exactly where her cousin was, but she'd die before giving in to her curiosity. Since their argument the week before, Cissy had been pointedly ignoring her. It was reminiscent of their childhood, although back then, Nellie was usually the one giving *her* the silent treatment. It was setting Nellie's teeth on edge – not ideal when her nerves were already shot to pieces.

The posh bloke – Francis – had returned once to pick up a couple more of the boxes, but there were still several left. And she'd still not been able to work out how to look inside undetected.

Francis's presence hadn't gone unnoticed by the customers. Adelaide Frost seemed to have positioned herself permanently at Jasper's old table by the counter in front of the kitchen door. Sometimes she was joined by Muriel Palmer or Mr Gallacher. It was as if they'd set up an unofficial surveillance.

As for Lou Carter, she'd disappeared. Probably off flogging her filthy mags. No doubt they brought in a lot more profit than the whelks. But what if there was something more sinister in her disappearance? Had Johnny Fox done away with her?

Nellie swallowed nervously. She *needed* that gun. If she knew she could protect herself maybe she'd manage to sleep a little better. As it was, every night, she'd lie awake, her ear cocked for trouble.

Muttering under her breath, she deposited the plates on the tables in front of her friends: Mavis Woodbridge, who ran the Royal Oak pub – since her daughter-in-law Daisy's death, the frown lines had deepened on her forehead, but not once had Nellie heard her complain about her lot; Ethel Turner, who ran the grocery store with her husband; and Phyllis Perkins, grandmother of Donny's friend Freddie, who owned the fish shop next door to that.

'Thought you was meant to be joinin' us, Nell?' Mavis said. 'This party won't plan itself.'

'Cissy's gone walkabout,' Nellie grumbled.

The three women exchanged a glance and a smile.

'Is there something I need to know?' She eyed them suspiciously.

Ethel shrugged and picked up her spoon. 'I'd've thought you'd know better than us.'

Nellie ground her teeth in frustration. 'Maybe you lot could make a start. We'll need a bit of booze, if there's any goin' spare, Mavis. And perhaps a nice piece of fish to roast, Phyllis. Ethel, if you could get us a bit of sugar and dried fruit, Marianne'll make a cake. And maybe some spuds. Keep a tab, and I'll settle up after.'

'Afternoon, all!'

Jasper's cheery voice made Nellie spin around. Hell's bells that was all she needed! She searched his expression for a clue as to whether his attitude towards her had changed since her outburst the previous week, but it was impossible to tell.

Spotting the four women, Jasper held out his arms. 'All my favourite girls in one place!' He was wearing his usual uniform of baggy brown trousers with braces and a blue shirt. But he wasn't looking at her. In fact, his eyes barely flicked in her direction. Was she included in that greeting or not?

'I'd like a bowl of that, if you don't mind, Nellie.' Finally, Jasper looked at her, but his expression was neutral. Well, there was her answer. Not even a flicker of remorse from him.

'What did your last slave die of,' she muttered. As she relayed the order to Marianne through the hatch, a burst of laughter erupted at the table and her back stiffened. It seemed no one had much time for her at the moment.

Someone cleared their throat, and she turned to see Bertha Bancroft standing at the counter, wearing a smart navy-blue suit, her blonde hair coifed to perfection. She looked more like she was on her way to Buckingham Palace than popping to the café for a cup of tea. Come to think of it, why was she here at all? Nellie felt a jolt of alarm. Last year she'd visited Bertha twice in search of answers from the spirit world, and received only cryptic nonsense back. Although in a roundabout way, she had predicted Colin's return and Jimmy's subsequent departure. She'd also implied she knew the truth about Donald's death. Which was impossible, unless she really could talk to spirits.

Since then, Nellie had tried to avoid her, which had been surprisingly easy. Even in a community as small as theirs, there were cliques and factions, and she steered clear of anyone who visited Bertha's spiritualist church.

'Mrs Bancroft.' She forced a smile. 'Cuppa, is it?'

Bertha shook her head. 'I'm not stoppin', love. But I had to come.' She leant over the counter. 'I've received a warnin'. You're dancin' with the devil, an' you need to watch out.'

Nellie went hot and then cold. 'Have you gone mad?' she snapped, glancing over the woman's shoulder and noting that almost everyone in the café – aside from the outsiders who didn't know who Bertha was – was staring at them curiously.

'Just deliverin' a message.' Her eyes bored into her with an intensity that raised goosebumps on Nellie's arms.

Nellie pursed her lips.

'Look,' Bertha sighed. 'I don't know what this is all about, but I'd heed the warnin' if I was you.' She turned and looked around, her gaze zeroing in on Jasper. 'As for you,' she said, pointing at him. 'You should let sleepin' dogs lie.'

Even the three ATS girls at the table by the window had stopped talking now and were staring unashamedly at Bertha.

The café door opened, and Adelaide Frost walked in, her knitting needles poking out of the bag over her arm. Catching sight of Bertha, she froze for a moment, before marching over, a thin finger pointing at the woman's chest. 'Beware of false prophets, which come to you in sheep's clothing, but inwardly they are ravening wolves.'

Nellie held her breath, waiting to see what Bertha would do. But the other woman merely smiled gently. 'You gotta let him go, Addy. He's suffered enough.' Then patting the woman's shoulder, she walked out.

Adelaide looked stricken, all belligerence draining from her.

Let who go? And Addy? She'd known the woman for most of her life, and no one had ever called her that. But then, Adelaide and Bertha were a good few years older than her, so maybe they'd been friends once.

She thought back to what she knew about the old busybody, realising that it wasn't a lot. She liked to knit, she liked the Bible, and she liked sticking her nose into other people's business. And that was it.

'My God, that woman gives me the shivers,' Mavis exclaimed when the door had closed behind Bertha. 'What was all that about anyway?' She glanced between Nellie and Adelaide, who, for the first time Nellie could remember, looked lost and uncertain.

'Is this about whatever them men are poppin' in and out of here for?' Ethel Turner asked. 'Everyone's talkin' about it, Nell. Word is, you're harbourin' secrets in your basement.'

Ethel was one of Nellie's very best friends, but right now she could have cheerfully throttled her. 'Don't you start, love. I get enough of that from everyone else.'

She glanced at Adelaide, expecting her to put in her tuppence worth, but the woman didn't seem to have heard. Instead, she was staring into space, her eyes large and haunted.

Jasper stood and held his chair to her. 'Here, take a seat, love. You're white as a ghost.'

Adelaide seemed to recover herself. 'There are no such things as ghosts,' she said sharply.

'What about the Holy Ghost?' someone called.

'Aside from that.' She sniffed. 'And that is not a real ghost. Thank you, Jasper. You are a true gentleman.' She looked over at Nellie. 'Bring me a bowl of that stew and a cup of tea, would you?'

Nellie bristled and opened her mouth to say something, but Jasper shook his head. So, she whirled round and called the order through to the kitchen.

When she turned to pour the tea, Jasper was leaning on the counter. 'So, no change with the whole storage situation then? I 'ear that bloke's been back. Looks like even the spirits are talkin' about it.'

'Talking to me now, are you?' She swiped a cloth over the counter a little more forcefully than necessary.

Jasper ignored the question. 'Well?'

Nellie sighed. 'That woman's full of strange little messages and I don't take no notice of her.'

'I wouldn't normally listen to her either, but I reckon she's got a point.'

'Maybe she also had a point about lettin' sleepin' dogs lie, too!' Nellie snapped.

Jasper coloured slightly. 'Reason I came in today was cos Cissy came to see me.'

Nellie sighed. Bloody Cissy.

'What did she 'ave to say this time?'

'She's worried about you, Nell. *I'm* worried about you. And this Johnny Fox bloke . . . I don't like the sound of 'im one bit.'

Nellie slammed her hands onto the counter. 'This is *not* your concern, Jasper.'

Jasper held up his hands. 'You're right. Nothin' to do with me. Not anymore.'

He muttered this last, and Nellie felt another moment of uncertainty. At this rate the party was going to be a disaster.

Jasper's gaze slid past her and his face broke into a wide smile. 'Well, look what the cat dragged in!'

Nellie looked round. Rodney was standing at the kitchen door, water dripping from his coat, his kitbag at his feet. She felt a flutter of joy, but it was quickly squashed by a sudden worry. She hoped he wasn't expecting to stay here. On the one hand, his presence would make her feel safer. But, on the other, she didn't want Rodney getting wind of what was going on.

'Come here, lad!' Jasper pulled him into a hug, not caring about the water dripping from his coat.

Rodney glanced at her over Jasper's shoulder. Nellie swallowed. Her feelings for her eldest son had always been complicated. She loved him, but she had never understood him. He'd saved her life once, pulling Donald off her when he'd tried to strangle her, and she could never forget that. Just twelve years old, bearing the brunt of his father's madness and seeing things a child should never see. But the incident had broken something in their relationship that had never healed. And ever since he'd persuaded her to give in to Mary Guthrie's blackmail at the trial last year, the rift between them felt as wide as the Atlantic.

But he was her firstborn. He'd brought such love and joy when he'd appeared thirty-two years ago. Donald had doted on him then, she remembered sadly. And so had she.

Jasper let go of Rodney and looked over at her with an expectant smile, so she stepped forward and held out her hand.

'You shoulda told us you was comin',' she said. 'We'd have killed the fatted calf.'

Rodney's disappointed expression and Jasper's disapproving one made her feel immediately contrite. She reached up and put her arms around his neck. 'I'm glad you're here, son,' she whispered. And she was. She was glad he was safe, but she was also worried. Somehow, she had to ensure that Rodney and Johnny Fox never crossed paths. Which meant he absolutely couldn't stay here. 'You're not expectin' to stay, are you?' she asked.

'Course 'e'll stay 'ere, Nell,' Jasper said indignantly.

Nellie forced a smile. 'Your room's been given to Marianne and the baby. Don's back in 'is little cubbyhole, an' Cissy's sharin' with Lily and Elodie for the moment. So . . .' She sighed deeply.

'You can come an' stay with me then,' Jasper said. 'It'd be good to 'ave some company.'

'For God's sake, Mum, of course Rod's staying,' Marianne snapped. 'Me and Ted'll move back in with Lily, and Cissy can share with you.'

Nellie blanched at the thought.

Rodney sighed impatiently. 'Calm down, everyone. I'll be bunking down at the castle. I just popped in to say hello.'

Nellie patted his arm. 'I'm sorry, love. We're packed in like sardines as it is. Marianne, get some food for the man.' She poured a cup of tea, deliberately avoiding Jasper's scowling disapproval.

# Chapter 19

Thank God he didn't actually have to stay here, Rodney reflected as he finally sat down to a large plate of stew after first being grilled by his mother's friends. He loved those women dearly, but they could talk a man to death in five minutes flat.

'Don't mind your mum; she's got a lot on her plate.' Jasper sat down opposite him.

Rodney grinned. 'Life on a warship is dangerous and noisy but believe me, compared to here, it's an oasis of calm.' He hadn't slept in the cramped apartment above the café since he'd left for naval training when he was eighteen, nor had he wanted to. The place held too many terrible memories for him to ever feel completely comfortable.

Jasper's blue eyes twinkled. 'When you put it like that, can't say as I blame you for wantin' to steer clear. Now, tell me about life on the ocean wave.'

'Oh, you know, a bit dicey.' Rodney looked over at his mother, who was bickering with a customer, her orange turban clashing with her pink apron and purple skirt. She was a force of nature and though they weren't close, they shared an unbreakable bond. He'd protected her when his father had tried to kill her. And a few years later, she'd returned the favour by killing his father. Or at least, like Gladys, he believed she had. No one really knew the truth except his mother. But for that one act alone, he owed her far more than she would ever understand.

'You said Mum has a lot on her plate?' he asked.

Jasper hesitated a moment, then shook his head. 'Just the usual. Life ain't easy for any of us.'

Rodney decided against delving further. He knew from bitter experience, it wasn't worth it. In any case, he wouldn't be here long enough to do anything. 'Well, I'm sure you'll all handle it.'

Jasper rubbed his hair. 'Course we will, son. Don't you worry about us. I'll keep 'em safe.'

Rodney smiled at him. 'I never doubted it.' When he was younger, he'd always wished Jasper was his father. It was only when he got older that he'd realised that in all the ways that mattered, he was. He couldn't imagine how grim their lives would have been without him. He reached out and clasped his hand. 'Thanks, Jasper. For everything.'

Jasper squeezed his hand. 'There ain't no thanks necessary. You kids mean the world to me. As does your mum.' He glanced over at Nellie with a look that was part affection, part exasperation. 'She ain't easy to love, but her heart beats for her kids. And that includes you. You know that, don't you? That's the only reason she—'

Did Jasper know? Rodney examined his face. Or was he trying to find out the truth? 'Only reason she what?' he asked innocently.

Jasper shook his head. 'Nothin'. Just know she loves you. As do I.'

He was beginning to feel uncomfortable at the turn in the conversation, so Rodney took a last mouthful of stew and put down his knife and fork. 'I better get off.' He stood up, clapped Jasper on the shoulder then took his dirty plate over to the counter.

'Leavin' so soon, love?' Nellie asked.

'Got a meeting up at the castle. And I want to pop in to see Edie and meet the new baby.'

His mother's lips tightened.

'She'll come round, Mum,' he said softly. 'You just need to give it time.'

'She's said that, has she?' Nellie snapped. 'Maybe she'd still be talkin' to me if it weren't for you makin' me say all them things in court.'

And maybe she wouldn't, he wanted to retort. But deciding discretion was the better part of valour, he kept his thoughts to himself as he leant forward to kiss his mother's cheek. 'I'll see you later.'

'Is that a promise or a threat?' she called after him as he walked into the kitchen.

Rodney rolled his eyes at Marianne, who gave him a sympathetic look. 'Come round for dinner tonight?' she asked. 'I miss you, big brother. Things don't feel right without you nearby. And I think Mum's in trouble . . .' She said this last bit quietly, casting a quick glance over her shoulder.

Not this again. 'Mum's always in trouble,' he said dryly. 'I'll come and say goodbye before I leave. By the way, I saw Marge at the station.'

Marianne frowned. 'Marge is here? She didn't tell me she was leaving Liverpool. Didn't she like it?'

'From what I saw, she was having a whale of a time up there.'

Marianne raised an eyebrow at him. 'Found another bloke, has she? Well, you had your chance, and you made a hash of it, so you've only got yourself to blame.'

Rodney felt his cheeks warm. 'You're right, as usual. Anyway, I'll see you later.' Shouldering his bag, he left by the back door.

Trudging up Castle Street, he started to wonder what sort of trouble his mother could be in this time. Then, realising what he was doing, he forced himself to put it to the back of his mind; it was none of his business anymore. Instead, he would focus his attention on trying to make things up with Marge. His next voyage might be his last, and at the very least, he didn't want to die without apologising.

At the castle, he was waved through by the guards with a smart salute, and he strolled towards the tunnel entrance feeling nostalgic. He'd grown up in the shadow of this castle never dreaming he'd end up living and working here. He might not have missed Dover, but he did miss this place.

He felt lighter as he wound his way through the tunnels towards his old offices deep underground. When he got there, Ruby, his old secretary, greeted him like a long-lost hero, rushing off to fetch him a cup of weak coffee and filling him in on everything that had happened since he'd been away.

He sipped his drink, listening with half an ear as she chattered on. Her talking had irritated him when he'd worked here, but now it calmed the noise in his mind.

'We miss you, sir. Your replacement's a right idiot, if you don't mind me saying. You were a stickler, but at least we knew where we stood.'

Rodney's lips twitched. He'd never have allowed her to talk about a superior officer like this when they worked together. But it was none of his business anymore. And it was gratifying to know the other secretaries had liked him.

The phone on her desk rang and she picked it up. 'Commander Worthing will see you now, sir,' she said primly.

Rodney put his cap on and stood up. 'Good to see you, Ruby.'

She blew him a kiss as he walked out. Really, he should admonish her, but since he'd been at sea, he didn't see the point. Discipline was all very well, but there should be room for a bit of fun as well.

He went into the commander's office and saluted smartly.

'At ease, Castle. Take a seat.'

Rodney sat down, assessing the other man. He was tall and thin with steel-grey hair and deep wrinkles at the corners of his eyes – a common affliction for old sailors, who'd spent years squinting into the distance. But despite the wrinkles, his eyes were bright and intelligent.

After some discussion about the Atlantic and the progress of the war, Commander Worthing clasped his hands together and put them on the desk in front of him.

'You must be wondering why I wanted to see you, Castle. The truth is, I need to talk to you about this damn stupid course. It's the talk of the mess, you know. Absolute bloody foolishness if you ask me. And run by a bunch of Wrens, you know.'

Rodney nodded, although he hadn't been aware of that. Was this why Marge was here? His heart leapt at the thought. There was something very attractive about the thought of her ordering him around . . . Realising he'd stopped listening, he hastily pushed the thought to the back of his mind and tuned in to the commander again.

'Well, obviously we can't let the little ladies run the show entirely by themselves, so they will be under the command of Captain Tom Bennett . . .' He paused and looked at Rodney expectantly.

When Rodney didn't respond, he sighed. 'I can see you don't know him. If you'd met him, you wouldn't forget him.

I don't like to say this about a fellow officer, but the man's a liability. Left the Navy under a cloud back in '35, and now back in the fold because we can't spare anyone else to supervise a bunch of women.'

'I see,' Rodney said. 'But what would you like me to do?'

'I want a full report. Efficiency, usefulness, behaviour of the women. But most especially, keep your eye on Bennett. Our female colleagues need our protection, no matter how much they bleat on about being as capable as the men, we both know they're not, what?'

Rodney imagined what Marge would say if she heard Worthing's opinions, and the thought made him want to grin. But he pursed his lips and nodded sagely.

'I understand, sir. Any idea of the names of the Wrens taking part, sir?' he asked casually. It was too much of a coincidence for Marge to have been sent down here just as the course was about to start, surely.

'Afraid not. But whoever they are, we need to be vigilant on their behalf, and I'm relying on you for that. Alert the other chaps as well. Even a sniff of any untoward behaviour from the man, and I'll get the whole thing shut down.' He slapped his palm on the table, then seemed to collect himself and cleared his throat. 'Or at the very least, I will find an excuse to remove Captain Bennett from his post so someone more trustworthy can take his place.'

'Why was he dismissed?' Rodney asked. If Worthing thought the women needed protection, then he could guess, but it would be useful to have specifics.

'Between you and me, he could never keep it in his trousers, Castle. Not normally a problem, but it is when you upset a senior officer . . . I imagine you get the picture.'

'Ahh.' Presumably the man had had an affair with some-one's wife then. Or several wives by the sound of it. 'I'll keep my eye out, and give you full assessment of the course on my return.'

'Good show, Castle.' He waved his hand towards the door. 'Dismissed.'

# Chapter 20

Edie was bent over the bonnet of an Austin 8, trying to work out why it wouldn't accelerate, while the driver paced the forecourt. She looked smart in her khaki uniform, with peaked cap and narrow skirt, her shoes polished to an intense shine, and Edie felt conscious of her oil-stained overalls and blackened fingernails.

On the floor beside her, Vivvy gurgled in her basket, playing with her feet and flashing a gummy smile at the wall every so often. What was it about walls that babies found so endlessly fascinating?

'Found anything?' The woman walked over. Everything about her was neat and purposeful, and Edie felt a flash of envy. She could do that job; driving officers around the country, tending to the cars and generally pulling her weight for the war effort.

Vivvy let out a squeal of delight, and Edie's heart softened. Of course she couldn't. Not when she'd promised Bill she'd stay at the garage and help his uncle, and not when she had this miraculous child to care for. Even national jeopardy faded into insignificance compared to Vivvy's wellbeing.

'I'm guessing spark plugs,' the woman said.

'Yup.' Edie wiped her hands on an oily rag. 'Give me forty-five minutes. An hour tops, and I'll replace them for you.'

The woman's eyebrows rose. 'Then you're a better woman than me,' she said. 'Last time I tried it took two hours.'

Edie smiled. 'First time?' she asked.

The women smiled ruefully. 'And last, I hope.' She looked down at Vivvy, who grinned gummily up at her. 'If it weren't for this little angel, I'd suggest you join the ATS.' She leant down to tickle Vivvy's plump tummy, currently covered with a blanket knitted by Adelaide Frost. Edie had been surprised and very touched when the woman had presented it to her. She'd only ever seen her through her mother's jaundiced view – a Bible-quoting busybody – but she was all right really.

'I'd love to join up,' Edie said.

'And I'd love a plump little cherub like this,' the driver said. 'Doubt it'll happen now.' Her grief-stricken tone spoke volumes, and Edie didn't pry. She should stop moaning and start counting her blessings. Yes, driving around in a smart uniform might be fun, but as long as she had Bill and Vivvy, nothing else really mattered.

'You can wait in the office if you prefer?' Edie gestured towards the single-storey white building next to the garage. Its red door was fading and chipped, the walls greying, but it was still one of her favourite places in the world and had been since she was young and used to come up here to watch Mr P fix the engines. This was where she'd first met Bill, too, when he'd stay at the garage during the holidays. Mrs P. had been alive then and used to feed them sandwiches, admonishing them to wash their hands before they ate. Which of course they never did.

'I'd rather watch how you do it, if you don't mind.' The woman pulled off a leather glove and held her hand out to Edie. 'Geraldine Ogilvie,' she said. 'Call me Gerry.'

Edie rubbed her hand down her blue overalls and shook her hand. 'Edie Castle—I mean Penfold, and this is Vivien.'

'Just married?' Gerry asked with a significant glance at Vivvy.

'It's been a year, actually, but I've not seen him since the day after the wedding. RAF.' Edie bent over the car again.

The woman gazed into the distance. 'The last time I saw my hubby was January 1940. We married a week before he left. But he never made it back from Dunkirk.' She blinked. 'Might go sit in the office after all. I could look after the baby for you.'

Edie nodded, watching as Gerry scooped Vivvy into her arms and hurried into the office, head bent. 'There but for the grace of God,' she murmured, bending to her task. She would always have Vivvy, at least. But as much as she loved her daughter, she wasn't Bill's. If he died, she wouldn't find him in her daughter's eyes or smile. He'd just be gone.

She was just finishing, when she heard her name being called by a familiar voice. She looked up to see her big brother, ramrod straight and not a hair out of place as usual. She and Rodney had always argued – he was too bossy, too judgemental – but if there was one person she knew she could always count on, it was her eldest brother.

Throwing down the oily rag, she ran across the forecourt and threw herself into his arms.

Laughing, he pushed her away. 'Steady on. Cleaning doesn't come cheap these days.'

She stepped back and rolled her eyes. 'I'd been hoping that a few months cramped on a boat with a bunch of smelly men might have lowered your standards, Rod.'

He smiled. 'You know me, Edie. I'm an old stick in the mud when it comes to things like getting oil all over my uniform.'

Edie examined him. Active duty had taken its toll: he'd lost weight and the shadows under his eyes were deeper. But then, so were hers.

'Mr P about?' he asked, looking around at the cars littering the forecourt.

Edie's smile slipped. 'He's resting. Touch of flu.' It was more than that, though. He'd been coughing for weeks and had lost a lot of weight. She'd asked Dr Palmer to come and see him as soon as he could.

'And where's my niece?' he asked.

She grinned. 'Come see her.'

They went into the office to find Gerry walking up and down, Vivvy fast asleep against her shoulder.

'You all done?' she asked, her eyes flitting to Rodney.

Edie tried to look at him through another woman's eyes. Tall, dark-haired, blue-eyed, smart. Her brothers were all handsome. But when you grew up with them you barely noticed. Apart from Bert, of course. Somehow, though he had the same colouring and features, he was better-looking than Jimmy and Rod. She could never work out why.

Rodney's eyes warmed as he looked at Gerry, and she blushed.

But her brother wasn't looking at the other woman; his eyes were fixed on Vivvy. 'Do you mind if I take her?' he asked. 'This is the first time I've met my niece.'

Gerry looked shamefaced as she handed the sleeping baby to him. Rodney held her in the crook of his arm and gazed down at her face. Vivvy's huge blue eyes blinked open and fixed on her uncle.

'God, Edie, she's miraculous,' he breathed. 'I've never seen a more beautiful baby.'

As though understanding he was talking about her, Vivvy broke into an angelic smile. Rodney smiled back. Edie had never seen her brother so entranced, and she liked it. Was his icy facade finally cracking?

'She is gorgeous,' Edie conceded. 'Until night falls, that is.' But Rodney didn't seem to hear her as he sat down in one of the chairs and started to coo at her daughter.

'Car's ready for you, Gerry,' she said, opening the door and leading the other woman back onto the forecourt.

The woman checked her watch. 'Under an hour! Amazing. Honestly, we could use someone like you. The other girls are good, but no one's as quick as you.'

'Just practice,' Edie said modestly. She handed her the keys. 'Good luck, love. Really.' She put a hand on her arm.

Gerry smiled brightly. 'You too.'

Edie watched her turn left onto Castle Hill, passing the postman as he cycled up towards the garage. Her heart always stopped at the sight of him, even though he wasn't the one to deliver bad news. But you just never knew with this bloody war.

'Afternoon, Edie,' he said cheerfully, hopping off the bike.

'Mr Edwards,' Edie said warily. Rodney had come to stand beside her, Vivvy gurgling in his arms.

'One from Lincolnshire for you,' he said with a wink.

Edie snatched the envelope from him. Bill's large, looping handwriting was unmistakable. She smiled brilliantly at the man. 'Bill,' she breathed.

The postman got back on his bike. 'You go and read it, love. And good to see you back safe and sound, young Rodney.'

Rodney smiled politely, but it was clear he had no idea who he was.

Edie rolled her eyes at him. 'You don't remember Mr Edwards? Been delivering our post for the past twelve years, for God's sake!'

She ripped open the envelope.

*Dear Edie,*

*If this letter reaches you before the 24th January, then guess what! I will be seeing you in a few days! I have a week's leave.*

*Can we spend the week kissing, my love? It's been so long, I fear I'm very out of practice, so we'll need to sort that – and other things – out!*

*I will tell you all my news when I see you, sweetheart.*

*Love always,*

*Bill*

*P.S. Give Vivvy a big kiss from her old dad!*

Tears came to her eyes. It seemed all her doubts and worries were unfounded. Bill would love Vivvy as fiercely as she did.

'Bad news, sis?' Rodney asked, seeing her tears.

Edie shook her head and grabbed Vivvy from Rodney's arms. 'He's coming home!' she cried. She swooped the baby through the air, making her giggle, then cuddled her close to her chest, planting a kiss on her blonde fluffy head. 'Daddy's coming home.'

# Chapter 21

It wasn't until Nellie was drawing the blackout curtain at half past four that afternoon that Cissy finally made an appearance.

'The wanderer returns,' Nellie said snippily. 'You knew I'd asked the girls for lunch today. Least you could've done was stay to help.' She glanced at the bag Cissy was carrying. 'Been out for a nice lunch and a spot of shoppin', 'ave you? Another lipstick, is it?' Cissy loved her cosmetics, although she'd be lucky to find anything worth buying at the moment.

'Treated myself to a new jumper, if you must know. And so what if I did get another lipstick?''

Nellie narrowed her eyes. 'Why this sudden urge to smarten yourself up?'

Cissy blushed slightly but refused to take the bait. 'Did you ask me to be 'ere today so's we could enjoy lunch with *our* friends, or did you just want me to serve you, like Lady Muck?' Cissy cocked her head, her small dark eyes glinting with anger. 'I came to live here to help, not be your skivvy. And when you invite *our* friends round, I don't expect to be left out of the invite.' With a toss of her head, she walked through to the kitchen, smiling at a few of the regulars on the way.

'At least tell me where you've been,' Nellie called after her.

Cissy glanced over her shoulder. 'That's for me to know and you to find out.' With that, she disappeared into the kitchen.

'That told you,' Mr Gallacher chuckled.

Ignoring him, Nellie turned back to the window and yanked the curtains across. 'Takin' advantage, she is,' she muttered. 'Thinks just cos she helped me out once she can swan in and out like she owns the place.'

'That ain't fair, Nell. Cissy comin' 'ere was the best thing that could've happened for the café, under the circs,' Mr Gallacher said.

'And what's that supposed to mean?' she snapped, picking up his half-drunk cup of tea.

'Hey! I ain't finished.'

'You were finished a long time ago, Arthur Gallagher.'

She went to deposit the cup and saucer on the counter.

The old man got up, grumbling. 'I don't know why I still come 'ere, when I could go to the community restaurant or the Pot an' Kettle.'

'You come 'ere for me charm, Arthur. And Marianne and Elodie's food. Won't get that from Muriel Palmer's bunch of cabbage boilers up the community restaurant. And you take your life in your hands when you eat at the Pot an' Kettle.' Nellie responded, one eye on Cissy as she went upstairs. 'Oy, Ciss! Sink's full to the brim with washin' up.'

'Better roll your sleeves up then,' her cousin called over her shoulder.

Nellie could feel her skin prickling with anger, but underneath was a hurt that she refused to acknowledge. Mr Gallacher wasn't wrong when he said Cissy was the best thing that could have happened to the café. Her cousin had helped her out of debt and been there for her when she was sure Gladys's ghost was haunting her; she'd even stuck by her after the trial. But now with both Cissy and Jasper angry with her she felt like the lone tree on top of a hill, waiting for lightning to strike.

She went to stand behind the counter and stuck her head through the hatch. 'Where's Don, Marianne? He might wanna give us a hand.'

'You know, Mum, you and Cissy sound just like you and Gladys these days. And Don and Fred have taken Teddy out.'

'For God's sake!' She slapped her hand against the wall, making Elodie jump.

'I will do the washing,' Elodie said, her eyes wide.

Nellie felt guilt snake around her. Sometimes she forgot the trauma the poor girl had suffered, but surely she'd learnt by now that no harm would come to her here. Not from Nellie anyway. 'No, love. You do enough. We'll manage somehow.' Sighing, she unbuttoned the cuffs on her blouse and rolled her sleeves up.

'Psst . . .'

Nellie turned to see Lou standing in front of the counter looking furtive. She felt a momentary flare of relief to see her. The whelk stall hadn't been up all week, and no one seemed to know or care where Lou had got to. She was furious with her, but she didn't want her to come to harm. 'Hope you're not expectin' a cuppa, Lou.'

The woman leant across the counter. 'You said I could come back if I sorted you out.' She raised her eyebrows. 'Well, I done what you asked.'

Nellie stilled. It was what she'd wanted, but suddenly being faced with the reality of her request the fear returned. 'You got what I wanted?' she asked, her voice barely a whisper.

Lou cast another glance over her shoulder. Arthur Gallacher was very slowly buttoning his coat, his eyes fixed on Nellie and Lou.

'You need help with that?' Nellie asked sharply. 'Or 'as the sight of Lou turned you to stone?'

Mr Gallacher picked up his hat and slapped it on his head. 'All right, all right. I'm off.' He flounced out of the door. Nellie hurried over and flipped the sign to closed. Then she gestured to one of the tables.

'I could murder a cuppa,' Lou said.

'Not till I see it,' Nellie responded.

Lou gestured to her pocket. 'I brung it, all right? But cuppa first.'

With a sigh, Nellie poured two cups of tea, but before she handed Lou's over, she peered into the hatch. She could hear the clink of crockery from the pantry, where Elodie, bless her, had ignored her instructions and had started on the washing up. Marianne was scrubbing the range down, a bucket of dirty water beside her. Cissy, presumably, was still sulking upstairs.

Satisfied they wouldn't be paying any attention, she took the cups over to the table and sat down. 'Where you been?' she asked. 'I been worried.'

'Aww, Nell. Always knew ya loved me really.' Lou grinned.

Nellie rolled her eyes and held her hand out. 'Show me.'

Lou glanced towards the kitchen door and then at the hatch, then reaching into her pocket she brought out a brown paper bag. 'Best I could do,' she whispered.

With trembling hands, Nellie peered inside the bag. Just the sight of the weapon brought back terrible memories of the night Donald had died. She'd vowed then never to hold a gun again, but desperate times called for desperate measures.

The revolver was similar to Donald's old service gun, although it was slightly lighter and had a brown wooden grip. But she assumed the mechanics were the same.

'Is it loaded?' she whispered.

Lou reached into her pocket again and brought out a small cardboard box. She shook it, making the contents rattle.

'What am I meant to do with those?' Nellie asked, taking the box from her and peering inside. The bullets looked like little gold cylinders, harmless and strangely beautiful, glinting under the lights.

'You tellin' me you don't know 'ow to load a gun?'

'Ain't gotta clue. Can you do it?' She pushed the box and bag across the table.

'*Me?*' Lou squeaked. 'Who do you think I am, Billy the bleedin' Kid?'

'You're the criminal mastermind, Lou, not me.'

Lou shook her head. 'Can't stand 'em. Terence'd know, but 'e's not here.'

Nellie looked up sharply. 'You ain't told him about this, 'ave ya?'

'Where d'you think I got it?'

'Did you tell 'im it was for me?'

She shook her head. 'But he got me one and all. Loaded it for me. I can be your backup person.'

'Christ,' Nellie sighed. 'You coulda got him to load it. What am I meant to do with this?'

'Look, Nell, you asked for a gun, I got you a bleedin' gun. What more do ya want from me?'

'I want you to load the bugger!' Nellie hissed.

Somebody cleared their throat then and she turned to find Cissy standing in the doorway, her eyes sharp and curious.

'This is a private conversation, Ciss,' Nellie snapped.

Cissy frowned. 'So, it's all right for you to 'ave secrets, but you expect me to spill mine?' She cast a disdainful glance at Lou. 'Look at you whisperin' and plottin' with old Mrs Whelks there. You should ask her to move in and get *her* to do the washin' up.' She turned and flounced back into the kitchen.

Lou grinned. 'She sounds like a jealous wife. Word of advice: you better stash that good an' proper if you don't want that one findin' it. Ciss always was a snooper.'

Nellie grabbed the bag and bullets and stuffed them in the capacious apron pocket. 'Least she ain't a criminal,' she snapped.

Lou picked up her cup and drained it in one gulp. She put it back on its saucer with a clink and stood up. 'That's rich, comin' from the woman what's asked for a gun.'

'Mum. That man's here again.' Marianne stood at the hatch watching them quizzically.

Nellie stiffened.

'Is it him?' Lou pulled her hat low and wrapped her scarf around her mouth. 'Don't tell 'im I'm 'ere."

It was terrifying to see Lou so scared.

'It'll be the posh bloke. He said he'd be here to pick up a couple more of the boxes. Johnny ain't been here since the first time, if that's what you're worried about. The supplies are gettin' low, though, so I reckon I'm due a visit soon. Come on, Lou, you must have an inkling what this is all about? If it's not dirty mags, what do you think it is?'

'I'm tellin' yer, Nell. I ain't got a clue. But if they've got toffs in on it, my guess is that whatever it is, it's worth serious dough.'

'Stay here and don't move a muscle,' Nellie whispered, pushing herself up from the chair.

When she went into the kitchen, the basement door was already open and she could hear a faint grunting. She could imagine the old bloke down on his hands and knees, pulling out the boxes. Well, he'd get no help from them this time.

Cissy, Elodie and Marianne were standing around the kitchen table, and if looks could kill, Nellie would have dropped dead then and there under the strength of her cousin's glare.

Nellie ignored her. While Francis was occupied, she intended to get a look at the car – it might give her a clue about who he was and what the hell was going on. She grabbed a torch from the shelf in the pantry and quietly let herself out of the back door. Outside the gate her torch beam landed on a sleek black car. She opened the door and shone the light inside. The interior smelt of leather and cigarettes, the seats maroon and the wooden dashboard polished, and a four-leaf clover charm hung from the rear-view mirror. There was nothing else to see, so she shut the door and examined the car. It looked like the military cars she'd seen driving around Dover. Usually, they'd have an officer sitting self-importantly in the back. Surely this Francis couldn't be a military man? Officers were meant to be honourable and upstanding, weren't they? People they could trust. Then again, who'd ever suspect them of nefarious dealings? It would be the perfect cover.

Deep in thought, she walked back across the yard, very aware of the gun in her pocket and the rattle of the bullets in their box. Even if it had been loaded, she'd not be pulling it out, but it was comforting to have all the same.

She almost bumped into the figure looming out of the darkness, a couple of boxes in his arms. 'While you're out here snooping around, you might as well make yourself useful and open the boot for me,' he said, his plummy accent even more pronounced than usual.

'You call standin' in me own back yard snooping? You're the one turnin' up out of the blue doin' God knows what in *my* basement.'

The man moved towards the back gate, and Nellie followed him, one hand in her pocket, gripping the gun.

'The less you know the better, Mrs Castle. You should thank your lucky stars that it's me here and not Mr Fox, who's not known for his tolerance. No doubt he'll be along shortly to bring more supplies. I'll see you in a few days. Now, boot, please.'

If she hadn't been so curious she'd have refused, but she went to the car and obediently pulled open the boot. She flashed the light quickly around it, but it was empty.

Francis pushed past her and deposited the boxes, then slammed the door shut.

'Till we meet again,' he said dryly. Then he got in the car and drove away.

She watched until the faint beam from his headlights turned right onto Castle Street. Suddenly her breath caught in her throat. A large man was standing at the corner. His features were obscured in the darkness, but there was no mistaking that bulk. Was Johnny Fox checking up on her, or Francis?

As he walked towards her, Nellie shivered and gripped the gun more tightly.

'Thought you should know, Mrs C,' he said, coming to a stop in front of her, 'that I saw your grandson and 'is friend racin' down Plum Puddin' Hill in the pram. Now, it ain't none of my business, but that's a dangerous game they're playin', so you might wanna 'ave a word.' Then he turned and walked away.

Nellie's ears buzzed with fear. He hadn't been watching her or Francis; he'd been watching Donny and Ted.

She watched, rooted to the spot with fear, until the man disappeared round the corner. Then she raced back inside, and nearly wept at the sight of Donny lifting Teddy out of his pram. Her sudden appearance made everyone turn and look at her in bemusement.

'Were you on Plum Puddin' Hill?' she snapped.

Donny blushed. 'We was just havin' fun, Gran. Some soldiers took us up in their truck, an' then we rode down on the pram.'

'Don! I've told you before not to do that. It's dangerous!' Marianne exclaimed.

Donny hung his head. 'I held on tight to Ted, I promise!'

Nellie softened. 'Your mum's right, Don, it is dangerous, so don't do it again.' She wanted to say that there were far more dangerous things than riding down the hill in a pram, but she kept that thought to herself.

# Chapter 22

After Mr Wainwright's bombshell about Katy, Marge sat shellshocked in front of the fire.

Her sister had been in London all this time? Why had she never let them know? Her disappearance had broken her mother's heart. She'd gone from a happy, fun-loving woman to a shadow, barely leaving the house, and talking only in whispers. She'd told Marge once that if Katy was dead, then she wished she could die too. As for her father, he'd become even more stiff and unyielding. He'd always run his house like he'd run his ships – with rigid discipline and routine. Her mother used to joke that when her father left for sea even the walls sagged with relief. But though he could be harsh and strict, she'd never doubted he loved them. So how could Katy have done this to them?

For years, she'd held on to the hope that her sister would come home to them. But after her parents had died, it had been easier to think that she was dead too. Deep down, though, she'd still had a tiny glimmer of hope. And now even that was gone. She hammered her fist on the table, grief and rage coursing through her. Rage at her sister for leaving and staying away. For dying. Rage at Bennett for preying on a young girl.

God, what she'd like to do to that man. Restlessly, she stood and paced the stone-flagged floor, trying to work out what to do.

She'd pretend she didn't know him, she decided eventually. But she'd be watching him. Leopards didn't change their spots, and she would lay money on him trying to seduce one of them.

She thought about the girls who would be in her charge. Becky, Emily and Maria. Emily was nineteen but looked several years younger, with her waif-like figure and flawless skin. No doubt about it, if he went for anyone, it would be her.

The clock on the mantelpiece chimed the hour, and she hurried to the bathroom to wash any trace of tears from her face, then she poked her head round Mr Wainwright's office door. 'I'm heading off now, Mr W.'

He stood and came round to stand in front of her. 'Take care, my dear,' he said, patting her awkwardly on the back. 'If you need anything – anything at all – just send for me, and I'll be there like a shot. And promise me there'll be no revenge plots or silly plans.'

She cocked her head and grinned. 'My plans are never silly.' She kissed his bald head, picked up her suitcase and left.

Marge shivered as she stood beneath the station canopy, straining her eyes for a sight of dimmed headlights coming towards her. The rain had stopped, but it was pitch-dark, and the temperature had dropped.

Finally, a car crawled to a stop beside her, and the window opened. 'Third Officer Atkinson?' It was a man's voice. 'Sorry I'm a little late, I had a few errands to run.'

Was it him? She couldn't be sure, but he certainly sounded like an officer, with his plummy accent.

'Captain Bennett?' she asked, saluting him smartly.

'The very same. Stick your case on the back seat and get in.'

She did as she was told and got into the passenger seat beside him.

It was too dark to make out his features, but she could feel his presence, and it made her blood run cold. He'd been nothing but polite and proper, but men like him didn't take long to show their true colours. She just had to be patient.

'Thank you for the lift, sir,' she said to break the silence. 'I could have made my own way.'

'Not a problem. Like I said, I had some errands to run in Dover. And, to be frank, there's not a lot for me to do at the moment. The house – such as it is – is ready, the supplies Captain Roberts asked me to prepare are here, and I've just been hanging around twiddling my thumbs. It's a relief to get out of the place, to be honest. It's bloody cold and draughty and stinks of damp.'

His tone was so charming that, had she not known better, she would have warmed to him.

'Are you from Dover?' she asked innocently.

'Served in Folkestone for a time in the twenties,' he responded. 'Dover and Folkestone were lovely back then. Shame what's happened. Where do you hail from, Atkinson?'

'Oh, I've lived in Dover all my life. Was stationed at the castle until a few months ago.'

'Must be nice to be back near the family,' he said.

Marge didn't reply; she wasn't going to give him any more information than necessary.

'Atkinson . . .' he said reflectively. 'Any relation to Captain Vic Atkinson?'

So, he did remember the name. But she didn't want the connection to come out just yet. 'Not that I know, sir. But then, Atkinson's a pretty common name.'

'As is Bennett – I dare say there are thousands of us running around England.' He chortled. 'So tell me about this game of yours. Fascinating stuff. But how can we be sure it works? No disrespect, but I can't see us beating those damn U-boats with chalk, string and wooden counters. And the names? Pineapple, Raspberry . . . Hardly words to send Jerry running for the hills, what?' He chuckled. 'No offence, of course, Atkinson. I know you've all worked dreadfully hard on this project.'

Marge was shocked. There'd been plenty of sceptics amongst the officers they'd trained so far, so she was used to it. But she hadn't expected her commanding officer to voice his thoughts so freely.

When she didn't respond, he turned the charm back on. 'Apologies, that was unbelievably rude of me. Rest assured I will keep my opinions to myself when the others arrive. I have a tendency to put my foot in it. Might have risen to the exalted position of commander if I wasn't so willing to speak up. Always speak truth to power, that's my motto.'

'Quite right, sir. I feel exactly the same. All I can say about Captain Roberts' game is that the officers we've trained so far have been very impressed. Only time will tell if it has any significant impact on our shipping losses. But naval command seem optimistic.'

'Well, who am I to argue with naval command,' Captain Bennett murmured. 'I hear that Roberts only employs the crème de la crème of Wrens, so I have no doubt it will be an enormous success. I look forward to learning all about it and meeting the other girls tomorrow.'

Marge held her tongue with difficulty. He was doing his best to cover his faux pas, and she might well have been taken in if she didn't know what a despicable man he was.

They drove the rest of the way in relative silence, although every so often the captain would ask after her welfare – was she warm enough? Was she comfortable? He was no doubt hoping that she'd be younger than she was. She wouldn't be at all surprised if he stopped trying so hard the minute he caught sight of her.

Finally, they took a sharp left off the road and drove up a bumpy track for a short way, before turning right onto a driveway. It was too dark to see anything, but gravel crunched under the tyres, indicating that they were approaching Abbots Cliff House. She was eager to see it. Captain Roberts had told her that it was perched right on the cliffs at Capel-le-Fern, so the views would be magnificent.

'Is there anyone else here at the moment, sir?' Marge didn't like the thought of being alone with him.

'Mrs Benson, the housekeeper, lives in the basement flat. She'll be cooking for us too, though going by what she's served up so far, don't get too excited. There's a gardener who lives around somewhere, but otherwise it'll just be us. Plenty of bedrooms to put the officers in when they come, and a large room across the attic to play your games.'

Once the car had stopped, he got out and came round to open her door. Marge reluctantly took his hand and stepped out. He then reached into the back and pulled her case off the back seat.

'Follow me, and mind the step,' he said, shining his torch at a small flight of steps that led up to the front door. 'Soon as you're settled, you and I should get to know each other a little better over a warming snifter of brandy, what?'

*I know you well enough*, Marge thought grimly, holding onto her hat as the salt-laden wind gusted around her, bringing the sound of the waves thundering onto the beach with it. Cautiously, she walked up the steps and through the front door, which the captain was holding open for her. Once inside, he shut the door and turned on the lights.

They were standing in a large hallway, wallpaper peeling off the walls, dark patches of damp showing through. Threadbare rugs covered the wooden floorboards and pushed against one wall was a mahogany side table containing a vase of dusty dried flowers, a notepad and pen, and a telephone. Several doors ran off the hall, each of them closed, although they rattled as the wind forced its way through cracks in the doors and windows. The whole place smelt musty.

'It's huge,' she said, her voice echoing off the walls, as she took off her coat and hat and looked up at the high ceilings, noting the cobwebs strung across it, swaying slightly in the draught.

'Unoccupied for years before we took it over, so I'm afraid it's not what it could be,' the captain said.

She turned to find him staring at her with wide eyes. She looked back boldly. He was a tall, handsome man, with deep grooves in his cheeks, grey hair and thin lips, which at this moment were hanging open in shock. Broken veins in his cheeks suggested he probably drank too much.

She raised her eyebrows. 'Is something wrong, sir?'

He shut his mouth and looked away. 'No, no ... You reminded me of someone I used to know for a moment. That hair ...'

'Did I, sir?' She patted her hair. 'My sister's hair is the exact same colour. Maybe you know her?' She smiled innocently.

His eyes narrowed. 'I thought you said you weren't related to—' He stopped abruptly. 'No, Atkinson, I've never met your sister. Now, why don't you go and get yourself settled.' He smiled, although it didn't reach his eyes. Those, she noticed, were assessing her coldly. 'Your room has been prepared. Top of the stairs, turn right. You'll be sharing with the other girls. If you're hungry, there's bread and cheese in the kitchen.' He pointed to one of the doors that led off the hall. Then, muttering something about needing to unload the car, he turned and left.

Marge let out a long breath and picked up her suitcase. Clearly the brandy was no longer on offer, she thought as she walked up the stairs. Maybe she should have pretended a little longer, but his attempts to be charming were making her skin crawl and she couldn't bear to be in his presence a moment longer.

The room they'd been assigned was large and plainly furnished with four beds – two on each side – each with a spindly wooden chair beside it. A desk, two chests of drawers and two wardrobes were crammed in on either side of a huge window, which had patches of damp around the frame and was rattling furiously as the wind battered against it.

She sat down on one of the beds, trying to process everything that had happened that day, from seeing Rodney at the station to finally finding out what had happened to Katy, and meeting the man she held responsible. It was almost too much to take in, and her head felt heavy with stress and grief. She needed sleep, so she could tackle the problem of what to do next with a clear head.

After a quick wash in the dingy bathroom, she changed and slipped between the sheets. Like everything else in this house, they felt damp and cold – they'd all end up with pneumonia at this rate.

Despite her exhaustion, though, sleep wouldn't come. Instead, she lay staring into the dark wondering if her sister had suffered when she died, or had death been immediate? The thought of her being burnt alive was too awful.

She got up and went to stand at the window, pulling the blackout curtain aside. But it was like looking into the abyss. Not a speck of light anywhere. She supposed the wind was too strong for an air raid, so the search lights were off. Intermittently, a glint of moonlight shone through the clouds scudding across the sky, but other than that, Marge felt like she was the only person left alive.

She was just about to turn back, when she noticed a tiny flicker of light below her. She watched as it bobbed towards the sea. It looked like someone was walking towards the clifftop with a torch. The light was extinguished briefly, but then she saw it again, walking off to the left on what must be a path. Was that Bennett? And if so, what was he up to? Nothing good, she'd wager.

She felt a thrill of excitement. Captain Bennett clearly had his secrets, and as she knew only too well, secrets made you vulnerable. Tomorrow, she would investigate. And if Tom Bennett was hiding something, then she'd find it. One way or another, she'd make him wish he'd never been born.

# Chapter 23

Casualty Hospital, Dover

Dot found the letter in her pigeonhole when she arrived for her shift first thing in the morning, and the sight of Bert's spidery handwriting made her heart leap – first with excitement and then with fear. Was he writing to tell her he'd been sentenced? Or would the army let him rejoin his regiment with just a slap on the wrist? It felt like years since she'd last seen him, though it was only three months. But in those months she'd imagined all manner of terrible fates for him. She'd even, in her worst moment, worried he'd be executed. But they didn't do that for stealing, did they?

Hurrying to the cloakroom, she threw down her bag and ripped open the envelope, her hands shaking as she unfolded the letter. It was dated the end of December. Three long weeks ago now. What had happened in the meantime?

*Aldershot Military Prison*

*My darling Dot,*
*You won't receive this till January, so Happy New Year!*
*Although obviously I don't envisage this one getting off to*
*the greatest start. Only to be expected when you've confessed*
*your sins and been banged up for your trouble.*

I have good news and bad news! The good news is that the court martial is off! The bad news is that I am being drafted into the Commandos – a special mission, apparently. It's either that or face prison.

It's my own fault, because as there's nothing to do here but stare at four walls, I've been building my strength. My muscles are so big now, I could wrestle four of your father's sheep without turning a hair! And the army has decided to put those muscles to good use.

Personally, I think they would be put to better use holding you, my love. But they didn't give me that option.

I hope you realise that those weeks at your parents' farm were the happiest of my life. Who knew I'd enjoy the farming life so much? I've always considered myself more of a city type (not that Dover's that big), but I think I found my true calling with you in Derbyshire. One day, I'd like to be able to live with you in a little cottage in the middle of the countryside. I'll wrestle the sheep – maybe we can throw in a few pigs and cows as well – and you can look after the hundreds of babies we'll have.

Haha! I bet that last bit annoyed you. Of course, you don't have to give up nursing if you don't want to. We'll find a way to make sure we're both happy.

Aside from building the hugest muscles anyone's ever seen (joke!), I dream a lot about our time together – and our wedding. You in your beautiful white dress and veil, your eyes shining brighter than the sun, my heart beating fit to burst with love. Meeting you has been the best thing that's ever happened to me. I was on the wrong path, Dot, but you saved me. I need you to understand how grateful I am. I know you feel guilty that I've ended up in prison – they call this place The Glasshouse, which makes it sound a lot nicer than it is — but in my mind, I feel better than I have in ages. I've let so many people down, and now, slowly, I hope I'm putting that right.

You'll be happy to hear that Captain Norman and his friend have been released, although he has been demoted — as has his friend. The fact that I was blackmailing him to steal for me didn't hold much sway with the army. As for the affair, it seems the top brass is a little less fussy about things like that while they need men to fight.

My guess is they'll be banging people up for loving the wrong person again after the war, which makes me worry for Jimmy and Colin. But that's a problem for another day. For now, I'm trying to put the whole sorry mess behind me, and that's thanks to you, my love.

Even better than all of that is that you don't have to be ashamed of me anymore. With this new posting, I'll prove that I'm not the selfish, feckless man Mum made me seem at the trial.

Tell the others about it, will you — but not the prison stuff, obviously! And if I get any time off, I will come and see you, even if it means we only get five minutes at the station together. Because five minutes with you is worth more than money could ever buy.

I'm being shipped out of here soon, apparently. God only knows where. I can't pretend I'm not nervous. The Commandos have a reputation for being hard as nails — although I bet I'll have the biggest muscles!

Take care, sweet love. I will write again soon. And if I can get back to Dover, I'll send you a telegram to let you know.

Lots and lots of love,

Bert xxxxxxxxxxxxxxxxx (These are just a small number of the kisses that I dream of giving you every night.)

The words blurred as Dot reread the letter. The Commandos? What were they? The fact that he had been offered immunity from prosecution in return for joining them could only mean one thing: no one else wanted to do it. And if no one else wanted to do it, then it was probably very dangerous. She supposed he'd already be with them now, training for something in some secret place.

Her breath hitched. This was all her fault! She would never have suggested Bert confess if she'd known the implications for his safety. Why hadn't she kept her stupid mouth shut!

And why had Bert accepted the deal when refusing would have kept him safe in prison? He should have just faced the court martial and lived with the consequences.

The answer was there in black and white. He thought she was ashamed of him. But that couldn't be further from the truth. It had taken courage to hand himself in, and he'd continued to show that courage in the way he'd accepted his punishment. She would have been proud of him no matter what.

'Oh, love, what have you done?' she whispered. She held the paper up to her nose, trying to catch even the most fleeting scent of him. But it just smelt a little mouldy.

Now, somehow, she had to break the news to his family. Just the thought of the song and dance Nellie would make exhausted her, and she dreaded seeing her again. If Nellie hadn't said those things about him at the trial, she might have been able to dissuade him from handing himself in. Because despite everything, Bert still loved his mother and wanted her to be proud of him.

She sighed. As her mum had said, marriage was all about compromise, and for Bert's sake, she would have to talk to Nellie, and she would have to keep her anger with the woman under control.

Alternatively, maybe she could persuade Lily to pass on the news. That's if she'd talk to her. It was unlike Lily to hold on to her anger, but there was a coolness between them since she'd told her where Bert was. They still met in the canteen from time to time, but never by arrangement as they used to. She had the feeling that something else was bothering her friend, but she wasn't sure she had the right to ask anymore. But this news changed everything. Lily would have to talk to her now. Tucking the letter in her pocket, she threw off her cloak and went off to find her.

Dot found Lily in the officers' ward where she was feeding breakfast to Colonel Mason. He'd been on the ward for weeks now, recovering from a broken ankle and two broken arms. He'd become a great favourite with the other nurses, due not only to his good looks, but to the fact that he had received his injuries while protecting some children during a shell attack. He was even being put forward for a medal, which he pretended to be humble about, but somehow managed to mention any time he met someone new. Something that she and Lily had often joked about.

She watched the pair for a moment, aware of a growing unease. Something was wrong. Lily's shoulders were stiff and her cheeks pale. If Dot didn't know better, she'd say that she was angry or frightened – possibly both.

She inched closer and watched as Colonel Mason smiled at her friend.

'Nurse Castle, what would I do without you to brighten my days.'

Lily smiled politely and placed the spoon back in the empty bowl. Taking the napkin tucked into the neck of the man's pyjamas, she wiped his mouth gently, retracting her hand quickly when he tried to kiss her fingers.

Dot gasped quietly. *The bloody cheek!*

'Colonel Mason, please,' Lily said quietly, her cheeks flushing.

The man smiled wryly at her. 'Can't blame a man for trying, eh?'

Dot gritted her teeth. *You really could!*

'Maybe one day you'll kiss my lips rather than wipe them.' He winked at her.

'Maybe one day, you can feed yourself.' Lily smiled sweetly and stood up.

*You tell him, Lily!* Dot cheered silently.

'And when that time comes, you better watch out, Nurse,' he said, his eyes raking over her. 'Because there'll be nothing to stop me.'

Dot pursed her lips. There was a threat buried in those words, she was sure of it. She glanced at her friend, remembering now that Colonel Mason had requested Lily attend him whenever she was on duty. And now she knew why. *Had he been harassing her all this time? Why hadn't Lily said anything?* The man was getting stronger by the day, and who knew what he'd try once he was able to get about more freely.

Lily smoothed his blankets, then picked up the bowl and spoon. 'Please stop talking to me like this,' she said quietly. 'I'm engaged and it's not appropriate.'

Colonel Mason's expression turned cold. 'I don't know what you're talking about, Nurse. It's just a bit of a fun.'

'Even so, I'd prefer it if you didn't talk like that.' Then Lily turned on her heel and walked away.

Dot was waiting at the door when she passed. 'Lily!' she hissed. 'What was all that about?'

Lily barely glanced at her as she walked past.

'How long has he been doing this?' she asked, hurrying after her.

'Leave it, Dot. I can handle it.'

'Are you sure? You look troubled.'

'Well, I'm not. In fact, I'd say you're the one who looks troubled.'

They were in the corridor now, and Dot put her hand on her friend's arm. Lily stopped and looked at her. Her blue eyes were clouded with worry, her brow furrowed. Lily was lying; she was definitely troubled. *But what could she do? Should she report it to Matron? Or should she do what her friend asked and keep her nose out?*

'Why did you want to see me?' Lily said impatiently. 'Have you heard from Bert? Has he been sentenced?' She whispered the last part, even though there was no one nearby to hear.

'I need to talk to you. Can you come to the cloakroom?'

Lily frowned. 'Now? I'm still doing the breakfasts.'

Dot gripped her arm. 'Please. Just for five minutes.'

'Tell me what's so important!'

With a sigh, Dot thrust Bert's letter into her hand. 'I got this. It's dated over three weeks ago.'

Lily took it and scanned the contents. 'He really loves you,' she said softly.

'Not that bit.' Dot took the letter from her and pointed to a sentence. 'This.'

Lily read the words with bewilderment. 'What does it mean?'

'I think it means he's volunteered for something dangerous. He wants to prove himself to your bloody mother. Will you tell her for me?'

'You want *me* to tell her, when Bert's specifically asked you to.'

Dot nodded. 'Please?'

'Absolutely not! You will come home with me, and tell everyone yourself. You're his *wife*, you're part of the family now, and you can't avoid us forever. So tonight, once we've finished, you are coming home with me, and I won't take no for an answer.'

Dot stared at her friend in disbelief. She'd never spoken to her so harshly. Even when she'd told her about Bert being in prison, her tone hadn't been this hard.

'Listen, Dot,' Lily continued. 'I've got enough on my plate. In case you haven't noticed, the trial didn't just affect *you*! Mum's in pieces, she and Dad barely speak, I've got Cissy bending my ear about the stupid boxes in the basement and gangsters visiting the café; Marianne doesn't seem to care a jot about her baby ... And then there's you, refusing to acknowledge my family. Well, I've had enough! So tonight, after work, we will go to the café together, and you will tell them yourself!' Then with a toss of her head, she marched away.

Dot stared after her, aghast. Her first instinct was to shout back at her, but she held her tongue. She had never seen Lily lose her temper like this. In fact, it was rare for Lily to be upset at all. Her family was always in crisis, and aside from that one occasion when she'd found out that Jasper was her real father, Lily had borne it all with long-suffering good humour.

Guilt trickled through her. She'd been so wrapped up in her own problems that she'd not paid enough attention to her friend. Well, she'd have to change that. She would face Bert's family, and she would need to keep an eye on Lily and Colonel Mason. Because though she might deny it, Lily definitely needed help.

# Chapter 24

*Abbots Cliff House*

Marge was woken the next morning by the rattle of the window-panes as the wind whistled around the house. Shivering, she switched on the lamp. The bulb fizzed and flickered for a moment, before settling. The threadbare brown curtains were fluttering in a draught, and the carpet beneath the windows was dark with damp. 'Well, isn't this lovely,' she murmured, as a particularly strong gust raised goosebumps on her arms. Flinging herself back on the pillows, she thought about the day ahead. The other girls were due to arrive this afternoon, but before that, she was expected to take Captain Bennett through the games. Which meant having to spend time alone in his company.

She looked around the dismal room, the three empty beds, the damp walls and musty curtains, and a wave of self-pity washed over her. It wasn't just the setting, or the man, it was the fact that her sister really was lost to her.

She pulled a cigarette from the packet on the chair beside her and lit it. There was no point moping, she thought, blowing smoke rings at the ceiling. Nothing in her life had changed with the news, so she'd just have to get on with it. The best thing she could do now was keep busy.

Finishing her cigarette, she flung back the covers and went to the window. A tinge of light brightened the horizon, glittering faintly off the sea, which she could hear battering against the shingle below the cliffs. As she'd suspected, the garden was directly below her, stretching towards the cliff, where it was bordered by a white fence. Given what she'd seen last night, there must be a path running along the cliff, but she couldn't see it from here. Hopefully at some point today, she'd get a chance to explore properly.

Suddenly full of purpose, she washed and dressed and went downstairs. The smell of cooking fat and sausages had banished the damp odour in the hallway, and the clink of crockery and burble of a wireless came from behind one of the doors. She pushed it open and found herself in the kitchen, which, like the rest of the house, had seen better days. But above the sink to her right, large picture windows looked out onto green rolling hills dotted with sheep, which more than made up for the shabby, mustard brown walls.

A middle-aged woman wearing a navy-blue turban and a grimy white apron was standing at the stove frying sausages, a cigarette dangling from the corner of her mouth.

'You must be Mrs Benson.'

The woman turned and nodded, ash from her cigarette dropping into the pan. 'That's me name. But you got the advantage on me.'

'I'm Marge. Sorry . . . I think some ash dropped onto the sausages.'

Tutting, the woman balanced the cigarette on the side of a glass ashtray and shook the pan. 'I won't tell if you don't.' She winked. 'I'll give these to Captain B. Cuppa?'

Marge grinned. Despite the questionable hygiene, she had a feeling she and Mrs Benson would get on. She sat down at the kitchen table, took a slice of cold, soggy toast from the rack and spread a thin layer of margarine over it. 'What's the captain like?' she asked, taking a bite of toast.

Mrs Benson snorted. 'Same as all them posh blokes. Talks like he's got a broom up his arse an' thinks he's cleverer than the rest of us. But he's got a shifty look in 'is eye. Wouldn't trust 'im to pour water out of a boot, if I told 'im the instructions were on the heel.'

Marge spluttered, sending toast crumbs across the table, just as the door opened and the man himself walked in.

'Ready for your sausages, Captain?' Mrs Benson said, tipping them onto a plate. 'Done just 'ow you instructed. Brown but not burnt.' Her eyes slid to Marge and she grinned wickedly. 'Oh, an' there's a letter by your plate. Found it on the mat when I come in. 'And delivered by the look of it.' She raised her eyebrows in question, but Captain Bennett ignored her.

He sat down opposite Marge but didn't look at her. After last night, she hadn't expected him to be friendly, especially if he'd worked out who she was. He would no doubt avoid all mention of it, but it was going to make working with him tricky.

She took a deep breath to steady her nerves and said, 'When you're ready, perhaps we should run through the game before the others arrive, sir. Captain Roberts told me he sent manoeuvres down for you to study, so it shouldn't take long.'

'Give me a chance to eat my breakfast, Atkinson.' He speared one of the sausages and took a bite.

Marge glanced over at Mrs Benson, who was eyeing the captain with a gleam in her eye.

'Hope the sausage is to yer likin', Captain.'

'Very nice, Mrs B. It's got a smoky flavour to it. Most unusual.' He shovelled another forkful into his mouth.

'Must be the new seasonin' I used.' Mrs Benson smirked.

Marge buried her face in her cup to hide her grin.

Captain Bennett was perusing his letter with a frown. He took a sip of tea and looked up at her briefly. 'I need to go out. Urgent navy business. Meantime you can set up the room. Right to the top of the house, large attic with skylights.'

'When will you have time to run through it with me, sir? The first course begins in a couple of days. You'll need to know how to—'

Captain Bennett held his hand up. 'I am the one who gives the orders round here, Atkinson, and I do not expect to be bossed around by a woman half my age and well below my rank, do I make myself clear?'

Marge felt her temper rise; so the gloves were off. Well, good. At least she didn't have to pretend anymore. She opened her mouth to give a sharp retort, but before she could say anything, Mrs Benson started to cough loudly.

Marge looked over at her, and the other woman shook her head.

Taking a deep breath, Marge managed to choke out, 'Yes, sir.' Pushing back her chair, she stood up.

'By the way, Atkinson, I'm afraid I won't be able to collect the girls today. I picked you up last night because it was dark. But it is *not* my job to be fetching and carrying like a common cabbie. I imagine they'll be quite capable of finding their own way here. And if they can't, then I fear for this project, I really do.'

Marge nodded sharply, and left the kitchen, shutting the door with a loud thump. She stomped up the stairs, muttering under her breath. 'Arrogant, jumped-up, two-bit, buffoon! Naval business, my foot!' Whatever the letter he'd received was, it wasn't an official navy summons. It was a bit early to be meeting a woman or going for a drink, so what else could it be?

Upstairs, on the floor above the bedrooms, she found a large attic room with a high ceiling and sloping eaves on either side. Piled in the corner were folded canvas sheets, balls of string and boxes of chalk. On a table against the far wall was a smaller box of wooden counters. Despite the winter sun that had now risen and was shining in from the east, casting shadows on the rough wooden planks of the floor, it was absolutely freezing. Marge rubbed her hands and went over to one of the windows that overlooked the front of the house. The condensation had frozen on the inside, so she needed to push it open to be able to see properly. The view was even more stunning from this vantage point than it was from the kitchen, but she only looked at it briefly, before training her eyes on the shiny black car that sat outside the house.

It took a while, but eventually the captain came outside, wearing his cap and navy blue great coat and carrying a box. She watched as he loaded it into the car and slammed the boot. Then he got in and drove away, the gravel crunching beneath the tyres.

# Chapter 25

*Folkestone, January 1942*

With her back resting against her pillows, Ellen counted out the cash sitting on her bedside table. Could be worse, she supposed. But she'd bloody earned every penny.

She winced as she got out of bed. Everything ached and her insides felt scraped raw. Grabbing a thick jersey and a pair of socks, she pulled them on and padded over to the other side of the room. Prising up a loose floorboard, she reached into the cavity and took out an old biscuit tin. It had a picture of the king and queen and the two princesses on it. Look at them, she thought scornfully. Frilly dresses, clean skin, a massive great painting on the wall behind them. They might say they were all in this together, but that lot didn't have a clue. When their house got bombed, they just moved into another wing. Whereas she . . . She stared around the dingy room, at its peeling wallpaper and threadbare carpet. It was better than nothing, but she couldn't see the queen having to lie on her back just to put a roof over her head.

She opened the lid, and counted the notes inside. Not bad for just a few weeks' work. If she kept this up, she'd soon have enough to get back to London, where she at least had some friends. She just needed a bit more so that she could live for a couple of weeks without working while she sorted herself out. She'd learnt from bitter experience that you should always have an emergency fund. Illness or a beating from a punter could mean having to take days or even weeks off, so it was best to be prepared. She thought sadly about the nice little nest egg she'd built up over the years. But it was all gone now. Still, no point crying over spilt milk. She'd survived far worse than this.

When she'd first started out, she'd made a fortune. Shame she'd not been in the frame of mind to enjoy it. She tried not to think of those days when it had felt like she lived under a permanent black cloud. The only thing that had kept her going was the little life inside her. She'd assumed that once she'd started to show it would've put paid to her earning capacity.

But men were beasts. A pretty face and big boobs and they didn't much care about anything else. And if that face looked barely old enough to be out in the wide world, so much the better. Filthy bastards, the lot of them. If she never had to touch a man again, it'd be too soon.

A creak outside her bedroom door made her look round sharply. She remained still until the footsteps had walked past, then she stuffed the notes back into the tin and slammed the lid before putting it back in its hiding place. The girls here seemed all right, but you couldn't be too careful.

Grabbing her towel, she went to the bathroom where she scrubbed herself in the four inches of water she was allowed. It didn't much matter to Ellen. Four inches, the River Thames, an entire fucking ocean: no matter how much water she had, it would never be enough.

After dressing carefully in a secondhand navy blue wool suit, sensible black lace-ups and a black wool coat, she took the small amount of money she'd left out and put it in her bag. In her line of work, you still needed to look good – particularly at her age. So, she needed to go on the hunt for some more makeup.

She crept down the stairs and opened the front door a crack to check the coast was clear. She didn't want anyone to see her coming or going from this place; if no one paid her any heed, it was easier to pretend she was just like them.

Seeing no one, she slipped outside and hurried down the hill towards Sandgate Road. She'd try her luck in Woolies first; the manager was a client who wouldn't dare refuse her anything in case she told his wife what he got up to when he said he was doing a stocktake. She'd never tell, of course. But he wasn't to know that, the dirty old goat.

As she turned into Sandgate Street, she saw a man in naval uniform getting out of a car. She had several clients who were naval officers, but this wasn't one of them. Something about the set of his shoulders was familiar, though. She watched as he opened the boot and took out a box. Then, with a quick look up and down the street, he crossed over to the newsagent's and disappeared inside.

Her breath caught. That brief glimpse of his profile had confirmed her growing suspicion. Could it really be him? Her heart was beating fast against her chest and the cup of tea she'd had before she came out swirled uncomfortably in her stomach. All thoughts of lipstick left her mind as she kept her eyes focused on the shop across the road. In there was the man who had destroyed her life. She had a choice: confront the bastard or wait. She'd dreamt about what she might do if she ever saw him again countless times. But now he was within her sights, she wasn't sure what to choose.

He'd promised her the world and then tricked her into running away. She'd waited for him for weeks, before she understood the truth. After her baby was born she'd had nothing left to lose, so she'd come back to Folkestone to confront him.

But a stranger had answered his door and told her he'd moved the month before. And no, they didn't know where to.

Afterwards, she'd gone to her own home, loitering around the corner, desperate to catch a glimpse of her mother. And then she'd seen her sister, bouncing along the road, linking arms with one of her friends. She'd looked happy and healthy and young. By contrast, Ellen had been gaunt, pale and any happiness she'd had had been ripped away from her when the midwife had placed her little boy in her arms. His lips had been blue and his skin so translucent she could see every vein on his tiny, closed eyelids. They'd fluttered open just once. And then closed for good.

Hot anger rose within her, and without thinking, she ran across the road, dodging through the cars, and went into the shop. A little bell rang on top of the door and a plump woman behind the counter smiled at her.

She looked around the small space; there was no sign of him.

'Can I help you, love?' the woman asked.

'The naval officer that just came in,' she said hesitantly. 'I wanted to say hello. He's a friend of my father's.'

The woman frowned. 'Ain't seen no one of that description,' she said firmly. But her gaze went to a closed door behind the counter.

'But I saw him,' Ellen persisted. 'He came in a few minutes ago.'

The woman shook her head. 'Do you want to buy anythin' or not?' she snapped.

Realising there was no chance of getting any more from her, Ellen turned and left. Why was the woman lying to her? And where was he?

Well, he'd have to come out eventually. He wasn't going to leave his car sitting there all day. And Ellen was used to waiting. She'd been waiting years to confront this man, and she wasn't going to pass up this opportunity.

# Chapter 26

## Castle's Café

Nellie lay in bed listening to the familiar sounds of the café coming to life: the murmur of voices, the clink of crockery. Cissy had been calling to her, but she couldn't face going downstairs after another sleepless night. The image of Johnny Fox looming out of the darkness had stayed with her all night. Much worse, though, was the thought that he'd been following Donny.

But it wasn't just the threat of him that had kept her awake. She'd hidden the gun and the bullets in her underwear drawer under some old girdles, bringing back terrible memories of the last time she'd hidden a gun in her room. She'd only meant to use it as protection that time as well. Instead, it had ended in death. Would it be the same this time?

She squeezed her eyes shut against the image of the red-splattered wall, Edie's small figure standing in the doorway screaming . . . Could she really go through that again?

If it was a choice between her family or these men, then no question. But she should probably find a better hiding place for now.

She cast her eyes around the room. On top of the wardrobe was an old brown suitcase that hadn't been touched for years – aside from the brief trip to London last year, she couldn't remember the last time she'd left Dover. Getting out of bed, she pulled the dressing table stool over and climbed onto it. Reaching up, she grabbed the handle and pulled the suitcase down, sneezing at the dust that swirled around her. The clasps were stiff, but once open, she put the gun and bullets inside. She had just slid the suitcase back into place when her bedroom door burst open and Cissy marched into the room.

'Thinkin' of goin' on holiday?' she snapped. 'Oh, wait, your life's already one long holiday. Standin' at the counter mouthin' off day in and day out while me, Marianne and Elodie slave away in the kitchen. And then there are days like today, when you don't bother even pretendin' to work! Well, I've 'ad it, Nell.'

Nellie wobbled and clutched the wardrobe. 'Hell's bells, Ciss! You tryin' to kill me?'

Cissy put her head on one side. 'Now you mention it, that ain't such a terrible idea. Are you gonna tell me what you're doin'?'

Thinking quickly, Nellie stepped down. Her instinct was to snap back at her cousin, but perhaps an apology would be better. Or, she thought, maybe she should confide in her. The idea of unburdening herself, of not being alone with this terror, was too seductive to ignore. 'Maybe it's time you an' me had things out. I know I've been like a bear with a sore head recently, but there's stuff goin' on that I wanted to protect everyone else from.' She sat on the bed, patting the space beside her.

Cissy shut the door and sat down. 'About time too. It's not fair to shut me out, Nellie. No good ever came of secrets. You of all people should know that.'

It must be wonderful to be Cissy. To go through life without dark clouds hanging over you. Some secrets she would never tell her, but this new one Cissy might just be able to help with.

'Well?' Cissy prompted.

'I know you want to know what's goin' on, but truth is, Ciss, I'm not too sure meself, and I'm scared.'

'You're not the only one, love. The minute I saw that big bloke, I knew 'e was trouble. Do you really not 'ave a clue?'

'I really don't. All I know is that big bugger's called Johnny Fox and Lou tells me he's some gangster from up London. It's her mess that we're in the middle of, nothin' to do with me. She got into some deal over dirty mags and ended up rippin' him off.'

'I shoulda known she'd be involved. What I don't understand is why you were givin' her cups of tea bein' all chummy. The woman's poison an' you need to cut her out of our lives.'

'I needed somethin' from her.' Nellie fiddled with the counterpane, wondering if she could ever cut Lou out of her life. For good or ill, she had been part of the fabric of her life for years, and she couldn't imagine things any other way. But deciding it was best not to voice these thoughts, she stood on the stool and pulled the suitcase down. Putting it on the bed, she waved her hand at it. 'Open it.' She looked away, not wanting to see Cissy's reaction.

The clasps made a loud click as the case was opened and she listened as the paper bag rustled, bracing herself. Sure enough, her cousin's high-pitched screech sent a shiver down her spine.

'Wh-what the hell do you think you're playin' at, Nellie Castle!' Cissy threw the bag back into the case. Cissy's chest was heaving, and her eyes were practically popping out of her head.

'We need protection, so I asked Lou to get me a gun. That man . . . He threatened the kids if I didn't help him. And this was the best I could do!' She put her head in her hands.

Cissy stared at the gun, as though it was about to leap up and shoot her. 'For pity's sake! You're gonna get us all killed. You can't go around wavin' guns at gangsters.' She paused for a moment. 'Well, those were words I never thought I'd say.' She broke into sudden laughter.

Nellie watched her in astonishment. This wasn't the reaction she'd been expecting. 'This ain't a laughin' matter.'

'You're tellin' me!' Cissy laughed harder, bending over at the waist and putting her hands on the bed. 'Gangsters, guns, mysterious boxes! There ain't nothin' funny about any of it,' she gasped, slumping down on the bed beside the suitcase and wiping her eyes with the corner of her apron. 'But if I don't laugh, I'll scream. And you'd hate that even more.'

They sat in silence for a moment. Outside her bedroom, she could hear Donny's footsteps thumping down the stairs, and Teddy's delighted giggle as he was jiggled about in his arms.

'If anythin' 'appens to those kids, I couldn't live with meself, Ciss. You must see that. What else could I do?'

Cissy nodded, not a trace of laughter remaining. 'You need to talk to Jasper.'

'No! I'm tellin' you cos I can't keep it to meself. But you're not to say a word about the gun. I mean it!'

'Gran!' Donny knocked on the door.

Hastily, she shut the suitcase. 'What is it, love?'

'Teddy wants to say hello.' He pushed the door open. 'Here she is! It's Gran Gran.' He put the little boy down, and he crawled towards the bed, a huge grin on his face, dribble rolling down his chin.

Nellie's heart swelled. She would die before she let anything happen to this little boy. Bending down, she scooped him into her arms and held him close, breathing in the warm scent of talcum powder.

Teddy reached over and patted Cissy's face, and she caught his chubby little hand in hers, holding it to her cheek.

The two women shared a long look, then Cissy nodded, as though to say, *We'll sort this together*. It felt like old times, the two of them against the world, and Nellie's heart lightened with relief that she was no longer alone.

But then Cissy leant over and whispered, 'I'm tellin' Jasper, no matter what you say. Now get downstairs and run your bloody café!'

# Chapter 27

*Abbots Cliff House*

Once she'd set up the room, Marge went downstairs into the large drawing room. It was furnished with several shabby sofas and armchairs, all upholstered in the same rose-patterned fabric. The cream-and-gold striped wallpaper had seen better days, but in her mind she could picture how this room might once have looked. Large French windows faced the endless sea, opening onto a stone-flagged terrace, and to the left, more windows looked out onto the lawn and driveway, beyond which was a field dotted with sheep.

Opening the French windows, she stepped out onto the terrace. She could picture girls in flapper dresses and headbands drinking cocktails with men in tuxedoes as the sun set over the sea. Her mother had loved to dance and dress up, and before Katy disappeared, she and her father were always going out to parties and dances. She used to say that after enduring the loss of so many men, it was their duty to enjoy life to the full – otherwise what was the point of all that sacrifice?

Is that what she'd do after this war ended? Personally, she couldn't see the point of waiting. She'd rather do the partying now. Mrs B, she suspected, would also love a party, and perhaps the sheep would be partial to a gin and orange. Once the girls had arrived, she was sure they could find some servicemen to invite round for the evening. If nothing else, it might help take her mind off everything that had happened.

She walked to the end of the garden, leaning against the flimsy wooden fence. The ground dropped steeply away and as she'd suspected a path snaked along the top of the cliffs. Further down towards the beach, she could see the railway track that ran between Dover and Folkestone. Swinging her leg over the fence, she jumped down onto the path and turned left, the wind at her back propelling her along and whipping the hair around her face.

After a brief walk, she noticed a strange round shape perched a few feet from the path. She went over to inspect it curiously. It was a huge concave structure that loomed over her like a concrete moon.

She'd not seen a sound mirror in real life before, but she recognised it from the pictures they'd been shown when she was training. Apparently, this is what the country would have used as an early warning system, if radar hadn't been invented, though she couldn't fathom how it worked. Rodney would know, she thought with a slight smile. And wouldn't he just love to tell her all about it. A wave of longing for his presence swept over her.

She should have at least talked to him yesterday, maybe even walked down to the café with him. Things had ended badly with them, but if Katy's death had taught her anything, it was that you shouldn't leave things too late. Yes, his judgemental expression the other week had annoyed her. But it was Rodney; he *always* looked a little disapproving. He'd probably come out of the womb looking disgusted at the mess. The thought made her giggle as she sat down on the lip of the sound mirror and took a cigarette from her pocket.

It was stubbornness and pride that were preventing her from speaking to him. Just as she imagined it was Katy's stubbornness and pride that had kept her away from her family. It was all so pointless. Rodney would be returning to sea soon, and if anything happened to him, she'd regret not talking to him for the rest of her life. Her eyes followed a convoy heading east, surrounded by smaller boats – the motor torpedo boats that accompanied all merchant shipping through the Channel. She glanced up at the sky above France; it was clear and blue, no planes in sight. The MTBs would have their guns trained on the sky nevertheless, everyone tense and ready.

She watched until the convoy was out of sight, then ground her cigarette under her heel and stood up. Enough thinking; she'd come here to try to work out what Bennett had been doing. And she suspected it was something to do with the little hut that sat a few feet from the sound mirror. She went across to it and tried the door, but it was locked. The ground in front of the door was heavily trodden, and a few cigarette butts were scattered around it, so clearly this was a regular haunt for someone. Cupping her hands around her face, she peered through the small window in the side, but the blackout blinds were drawn. She'd either need to learn to pick a lock or find the key.

Stuffing her hands into her pockets, she walked up the slope away from the sea. At the top, a path ran between two fields, the one on her left was full of nettles and brambles, and she could see all the way to the drawing room windows of Abbots Cliff House; in the field to her right, a flock of sheep clustered against the dry stone wall, sheltering from the wind, and on the far side, a land girl appeared to be breaking the ice on a trough of water. It made her think of Reenie Turner. Her friend was never happier than when her hands were deep in the mud. She would never forget how Reenie had run to her allotment in her wedding dress after Jimmy Castle had left her in the middle of their reception. She hoped she'd recovered from that heartbreak now. Considering Jimmy was in love with a man, the marriage would never have worked.

She turned and looked back at the sound mirror, silhouetted against the bright blue sky. She'd love to bring Rodney here. She could imagine him enthusiastically explaining in intricate detail how it worked. She'd complain he was boring her to death and kiss him to shut him up . . . She touched her lips. Stupid dreams.

As she walked on, a black car drove up the track towards her and turned right into the drive, and pressed up against the window was Becky. She let out a whoop, and ran down the path, skidding into the drive as she chased after the car.

The girls wound down the windows and stuck their heads out, yelling her name. For the first time since she'd left Liverpool, Marge felt a rush of happiness. It was wonderful to have them here, and even better to know that she wouldn't be alone with Captain Bennett anymore. His car was back, she noticed, so he could have collected them if he'd really wanted. He just couldn't be bothered.

As soon as the car came to a stop, Becky threw open the door and jumped out. Maria and Emily followed, and with their arms around each other, the four women hopped in a circle, squealing with excitement.

The front door of the house opened, and Captain Bennett came out and stood at the top of the steps. 'What on earth do you think you're doing? Get inside and get unpacked immediately!'

The women jumped apart and saluted smartly.

'I didn't think you'd be here, sir. Didn't you say you wouldn't be able to pick the girls up?' Marge said, while the others pulled their suitcases out of the boot.

'I *said* that they were quite capable of finding their own way.' He gestured towards them. 'And so it's proved.' He narrowed his eyes at her. 'In future, I expect you to maintain discipline to the standards the Navy expects.'

Marge saluted, but inwardly she was seething.

Captain Bennett watched the girls approach, and Marge saw the exact moment he caught sight of Emily. His expression changed and a smarmy smile appeared on his face as he stepped forward to take her case.

Emily smiled prettily at him, and Marge suppressed a sigh. Unless she could find something to discredit the man, the next few weeks were going to be very difficult.

# Chapter 28

*Falmouth, January 1942*

Bert's breath was coming in short pants and despite the cold rain that lashed his face, sweat was trickling down his back. Since he'd arrived, the training had been relentless. Today's torture involved running up to Pendennis Castle and back ten times. He could hear the laboured breaths and groans of the men behind him and forced his legs to go faster. He was out in front, and he needed to win this race. If he had any hopes of surviving this crazy mission, then he needed to be in the first boat with Commander Stephens.

And for that, he had to be the best runner, the best shot, the strongest. If pushing himself to the very limits of his endurance meant that he'd get back to Dot, then he'd bloody well do it.

The commander was standing in front of the hut, a stop-watch in his hand.

'Well done, Castle!' Stephens clapped him on the back as Bert bent over, hands on his knees. 'No time to rest. You need to get to the firing range.'

Somehow, Bert managed to stagger up the hill to a field where man-shaped targets had been set up. Someone handed him a rifle, and he advanced into the field.

'Get the fuck down!' A drill sergeant stood to the side, his hair plastered to his face with rain, his cheeks red with anger.

Bert dropped onto his stomach, mud soaking through his jacket, and started to crawl. There were thirty targets and he needed to hit each in the chest before he could leave. Steadying his breathing, he forced himself to lie still, assessing each one. He'd always been a good shot, and he was determined not to falter now. He *had* to win this challenge.

Dot's face floated into his mind. She smiled at him gently and nodded. *You can do anything, love.* Her voice whispered through him, slowing his heartbeat. He raised his head and forgetting the pain in his muscles, the damp seeping through his trousers and the fear that had been an ever-present companion since that first briefing, he began to fire.

And, one by one, he punched a neat hole right in the centre of the targets.

'I said, stand down, Castle!'

Bert had been so focused on his task that he hadn't heard the order at first. Gratefully, he dropped the gun and rolled onto his back, spreading his arms wide. Around him, others were still firing, the shots reverberating through the air. Since training had started, his ears were constantly ringing from the sound of gunfire.

He squeezed his eyes shut against the memories that accompanied each shot: his mates dropping dead on the beach at Dunkirk; Gladys falling outside the café; the sudden burst of pain in his face and shoulder on the football field. He drew in a deep breath. He couldn't afford to lose it in the middle of a training session. Right now, he was safe. He was succeeding. He had done everything he'd promised Dot he would do. And he would get out of this alive, if it was the last thing he did.

# Chapter 29



*Castle's Café*

Later that night, Nellie turned on the wireless and poured herself a sherry, sighing with relief that the day was finally over.

The momentary comfort she'd felt after confiding in Cissy was long gone, and she was bitterly regretting telling her anything. Everything might have been fine, if not for the air raid at lunchtime. Cissy had ostentatiously moved a chair in front of the curtain, where she sat bolt upright, her eyes wandering watchfully around the assembled group. It was so unlike her to sit away from everyone, that of course it hadn't gone unnoticed.

'Why you sittin' there, Auntie Cissy?' Donny had asked.

Adelaide had tutted. 'Looks like she's guarding something to me. Contraband goods, perhaps?'

'Just because I choose to sit away from you,' Cissy had said with uncharacteristic rudeness, 'it don't mean I have anythin' to hide.'

'Luke said, "For there is nothing covered that shall not be revealed; neither hid, that shall not be known". What he didn't say was that it doesn't matter where you sit, Cissy, the whole town knows there's been strange goings-on here.'

'She ain't wrong.' Mr Gallacher clearly couldn't resist throwing in his tuppence worth, the old goat. 'I been sayin' it ever since that big bloke arrived.'

'Oh honestly,' Cissy had twittered. 'You're all so dramatic. Chuck me the fiddle, Nell. Let's have a tune.'

And for the next hour, she'd sat trapped in the basement while Cissy played tune after tune and Adelaide and Mr Gallacher kept casting glances at the curtain. By the time the all-clear sounded her nerves were wrung out.

Now, Marianne was upstairs putting Teddy to bed, while Donny lay in his usual place on the rug by the fire engrossed in the latest edition of *The Beano*. Elodie had retired to bed, and Cissy was knitting a jumper for Teddy, her lips pursed. They'd had words after everyone had left the basement, and unsurprisingly her cousin had taken exception to being called as subtle as Belisha beacon. Looking at her now with her recently dyed orange hair glowing in the lamplight, Nellie almost laughed. Her statement was true in more ways than one.

But the humour left her almost as quickly as it had arrived. She wasn't sure how much more she could take of this. What with waiting for the next visit from Johnny Fox and the posh bloke, the gun in her bedroom and the siren going off every single day . . . If this went on, Cissy would have to have her carted off to the loony bin. Although the thought of lying quietly in a padded cell seemed quite appealing right now.

The radio was playing military band music, and the endless marchiness was irritating her. As if they needed any more reminders they were at war. Air raids, ruined buildings and sleepless nights in the basement were all the reminder she needed. She switched it off with an irritated flick and laid her head back on the lace antimacassar. All was peaceful until downstairs she heard the back door open, and she stiffened, her eyes shooting open. Cissy, too, was sitting straighter, her needles paused mid-stitch.

'I've brought someone to see you, Mum?'

Nellie relaxed at the sound of Lily's voice. She could also hear the unmistakable rumble of a man's voice.

Jasper. Her heart lifted. Was it possible he just wanted to come round, like old times? For the first time that evening, she felt a smile forming at the corner of her lips. Until she remembered that it was far more likely he was here to nag her about Johnny Fox. She glanced at Cissy, eyebrows raised – she wouldn't put it past her cousin to have blabbed again. But her cousin looked just as bemused.

Lily walked through the door, followed, much to Nellie's surprise, by Dot, who looked pale and thin. Jasper brought up the rear, and any illusions that this was a social visit disappeared as she looked at their grim expressions.

She half rose from the chair; Dot's presence could only mean one thing. 'Has something happened to Bert?'

'He's fine, Mum,' Lily said. 'But Dot does have some news she wanted to share.'

'And why's Jasper here?' She looked at him, but he merely shrugged.

'Because I want him to hear this too. And it's about time he came round, don't you think?' Lily said pointedly.

Cissy stood. 'I'll make some tea.'

Donny had sat up, his expression fearful. 'Uncle Bert's all right, isn't he, Auntie Dot?'

'He's all right, Donny, don't worry,' Dot replied. She looked at Nellie and nodded. 'Good evening, Mrs Castle.'

'Oh, come on!' Nellie responded, irritated at her formal tone. 'You're my daughter-in-law, so scrap the Mrs Castle nonsense. Though I'd've appreciated an invite to the weddin', or at least a notification.'

'Mum!' Lily said. 'Will you shut up and listen!'

Nellie sank back into her chair. 'Sorry, love,' she said to Dot, trying to keep her tone even. 'I understand I might not be your favourite person, but there ain't no need to stand on ceremony. We're your family now.'

Dot nodded, but her expression didn't warm. Nellie suppressed a sigh; somehow, she needed to win the girl over, or Bert might never speak to her again.

Jasper sat on one of the wooden chairs by the table, while Dot and Lily sat on the sofa. Marianne, who had heard the commotion, came downstairs, and smiled widely at Dot, going straight over to give her a kiss.

Cissy returned with a tray of cups and saucers and a pot of tea, which she poured at the table.

'Put us out of our misery, then. What's goin' on?' Nellie said sharply.

Dot cast a glance at Lily who nodded back. Nellie didn't miss the slight frostiness in her daughter's look. Something was up between those two. No doubt she was about to find out what.

'Commandos!' Nellie gasped, after Dot had delivered the news. 'What does that even mean?' She wouldn't have been so concerned about this, if not for Jasper putting his head in his hands as soon as the words were out. 'Jasper?'

Jasper sighed. 'From what I've heard, Nell, they've been set up to do special raids. Dangerous missions, I imagine. They won't take just any old soldier, that lot. They'll be takin' the blokes who either love the danger or who just don't care what happens to 'em.'

'Bert don't love danger! He's been strugglin' as it is . . .' Her voice trailed off. 'And he's just got married . . . He's got so much to live for.' She glared at Dot.

'That's not why he's joined.' Dot's tone was firm. She cast a look at Lily who shook her head slightly. Those two were hiding something.

'Then why?'

Dot turned to her, her eyes sparkling with anger. 'Because, *Mrs Castle*, he wants to prove to himself and the world that he's not the man *you* painted him in court. He's joined that regiment to make *you* proud. God knows why he cares, but he does.'

Nellie felt as though she'd been punched. Was this really her fault? She could handle the thought of Bert not talking to her out of anger, but the thought of him never being able to talk to her again because she'd driven him into danger was something else entirely.

'What does she mean, Gran?' Donny broke the silence. 'What did you do?'

Somehow, they'd kept the truth of what had happened at the trial away from Donny, and she intended to keep it that way. She looked at Jasper beseechingly.

'Bert and your gran 'ad a little disagreement is all, Don. You know what Gran's like; she could argue with a paper bag when she's in a mood.'

'But Uncle Bert'll be all right, won't he?'

'Course he will.' Marianne leant forward and put a hand on her son's shoulder. 'He was born lucky, and he'll stay lucky. You mustn't worry about him.'

Dot stood up. 'I really hope you're right, Marianne. Because after everything that's happened over the last year, he doesn't seem all that lucky to me.' She turned to Lily. 'I'll see you tomorrow.' Then she walked out, without bothering to even look at Nellie.

# Chapter 30

After Dot left, the silence was deafening. Jasper glanced at Nellie. She'd lost even more weight recently, and it showed in her face where new lines were etched onto her forehead and beside her mouth. Her eyes, too, seemed dull and lifeless. The only thing that hadn't changed was the brightness of her clothes, but they seemed to hang off her diminished frame. He knew that some of her misery was down to him. He'd loved her for years, and yet when she needed his support the most, he'd withdrawn from her, more concerned with his own bruised ego than he was with her obvious distress.

Nellie's words and Bertha's admonition that he should let sleeping dogs lie had finally made him think about recent events from Nellie's point of view. Something he should have done before. The thought that it was unfair of him to expect Nellie to dredge up the trauma of Donald's death just to soothe his ego had never occurred to him. She'd lied, that was true, but could he really blame her?

How could he have been so blind to it for so long? He'd seen the cost on Nellie of Donald's life, and he'd seen the cost of his death. He'd watched for years as she'd battled to keep this family afloat with fierce tenacity. It was one of the things he loved most about her. But looking at her now, he realised that some of the fight had gone out of her. One by one, she was losing her family, and in his arrogance, he had decided that unless she told him everything then she wasn't worthy of him.

How could he have done that to her?

As though feeling the weight of his thoughts, Nellie looked over at him and their eyes locked. There was a wealth of pain in her expression, and he ached to ease it.

But what else was she hiding? Who were these men that kept turning up, using the café as some sort of headquarters for their activities? He needed to know if Nellie was lying about not knowing what they were doing. The old Nellie would never have stood for being used. But that was before everything that had happened, before he'd demanded something she couldn't give. Before she'd lost Jimmy, Bert and Edie.

Upstairs, Teddy began to cry, and it was as if a spell was broken. Marianne huffed an impatient sigh and left the room.

'Time for bed, Donny,' Nellie said.

Donny looked at Jasper, and he nodded. 'And don't worry about your Uncle Bert. Them lads is brave as lions, and so's your uncle.' He reached out and ruffled the boy's hair, but Donny pushed his hand away.

'Just cos he's brave, don't mean he can't get hurt. Stop treatin' me like I'm a baby.' He got up and went into his little cubbyhole beside the sitting room, but where once he'd have slammed the door, now he shut it carefully, so as not to scare the baby.

Lily yawned. 'I'm going to turn in too. Try not to worry, Mum.' She stood and kissed her mother's cheek.

'You all right, love?' Jasper asked. Lily looked more troubled than the news about her brother warranted.

She smiled. 'Course I am. Aren't I always?'

Jasper stared after his daughter as she left the room. There had been a hint of bitterness in her words, which was unlike her. He'd find out what was going on when they went for his birthday lunch, he decided. One problem at a time. First, Nellie.

Cissy, who had been uncharacteristically silent throughout, looked between the two of them. 'I'll leave you to it then, shall I?'

He nodded at her gratefully.

'I just 'ave one thing to say to you . . .' Cissy waited until they were both looking at her. 'Love don't come along every day. So when it does, you gotta hold on tight to it an' never let it go.'

After she left, Nellie hung her head, the empty sherry glass clasped in her hands. 'It's my fault Bert's done this,' she whispered.

'The man makes 'is own decisions. Not everythin's about you.'

Nellie looked up at him angrily. 'If you're just gonna insult me, then you know where the door is.'

The familiar frustration and anger rose inside him, but he swallowed it back. 'I'm sorry, Nell,' he said quietly.

'Sorry for what, exactly, Jasper? For walkin' out when I needed you? For treatin' me like I'm some sort of leper? Or sorry that you're determined to make me talk about the past when you know it kills me to think about it?' Her voice broke on this last, but she took a breath and glared at him, the old fire back in her eyes.

'For all of it, love.' He could feel his own throat burning. He'd spent years loving this woman, and yet when she'd finally admitted it too, he'd thrown his chance away. He'd noticed the heart-shaped diamond engagement ring on Dot's finger, flashing in the light. The ring he'd bought for Nellie so many years ago. The ring he'd been waiting to give her.

But as soon as he'd had the chance, he'd given it away. Even so, he wasn't ready to buy another one quite yet. Not while she was still keeping so many secrets from him.

'I mean it, love. I really am sorry. For everythin'.' He went over to her and rested his hand on her shoulder. Instinctively, her own hand came up and clasped it.

'Stay for a bit, Jasper?' Her eyes were imploring him, and he longed to sit down and chat into the night like they'd done on so many evenings over the years.

First, though, he needed to find out what was going on here. 'Another time, love,' he said gruffly. 'I'm on duty in an hour, so I best go get changed. Soon, though, I promise.' Ignoring her disappointed look, he walked out of the room and down the stairs. Opening the back door, he waited a moment then shut it very quietly. But he didn't leave.

Upstairs, he heard Nellie switch on the wireless, and reassured that she wouldn't hear him, he opened the basement door and went downstairs.

Crawling beneath the sloping ceiling, he pulled one of the boxes into the light and contemplated it. It was tied with rope, the knot sealed with a large blob of white wax. If he broke it, they would know, but if he didn't, he wouldn't be able to gauge the danger. He studied the pattern of the wax carefully. All he needed to do was try to make it the same sort of shape and size, and it didn't look too hard.

With a decisive tug, he broke the seal, then spent several minutes trying to untie the rope; whoever had tied it certainly knew their knots. Finally, he managed to unpick it, and after pulling back the flaps, he pushed the hay that was being used to protect the contents aside and stared in puzzlement.

It took a while for the significance of what he was seeing to register, but when it did, his heart started to thump heavily and he let out a long, shaky breath. 'Oh, sweet Jesus,' he muttered. Reaching in, he took one off the top and studied it. Never in his wildest dreams had he suspected this.

Hastily, he put the straw back into place and closed the box. Somehow, despite his shaking hands, he managed to retie the rope, then he grabbed a candle and dripped wax onto the knot making it look as much like the others as he could.

Because if Johnny Fox realised anyone knew what was inside, he dreaded to think what he'd do.

# Chapter 31

*Abbots Cliff House*

Reenie Turner blew on her numb hands and fumbled with the latch on the gate. She'd lived by the sea all her life, so she was used to the bitter gusts that penetrated to your bones during the winter. But even so, there was a difference between living snug and warm in a shop a few hundred yards from the seafront in Dover to herding sheep on a clifftop. The sun was just coming up over the sea and once the sheep were secure and munching at the sparse grass, she went to stand at the end of the field to gaze out at the view.

To her right, the majestic Abbots Cliff House rose white and glowing, its windows glinting, and directly in front of her the strange ugly circular structure, and beyond that, the endless sea. She smiled. It was good to be back in Kent; she'd missed standing on the clifftop with the wind buffeting her and the water glinting below.

She thought back to the last time she'd done this. It had been just before she left Dover in the early spring. She and Jimmy Castle had watched as a lifeboat sped towards a bomb-damaged ship. Where was Jim now? she wondered, gazing at the faint outline of the French coast. Despite everything he'd done, she hoped he and Colin were safe. The pain of his betrayal had faded over the months, and she'd finally accepted that no matter how strong their friendship, the marriage would have been a disaster with the spectre of Colin forever between them. But even so, the humiliation of being left on her wedding day still stung.

If she were honest, these days she thought more about Wilf Perkins and the kiss he'd given her in the potting shed at the allotment than she did about Jimmy. Both men had hurt her. Jim had abandoned her to run off with a man. Whereas Wilf, her childhood best friend, had married her sister. June had been dead a long time now, and as for Wilf . . . she'd not heard a word from him since she'd left Dover. She sighed. She'd thought he'd understand that when she left, she just needed some time to think. But he'd never been very good at reading subtext.

It was Aunt Ethel who'd told her that he'd left the lifeboat service to join the navy and was working on the MTBs. Now, whenever she saw one skimming across the waves, she thought of him.

She thrust her hands into her pockets and walked back to the end of the field. She picked up the pitchfork and began to break the ice in the trough with the wooden handle. It was only when she'd finished that she heard a plane. Shielding her eyes, she squinted into the sun.

Suddenly it came into view. It was flying very low, its wings wobbling from side to side, the engine sputtering. She watched, frozen to the spot, as the yellow nose of a Messerschmidt came closer, losing height all the time. And as it crested the top of the cliff, she fell to the ground and put her hands over her head, memories of another day running through her mind: the ground littered with bodies, the little boy sitting by his dead grandfather, the desperate dash to safety as a plane fired indiscriminately at the field full of people. In her mind's eye, she could still see Bert Castle lying motionless in the centre.

The air started to vibrate with noise and she curled into a tighter ball, her breath coming in short, sharp gasps as she fought the panic.

Suddenly the screaming of the engine stopped and the ground shook as the plane thumped down. She peeped under her arms to see it skidding across the grass, smoke pouring from its engines, as the sheep scattered, bleating in panic.

She watched wide-eyed as it crashed into the drystone wall and came to a stop. After a moment, the pilot leapt down. He hesitated briefly, seemingly undecided about what to do, then started to climb over the wall.

Without thinking, Reenie picked up the pitchfork, leapt to her feet and charged towards him.

'Stop!'

As he glanced back, he lost his footing and fell over.

Reenie approached him, wielding the pitchfork in front of her. Behind her, she could hear the sheep, whickering in distress, but they'd have to wait. This bastard might have been the one who'd fired on the field; if not for him she'd probably never have married Jimmy. Pastor Philip would still have his leg, and that poor little boy wouldn't have seen his grandfather die.

The fear left her and fury propelled her forward. 'Do you know what you did?' she cried. In the back of her mind, she knew it was irrational, but she didn't care. She watched with satisfaction as the man cowered against the wall, his hands over his head.

She waved the prongs of the pitchfork in the man's face. 'Take your trousers off now, or I'll poke your bloody eyes out!'

# Chapter 32

Marge stood at the large bay window in the drawing room drinking a cup of tea, her head thumping unpleasantly after celebrating the arrival of her friends a little too hard the night before.

Captain Bennett had stayed up with them for a while, his eyes rarely leaving Emily. Finally, though, he'd fallen asleep, and they'd tiptoed out, leaving him to the draught coming through the French windows, and continued drinking in their dormitory. It had been fun, and for the first time since Captain Roberts had uttered Tom Bennett's name, Marge had slept undisturbed by dreams of Katy and the past.

And this morning, she intended to keep her dismal thoughts at bay with hard work. The first group of men was arriving tomorrow, and she and the girls needed to run through the games to ensure everything went smoothly. Captain Roberts had put his faith in them, and she was determined they wouldn't let him down.

A familiar droning noise reached her and she squinted out of the window, spotting the plane just as the rat-a-tat of the anti-aircraft guns started to ring out. 'Oh my God!' she exclaimed, watching the plane, with its distinctive cross on the side and yellow nose, fly towards the cliffs.

'What's up?' Becky came to join her and gasped. 'Bloody hell. It's going to come down in the field.'

Marge deposited her cup and saucer on a side table. 'I want to see this.' She ran out of the room and made for the stairs.

'There's a plane about to crash!' Becky called out to the others, who were in the kitchen. 'Come on!'

'Let me know if it drops a bomb, otherwise, I'm not budging,' Maria muttered into her tea. She had been very drunk the night before.

Upstairs in the attic, the windows gave them a perfect view. As the plane drew closer, they moved to the window that overlooked the field, keeping it in their sights. Another explosion from the ack-ack guns made the windows rattle. 'It's better than the pictures,' Emily gasped.

'It was like this every day back in the summer of 1940,' Marge said. 'It almost got boring.' She decided not to mention the bloodbath at the football field last year. She still had nightmares about tying a tourniquet around Philip's leg as he lay begging her to tell him he was going to be all right. For a moment her eyes misted with regret. He'd been a good man, but she had been right to turn down his proposal. She'd heard he'd gone to Roehampton to be fitted with a prosthetic leg. She hoped he'd find the happiness he deserved.

'It's coming down!' Becky shouted.

Marge switched her attention back to the field, her hand flying to her mouth as the plane skidded across the grass and smashed through the drystone wall. For a moment, all was quiet and the women stood in stunned silence. Then she noticed a figure running towards it.

'Someone's there! We should help them!'

She turned and ran back down the stairs, the others clatter-
ing after her.

Captain Bennett was just emerging from his bedroom and
called down the stairs after them.

'Ladies! What are you doing dashing around the house like
a bunch of schoolgirls?'

'A plane's come down in the field, sir,' Emily called back.
'We can't let the pilot escape!'

He tutted with annoyance, but followed them out, running
behind them down the long driveway, then he stopped. 'I'll get
my gun,' he called. 'Try to hold him till I get there.'

Marge glanced behind her and almost laughed at the sight
of him running back towards the house. 'Get his gun, my foot,'
she panted. 'He just doesn't want to be shown up.'

They could see smoke from the plane's damaged engine rising up behind the hedge, but by the time they reached it, no one
was there. They skidded to a halt, looking in either direction.
'He's escaped!' Becky bent over with her hands on her thighs.

Marge coughed, her chest felt tight and wheezy – she really
needed to cut down on the fags. 'Come on,' she said. 'Let's keep
going.' They walked along the lane, bordered on either side by
drystone walls, keeping their eyes out for signs of the pilot.

It wasn't long before they saw a man and woman coming
towards them. The woman's curly blonde hair was escaping from
beneath a green woollen hat and she was wearing baggy cordu-
roy trousers and a thick sweater. She was brandishing a pitchfork,
which she stabbed into the back of a short, brown-haired man
walking in front of her with his arms held out by his sides, a boot
in each hand. His top half was wrapped in a flying jacket, but
beneath that they could see a pair of pale, skinny legs.

'Where are his trousers?' Marge said.

They watched in astonishment as the pair came closer. 'Who is that?' Emily pointed at the woman who was poking the pilot in the back with a pitchfork. 'Did she really catch him on her own?'

Marge squinted at the figure. Surely that wasn't … The clouds parted for a moment, throwing a beam of sunlight onto the pair. The woman's hair gleamed gold in the sunlight.

'Reenie, is that you?' She started to run towards the pair. 'Oh my God, Reenie!'

Reenie looked up at her and grinned in disbelief. 'Marge?'

They gazed at each other in delight for a moment, then Marge turned her attention to the trouser-less pilot and raised an eyebrow. 'Why didn't we think about that before Jimmy Castle ran off!' Then her hand flew to her mouth. How could she be so insensitive!

For a moment Reenie looked shocked, then she started to giggle. 'Well, once we've called the police, you can have the pitchfork and try this tactic on Rodney.'

The others reached them just as Reenie threw her pitchfork down and ran at Marge. Becky hastily picked up the discarded weapon and waved it in the pilot's direction, but her eyes were on Marge as she cried with laughter in the land girl's arms.

'What's going on?' Becky's voice was panicked as she waved the pitchfork at the hapless pilot, who stood with his head down, his shoulders slumped with humiliation.

Marge disentangled herself and wiped her eyes. 'This is one of my oldest and best friends. I haven't seen her since—' She stopped herself, shooting a glance at Reenie.

Reenie just smiled. 'She hasn't seen me since my wedding day when my groom ran away, and I ended up kissing someone else in the potting shed. Fun times.'

'Is that how things are done here in the sticks? My mum'd have a fit if she realised that me joining the Wrens meant I'd see a man without his trousers.'

'Your mum would have a fit if she knew you'd seen a man without a lot more than his trousers,' Becky smirked, her gaze never wavering from the pilot.

Emily giggled and hit her on the arm. 'Fair point.'

Marge linked her arm through Reenie's and began walking up the lane. 'Becky, bring him back to the house and we can call the police. You never know, Bennett might have managed to locate his gun by the time we get back.'

Becky snorted. 'He's probably hiding under his bed with a hip flask of brandy.'

Emily shuddered. 'He's such a creep.'

'You have no idea just how much,' Marge muttered.

Reenie shot her a look. 'Has something happened?'

Her friend knew her too well. But now wasn't the time to explain. After all these years of lying about her sister, she wasn't even sure where she'd start.

She shook her head and smiled reassuringly. 'Our new CO turns out to be not only incompetent, but also a lecherous bastard.'

Reenie wrinkled her nose. 'Well, if anyone can give him his just deserts, that'd be you, Marge.'

God, she really hoped so, but she still wasn't sure how. She couldn't imagine the top brass giving two figs about Bennett's lechery – unless it was their own wife or daughter on the receiving end. Still, she'd only been here a couple of days. She was sure something would turn up soon.

By the time they made it back to the house, Maria and Mrs Benson were waiting on the doorstep, gabbling excitedly as they watched the procession of three Wrens, a land girl and a trouser-less enemy pilot make its way towards them.

Captain Bennett emerged as they reached the door and pointed a gun at the German. 'The game's up, man.' His eyes flickered with some surprise to the pilot's bare legs. 'Bring him into the kitchen. I've called the police.'

'Very brave of you, sir,' Marge said wryly. 'You deserve a whisky.'

He scowled at her. 'Shut your mouth,' he murmured as she passed.

Marge nearly gagged at the alcohol fumes, but she held his gaze. 'Or what, *sir*?' she whispered back.

His eyes narrowed threateningly, but Marge stared back, until finally he turned and followed the others into the kitchen.

'What was all that about?' Reenie asked.

'Like I said, the man's a creep,' Marge said shortly. The adrenaline of the morning was draining away, and she reached into her pocket for a cigarette, lighting it with a shaking hand.

Reenie watched her with concern. 'What's going on, Marge?'

Marge smiled at her. 'Later,' she murmured. 'Don't suppose you get any time off, do you? Maybe you and me could go for a cup of tea . . . or preferably something stronger?'

Reenie smiled. 'I get Sundays off.'

Marge thought for a moment. Sunday would be a half day, and she'd been planning on going to Dover to see Marianne and Mr W in the afternoon. 'Let's go to Castle's. You can see

Marianne and meet the baby. It'll be great to get the old gang back together.'

Reenie's eyes clouded over. 'The old gang will never be back together,' she said quietly.

They were silent for a moment, Daisy's ghost hanging between them. But then Reenie rallied. 'All right. I'll come over in the morning, then we can go to the café together. But let's not go to the Oak. I'm not ready to face that memory just yet.' She shuddered.

Marge nodded understandingly. Reenie's wedding reception had been held at the pub, so she couldn't blame her for not wanting to return just yet.

Captain Bennett came out of the kitchen. 'Young lady, thank you for your bravery, but we've got it all in hand. This property is classified. Very important and *secret* war work is taking place here and we can't risk any old Tom, Dick and Harry finding us out.'

Marge rolled her eyes and led Reenie out of the front door. 'See you on Sunday.' She leant forward and gave her another hug. Reenie's heavy jumper smelt of manure and sheep. 'You've lost weight,' she said, pulling back.

'Heartbreak's got to be good for something.' Reenie smiled.

'Oh, love. Are you really still heartbroken about Jimmy? You know your marriage would've been a disaster.'

Reenie sighed. 'I know. But that doesn't make the humili- ation any easier.'

'What about you and Wilf? You been in touch?'

'Course not. The man is incapable of communicating. But Aunt Ethel told me that he's on the MTBs now.'

'You do know he loves you, don't you? He actually told me that.'

Reenie pushed a stray lock of hair from her face. 'Then he should have written and told *me*. Anyway, I still find it hard to forgive him for marrying my sister.'

Marge sighed. 'Nothing's ever simple when it comes to love, is it.'

'Ladies, this is not the place for organising your social life and talking about your boyfriends. I'd have thought you two were old enough to have grown out of that stage.'

Marge felt an angry flush rise up her cheeks, but Reenie seemed unfazed.

'Nice to meet you too, Captain Bennett.' She smiled winningly at him. 'I really hope we have the chance to get to know each other better.' She winked at Marge. 'And you and me will discuss Rodney next time we meet.' Then with a final wave, she left.

When the front door had closed behind them, Captain Bennett looked around furtively, then grabbed Marge's arm. 'If you *ever* talk to me like that again, you'll be sorry,' he ground out.

Pulling her arm free, Marge raised an eyebrow. 'What exactly will you do?' she asked. 'Report me? Well, go ahead. As you can see, I'm shaking in my boots.' She leant forward, trying not to breathe in the stench of Old Spice mixed with alcohol. 'Never forget I know *who* you really are. And I know *what* you really are. So go ahead and do your worst.'

A knock on the front door interrupted them, and Marge tossed her head as she went to answer it.

'Welcome, officers. The prisoner's in the kitchen.' Then with a last contemptuous glance at Captain Bennett, whose flushed cheeks now matched the redness of his nose, she went after them.

# Chapter 33

After a restless night, Jasper had realised three things: he'd been wrong when he'd told Nellie that sometimes love wasn't enough. Love was *always* enough. He just hoped that she'd forgive him for being so pig-headed.

Secondly, and this was the one that had kept him up all night: whoever was using the café's basement was playing a very dangerous game.

Thirdly, he couldn't go to the police. Just having those boxes in her basement would implicate Nellie, and she would be arrested.

Opening the drawer in his bedside table, he looked again at the papers he'd taken from the box. He couldn't understand how they were even producing them – or where. Was it nearby? Or did they produce them somewhere else and distribute around the country? If only he knew where their centre of operations was, then he could report it. But who to? This needed to go right to the top. He thought for a moment. First things first, he needed to find out what Lou Carter knew. After that, he knew exactly who he needed to talk to.

After he'd dressed, Jasper sat in his worn brown armchair and considered the best thing to do. He would talk to Mr Wainwright, but he also needed an alternative plan. If he could find out where they worked, perhaps he could keep the authorities away from Nellie's door and reduce the risk of her being implicated. But to do that, he'd need to be able to follow them when they picked up their supplies. Maybe Clive Pearson could lend him a car and some petrol, although he had no way of knowing how much he'd need. Plus, it was a dangerous plan; he'd need to be prepared if he was going to go down that route.

Going back into his bedroom, he knelt on the floor, his knees creaking, reminding him that he was probably too old to go chasing gangsters around the country. Still, it wouldn't hurt to have some protection. Reaching under the wardrobe, he pulled out a shoebox and opened the lid. Inside was his old service revolver and a box of bullets, untouched since he'd put them there when he'd returned from war in 1919. He hesitated before he touched it. He wasn't a superstitious man, but this gun had been with him through some of the worst of times. It had protected him, but the cost of that protection was the lives of boys his own age, and he had hoped never to have to use a gun again. This was why he'd become an ARP warden rather than join the Home Guard.

He picked it up and pointed it at the wall. It felt familiar, as though he'd put it down only yesterday. In decent condition too. A thorough clean and oil, and it'd be good as new.

Later, as he walked past the café, he could see Nellie's bright orange jumper through the plastic window. He doubted she'd have slept last night after Dot's revelations on top of everything else. Bert might not be his son, but he loved him as though he was, and he'd watched helplessly as he'd gone off the rails after Gladys's death. Only Dot had been able to pull him back from the brink, and now they were married, he couldn't fathom why he'd have joined the Commandos. He didn't buy Dot's accusation that he'd done it to make Nellie proud; Bert just wasn't the type, and reformed character or not, he couldn't imagine marriage had changed him *that* much.

Still, there was nothing he could do for him; he needed to concentrate on the immediate danger – the one that threatened not just Nellie but everyone living above the cafe, including Lily, the daughter he had loved from afar for so many years and who had only recently started to call him 'Dad'. He swallowed back a wave of fear. He loved all the Castles as though they were his own family, but Lily was his only blood relative in the world. Anyone who came for her would have to step over his cold, dead body first.

Beside the ruined Market Hall, Lou was setting up her stall. He watched her for a moment, fighting back the anger. She was the reason Nellie was mixed up in this dangerous business, but he needed to stay calm. Once he'd got himself under control, he jogged across the road and went to stand in front of the stall, examining the whelks lying in a slimy grey and orange pile at the bottom of a wooden bowl.

Lou had been rummaging beneath the stall and jumped when she stood up to find him glowering at her. But then she smiled. 'To what do I owe the pleasure, Jasper? Fish for breakfast, is it?'

Any sense of control he thought he'd had fled. 'What the hell 'ave you got Nellie mixed up in?'

Lou's usually ruddy cheeks paled. 'I don't know what you're talkin' about,' she snapped back, but Jasper could tell she knew exactly what he was talking about.

'You brought that man to her door to save your own skin.' He leant towards her. 'Do you 'ave any idea what you've done?'

'Look, Nellie's a grown woman 'as can make 'er own decisions. I merely suggested that 'er basement might be a useful drop-off point for an acquaintance's new business venture.'

Jasper rarely lost his temper, but he was fighting the urge to grab the bowl of whelks and tip it over the woman's head. 'And what is this *business* venture? Legal and above board, is it?'

Lou looked away. 'Well, I mean, it ain't entirely legit, but it's just printin' of some sort, I think.'

'Printin' what?'

'Does it matter? Not exactly the crime of the century to print a few dirty mags, is it?'

'If that's what it is.' His hands twitched with the desire to shake her.

'Look, I don't know what it is. Honest to God, I don't. An' I told Nellie the same, so lay off, all right?'

Jasper examined her face, trying to gauge whether she was lying. It was impossible to tell; Lou told lies for a living and you couldn't trust her to tell you what day it was.

Her eyes narrowed. 'What's all this got to do with you, anyway? I got the impression you was keepin' your distance ever since the trial. Do *you* know what they're doin'?'

Jasper's expression must have given him away, and Lou gasped. 'Bloody 'ell, you do, don'tcha? Don't tell me you've opened one of them boxes. Johnny Fox ain't a man to cross.'

Jasper ignored the question. 'Why'd you get Nellie involved?'

'Well, she owed me a favour,' she mumbled, fiddling with the bowls.

'She owed you nothin'! *You* owed *her*, for puttin' up with you all these years. For bein' friends with you when no one else wants anythin' to do with you. Ye gods, you've got no bloody idea what you've done!'

Lou looked hurt. 'You an' me are friends.'

'No. You an' me are acquaintances. I've tolerated you, I've felt sorry for you. But friends? Nah. And unless you can sort this out, then we ain't even gonna be acquainted. An' I mean that, Lou.'

He turned on his heel and walked away, but as his temper cooled, he began to regret his impulsiveness. If Lou told Johnny Fox that he'd opened one of the boxes, then he'd just put them all in even more danger.

# Chapter 34



*Dover Castle*

After a couple of days spent catching up with old colleagues, Rodney shouldered his kitbag and walked down to the café. Slipping in through the back door, he called a greeting to Marianne and Elodie as he walked through the kitchen.

In the café, Cissy smiled at him distractedly, but immediately turned her attention back to his mother, who was standing by the window, hands on hips, her eyes fixed on the square.

'What's going on?' he asked.

'It's Jasper,' Cissy hissed. 'He's havin' a barney with Lou Carter!'

Rodney's eyebrows rose. The only person he'd seen Jasper argue with was his mum, but everyone argued with her. Curious, he went to stand beside his mother. Jasper was leaning forward, almost spitting in Lou's face.

'What's all that about?' he murmured.

The customers at the table were also riveted on the action. 'Probably got the runs from her dodgy whelks. 'Ad them meself the other week,' a soldier sitting at the table remarked.

'Have some decency, Private! People are trying to eat,' Nellie snapped. But her eyes never left Jasper, as he turned on his heel and marched away. It was hard to see his expression, but from the stiffness of his shoulders, it was clear he was furious.

Nellie turned and attempted to smile but she looked upset. 'You after some breakfast, love?'

Rodney bit his tongue to stop the questions that came to his lips. He'd promised himself he wouldn't get involved, and he needed to stick to that. And frankly, he had neither the time nor the energy. So, he nodded. 'Wouldn't say no, Mum. If you've got spare.'

'Take a seat an' I'll bring you a cuppa.'

He sat down at the table by the counter, while his mother bustled off to make the tea. Cissy was hovering in the kitchen door, her eyes fixed on him. She flicked a glance at Nellie, then came to perch on the chair opposite, looking ready to take flight at any moment.

'Your mum's in trouble,' she hissed.

Rodney's heart sank. 'Mum's always in trouble of some sort.'

'But this is bad.' She leant towards him. 'You gotta do something, Rod. She's gone an' got 'erself a g—'

'Cissy!' Nellie's sharp voice rang out across the room, and a sudden hush fell as everyone turned to look.

Cissy blushed. 'I'm just chattin' to my nephew, Nell.'

'He's not your nephew.'

Rodney watched the exchange in exasperation. 'I'm sorry, Cissy, whatever's going on, I'm not getting involved. Last time I did, I made everything worse, and believe me, Mum wouldn't listen to a word I say.'

'He's right. I won't listen, an' I won't brook no interference in my business, do you understand?'

'I'll tell you what I understand, Nell. I understand that your stubborn pride'll get us all *killed* if you're not careful.'

'I think *you're* the one in danger of bein' killed, Cissy. Cos if you don't stop your hysterics, I'll do it meself.'

The two women stared at each other, some sort of silent message passing between them.

'I'm not surprised she's hysterical, Nellie. Something's not right about this place at the moment. And now poor dear Jasper's shouting in the square. I've known that man all his life and I've never seen him behave like that. It makes me wonder what could be next,' Adelaide Frost remarked.

'What's next, Adelaide, is you leavin' and not comin' back,' Nellie retorted.

Adelaide took a sip of tea. 'You know, I think you're right. I've a feeling in my water that something bad's going to happen.'

'You been speakin' to Bertha again?' Nellie mocked, putting a plate of sausage and egg in front of Rodney.

He heaved a sigh as he picked up his knife and fork. On the one hand he wanted to know what the problem was. On the other, as Marge had always told him, he had to stop feeling responsible for his family. He hadn't listened when she'd warned him not to get involved with the trial, but he intended to take her advice now.

'Ladies.' He turned and smiled at Miss Frost over his shoulder. 'I can't stay long, and much as I would love to help, just this once, would you mind if I ate my breakfast in peace.'

'Quite right, Rodney. Cissy, there're orders to take. An', Adelaide, if you're worried about your safety, you know where the door is.' With a toss of her head, Nellie returned to her usual place behind the counter.

'Rodney, you gotta listen.' Cissy wasn't about to be put off. 'I'm tellin' you, your mum 'as a gun hidden upstairs.' She mouthed the word 'gun', mindful of Adelaide's flapping ears.

Rodney put down his knife and fork, his appetite suddenly deserting him, and stared at her. 'What?' The idea of his mother with a gun brought terrible thoughts racing to the forefront of his mind. Was it the same gun? He had no idea what had happened to his father's gun after he'd died and had never thought to question it. But had she kept it?

Nellie came over and laid a hand on her cousin's arm. 'Please,' she said softly. 'For me.'

Cissy shook her head slightly. 'How can I, love? You need help.'

'For the love of God! I'm beggin' you.' Nellie's fingers dug into Cissy's sleeve.

Was it his imagination or was there genuine panic in his mother's tone? 'Mum?' Rodney looked between the two women.

Cissy threw up her hands. 'Well, if we're all murdered in our beds, don't say I didn't warn you,' she muttered before stamping back to the kitchen.

Rodney swallowed nervously. 'Mum, if there was something, you would tell me, wouldn't you?'

Nellie tutted. 'Don't listen to her. She's always made mountains out of molehills.' She patted his hand. 'Anyway, I don't ask you about what's goin' on in the war, do I? And I wouldn't, cos that's *your* business. And the café is *my* business. You've got more important things to worry about. Like winnin' this damn war so we can all get back to normal. Now, eat your breakfast and get off to whatever important stuff you've gotta do. I ain't askin' what it is, cos . . .' She raised her eyebrow at him.

Rodney smiled reluctantly. She had a point. In any case, there wasn't a lot he could do, so he picked up his knife and fork and cut into his sausage.

'If I might venture an opinion, Lieutenant Castle.'

Rodney turned to look at Miss Frost. Despite her judgemental ways and her habit of quoting Bible passages, he'd always had a soft spot for her. She'd been the one who'd fuelled his desire to join the Navy when she'd given him a collection of Captain Marryat's books. He'd read *Peter Simple* and *Mr Midshipman Easy* so many times the books had fallen apart. It was a kindness he would never forget.

'Do you know what's going on, Miss Frost?'

'I could never pretend to know what goes on in your mother's mind, Rodney. But I can tell you there have been some very unsavoury characters coming in and out of the back door as if they owned the place.'

'You mean Terence Carter?'

'Good heavens, Terence Carter is a minnow compared to the men I've seen. But you have duties to perform, and I am due at the community restaurant for my shift.' She smiled slightly at him. 'Take care, Rodney, won't you? Those seas can be so terribly dangerous.'

'I'll do my best, Miss Frost. You take care too.'

'Oh, when it's time, it's time. A lesson I learnt when my sweetheart was killed in the Boer War back in 1901. But don't worry. Me and your mum might disagree on a lot, but she's an integral part of this community. I'll keep my eye out.'

A lump came to Rodney's throat as he stood and kissed the woman's cheek. 'I didn't know. I'm sorry.'

She tilted her head. 'Those books I gave you were his. Anyway, must be off.' After buttoning her coat and picking up her knitting bag, she walked away, leaving Rodney bemused and strangely touched. He sat back down and picked up his teacup thoughtfully. Like most people, he'd assumed she'd remained a spinster out of choice. It was easy to forget that women had been losing their sweethearts to battle long before the Great War. It was a long line of tragedy and loss that never seemed to end.

'And don't take no notice of her, either!' His mother's sharp voice brought him back to the present. 'Thinks she knows better than everyone, but she's just a stuck-up busybody.'

Rodney put down his cup with a clink. 'Well, I like her. And you should go easy on her, Mum. She's just lonely.'

Nellie raised her eyebrows. 'Lonely, my arse. Nosy, is what she is.'

There was no point arguing the point with this mother so he stood up. 'I have to go. But take care, Mum.' He looked at her intently. 'And if you do have a gun . . .' He hesitated, not sure how to say this. 'If you do have one, please don't use it. You don't want to go through that again.'

Nellie paled, and when she spoke, her voice trembled. 'I will do what has to be done, just like I always have, no matter the consequences.' Then she grasped his arms and standing on tiptoe, kissed his cheek. 'Take care, love.'

To his surprise, his mother's eyes were glassy with tears. She'd never been this demonstrative to him before, and it made his chest ache. 'I'll only be in Folkestone, Mum. I'll be back to say goodbye before I go to sea.'

Putting his hat on, he went through to the kitchen, and after kissing Marianne and Cissy, and waving at Elodie, he left. But despite his determination to stay out of his mother's business, he found he could think of little else as he sat on the bus to Folkestone. No matter what he told himself, he knew that as soon as he came back, he'd have to find out what was really going on.

# Chapter 35

*Abbots Cliff House*

After the confrontation with Captain Bennett, Marge felt a little shaken as she led the two military policemen into the kitchen. She had no power over that man at all. The Navy was rigidly hierarchical in all things, and though she might be an officer now, women came beneath midshipmen as far as the navy were concerned. So in a clash between her and Captain Bennett, she would undoubtedly come off the worst.

Her gloomy thoughts fled as she took in the sight in front of her. The pilot was sitting at the kitchen table looking bemused. He had a cigarette between his fingers and a cup of tea in front of him. Opposite him, Mrs Benson was plying him with questions while the other girls looked on with amusement.

'So, 'ow many d'you reckon you've shot down then?' Mrs Benson asked, tapping her cigarette against the bowl serving as an ashtray. 'You reckon you've dropped a bomb on Folkestone or Dover? What about London? Coventry?'

Becky laughed. 'He's not going to answer, Mrs B.'

'Thing is' – she took a long drag of her cigarette, her narrowed eyes never leaving the pilot's face – 'Mr B were killed the first day of the Blitz up in London. An' if this bloke dropped them bombs then 'e'll be losin' a lot more than 'is trousers.' A bread knife was sitting on the table, and she picked it up and sliced at the pad of her thumb, drawing a small bead of blood. 'This one'd do nicely.' She gave him a hard stare.

The pilot didn't need an interpreter to get the gist of what she was saying, and he gulped, cowering away from her.

As she raised the knife and pointed it at the pilot, one of the MPs muttered, 'Bloody hell. Is she really going to geld him at the kitchen table?'

Marge laughed at the sight of the little woman pointing the big knife at the trouser-less pilot. And once she'd started, she found she couldn't stop.

'Your face!' She pointed at Becky. 'She's not really going to do anything, are you, Mrs B?'

Mrs Benson put the knife down and took another drag of her cigarette. 'Aren't I? I 'ad a fondness for Mr B, so only seems fair. He took mine, so I should take 'is.' She gestured towards the pilot's lap.

One of the MPs stepped forward and took the knife from the table. 'If you don't mind, madam, we'll deal with him now.' He grasped the pilot's arm and pulled him from his seat. If anything, the man looked relieved to be leaving.

'Bye, then, love,' Mrs Benson called after him.

The other girls stood and followed the police out of the house. 'Don't suppose you'd like to come back for a drink when you're off duty?' Becky called after them. 'Say, six o'clock?'

The younger of the two grinned at her. 'Only if you promise to hide the knives from that madwoman. We'll bring some mates, shall we?'

'Only if they're handsome!' Maria called.

The man saluted and got into the driver's seat of the car parked outside, while the other policeman sat in the back with the prisoner.

'Well, that was entertaining.' Emily turned to go back inside. 'Is there a record player in this place? We can't invite a load of men around if we don't have a record player.'

'Who's invited men around?' Captain Bennett was hovering by the stairs. 'This isn't a party venue, ladies.'

Emily smiled at him. 'You don't really mind, do you, sir? We all need a little fun in our lives. It can't be all war, war, war.'

The captain softened. 'As long as you save a dance for me.' He smiled. He no doubt thought it was charming, but in fact it just made him look like a dirty old man.

Emily's smile stayed in place. 'Of course, sir.' She glanced over at Maria and wrinkled her nose.

'We need to get to work,' Marge said firmly. 'And that includes you, sir. We need to teach you how to play before the men arrive tomorrow. Come on, girls, we'll set it up, then you can join us, Captain.'

She was halfway up the stairs, when she stopped and turned back to him. 'By the way, sir, what's that hut for by the sound mirror?'

The captain had been about to go into the study, but he stopped and looked back at her. 'What were you doing snooping around there?'

She frowned. 'I wasn't snooping. I was just curious.'

'Well, don't be. That place is out of bounds to you. There's some hush-hush equipment in there that I'm keeping an eye on, so you need to stay well away.'

'What do you suppose the hush-hush equipment is?' Becky said as they went into the room.

'I don't know, but if it's secret, I sort of want to know what it is,' Marge said, slightly disappointed at the thought. It suggested that Bennett was more important to the Navy than she'd thought.

'I wouldn't, if I were you, Marge,' Maria said. She always had been a rule follower.

'Probably just listening equipment,' Emily said. 'This is the perfect location to listen to Nazi shipping.'

'Hmm.' Marge wanted to be sure though. The captain had probably been lying to everyone all his life – most especially his wife. Somehow she needed to find out if he was lying now, because she needed all the ammunition she could get if she was going to bring this man down.

# Chapter 36



Jasper was wheezing by the time he reached Victoria Crescent, his breath puffing out in clouds in front of him. He was furious with himself for losing his temper with Lou, and the thought that he might have put Nellie and everyone at the café in even more danger made him bang the brass knocker with such force that it made his ears ring.

The door was opened by a severe-looking woman with scraped-back hair and an old-fashioned high-necked blouse and long black skirt. Jasper cocked his head and looked at her closely.

'Mr Wainwright is unavailable,' she said before he'd had a chance to say a word.

'Gertie . . . Gertie Bright?' he asked.

The woman squinted at him, frown lines prominent between her brows. 'J-Jasper Cane?'

He smiled. 'I can't believe it! 'Ow long's it been since I saw you?' He stepped forward and took her hand, holding it in both his.

'It's Gertrude Frobisher now. Although I'm widowed.' She pulled her hand away.

'Well, well. Little Gertie. I cried when you left Dover.'

She smiled thinly. 'Did you? I didn't. I'm afraid Mr Wainwright isn't available. He's a very important man, and I'm trying to discourage people from knocking on the door day in and day out, expecting him to help them. It's not right. And now he has his lady friend popping by . . .' She shook her head. 'Totally unsuitable she is as well. Dyed hair, you know. Orange. Not at all the sort of woman a man like Mr Wainwright should be associating with.'

Jasper felt his good humour fade. Her icy demeanour was one thing, but insulting his friend was going too far. 'Cissy's a friend of mine, and I think they're perfectly matched. And I need to see Mr W on a matter of urgency.'

Mrs Frobisher flushed. 'I'm allowed opinions. And I'll tell you another one. You've aged, Jasper.' She nodded towards his wiry white hair. 'What happened to all that blond hair?'

'You ain't no spring chicken yourself, Gertie, so watch yerself. Now, if you wouldn't mind, this really is urgent.'

With a sniff, she bustled away. He could hardly believe the change in her. But then, the last time he'd seen her they'd been twelve, and who knew what her life had been like since.

'He'll see you now, Jasper.' Gertie called down the corridor. 'He's having his breakfast but he said you could join him.'

Jasper took a deep breath and walked towards the door. Mr Wainwright was seated at a large dark-wood table, a white napkin tucked into his shirt as he ate sardines on toast.

'Jasper!' He stood up and gestured him towards a seat. 'This is a surprise. I hope you're not in trouble.'

Jasper sat down. 'It's not me, Mr W. It's Nellie.'

Mr Wainwright rolled his eyes. 'When isn't it one of the Castles,' he replied.

'Thing is, though, this is bad.' He reached into his pocket and threw some papers on the table in front of him. 'What do you make of that?'

Mr Wainwright peered through the spectacles perched on the end of his nose.

'What should I make of it?' he asked, turning it over.

'It's a forgery.'

Mr Wainwright frowned. 'Are you sure?'

'Gotta be.' Jasper nodded grimly. 'There's boxes and boxes of them at the café.'

'Good God! Who else knows about this? Is Mrs Castle aware?'

'She don't 'ave a clue. The bloke what brought them threatened the babies and she's scared witless.'

'I'm not surprised,' he murmured, staring thoughtfully into the distance.

Jasper continued. 'Whoever's makin' them, is usin' the café as the drop-off and pick-up. They must be producin' them somewhere else.'

Mr Wainwright whistled. 'Who could have the means to produce these?'

'Some bloke called Johnny Fox. Nellie's so scared of 'im that she's bought a gun.'

Mr Wainwright looked up sharply.

'This is too big for the police, Mr W. That's why I come to you. You know people in high places, or so it's always seemed. An' you an' me 'ave a lot at stake in that café, don't we?'

Mr Wainwright nodded. 'We do indeed, Jasper.'

'Lily's my only blood and as for Nellie . . .' He shook his head, words failing him.

'I know exactly what you mean, man. And this is an outrage.' He threw the papers on the table. 'It's undermining everything the government is trying to do. Whoever these people are, they have to be stopped. And I think I know just who to call.' He wiped his mouth with his napkin. 'Stay here. I'll be back in a moment. Oh, and help yourself to a cup of tea.'

After he'd left, Jasper paced around the room, his eyes roaming over the panelled walls, and fussy china ornaments on the mantelpiece that he couldn't imagine Mr Wainwright would have chosen.

After half an hour, the lawyer returned, his expression grim. 'It seems, Jasper, you've stumbled on something the authorities have been trying to pin down for some time. These are indeed extremely dangerous men. They'll be sending people down to investigate.'

'But what about Nellie? Will she be implicated in this?'

Mr Wainwright sighed. 'I've explained the situation as best I can, so we'll just have to hope not. And if she is, I know of a very good lawyer.' He smiled reassuringly.

But Jasper didn't return his smile. Mr W could be the best lawyer in the world, but he wasn't sure anyone would get away with this sort of thing. 'What 'appens now?'

'We sit tight and they'll send some people to deal with the situation. But you're not to alert anyone about this. Not even Mrs Castle. It's important that these men are caught red-handed, so there can't be a whiff that anything has changed, or they'll go to ground.'

Jasper thought it best not to mention that Lou Carter might have guessed he knew what Johnny Fox was up to. He didn't trust Lou as far as he could throw her, but she had a soft spot for Nellie, so he just had to hope she'd keep her mouth shut.

'Do you understand, Jasper?' Mr Wainwright urged. 'We can't alert anyone.'

Jasper nodded. He wouldn't say a word, but he needed to be prepared to do whatever it took to protect the people he loved.

# Chapter 37

*Abbots Cliff House*

After the excitement of the morning, the girls went upstairs to prepare for the first group of officers, who were due to arrive the next day. Captain Bennett joined them, but he proved to be an inept student and refused to take the game seriously. It didn't help that he made no effort to disguise his dislike of Marge.

Finally, Marge snapped. 'With respect, sir, perhaps it might be better if you left us to it.'

He turned an icy stare in her direction. 'With *respect*, Atkinson, as your commanding officer, it's not up to you what I do. Perhaps you need to reflect on how you teach the game. I can't think what Captain Roberts was thinking, sending you here. The man always was a liability.'

Marge clenched her fists, fury fizzing through her. After the way he'd talked to her that morning, and then the nonsense about secret equipment in the hut, now he chose to insult not only her but possibly one of the best officers she had ever worked for.

She opened her mouth to respond, but Becky got there first.

'How about we all take a break,' she said evenly. 'It's very cold in here, so I think a cup of tea is in order.' She gave Marge a warning glance.

'Capital idea, Purviss. Tea it is. And maybe something a little stronger. I'm sure it's six o'clock somewhere.' Captain Bennett left the room with alacrity.

Marge blew out her cheeks. 'I swear to God, I will strangle him if he comes back up here.'

'Best not, Marge,' Emily said. 'Navy takes a dim view of murder. Come on, one more run-through of Raspberry, then we'll have a cup of tea.'

While Maria and Emily put the pieces back into position, Becky came over to her. 'What the hell's wrong with you? He's not the first incompetent drunkard you've had to deal with.'

'If only that was all he was,' Marge gritted.

Becky regarded her seriously. 'Ever since Roberts told us about Dover, you've been different, and now that we're here, it clearly has something to do with Bennett. Do you two know each other?'

Marge hesitated, but she'd been carrying this secret for far too long, and she was tired of it. And maybe the girls could help her.

She nodded. 'All right, I'll tell you.' She went over to the door and checked the corridor. Bennett was nowhere in sight, but even so she couldn't be too careful. Shutting the door, she arranged some chairs in a small circle and asked the others to join her.

'What's this about?' Maria asked. 'Is it the captain?'

Marge nodded. Then, sitting forward, she began to talk in a hushed voice, forcing the others to lean in until their heads were almost touching.

When she'd finished, she sat back.

'Bloody hell,' Emily gasped. 'This place might look like the back of beyond, but you don't half keep yourselves entertained.

There's your mate kissing someone in the potting shed on her wedding day, your sister and the filthy captain. There's the trouser-less pilot in the kitchen . . . What else goes on in this part of Kent?'

Marge smiled wearily. 'That's not even the half of it.' She felt better for telling them. Until recently she'd not realised what a burden this secret had put on her. She should have confided in her friends years ago, instead of perpetuating a fairy tale dreamt up by her heartbroken parents.

'That little weasel!' Maria exclaimed. 'No wonder you hate his guts. How old was your sister when she met him?'

'Around fourteen. She left when she was fifteen.'

'Pervert. Revolting, disgusting . . . I'm so sorry, Marge.' Becky scrabbled in her jacket pocket and pulled out a crumpled packet of cigarettes. 'Personally, I'd rather have a drink, but I bet you could use one of these right now?'

Marge took one gratefully, and the women smoked in silence for a while.

'I reckon he's hiding something in that hut as well,' Marge said. 'No one in their right mind would trust a drunk like him with secret equipment.'

Emily sat forward. 'Let's break in and find out!' she exclaimed, her brown eyes gleaming with excitement.

'Yes!' Marge stubbed out her cigarette in a glass ashtray on the floor. 'No time like the present.'

Becky held up a hand. 'Girls, are you forgetting something? The captain is somewhere in the house, it's broad daylight, and I'm betting none of you can pick a lock.'

Marge slumped back and folded her arms. 'All good points. But he's up to something, I'm sure of it. And for Katy's sake, I need to find out what it is and bring him down.'

'Tonight then?' Emily said.

'The policemen are coming round,' Maria said. 'And tomorrow the men arrive first thing. Let's be sensible and bide our time.'

Reluctantly, Marge had to agree. 'Fine. We'll postpone operations for now. But remember, don't let yourself be alone with that man. He may seem like a bumbling old buffoon, but he's a predator. You, especially, Emily. He's had his eye on you ever since you arrived.'

'Yeah, I know. Don't worry, I can take care of myself.' She grinned and flexed her arm.

'Katy probably thought that too,' Marge said grimly. 'Go on, you lot, go down and see what delights Mrs B's scared up for lunch.'

'Scared is the right word.' Becky grimaced as they stood up.

Marge watched as they left the room, a surge of emotion rushing through her. It was true what they said – a problem shared is a problem halved. She lit another cigarette and strolled over to the window. Above her, the clouds scudded across the sky, while below, white horses raced towards the shore. Just for a moment, the sun peeked out from behind a cloud, spotlighting a seagull that was riding the air currents, wings outstretched. For a fanciful moment, she imagined it was Katy, flying free and happy. 'I won't let you down again, love,' she whispered. 'No matter what it takes.'

# Chapter 38

*Folkestone*

Sitting in front of her dressing table, Ellen leant forward and carefully painted her lips a bright, cherry red. She'd brushed her lids with green eyeshadow, mixed with brilliance oil to make them shimmer, and her cheekbones were highlighted with rouge. Blotting her lips with a tissue, she sat back and examined herself. She looked overblown and tarty. Exactly what she'd been going for.

After she'd seen Tom the day before, she'd waited for half an hour for him to come out, and when he had finally returned to the car, she'd walked towards him, hoping he'd recognise her. But he'd not even looked at her. His eyes had been fixed on a couple of schoolgirls walking along the road arm in arm, their gas masks slung across their chests. He'd smiled and tipped his hat at them, making them giggle, and she'd had to fight the urge to scratch his eyes out.

She'd been like those girls once: young, carefree, beautiful. But he'd taken all that away from her. Now she was just an ageing whore. She blinked back the tears. She hadn't cried in years, not since she'd lost her little boy, and she wasn't about to start now. Especially not over a nasty pervert like Tom Bennett.

Now, of course, she understood all too well what sort of a man he was, if only she could find a way to make sure the rest of the world knew too.

She stood up and slipped her feet into a pair of strappy high-heeled gold shoes, then stood in front of the full-length mirror and smoothed her tight green satin dress over her hips. After checking she had everything she needed in her gold clutch bag, she put on her fur coat and left the room.

It was dark by the time Rodney and the officers he'd be taking the course with left the surprisingly comfortable East Battery after a long, boozy lunch. There were six of them in all. George Fry was a middle-aged captain who, as the most senior member of the group, had appointed himself their leader.

'One more for the road, chaps?' Gordon Lacey, a tall, handsome lieutenant with silver-grey hair, said.

Rodney suppressed a sigh. Lacey had already sunk the better part of two bottles of wine. 'I quite fancy getting to bed. It's an early start tomorrow,' he said.

'Come on, man!' Alan Greengage, a short, skinny man with a large nose and an irritating sniff, clapped him on the shoulder. 'We're on holiday, so let's have some fun. Not as if this course is going to teach us much that we don't already know. And run by a bunch of women, who I'd wager have never seen the inside of a ship.' He shook his head. 'I don't mind them typing our letters, cooking our food and making our coffee, but it's a damn impertinence to think they can teach us old sea dogs anything new.'

'I'll tell you what else women are good for . . .' George Fry winked. 'Just so happens, I know of a nice little place where we can relax over a couple of glasses and find some company.'

Rodney closed his eyes. This just got worse. 'Really, I think I'll get an early night and go back to the barracks.'

George Fry snorted. 'Let's take a vote. Hands up all those who fancy a little snifter and a little lady.'

Five hands went up. 'Outvoted, Castle, old chap. Let's go. All for one and one for all, what!'

Rodney trailed after them into the dark night, the sea pounding heavily against the beach to his left, the sky inky and scattered with stars. It was a good thirty minutes' walk into town, but on the bright side, it would at least sober the men up. One drink, he promised himself, then he'd make his excuses.

Finally, they walked down the High Street, George Fry's torch beam wobbling in front of them, revealing only a fraction of the damage that he knew was there. Like Dover, Folkestone had once been a beautiful seaside town, and though it had fared a little better than his hometown, much of the seafront and the Harbour Arm had suffered serious damage.

The captain stopped outside a door. 'Here we are, chaps. You're in for a treat.' Chuckling, he knocked on a door.

It was opened by a man in an ill-fitting tuxedo, and they trooped through the blackout curtain and into a cramped hallway, with red wallpaper and a large chandelier hanging so low that Rodney had to duck.

A beautiful woman wearing a skintight black satin dress swept through a beaded curtain. Her blonde hair was immaculately styled, and her bright red lips stood out against her pale face.

'Welcome, gentlemen. You look like you could do with a stiff drink and some good company.'

Rodney wanted nothing more than to walk straight back outside. When he'd been young, he'd visited countless places like this all over the world. But everything had changed after an encounter in a seedy place in Hong Kong, where the woman he was with had started to cry. For the first time it had occurred to him that some of these women didn't want to be there. He'd instinctively put his arm around her, but she'd flinched away. So, he did the only thing he could: paid and left, shame roiling through him as he thought of his sisters. Imagine if they became so desperate they found themselves having to work in a place like this?

He'd vowed never to visit a brothel again, and though he'd been mocked for it, he'd kept to his word. Until now.

As he walked into the smoky room, the tables crammed with soldiers, sailors and the occasional airman, each accompanied by a beautifully dressed and made-up woman, a flash of red caught his eye. He turned his head slightly and a shock of recognition stopped him in his tracks.

A tall redhead stood by the bar, her back to him. She was wearing a tight green satin dress, the shiny fabric clinging to the indent of her waist and flaring out over her hips. A much shorter man had his arm around her, and he resisted the urge to run over and drive his fist into the little toad's face.

'Nice little filly, eh?' Captain Fry stopped beside him, his eyes trained on the woman's back. 'And that hair . . . Bet she'd be a handful!' He guffawed. 'Looks like you're out of luck, though.'

Rodney watched in mounting disbelief as the woman leant towards the man beside her and kissed him on the lips.

Without thinking, he strode towards them, bumping into several couples who were swaying on the dance floor. Somewhere in the back of his mind, he was aware he was being stupid. He and Marge weren't together and she had the right to kiss whoever she chose. But not *here*, in this *gentlemen's* club! What the *hell* was she thinking? If she was kissing anyone, it should be him!

'Marge!' It was the loud, sonorous voice he'd perfected over the previous few months to make himself heard on board.

The woman turned and her eyes widened. In one swift movement, she pulled herself out of the man's grasp and fled through a door by the bar.

Rodney followed. 'Wait, Marge!' he called after her. 'I just want to talk . . .'

She didn't pause, disappearing through a door at the end of the hallway.

Rodney pushed through the door a few seconds after her and found himself in a narrow alleyway. But though he could hear Marge's heels clip-clopping away, her form was lost in the darkness.

With one hand on the brick wall to guide him, he followed the sound of her footsteps. It was dangerous enough for women in the blackout, but in that dress, either she'd be attacked or freeze to death.

When he reached the main street, he stood still, straining his ears to work out in which direction she had gone. But all he could hear was the wind whistling around the buildings and the distant shouts of drunken men.

Marge had disappeared.

# Chapter 39

Ellen limped along the road, shivering in the cold wind. Stopping for a moment, she balanced one arm against a rough brick wall and wrenched off her shoes.

She shouldn't have run away. But hearing that name after all these years . . . it had felt like a knife in her heart. So many times she'd wanted to go back home to her sister. But after seeing her that one time, happy and carefree, she couldn't bring herself to blight her life. And then, when she'd finally plucked up the courage, she'd been too late. Her parents were dead, and Marge had left.

She could easily have tracked down one of her sister's old friends, but she'd been too scared to face anyone. She had no idea what her parents had said about her disappearance, or what people would think when she turned up again out of the blue. Did they even remember her?

She shivered as the wind cut through her clothing. She shouldn't have run from the handsome naval officer. She'd only caught a glimpse, but she was sure she recognised him. He might know where Marge was. Then again, maybe it was better not to know. She wasn't sure she could cope if her sister didn't want to see her.

Ellen was breathless by the time she reached her lodgings and once inside, she ran upstairs and fell into her room, locking the door behind her. Sitting down heavily at her dressing table, she stared at herself. Her cheeks were streaked with mascara, the eyeshadow smudged, and the rouge stood out on her cheeks making her look like a clown. She reached for the cold cream and rubbed it into her skin, then took some cotton wool and cleaned off the makeup.

When she'd finished, she leant forward to examine herself. The freckles she took such pains to cover stood out on her pale skin, fine lines fanned out from her eyes, and there were worry lines across her forehead. She looked like a ghost. An old ghost. But maybe seeing Tom and the naval officer at the club was a sign that she needed to face up to her mistakes and make it up to the people she'd hurt by running away. Perhaps then she'd be able to find the peace of mind she'd lost all those years ago.

Rodney hunched his shoulders against the cold and returned to the smoky bar, his mind in turmoil. Had he been mistaken? He couldn't think of any reason Marge would be in a place like this: she had a good job and a place to live . . . There was no way it could have been her.

In his mind's eye, he saw the figure again. Red hair, green satin dress, that tiny waist, those generous hips. And those long, long legs. No one else looked like Marge. But though his head told him it couldn't be Marge, his jealous heart wouldn't accept it.

His stomach churned with a mixture of shock and outrage. Every time he'd seen her recently, she'd been with a different man, so was it that unlikely? Maybe this was how she got her kicks now.

Stumbling into the bar, he spotted his colleagues sitting at a table, glasses of whisky in front of them. George Fry had a girl sitting on his knee, and Gordon Lacey had an arm around the waist of the woman next to him. The other three were on the dance floor.

'Castle!' Fry beckoned him over and pushed a tumbler towards him. 'Don't tell me you went chasing after that girl? There's always plenty more fish in the sea.' He laughed heartily and the girl on his knee smiled dutifully.

Rodney leant across to her. 'Do you know the woman with the red hair and green satin dress?' he asked urgently.

The girl shrugged. 'Might do.'

'What's her name? And do you know where she's from?' Rodney resisted the urge to grab her arm and pull her away so he could talk to her properly.

'Enough, Castle! This one's mine, go find your own.' He squeezed the girl's waist.

Reaching for his whisky, Rodney took a large gulp and stared at the stage where a beautiful woman with shining dark hair started to sing 'Chattanooga Choo Choo'. His companions immediately stood up to dance. Rodney barely noticed; all he could think about was finding the woman in the green satin dress.

He downed the rest of his drink and was about to leave when the hostess who'd welcomed them walked across. 'I noticed you run after Ellen,' she said. 'Perhaps you'd like another girl?'

Ellen . . . So not Marge. But she could be using a false name. He scoffed at himself. Marge loved a party, but she wouldn't do this, would she? 'How long has she worked here?' he asked. Up close, he noticed the woman was a lot older than she first appeared.

She put her hand on his knee and leant in close. 'Forget her. Look around you, there's plenty of other gorgeous women.' She smiled seductively at him.

Rodney tried to hide his impatience. 'It's just, she looked like an old friend of mine. Do you know her?'

'Look, love, I know she's called Ellen, I know she came with a friend, and that's it. Don't know how long she's been here, or where she's from. But if you fancy a redhead, then there's always Poppy who's around somewhere. Alternatively, you and me could get to know each other.'

'Who's her friend?' he asked, ignoring her invitation.

The woman huffed. 'Fine. Her name's Scarlett.' She looked around and beckoned to a petite brunette sitting at a table with a group of men in suits.

The girl came over and smiled at Rodney. 'Scarlett, this bloke wants to know about Ellen. Do you know where she lives?'

'Might do. Thing is, though, I saw her run out, so I reckon she's not keen on you knowin'. Only met her yesterday, though.'

Rodney frowned. 'So she's new to Folkestone?'

'No, I didn't say that. Just that I only met her yesterday. If you want to know where she's stayin', then you'll 'ave to buy me a drink.' She smiled coyly.

Rodney's first instinct was to leave; the woman's perfume was making his nose itch. And now the shock of seeing her had worn off, he was certain the woman couldn't have been Marge, but still . . . He hated himself for that small kernel of doubt. He'd always considered himself a rational man, but this suspicion was completely irrational. That was the problem with love. It stripped you of your intelligence and discipline and left you at the mercy of impulse and passion. And the only way for him to regain some semblance of control was to find out who the woman that looked like Marge was.

So, plastering on a smile, he raised his arm and signalled to a waitress to bring them a drink. Then he sat back and prepared himself for a long night.

# Chapter 40

*Castle's Café*

As soon as Nellie unbolted the door the following morning, Jasper pushed in, looking like he'd slept in a hedge.

'Good God, you look like you've been out on the tiles all night.'

'Good to see you too, Nell,' he remarked dryly, rubbing a hand through his hair. Always unkempt, this morning it looked like he'd stuck his finger in an electrical socket.

He'd been behaving strangely yesterday as well. An hour after his row with Lou, he'd returned to the café and sat by the window for the entire day, jumpy as a cat, his eyes never leaving the square.

'Are you gonna tell me what's goin' on, love? You've given me a wide berth for months, but suddenly you're hauntin' the place like a hungry ghost.'

Jasper smiled, but it didn't reach his bloodshot eyes. 'Speakin' of hunger. I could murder a cup of tea and a bacon sarnie.' Before sitting down at the same table by the window, he opened the blackout curtain.

'Excuse me! It's still bloody dark. If I get fined for this, you're payin'.'

229

He waved her away. 'It'll be gettin' light in sixteen minutes. No one's gonna fine you.'

A soldier came in. 'Ahh, does me heart good to see light spillin' onto the streets again. Just 'ope you don't bring the Luftwaffe down on our heads.'

'Don't worry, Private. Accordin' to our resident ARP warden, these lights can't be seen.'

Jasper ignored her.

With a huff, she went back to fetch Jasper's breakfast. Cissy was standing by the counter. 'I think someone's slept in the basement, Nell,' she hissed. 'I just went down an' the cushions are laid out like a bed.'

Nellie's heart thumped with fear. 'Were the boxes still there?'

Cissy nodded. 'I checked cos my first thought was that man 'ad come in the night and taken the lot.'

'If only.' Nellie looked back at Jasper thoughtfully. 'Does that look like a bloke what's slept peacefully in 'is own bed?'

Cissy studied him and frowned. 'But why would 'e sleep downstairs without sayin' a word?'

''E sat in the café all day yesterday. Ate 'is dinner with us and only left when I threw 'im out.'

'Do you reckon it's got somethin' to do with his row with Lou?'

'Wouldn't surprise me; the woman could drive a saint to madness.' Pouring a cup of tea, she took it over and put it down in front of him. 'Drink this, then go home and take a nap. After that, you're gonna come back 'ere an' tell me why you slept in the basement last night.'

Jasper's eyes snapped to her face. 'Why would I do that?' he replied gruffly.

'My question exactly. Please, Jasper, you're behavin' like a lunatic. Go home, sleep. Then when you come back, you can tell me what's goin' on.'

Jasper's shoulders slumped and he shook his head. 'I'm stayin' right here, Nell.'

'No, you ain't. Now, drink up and I'll see ya later.'

Cissy brought over a bacon sandwich for him and Nellie thrust it into his hand. 'Go on, out.'

Jasper looked between the two women, then nodded in defeat. 'All right. I'll be back at lunch.' He stood up and shuffled out.

'Something's off, Nell. I can feel it in me bones.'

Nellie let out a laugh. 'You don't need to be Bertha Bancroft to work that out, Ciss. It's been off for ages.'

'I know that, but now me guts are all over the place.' She put a hand on her stomach. 'They was like this the day before my Ernie died. Me gut's never wrong, Nell. Things are only gonna get worse.'

Despite her outward disdain, Cissy's words sent a chill down Nellie's spine.

'Where's the you know what?' Cissy hissed. 'I think we need it close.'

Nellie nodded. The gun was still in its paper bag in the suitcase, but perhaps it was time. Jasper's strange behaviour alone was giving her the heebie-jeebies.

The conversation was ended when a large group came into the café and for the next hour, they were so busy that she didn't have time to think about Jasper's strange behaviour or Cissy's fortune-telling gut. But as the breakfast rush calmed, Nellie glanced out of the window and the fear returned full force.

Through the cloudy plastic window, she could see the usual queue of people outside Turners' Grocery. And parked directly outside the shop was a highly polished black car, very similar to the one the posh bloke used to pick up the boxes. She couldn't swear to it, because it had been dark when she'd gone to examine it, but maybe if she could take a look inside, she'd be able to confirm it.

Without bothering to put on a coat, she went outside and crossed the square, glancing through the windscreen of the car as she passed it. A young woman wearing a khaki uniform and cap was sitting in the driver's seat, reading a book. And hanging from the rear-view mirror was a small silver four-leaf clover. It must be the same car. Did that mean Francis would come to the café today? Was the girl in on it? What the hell was going on?

She edged past the women standing in the shop doorway and went inside. Ethel Turner, her head wrapped in a green scarf and with a matching pinny tied round her thin frame, was filling a wicker basket for a customer.

'What's with the car? You in trouble?' Nellie asked casually, gesturing outside.

Ethel glanced up and smiled a greeting. 'Trouble's your department, love. I ain't been in trouble since I got drunk on Mum's gin back in '05. Why d'you ask?'

'That car out there. Don't tell me Winston's popped in fer a tin of tomatoes?'

'He'd be out of luck if he did,' Ethel chuckled. 'No, it's the Ministry of Food doin' spot-checks on ration books. They was in earlier, peekin' over me shoulder, askin' me questions.'

Ministry of Food? Surely Francis wasn't a ministry man?

'They're cheeky bastards!' the woman Ethel was serving exclaimed. She was wearing a moth-eaten fur coat and hat. 'The bloke went down the line lookin' at our books. Like I said to him, you ain't gonna find much in a line of old women waitin' to buy a tin of pilchards. They should be out catchin' the real criminals.'

'It's just routine, Mrs Langley,' Ethel replied. 'They like to show up once in a while to put the fear of God into us shop-keepers. That lot could give the Nazis a run for their money.'

'Ministry of Food, my foot,' the woman grumbled. 'Ministry of No Bloody Food more like. Every day a new rule, a new ration. And don't get me started on the ARP wardens! I got fined three shillings for a chink of light round me blackout curtain the other night. A chink! As if we ain't bein' hammered enough by taxes. Sick and tired of the lot of it.'

'You'll get no disagreement from me.' Ethel stamped the woman's ration book. 'All we can do is keep our noses clean and hope it all turns out for the best.'

Mrs Langley tutted. 'Best for who? Cos sure as eggs is eggs, the working man's lot won't be any easier after the war. And as for that' – she pointed at the car – 'the sooner it goes, the better. Gives me the willies, sittin' out there like a big black crow.'

Nellie agreed with every word of this diatribe, even though it was coming from Mrs Langley, who she'd barred from the café some years before. But was it really possible that one of the men she'd come to fear was part of the Establishment?

'Why you interested anyway, Mrs C?' Mrs Langley fixed her beady eyes on her. 'Worried it's come for you, are ya? Miss Frost's been bendin' me ear over at the community restaurant about the shenanigans at your café. Almost enough to tempt me back.' She grinned, revealing small, yellow teeth.

Nellie raised her eyebrows. 'Gladdens me heart to hear you've found a friend, Mrs L. An' when you give me the half-crown you owe after your kids ran off without payin', then you'll be welcome.'

'That were ten years ago, Nell!' Mrs Langley spluttered.

'Ten years, ten days, ten minutes . . . a debt's a debt. And once it's paid, I'll be ready to welcome you back with open arms. Anyway, Ethel, see you Sunday. Two p.m. sharp. Lily's bringin' Jasper over at quarter past.'

'Wouldn't miss it for the world, love,' Ethel replied. 'I'll bring our contribution round first thing Sunday morning. Nice bit of spam, some tinned salmon and a lovely lump of Cheddar I've been savin' for a special occasion.'

'Party, is it?' Mrs Langley said resentfully. 'All right for some. Funny how there ain't no spam on the shelves today, Mrs Turner. Maybe the ministry man were 'ere for good reason.'

Ethel gave her a steely glare. 'You know, I ain't above followin' Nellie's example and barring you, Mrs L.'

The woman sniffed. 'I were just makin' an observation.' She picked up her basket and flounced out.

'Strewth, some people, eh?'

'Yeah,' Nellie said distractedly. 'Sorry, love, gotta go.'

She hurried outside and tapped on the car's window.

The girl wound it down. Her nose was red and her cheeks flushed. 'Fancy a cuppa, love. Perishin' cold out 'ere. Come in and get warm.' She gestured across the square towards the café.

The girl smiled. 'Thank you, but I'm not allowed to leave the car unattended.'

'Worried we'll nick it, are they? Come on. Biggest danger here would be if a shell dropped, an' you'll be better off in the café than sittin' in this hunk of metal if that happens. Look, you can see the car from the winder.'

The girl hesitated, sneezed and fished in her pocket for a hankie.

'Love, you'll catch your death. Come on.'

After a moment's hesitation, the girl nodded. 'All right. Just for a minute to warm up.' She sneezed again, then got out of the car and followed Nellie across the square.

'Sit down there, an' I'll bring you a cuppa and a slice of toast.' Nellie indicated a table by the window.

When she returned with the food, she sat down opposite. She couldn't see how this girl would have anything to do with the posh bloke, but there was only one way to find out. 'What's your name, love?'

'Geraldine – but call me Gerry. I've only been posted here recently. ATS.'

'An' what's the to-do with the car? Belongs to the Ministry of Food, does it?'

'No. It's just one of the pool cars. There are loads of them.'

'Is that your four-leaf clover on the mirror?'

'No. Lots of people drive the car though, so could be anyone's.'

Nellie wanted to grind her teeth in frustration. The girl clearly had nothing to do with anything, but she really wanted to know who she was driving. 'So you just drive who you're told to, do you? Sounds fun.'

At the counter she could see Cissy watching her curiously. She had five minutes, she reckoned, until her cousin's curiosity got the better of her and she came over to hijack the conversation.

Gerry shrugged. 'Sometimes. But not today when I feel so rotten.' She wiped her streaming nose. 'I had to meet them at the station at the crack of dawn, and now we've been driving all over the town, and when I'm not driving, I'm just sitting in a freezing car like a lemon. You're the first person to even offer me a cuppa. They were in someone's house for ages, so I knocked on the door to ask to use the loo and the woman that answered wouldn't give me so much as a glass of water.'

'House, was it?' Nellie's ears pricked up.

'Yeah. Some lawyer bloke.'

Nellie sat up straighter. Noticing her interest, Gerry seemed to realise she'd probably been a bit indiscreet, so Nellie changed tack and asked her about the ATS. Gerry began to chat about the difficulties of driving in the blackout and having to learn to fix the car.

Nellie listened with half an ear. Did she know a house with a mean old woman in it? She almost laughed. Only half of Dover. But she couldn't see why someone from the Ministry of Food would be visiting Adelaide Frost first thing in the morning.

Mean old woman, lawyer ... surely that could only be Mr Wainwright and Mrs Frobisher.

Mr Wainwright might appear to be just a parochial lawyer, but it was he who had been instrumental in having Hester Erskine and Elspeth Fanshawe arrested for spying. And he who'd pulled strings to get Mr Pearson and Donny out of prison. And he'd sorted things out for Lily when she'd been suspected of helping that German prisoner escape as well. That man always seemed to know what string to pull, so why was he having visits from the Ministry of Food?

Her thoughts were interrupted when Gerry pushed back her chair. 'Yikes, looks like the boss is back. I better go. Thanks ever so for the tea, Mrs Castle.'

She nodded, but once Gerry was crossing the square, she hurried out of the door, and looked up Cannon Street. And there, coming towards her, was a tall figure in a dark coat. Was this the same man? She'd never seen his face, but she remembered he had a limp. And sure enough, one foot dragged slightly behind him. Hurrying back inside, she watched as he got into the car and it drove away.

What on earth was going on? How were Mr Wainwright, the Ministry of Food, Johnny Fox and whatever was being stored in her basement connected?

She needed to find out. Because when it all came to a head, her family and the café would be trapped in the middle.

# Chapter 41

*Abbots Cliff House*

'This is it, girls! Everything's got to be perfect today. No arguing, no messing, no forgetting the manoeuvres. One step out of line, and those men'll be down on us like a ton of bricks.'

Marge stood in the middle of the large attic room and looked around her one last time. It wasn't unnecessary; she had complete faith in the other women – not only to run the game impeccably, but also to help her bring the captain down. After he'd stomped away in a huff the day before, they'd not seen him again, until the policemen they'd invited for a drink had turned up with several of their friends. The evening had been fun, and the captain had been relegated to the sidelines watching moodily as the younger men monopolised the women. Finally, he'd given her a malignant look and stumbled away to bed.

The gloves were off, it seemed, and she had a horrible feeling that unless she was very careful, he'd do what he could to have her transferred away from here. She'd never had issues with any of her commanding officers before, and she was only just starting to realise how damaging it could be for her career. If she wasn't careful, she'd find herself back at the plotting table. So, as soon as this course was over, she and the girls would have to investigate the mysterious hut. She just hoped her instincts were right and Bennett was harbouring secrets in there that she could use to bring him down.

'Hey, Marge!' Becky clicked her fingers in front of her face, and Marge started. 'Are you happy with the screen placement?' she asked, indicating the grey canvas screens around the room. Behind each was a chair where one of them would sit and pass orders to their partner playing in the centre of the room.

'It all looks perfect. I wonder what sort of men they'll be. Remember that bald admiral Captain Roberts had to throw out because he refused to work with a bunch of useless girls?'

Becky laughed. 'The bugger was back with his tail between his legs soon enough, though.'

'I can't see Bennett sticking up for us like that,' Emily remarked, smoothing down her hair. 'You know he pinched my bum twice last night.' She shuddered. 'Not for the first time either, but after what you told us yesterday, it's as much as I can do not to kick him in the balls.'

'If any of the men so much as breathe on you, let me know.' Marge eyed Emily. 'As for Captain Bennett . . . He'll get what he deserves. We'll make sure of that.'

'If only I didn't have a hangover,' Becky moaned. 'I thought the navy boys were bad, but those MPs really know how to party.'

Just then Captain Bennett's voice called up the stairs. 'Action stations, girls. I want you lined up in the hall ready to greet the men.'

Marge rolled her eyes. 'Will he want us to curtsey as well?'

'Oh, let's!' Maria giggled.

Marge gave her a warning look. 'We will be firm, we will be dignified, and we will keep them in their place,' she said. 'By the end, they will be the ones bending their knees to us in gratitude and amazement. Ready, girls? Best foot forward!'

Downstairs, the women lined up obediently against the shabby wall in height order – as per Captain Bennett's instructions. The captain, meanwhile, stood by the door and greeted each man with a salute as they came in. They were the usual type, Marge noted, suppressing a sigh. Middle-aged, some of them paunchy, but all with that look of superiority that she'd become used to after two years in the Wrens.

She was saluting an officer several inches shorter and wider than her, when Becky, who was standing next to her, nudged her and raised her eyebrows. Marge looked over and her heart stopped as Rodney walked in. When he saw her, he paused for a moment, his brow furrowed.

Marge couldn't help the grin that broke out on her face. Despite what had happened, despite their uncomfortable meetings in Liverpool and a few days before at the station, she was just so damn glad to see him. She'd wanted a chance to talk to him, and now she had it. He looked tired, though, and a little more rumpled than usual. As he approached, he stared at her as though he'd seen ghost.

'I can't believe it,' he murmured, returning her salute. 'You're here! So it *was* you last night.'

Her eyes snapped to his. 'What?'

'In the bar with that fat little officer.' He laughed shortly. 'You really get around, don't you?'

Marge was stunned. Why had she ever thought she should give this man another chance? All he did was make her feel like a piece of dirt. Well, she wasn't going to stand for it anymore. She stared straight in front of her, unsure what to say, hurt and anger churning within her. Rodney was one of the few men she knew who was taller than her, and her eyes lined up with his shirt collar. She squinted. Was that lipstick? 'Well, whatever you think I was doing last night, it seems you were having a better time than me.'

Colour flooded his cheeks. 'What's sauce for the goose is sauce for the gander,' he responded, tight-lipped, before moving on.

'Do you know him?' Becky hissed, after he'd passed down the line and disappeared into the drawing room where they were to take tea before the course started. 'He doesn't seem to like you much.'

'That's nothing compared to how I feel about him,' she muttered. 'I need some air.' Turning, she hurried out of the front door, one hand already reaching into her jacket pocket for her cigarettes.

She could barely contain her fury. But the anger was directed at herself as well as at him. Her head *knew* that he didn't love her, that he disapproved of her and there was no future for them. So why could her heart not get the message?

# Chapter 42

*Castle's Café*

The feeling of confusion and dread stayed with Nellie for the rest of the morning, and she kept checking the clock, wishing that Jasper would return. She was certain, now, that he had slept in the basement, and his obvious worry only fuelled her own anxiety.

Lily appeared beside her, dressed in her uniform and cape. 'How're the arrangements for the party going?' she asked.

Lily's beauty usually radiated from her, but this morning she seemed muted. 'Everythin' all right, love?' Nellie couldn't remember the last time she'd asked Lily that, she realised with a spurt of guilt. And if she thought about it, Lily hadn't seemed herself for a few days now.

'Aren't I always?' Lily poured herself a cup of tea.

Was there a note of bitterness in her daughter's voice?

'I'm just busy. And I'm worried about Bert. Dot's beside herself.'

Nellie relaxed slightly. Not that worrying about Bert wasn't justified, but it was, at least, something she understood.

'Try not to worry. He were born lucky.'

'Why do people keep saying that? There's no such thing, Mum. Luck comes and goes.'

Nellie frowned at her. 'What's up, love? Somethin' else is botherin' you.'

Lily flashed a bright smile. 'I'm fine, Mum.' She drained her cup. 'Better go.' With a brief wave, she left through the front door.

Was it Nellie's imagination or were her shoulders a little slumped? Was this something to do with Charlie? Sometimes she forgot her daughter was engaged. In fact, most days she forgot. But Lily wouldn't have. That girl didn't make promises lightly, and nothing short of death could make her break them. She was like her father in that way.

'You spoken much to Lily lately?' she asked Cissy, when she passed.

Cissy nodded. 'Poor girl. It's not right, is it?'

Nellie frowned. 'What's not right?'

Cissy gave her a judgemental look. 'Maybe you'd know if you wasn't so wrapped up in yer own business. She mentioned that some bloke at the hospital's givin' her a hard time. Speakin' of your kids' troubles, when are you goin' to have a chat with Marianne about Teddy? She left 'im to Don again yesterday evenin' to go up to the garage.'

Nellie tensed. Cissy was right; she needed to address this problem before Teddy became aware of it.

Donny came crashing down the stairs at that moment, carrying Teddy who was dressed in a blue woollen knitted one-piece suit and matching hat that Cissy had made.

'Me, Ted an' Fred are goin' out,' he announced.

Teddy squealed joyfully, batting his hand on Donny's head.

'Not up Plum Puddin' Hill again?' Nellie asked sharply. She wished he'd stay in. What if Johnny Fox decided to kidnap him? Or worse. But how could she say anything without making everyone as scared as she was?

'No, just for a little walk.'

'Does your mum know?' Cissy asked.

'She does now,' he said, looking at his mother.

Marianne was putting a tray of biscuits into the range. 'They always go out. And it's a nice day.' She stood and kicked the door shut.

It was true, they did always go out, and Marianne would find it strange if she suggested they stay in, but she had to try. 'Are you sure it's safe, love?'

Marianne narrowed her eyes. 'Donny's brilliant with his brother. I trust him completely.'

'There, you see, Gran!' Donny said triumphantly. 'I always look after Ted.'

'But just this once . . . Maybe stay here for a bit.'

'But Gran . . .' Donny wheedled.

Marianne faced her. 'What's this really about, Mum? They're my kids, and if I say they can go, they can go!'

'Yes, Nellie. What's this really about?' Cissy echoed.

She looked between the two of them, then sighed with resignation. 'Fine, like you say, they're *your* kids, Marianne. An' that includes Teddy!'

Marianne narrowed her eyes. 'Yes, Mum. That includes Teddy.' She turned back to the boys. 'Go on, get out and have fun. Just be careful.'

'I promise!' Donny yelled, shoving Teddy into the pram and pushing it out of the back door.

'Stick to the streets, Donny!' Nellie called after him. As long as there were plenty of people around, surely they'd be all right.

Nellie watched them leave with a sinking feeling in her chest. This was all her fault. She'd brought this danger to their door, and now it was too late to do anything.

With a weary sigh, she went back into the café, surprised to see Lou Carter standing there, and reminding her that she wasn't the only one to blame for this mess!

'What do you want?' she snapped.

Lou leant towards her. 'Did you see the car?'

'Could 'ardly miss it.' Was it possible that Lou knew Francis? Should she mention she'd seen him. Or would that complicate matters? 'Ethel said it was blokes from the Ministry of Food doin' spot checks on ration books.'

'I don't buy it. Somethin' fishy's goin' on.'

Cissy came to stand beside her. 'What's fishy, Lou, is your dirty business. And I ain't talkin' about the whelks! I'm talkin' about your dirty mags, Johnny flamin' Fox, and dealin' in firearms.'

Lou gave Nellie a sharp look, then turned her attention back to Cissy. 'You an' me've never been mates, Ciss, but I don't know why you got it in for me so bad.'

'I got it in fer you cos Nellie should never've 'ad to buy a gun. It's ironic, ain't it, that the person who puts her in danger, is the person she goes to to get protection. I don't know what your game is, but I warn you, I'm this far from callin' the police.' She held up a finger and thumb.

'I wouldn't do that if I was you. That's what I'm tryin' to tell ya. It ain't just the car. There's been other blokes I ain't never seen before hangin' around the place.' Lou glanced towards the window. 'See over there: bloke readin' the paper leanin' against the Market Hall. Never seen 'im before.' She lowered her voice. 'I think we're under severance.'

Nellie frowned. 'What's that even mean, Lou?'

'We're bein' watched!'

Nellie felt a jolt of alarm. 'Who by? And why?' It was on the tip of her tongue to mention Francis, but Lou spoke before she could.

'It's gotta be Jasper's fault.'

'Cos of your row?' Nellie asked. 'What was that all about?'

'I think 'e's been snoopin' in the boxes. It's the only explanation.'

Nellie suppressed a gasp. Of course he had! Why else would he suddenly be sleeping here? Why else would he have been arguing with Lou? But that still didn't explain everything.

'But even if 'e has, Jasper don't know the sort of blokes who drive around in fancy cars and do surveillance.' *But Mr Wainwright did.* The thought shivered across her like an icy breeze. And from what Gerry had said, it seemed likely that Francis had been to see him this morning.

'Maybe none of us knows Jasper as well as we thought,' Lou rasped. 'I always thought he were a stand-up bloke, but he ain't.'

Nellie was shocked by her vehemence. Jasper must really have laid into her.

'In the end, though, it don't really matter who did what. Fact remains, I'm scared, love. So I'm goin' to ground and I suggest you do the same.'

'I can't just disappear. People rely on me. You can scuttle off like a frightened mouse if you want, but I'm stayin' put.' Nellie only realised she'd raised her voice when she noticed the room had gone deathly quiet as everyone turned to look at them.

'Mum, what's going on?' Marianne and Elodie were leaning on the hatch.

'You better leave, Lou,' Nellie said hastily.

'Don't worry, I'm goin'. And I won't be back till this is sorted.' She looked at Cissy thoughtfully for a moment. 'Hang on! I know exactly who's got the big guns down here. Your bleedin' boyfriend! After all, he were the one that sorted out Hester, weren't he?'

Nellie's head whipped round. 'Boyfriend? What boyfriend?'

But she knew. Of course she did. And suddenly it all made sense: Cissy's absences, her new lipstick, her re-dyed hair . . . Singing that awful Algernon song while she was washing up . . . Algernon Wainwright!

Cissy's cheeks were bright red. 'I never breathed a word to him.'

'Who's your boyfriend?' Nellie said. 'And how come Lou knows about it?' She glanced at Marianne and Elodie, who looked guilty. Clearly *everyone* knew – apart from her.

'It weren't like that, Nell. I ain't *told* anyone. People guessed. And maybe if you thought about anythin' other than your own problems, you would've too!'

The words hit Nellie like a slap in the face. Not least because she was right. While she'd been wallowing in self-pity, her cousin had not only quietly taken over her family, she'd fallen in love. And never breathed a word to her.

'What did you tell 'im?' she growled.

'Nothing! I've not said anythin' about what's goin' on, cos I didn't want to worry 'im.'

'Well, it don't make no difference who told who what. I've got a nose for danger, and it's stinkin' the place out right now. So if you insist on stayin, then I suggest you get practisin' with your new toy,' Lou said.

'Is this a private conversation or can anyone join in?' Jasper suddenly appeared and stood behind Lou, his expression inscrutable.

Lou turned and poked her finger into his chest. 'Did you talk to Mr W after we spoke yesterday?'

'That's none of your business.'

'I 'ope to God you don't regret it, Jasper,' she said darkly, before brushing past him and stomping away.

'What's up with Lou?' he asked.

Nellie shook her head. 'She says we're bein' watched, and what's more—' She stopped and looked around. 'Let's talk upstairs. I'll be five minutes, Ciss.'

She left before Cissy could protest.

Upstairs she told Jasper everything that had happened while he'd been gone. It was no comfort to see that he took it as seriously as she did. 'That bloke Donny helped that first time?' he asked in astonishment.

She nodded. 'I'm sure it was him.'

Jasper rubbed his face. 'I need to let Mr W know. Meantime, you need to carry on as normal. If you are bein' watched, you don't want to alert anyone.' He stood up.

'Hang on, don't you think you owe me an explanation? You know what Johnny Fox is up to, don't you?'

He nodded. 'I've got an inklin'. But there ain't time to explain. I'll be back later.'

Marvellous, Nellie thought. Everyone was keeping secrets from her, it seemed. Well, she wasn't going to stand for it anymore. This was her house, and her business. She should never have allowed things to get this far.

Marching down the stairs, she grabbed a kitchen knife and went to the basement. Pulling out one of the boxes, she hesitated for just a moment before she broke the seal and sliced through the rope.

# Chapter 43

As Lily neared the hospital, the dread settled deep into her bones. Colonel Mason was making her life a misery and now the plaster cast was off his leg, she was frankly terrified that he might start stalking the corridors in search of her.

Cissy had advised her to talk to Matron, but Lily wasn't sure that would help. She had a lot of respect for the woman, but Matron was a firm believer in hierarchy, which meant that if it came to a choice between taking Lily's word against that of a decorated colonel, she knew exactly which side she'd opt for. Which was exactly why Lily found herself in this situation in the first place. Because the colonel had requested her specifically and Matron would never dream of refusing him.

The person she really wished she could speak to was Charlie, but the longer she went without any word, the more she believed that he'd changed his mind about marrying her. And who could blame him? She was just a young nurse in training at a small hospital, while he was a qualified doctor. He was so far ahead of her in terms of life and experience, she was now beginning to wonder why he wanted to spend the rest of his life with her.

Lily wiped at the tear that slipped from her eye. She would not bloody cry about this! She would find a solution. But no matter how hard she tried, she couldn't think of any way to avoid the colonel without appearing difficult and obstructive. She still had a year and a half of training left, and if she was considered a troublemaker, they wouldn't think twice about dismissing her.

It seemed that there really was only one choice: put up and shut up. But perhaps she would try to recruit some of the other nurses to help her. They were none of them strangers to some of the patients making a nuisance of themselves.

After hanging her cloak up, she washed the traces of tears from her cheeks, tidied her hair and straightened her shoulders. Everything would be fine. And Charlie still loved her. She reached inside her dress and pulled out the ring. Taking it off the chain, she slipped it onto her finger, admiring the way the diamonds threw rainbows on the wall. Charlie wasn't the sort to ask a woman to marry him then change his mind, was he?

She remembered how he'd carried the ring with him for weeks, hoping she'd change her mind after her initial refusal. He'd showered her with love and attention until she couldn't hold out any longer. But maybe that had been the attraction for him, and once he had her, he wasn't interested anymore.

Closing her eyes, she wrapped her arms around herself, squeezing tight as she imagined Charlie standing behind her, holding her against his chest. 'Charlie, I need you,' she whispered. 'Please don't forget me.'

Opening her eyes, she took a deep breath. It was time to pull herself together. She threaded the ring back on the chain, then, straightening her shoulders, she went to check her pigeonhole, surprised to see an envelope in there.

Taking it out, she opened it and pulled out the single sheet of thick writing paper.

*My dear Lily,*

*I wanted to write to express my gratitude for all you've done to aid my recovery.*

*As the time for me to leave this place creeps ever closer, I wanted to assure you of my everlasting admiration and respect. You have told me many times that you are an engaged woman, and it tears my heart in two to hear it. But such is the lot of a man in the grip of unrequited love.*

*But even as I write the word 'unrequited', I find I can't quite believe that you don't feel this passion too? I've seen it in your eyes, and though you may be hiding it for decency's sake, you must know you never have to hide yourself from me. One day, when I am strong again, you and I will meet, and then we shall see . . . Perhaps then your fiancé might not seem quite so attractive.*

*But I jest. Of course, you must do as your heart tells you. Just know that when I depart from here, I will leave my heart in your hands.*

*Always yours,*

*Jeremy*

*PS Apologies for the scrawl. Writing with a plaster cast has rather cramped my style — in more ways than one.*

The fury rose so suddenly that it made her hands shake. What made him think she felt anything for him at all? This had to end now. No more self-pity, no more expecting someone else to save her. She was on her own. And he needed to know that she would not put up with this anymore!

The colonel was lying on top of his blankets wearing navy blue silk pyjamas and smoking a cigarette when Lily reached the ward. He watched as she walked towards him, a smug grin on his face, his blue eyes twinkling. 'My very favourite person in the world,' he said. 'I see you've received my letter. I meant every word.'

Lily couldn't think of a single word that could convey how deeply she despised this man, but she didn't want to cause a scene.

'Thank you for your respect and gratitude, sir,' she said through gritted teeth. 'Sadly, your feelings are definitely *not* reciprocated, so I would be grateful if you didn't refer to this again.'

The colonel's face hardened. 'Oh, my sweet Lily, I fear you are deceiving yourself. But one day, you will see how things will be.'

'I think not, Colonel. My fiancé will be home on leave soon and we will be married.'

He stared at her steadily. 'Are you really sure about that?' he murmured, one eyebrow raised superciliously.

'Quite sure, Colonel.' Then she turned on her heel and left. But she was quivering inside. And his words wouldn't leave her mind. *Are you really sure about that?* He hadn't meant about Charlie's leave. He was asking whether she was sure Charlie *would* marry her at all. And the truth was, she wasn't sure about anything anymore.

# Chapter 44

*What the hell have I done?* Jasper thought, as he once again hurried up High Street towards Mr Wainwright's house. He'd thought the lawyer would sort things out, not make them worse. Maybe he should have resolved this problem himself: man to man; gun to gun. His chest wheezed as he broke into a trot, and he smiled ruefully.

His days of fighting man to man were long gone. They had been over the moment the first war ended. He'd not raised a hand in anger to anyone since, even though he'd been tempted once or twice when it came to Donald Castle. But he'd stuck to his word, and though he wouldn't hesitate to hurt someone if it meant protecting the people he loved, he wasn't going to go looking for trouble.

'Bit late for that, Jasper, mate,' he muttered. On reaching Victoria Crescent, he paused for a moment and caught his breath before knocking.

Mrs Frobisher answered as usual, but this time she didn't chat, merely ushered him in and went back to her own office where she started to bash on the typewriter as though her life depended upon it.

Brimming with anger, Jasper barged into Mr Wainwright's office without knocking.

'Do you realise what you done?' he snapped. 'Whoever you called 'as the streets swarmin' with blokes who stick out like sore thumbs. Mark my words, it won't be long till Johnny Fox gets wind of this. Lou Carter's probably already told him, so he'll be on 'is way down now. And that's not the only thing . . .' He paused to take a breath.

Mr Wainwright waved him to the chair. 'Come, come, Jasper, there's no need to panic. You need to learn to trust in the process,' he said calmly.

'Trust in the bloody process?! When there's—' He shook his head. 'Them boxes are worth a bloody mint, so Johnny won't be messin' around if he gets wind that others know. He'll be down here, all guns blazin'. An' who do you think'll get caught in the crossfire? Anyone what happens to be sittin' in the café at that moment. It ain't good enough, Mr W!' He sat down and ran his hands through his bushy white hair. 'I'm sorry, but I'm scared. Not for meself, but for Lilly, Don, little Teddy, Nellie . . .' He looked Mr Wainwright in the eye and said, 'Cissy.'

Mr Wainwright swallowed and sat back, steepling his fingers in front of his mouth. 'I do understand your concern, Jasper. I really do.'

'And then there's the fact that it seems that the bloke what's been pickin' up the boxes is a Ministry man!'

Mr Wainwright's eyes sharpened behind his spectacles. 'I beg your pardon?'

'That's right. Seems it's a bloke from the Ministry of Food, an' he were in your house this mornin'!'

Mr Wainwright slumped back in the chair. 'Good heavens.' He pulled his hankie out of his top pocket and blew his nose. 'Are you quite sure?'

'Nellie thought so. Same car. Same limp. Told her his name were Francis. So don't you bloody tell me to trust the flippin' process! Cos the process is as crooked as Johnny Fox! They're in cahoots!

'And then there's them blokes hangin' around thinkin' they're Richard bleedin' Hannay! I ain't got a clue if they're involved or not, but if they're not, then they need to sort themselves out, instead of swannin' round town in their long coats an' hats. They're as subtle as a Nazi rally. One of 'em were standin' right by Lou Carter's stall, for God's sake.'

Mr Wainwright clutched his hands tightly together on the desk, his brow furrowed. 'Yes, yes, it is very unsatisfactory,' he muttered. He thought for a moment. 'I need to make a phone call. But it is rather delicate, so if you wouldn't mind stepping out of the room.'

'You think I don't know how to keep me trap shut?' Jasper ground out.

'Please, Jasper. It's not about you at all.'

With a sigh, Jasper heaved himself up and left the room, only just managing to stop himself slamming the door. He liked the lawyer, but he seemed to have the blind faith that most of the higher-ups had in their superiors. He'd bet his life Algernon Wainwright hadn't been in the trenches; anyone who had knew from bitter experience that the blokes at the top rarely had a clue what they were doing.

Jasper pressed his ear to the office door, trying to make out what was being said. But the wood was too thick and all he could catch was Mr Wainwright saying things like, 'Yes, I understand.' 'Of course, I'll let them know.' Which didn't sound like a man laying down the law. He was tempted to go and grab the phone from him and give whoever he was talking to a piece of his mind.

Finally, he heard the click of the telephone being replaced in its cradle, and he barged back in. 'Well?'

Mr Wainwright smiled tightly. 'Our instructions are to behave as if nothing at all is out of the ordinary. '

'Very helpful,' Jasper snorted.

'What you have to understand is that this problem started back in 1940.'

'No, Mr W, as far as I'm concerned, this problem started about two weeks ago. An' that's what needs sortin'. Then they can take their own sweet time sortin' out whatever mess started nearly two years ago.'

'That mess and this mess are one and the same. Because that's when the factory was bombed and the printing equipment was stolen. And no one knows where they've set it up. That's what my contact needs to find. And he was most interested in your information about this Francis. It means they have to act swiftly. Because if the man I saw this morning really is involved, then they suspect this Johnny Fox will be here sooner rather than later. But if you see the man again, behave as if you don't know him. He mustn't get a sniff that his cover has been blown. The other men on the ground will be briefed accordingly.'

Jasper sat back and ran his hand through his hair. 'But what about Nell and Lily? The kids? Cissy?'

Mr Wainwright sighed deeply. 'Believe me, I share your concern. Really, I do.'

To be fair, he didn't look happy. Jasper softened his tone. 'And what are they gonna do about those blokes hangin' round the place?'

'They said they will advise them to be more discreet. This is something of a coup for my contact, and he needs this operation to succeed. They've known about Johnny Fox for quite some time, and they've known about his little business. They've just not been able to catch him, because he hops about the country, never staying long in each place. And now they realise there's someone working on the inside, it makes a lot more sense. They want this stopped as much as you do. So, all I can advise is that you go to the café, let them know they're not on their own and carry on as though nothing's happening.'

Jasper huffed out a frustrated breath. 'You might trust these people, but if they don't pull their finger out, then things could turn very ugly. And frankly, Mr W, I'm not willin' to take the risk. So I'm gonna sit up all night at the café if necessary. Cos if they think they've been rumbled, they're won't hang around. And I'm not gonna sit on my backside waitin' for a load of suits to tell me what to do.'

He turned on his heel and left the room. This time he did slam the door.

# Chapter 45

*Abbots Cliff House*

Marge clapped her hands. 'Thank you very much, gentlemen. Mrs Benson will have some tea and biscuits waiting for you in the drawing room, then supper will be at seven in the dining room.'

It had been a challenging day, made worse by Rodney's brooding presence, and Marge's temper was simmering very close to the surface. The girls had been wonderfully patient and professional, but even so it had taken them some time to overcome the men's prejudices.

Captain Bennett had deigned to make an appearance at the start, but had once again disappeared on his own business, returning for lunch, after which he spent the rest of the day in his study.

'I must say, Third Officer Atkinson, that was most enlightening,' Captain Fry said. 'I had my doubts, but this was very thorough. Most impressive. I'll be passing on my compliments to the admiral when I see him.'

Marge smiled graciously. 'Thank you. I'm sure Captain Roberts will be delighted.'

He rocked back on his heels and cleared his throat. 'And you young ladies have surprised me. Wherever did he manage to find four such clever women?' He patted her arm and followed his colleagues out of the door.

*Bloody cheek!* Marge narrowed her eyes as she watched him leave. It had taken them all morning to convince the men they knew what they were doing, then Captain Fry had thrown a tantrum when his ship had been sunk by Becky's torpedo, insisting that his tactic had been correct and had got him out of more than one tight hole. Which was a lie. Captain Fry's ship had been sunk in the middle of the Atlantic, with the loss of thirty men.

A slow hand clap made her whirl around. Rodney emerged from behind one of the canvas screens. 'It's a wonder you've managed to keep it all on track considering your late night.'

Marge raked her eyes over him disdainfully, acutely aware of Maria standing by the door watching them. 'Says the man with lipstick on his collar.' She stalked towards him and glared up into his eyes. 'I don't know what your problem with me is, Rodders, but keep your thoughts to yourself. You're undermining my authority and making an already difficult job bloody *impossible.*'

'What have I done?' he asked indignantly.

To be fair, he'd been the only one who'd been professional and attentive throughout, and he'd played the game to perfection. It reassured her a little that he'd have these tricks up his sleeve the next time he came under threat from a pack of U-boats.

Although why she still cared was beyond her. 'If you don't mind, I need to clear up this mess and prepare for tomorrow morning's games.'

She didn't. The girls had already tidied the counters away, swept the floor and redrawn the chalk grids on the boards.

'Will I see you at supper?'

His question surprised her. From the way he'd been talking she assumed he never wanted to see her again. Something had really put a bee up his arse – as his mother was fond of saying.

'Nope. I have plans.' Which consisted of a bowl of soup in her room and an early night. After spending the day with this lot, the last thing she wanted was to have to eat with them as well. Captain Bennett had graciously promised to entertain them. Typical of the man. Absent all day, but back in time for a snifter and a cigar.

'I just bet you have,' Rodney murmured. 'Navy not paying enough it seems.'

Marge was too shocked by his implication to think of a response, and by the time she opened her mouth to give him a piece of her mind, she could hear his footsteps running down the steep wooden staircase.

'If I didn't know better, I'd say he had a bad case of the green-eyed monster,' Maria said.

'The man can't stand me,' Marge gritted, blinking back tears. 'I can't imagine what he'd be jealous about.'

Maria came over and put an arm around her shoulders. 'He couldn't take his eyes off you all day – he's clearly got it bad. He's just doing the classic pulling pigtails trick because he's desperate to get your attention.'

Marge turned away and wiped her eyes with her sleeve. Why, why, why couldn't she get this man out of her system? 'Well, he'll be gone in a couple of days. And good riddance.'

'But it goes two ways, doesn't it? Don't think I didn't notice you watching him out of the corner of your eye. I suppose he's the reason you've never really been interested in other blokes.'

He was. But no longer.

The first opportunity she got, she was going to go dancing and kiss the first decent man she saw. And if he was a good kisser, maybe she'd even see him again. And again. Over time, surely she could cut Rodney out of her heart for good.

Rodney cursed himself as he went down the stairs. Why was he baiting her like this? He'd questioned the other girls earlier about what they'd been up to the previous night, and he knew for certain the girl he'd seen last night wasn't Marge.

He paused in the entrance hall, wondering whether he should go back and apologise. His plan to win her back wasn't going so well, he thought grimly. But if he wanted her, then he needed to accept that he couldn't control her. He knocked his forehead against the wall gently. Stupid, stupid Rodney. Only Marge had the ability to make him act so irrationally. And only Marge could make him feel better.

'You joining us, Castle?' Captain Fry's gratingly posh voice called from the drawing room door.

Pulling himself together, he turned to face him. 'In a moment, sir. Think I might get a bit of air first.'

'Suit yourself. Saw you had your eye on the redhead. You seem to have a bit of a fancy for them, what? I could've sworn that was the same girl you chased after last night.' He guffawed and slapped him on the shoulder. 'Better off with this one, old chap. Much cleaner.' He winked and went back to join the others.

Rodney went out of the front door and walked down the steps. He could hear the crash of the sea from the other side of the house and followed the sound. Dusk was falling, the light leaching from the sky and the salty air on his face soothed him as he thought about what Fry had said. So, he wasn't going mad. The woman really had looked like Marge. Over the course of the day, he'd remembered that Marge had a sister. Now, he put his hands in his pockets and squinted into the distance, trying to remember what he knew about her.

She'd been in the year below him at school, but he hadn't thought about her in years, and Marge never spoke about her. No one ever spoke about her, come to think of it.

He suddenly realised how little he really knew about Marge's family. His own family was so noisy and so large that it sucked all the attention away from anyone else. And she'd never volunteered the information. Shame washed through him. If he managed to win her back, he'd ask more questions, be less self-absorbed. It was the least she deserved.

He stepped over the low wooden fence at the bottom of the lawn and turned left along the path towards the old sound mirror. Someone had mentioned it at lunch, and it seemed like the perfect place to get a bit of solitude while he contemplated his utter stupidity. The wind cut through his jacket, but he welcomed the chill. It cooled his mind and helped him think. He'd been behaving like a stupid, spoilt boy whose favourite toy had been taken away. Even though, rationally, he'd known it wasn't Marge at the club.

He pictured that shapely back, the red hair, and shook his head. The resemblance was uncanny.

To his left, the steep bank widened into a grassy patch and the sound mirror rose up before him, silhouetted against the darkening sky. Beside it was an old hut, which back in the day had probably been used by the poor sap who had to sit out here with a stethoscope listening for the faint drone of aircraft. When he was doing his naval training, they'd spent a day over in Denge sitting in front of an enormous concrete wall trying to discern the rumblings from the ferries that crossed the water. Thank God someone had managed to come up with radar before this war started.

He went and sat on the lip of the concrete block and patted it with affection; it might be obsolete, but it was still a magnificent and deceptively simple piece of equipment.

He sat for a while, thinking about all the ways he'd messed things up with Marge. The woman addled his brain and made him lose his wits, and the time had come to put things right between them.

Suddenly, the door of the hut opened, and he turned to look in surprise as Captain Bennett stepped out. He was carrying a box and didn't notice him, as he locked the door, before walking along the path back towards the house.

Mindful of Commander Worthing's warning about him, Rodney dithered about whether to call out and question him, but decided against it. Instead, he stepped over to the hut and rattled the doorknob. The lock looked new, but from the trampled earth around it, it was clear he came here frequently. So, the commander was right: something was off about Captain Bennett. He was tempted to break in, but speaking to Marge felt more important right now.

Deliberately choosing a different path to the captain, he walked up the slight incline and followed the track down to the house. He would go down on bended knee and beg her forgiveness, he decided. And if she wouldn't listen, then he'd have to come up with another plan. Because he wasn't going to give her up without a fight.

# Chapter 46

*Castle's Café*

The café was finally empty, and the boys were home safe, but Nellie couldn't relax. She went and stood on the pavement, her eyes searching the darkness. Now she knew what she'd been storing in her basement, her nerves felt even more strung out. Nothing made sense anymore, and she had no idea who to trust.

Jasper had returned earlier looking flustered and told her to act as though nothing was out of the ordinary. And though she'd done her best, she'd been jumpy all day, suspicious of everyone who came in, unable to concentrate on the orders as she weighed each customer up as a potential threat. And every time the door opened, she'd expected to see Johnny Fox, his gun pointing straight at her chest.

All she wanted now was to collapse into bed, but the place still needed cleaning up, and, as per her orders, she needed to pretend everything was normal.

She went back inside and shrieked. Johnny Fox had crawled out of her nightmares and was now sitting at a table, looking as menacing as ever, his broad shoulders straining against his overcoat.

And then she noticed the silence. Normally after a busy day, the kitchen would be a hive of activity, with Cissy singing tunelessly in the scullery, Elodie scrubbing the floor, Marianne cleaning the range or preparing the following day's pastry. 'What've you done with them?' she asked, her voice as high as Cissy's.

'Don't worry, Mrs C. They're safe upstairs. I just wanted a quiet word.' He gestured to the chair opposite him.

Swallowing, Nellie perched on the edge, smoothing down her red skirt while Johnny Fox contemplated her.

'You know, my mum always said that red and green should never be seen. Especially that shade of green.' He nodded towards her lime green jersey.

'Your mum clearly didn't have much taste,' she muttered. 'But I don't suppose you're 'ere to discuss my clothes.'

He leant across the table. 'A little dicky bird told me that there's been unusual activity round abouts. Strikes me that someone might've disregarded my orders. Who's been snoopin' round my stuff, Mrs C? Was it you? Or was it that old white-haired fella? Maybe it were the boy?' He tutted. 'Kids these days are runnin' wild.'

Nellie twisted her hands together, her knuckles white.

'Now, I'm gonna go downstairs to check what's what. An' if I find that you've peeked, then don't say I didn't warn ya. Kids back 'ome safe, are they?' He smiled coldly as he stood.

Nellie wished she had her gun on her. But would it have made a difference? He had one too, and he was probably a damn sight more used to using it. 'I warned you when you came: my basement is a shelter – people are in and out like jack-in-the-boxes. If someone took a peek, then that ain't my fault. That's yours for puttin' them in a bloody public place!'

Planting his giant fists on the table, Johnny Fox leant over her. 'No, Mrs C. This is on you. Now, you better come with me.' He stood up and grasped her arm, dragging her out of her seat.

There was no point resisting, so she went with him, her ears buzzing with fear. They'd only taken a few steps when the rumble of an explosion made the floor shake. A second later, the air was torn by the insistent cry of the shell warning. Johnny froze, his grip tightening painfully around her upper arm.

Nellie's heart lightened. Never, in her wildest dreams, did she think she'd be happy that the town was being shelled. 'Any minute now that back door will open and a load of people'll rush in,' she said. 'You all right with that?' She glanced up at him, gratified to see indecision on his face.

He bent towards her and whispered, 'I'll go now. But you ain't heard the last of this. An' if I find out that you ain't kept your promise, Mrs C, you know exactly what'll happen.'

His breath in her ear sent shivers down her spine, and she kept her head lowered, not wanting him to see her bone-deep fear. He pushed her away from him, and walked out of the back door, not bothering to close it behind him, allowing light to spill out into the yard.

After shutting it quickly, Nellie ran back into the kitchen. Cissy was standing at the bottom of the stairs, her hand in her pocket, a determined look on her face.

'He's gone,' Nellie choked out. She looked suspiciously at Cissy's pocket and her breath hitched. 'You don't even know 'ow to use it.' She'd worked out how to load the thing the night before, although she couldn't be entirely sure she'd done it correctly.

'Everyone knows 'ow to use a gun,' Cissy hissed. 'You point an' you pull the trigger. To be honest, I wasn't sure who to shoot first.'

The others had followed Cissy down. 'Christ, Mum. That man scares the living daylights out of me,' Marianne said. Teddy was squirming in her arms, but she held him firmly.

Donny and Elodie followed behind, eyes wide and confused. 'Get downstairs, all of you. I'll bring the tea,' she said. She needed a moment to collect herself.

Cissy remained behind and as soon as the basement door had shut behind the others, she took the gun from her pocket and handed it to her. 'Bloody Lou Carter's gone an' stitched us all up an' then scarpered, leavin' us to face the consequences.'

After ensuring the safety catch was on, Nellie put the gun in her apron pocket. 'It's not entirely Lou's fault,' she said. 'Gawd, that makes two things in a row I never thought I'd say.'

'What was the first?' Cissy asked, as she loaded a tray with cups and saucers.

'Thank God for the bloody shells.'

Cissy choked out a laugh. The rouge on her cheeks was standing out in sharp contrast to the pallor of her skin, and Nellie felt a rush of affection for her. She'd come down here ready to shoot a man to protect her. They might have been at odds since Johnny Fox had first walked into the café, but Cissy would be by her side no matter what happened. 'Thanks, love,' she said softly, reaching out to touch her cousin's shoulder.

Cissy's smile dropped and she shrugged Nellie's hand off. 'This ends tomorrow, Nell. One way or another, you an' me's gonna get rid of everythin' downstairs, or so help me, I'll bring the police 'ere meself.'

Nellie blanched at the thought. Considering what was down there, it would probably mean she would be arrested too. Frankly, though, she'd welcome the rest. And if it kept everyone safe, then so be it. 'One more day, Ciss. Jasper said we needed to behave as if everythin's normal.'

'Normal? Bloody hell, we got shells fallin' outside, gangsters in and out, bloody men standin' round the square lookin' shifty. There ain't nothin' normal about this.'

'What are we gonna do about the party tomorrow? Don and Lily 'ave their hearts set on it.'

Cissy rolled her eyes. 'Don and Lily also 'ave their hearts set on stayin' alive a good few more years. As do I!'

'You're right. We'll cancel. I'll make it up to them.'

'Agreed. Tomorrow, we sort this out.' She picked up the tray and left the kitchen.

Nellie followed more slowly, her hand clutched around the gun in her pocket. Another explosion rumbled through the building, and it brought to mind a poem she'd heard on the radio a few years back. She wasn't one for poetry usually, but this one had tickled her. 'Come friendly shells and fall on Johnny Fox,' she murmured, and despite everything, she giggled.

# Chapter 47



*Abbots Cliff House*

Taking a deep drag of her cigarette, Marge watched Rodney's dark figure walk up the long drive, his feet crunching on the gravel. The light was almost gone now, so with any luck he wouldn't notice her standing by the wall huddled in her coat.

As he climbed the steps to the front door, he paused and sniffed the air. 'Is that you, Marge?'

Dammit. Stupid fags. Another good reason to cut down.

'I know it's you.' He walked back down the steps. 'I really do need to talk to you . . . Please. It's important.'

Despite herself, Marge was interested.

'I've been a complete idiot.'

Marge raised her eyebrows. She'd have put it a bit more strongly than that. He'd been an utter bastard, and she wasn't going to let him get away with it quite so easily.

'I can see you, you know. Your cigarette is glowing.'

She took another drag and blew the smoke towards him.

He laughed slightly. 'Will you let me explain?'

'Explain why you basically accused me of being a prostitute, you mean? Why, yes Rodney, please do. I'm sure there's a perfectly *rational* explanation. No need for me to be offended at all.'

He sighed and sank down onto one of the steps, a dark shadow against the white walls of the house. 'I deserved that. The thing is, though . . . It's so hard to explain, but I thought I saw you last night at a club in Folkestone.'

'I see. I presume this is a club that it's perfectly fine for a man to go to, but if a woman dares set her dainty little foot over the threshold, then she deserves to be insulted in front of her colleagues.' The more she thought about it, the angrier she was becoming.

'That's about the size of it. But don't shoot the messenger. It's just the way it is.'

'So what if I was at a disreputable club. Why does that give you the right to insult me?'

'You mean it *was* you?' He jumped up and walked towards her.

Marge resisted the temptation to scream. 'Let me get this straight. You expect me to believe that you insulted me because you *thought* you saw me somewhere where you didn't want me to be? Do you know how ridiculous that makes you sound? Whether I was there or not is moot. The point is you have no right to talk to me like that. And even if I had been there, it's none of your business. Just like it was none of your business in Liverpool, and none of your business when I saw you at the station. Who I spend my time with, what I choose to do with them, is none of your business.'

She threw her cigarette on the ground and made to walk away. But he grabbed her arm.

'You're right. I feel so stupid. But I swear, there was a woman who looked exactly like you, and I . . .' He sighed heavily. 'I was jealous.'

Marge had been about to pull away, but she paused at this. 'Why were you jealous?'

Rodney ignored the question. 'I called out your name and the woman looked back at me then ran away. She looked exactly like you.'

Marge wasn't sure what to make of this. It was odd to think there was someone who looked like her running around Folkestone.

'Almost like a twin,' he continued.

Marge's breath caught in the back of her throat. 'I don't have a twin.' But she used to. They might not have been the same age, but people had often mistaken them for twins.

'What happened to Katy?' Rodney said suddenly. 'One minute she was in Dover and the next she'd left. You never speak about her or your mum and dad.'

'That's because they're all dead, Rodney.'

'Katy died?' he breathed. 'Oh God, I didn't know. I'm so sorry. But . . . I swear, Marge. She was identical. Red hair, tall, curvy.'

Marge felt a flare of jealousy. 'Fancy her, did you? Well, speaking from experience, I'm not sure tall redheads are your type.' She hated herself for the tremor of hurt she could hear in her voice.

He grasped her shoulders and pulled her into his arms. 'I'm so sorry. I've been so stupid and messed everything up.' He brushed his lips over her cheek. 'When did she die? You never said a word.'

Marge tried to pull away from him. 'That's because I only just found out. Apparently, she died in an air raid in London.' She could feel the burn of tears at the back of her throat, but she refused to let them fall in front of him. She needed to go back to her room so she could cry for her sister in peace.

'Christ.' He tightened his arms around her. 'But are you sure? This woman . . . They called her Ellen. She was you. She was definitely you.'

'I'm sure.' Her voice broke and the tears came, soaking into the wool of his coat. 'Mr Wainwright said her house took a direct hit. He's been looking for her for years.'

'Why have you never told me any of this? I would have helped you search.'

'Firstly, you only returned to Dover a couple of years ago. And secondly, because you never asked.'

There was a long pause.

'No, I never did. Because I'm a selfish ass. I've taken you for granted, haven't I?'

'No, you've taken me for a fool. I put my bloody heart – and my job – on the line when I came to your room last year. Do you remember what you said? "I don't feel anything for you except desire." Do you remember that, Rodders? Basically you were saying I'm good for a quick fumble but forget anything else. Is it any wonder I never talked to you about stuff? Because I could never trust you!'

She thrust him away from her and went back inside. Did he really think he could just apologise and she'd fall gratefully into his arms? He'd rejected her, insulted her and ripped her heart to shreds.

Inside, she could hear the low rumble of voices coming from the drawing room. Captain Bennett's laugh rang out and she cringed. She couldn't be anywhere near that man right now.

She hurried upstairs and threw herself onto her bed, the conversation with Rodney running through her mind. A woman named Ellen who looked like her.

Something niggled at the back of her mind. That name brought back memories of a happier time. A time when she and Katy would curl in their mother's lap while she read them their favourite story. *The Light Princess*. Ellen. The princess who had no gravity and never cried. She had to be weighed down in case a puff of wind blew her away. Katy used to say that if she'd been the princess she'd have taken the weights off so she could float out across the world.

Marge sat up. Is that what Katy had done? Floated out across the world and landed in a seedy club in Folkestone? 'She's dead, Marge,' she told herself sternly. She turned off the light and went to stand at the window. The beams from the searchlights shot into the sky like tunnels of light. She tried to picture Katy inside one, arms stretched to the heavens as she floated up towards the stars. She was definitely dead.

But it didn't matter how much she repeated the words, a tiny flicker of hope had started up inside her, and she clung to it as tightly as the princess had held the prince's body as she dragged him out of the water.

After Marge had gone, Rodney let out a long breath. He couldn't feel worse if someone had taken his heart out of his chest, scraped it with a knife and stuck it back in. He sat down on the steps and put his head in his hands. They'd been so close to something special just a few short months ago and he'd ruined it.

But he refused to give up on her. He sat for a long time, staring up at the scattering of stars. It was a good night for a bombing raid, he thought absently. He stood and walked to the end of the garden again. To his right, Folkestone was visible only because of the searchlights that swept restlessly through the sky. But otherwise, the place was pitch-black.

He thought again about the woman he'd seen and the address Scarlett had finally given him, after he'd bought two bottles of champagne and danced with some of the girls.

As soon as he could, he'd go to Folkestone and find out who the woman really was.

The entrance hall was in darkness when he pushed inside, but from the loud laughter from the drawing room, they had already substituted the tea for something a little stronger. A drink was exactly what he needed right now.

Before he could walk across the hall though, his arm was grabbed.

'Where did you see this woman?' He could smell Marge's perfume, and the lingering scent of her cigarette.

He pulled away and walked over to the wall to turn on the light, illuminating her blotchy face. 'Have you been crying?' His heart ached. He'd done this to her.

'I just want to know what club you went to last night and if you know where this Ellen lives.'

He nodded. 'The lipstick was the price I paid for the information.' He grinned, but she didn't return the smile.

Going over to the telephone table, she ripped a piece of paper from the pad and picked up a pen. 'Tell me then.'

'You're not going on your own, Marge. Let me come with you. We'll go after lunch tomorrow.'

'Address, Rodney. Now.'

'I said no. Anyway, if your sister is dead, then clearly it can't be her.'

She seemed to recoil at his words, and he felt instantly contrite. 'Will you tell me what's going on,' he asked more softly.

'I just want the bloody address, Rod! After everything you've said and done to me, it's the least you can do.'

Guilt wrapped around him. 'I've apologised for that. I know I've been in the wrong.'

'Well, show me you mean it by giving me the information.'

Her expression was hard, her jaw set. He'd seen this look on her face so many times that he had to resist the temptation to kiss it away. He also knew that Marge wouldn't budge. And she had a point: he'd behaved abominably; it really was the least he could do.

'I'll give it to you on one condition.'

She raised an eyebrow in query.

'You and I will go together tomorrow.'

She nodded.

He took the pen from her and wrote the address. 'Tomorrow, Marge. I promise we'll sort this out.' He held the paper out to her and she snatched it from him, then letting out a long breath, her shoulders dropped.

'Go through to the others. I need to check something with Mrs Benson in the kitchen.'

She disappeared through the kitchen door, and he couldn't help feeling he'd just made a terrible mistake.

# Chapter 48

Jasper had packed himself a small bag, put his gun in his old over-the-shoulder holster under his shirt, and was on his way to the café when the first shell fell and the siren gave two short, sharp bursts. The sky lit up with searchlights, and he could hear the boom of the British guns returning fire across the Channel from St Margaret's Bay in the usual pointless exchange.

The streets were deserted, as people preferred to be home before darkness fell and he assumed the men who'd been watching the café earlier would be gone now too. He turned into Church Street and was just approaching the back gate to the café, when it crashed open and a figure brushed past him, hurrying towards Castle Street. It was impossible to see the man's face in the darkness, but he sensed his size and bulk. Heart in his mouth, he dithered for a second. On the one hand, he was desperate to check everyone was all right, but on the other, Johnny Fox – if that was who it was – needed to be found. Dropping his bag, he put one hand on his gun and followed him.

But they'd had too much of a head start, and when he reached the junction of Castle Street and Church Street, there was no sign of him. Suddenly a torch beam caught him, and a man's voice ordered him to the shelter

'Keep yer hair on, Joe. It's me, Jasper. You ain't seen a big bloke runnin' around here tonight, 'ave you?'

A loud crash made the ground shake beneath them. It was hard to tell where the shell had fallen, but it wasn't in the immediate vicinity, so they ignored it.

'I ain't seen a soul, Jasper,' he replied. 'Folk know better than to run around town in the middle of a shell attack, so get outta here.'

'All right, all right. But seriously, mate, you see anyone suspicious, anyone you ain't never seen, you let me know.'

'There's been a couple of cagey-lookin' blokes in long coats and hats round today.'

'Yeah, I don't mean those numpties. I mean a big bloke, squashed nose. Sometimes drivin' a posh motor.'

'Nope not seen 'im, but if I do, I'll let you know.'

'Pass it round to the others, will ya? Bloke needs findin'.'

Another shell landed somewhere, and a piercing scream rang out, followed by shouts. 'I gotta go, mate. I'll keep me eyes peeled.'

He ran off and Jasper hurried back to the café. When he pushed open the basement door, both Cissy and Nellie started out of their chairs. He narrowed his eyes at them, then looked around the room. 'Lily at work?' he asked, noting with relief that everyone else was here and seemed unharmed.

Nellie nodded warily. Both she and Cissy looked as nervous as kittens and the anger he'd felt when he'd spoken to Mr Wainwright bubbled up in him again. If nothing happened tomorrow, he was going to demand action. At the very least they should remove the bloody boxes and station men *inside* the café.

'Just saw your visitor leave,' he said casually, as Nellie poured him a cup of tea.

She gave him a sharp glance and pursed her lips. 'He weren't here long.'

'What did he want?' His gaze flicked towards the curtain. If Johnny Fox had discovered he'd tampered with one of the boxes, he doubted he'd have left, but he needed to be sure.

'It was that man again,' Donny piped up. 'The one that scares Gran and makes Auntie Cissy angry. But he's all right, really.'

'What do you know about him, Don?' Nellie snapped.

Donny shrugged and handed a crust of bread to Teddy, who was fussing on Marianne's knee.

'Yes, what do you know, Don?' Marianne repeated.

'Don't know nothing.' Teddy knocked the crust out of his hand, and sighing, Donny dug into his pocket and pulled out a paper bag. Reaching into it, he produced a barley sugar twist and handed it to his brother. 'But 'e gave me these today!'

Marianne snatched it from his hand before Teddy could put it in his mouth. 'He can't eat this, Don! He'll choke!'

'Sorry, Mum. You have it then.' He popped one into his mouth then handed the bag to Elodie. 'You'll love these, Ellie,' he said shyly.

She smiled and dipped her hand into the bag. '*Merci*, Donny. You are kind to give me your sweets.'

His cheeks turned a deep crimson, and he dropped his gaze back to the bag and pulled out a long liquorice shoestring. 'Can Teddy have this, Mum?'

Nellie had been watching the scene aghast. 'Where did you see him?' she asked, grabbing the sweets out of his hand.

'Hey, they're mine! He were just down by the seafront, that's all!' He snatched it back.

'The man who left the boxes?' Marianne looked at Nellie. 'He was talking to you and Ted?' Her voice rose with concern. 'Didn't Gran tell you not to talk to strangers, Don!' She hugged Teddy to her.

'You didn't seem to care much when Don was takin' 'im out,' Nellie said caustically.

Marianne's cheeks reddened. 'I'm not the one who brought that man to our door! And you don't know how I feel about anything,' she said in a low voice. 'So don't you dare judge me.'

'Hey,' Jasper intervened. 'Can we all calm down.' Although he didn't feel calm. The fact that the man had approached Donny felt more threatening than the boxes sitting behind the curtain.

He moved to sit next to Nellie, who had her hands clasped tightly on the table.

'Are you gonna tell me what happened tonight?' he asked quietly.

'This is your doin', Jasper – all them blokes hangin' around. Talkin' to Mr Wainwright's made everythin' worse. That's why he was here. Cos he thinks we've grassed. The shells saved us.'

'Did he come down here?' he asked tensely.

'Didn't have a chance.' She glanced around her. 'I know what's in them, and I think you do too,' she whispered.

Jasper stared at her aghast. 'You opened one? Tell me you sealed it again, Nell.'

She looked away with a small shake of her head. 'Didn't have time,' she murmured.

'What are you two whisperin' about?' Cissy asked.

'Are you talkin' about the party?'

Marianne slapped Donny on the head. 'For God's sake, Don!'

Jasper looked at him. 'What party?'

Donny scratched his head. 'Umm, my mate Barry Cannon's birthday party.'

Jasper looked around. Marianne was fussing with Teddy's hair, Elodie had leant her head back against the wall and closed her eyes. Cissy poured another cup of tea and pushed it towards him, while Nellie glared daggers at Donny.

None of them were looking at him. And then it hit him.

'You ain't havin' a party for me, I hope?' he said in a strangled voice.

Nellie raised her eyebrows at him. 'Now, why would I go an' do somethin' like that, when you'd clearly love it so much.'

'You swear?' he asked.

Nellie looked him right in the eye. 'I *swear.*'

She sounded sincere, but she'd always been a good liar. He looked at Donny, who appeared close to tears. They were definitely having a party for him. He needed to stop it. But Donny looked so upset and the boy had little enough fun in his life. How could he disappoint him?

'Well, that's a shame. I'd've loved it.'

Donny's eyes brightened. 'Maybe we should have one then. Don't you think, Gran?'

'Maybe next year, love,' she said with a wink.

Seemingly satisfied, Donny handed around the sweets again.

But Jasper was far from satisfied. Nellie was right about one thing: he was partly to blame. By talking to Mr Wainwright he'd set a chain of events in motion that threatened to spin out of control, and he had no idea if he'd be able to keep everyone safe.

*We should call off the party*, Nellie thought, wishing she'd not looked in the box. Everything was starting to make sense to her now: Francis, the men from the Ministry of Food, the café under surveillance, Johnny Fox . . . She put a hand to her mouth, swallowing back the nausea as she watched Teddy, his lips smeared black, sucking on the liquorice lace. Johnny Fox was getting too close to the kids, and now he seemed to have earned Donny's trust. Until the man was caught the boys would leave the café over her dead body.

'This has to end now, Jasper. If anything happened to the kids . . .' She gulped.

Cissy sighed loudly. 'Are you two gonna sit there whisperin' like a couple of kids in assembly all evenin', or are you gonna let us in on your secrets?'

'Sorry, Ciss. I were just explainin' to Nell that the electric's gone at my flat, so I was wonderin' whether I could stay here tonight.'

Cissy's eyebrows rose. 'Oh, so you're gonna do it above board this time, are you?'

'What do you mean above board?' Marianne asked, wiping Teddy's mouth. She still looked furious, but Nellie wasn't about to apologise to her. Who knew? Maybe having Johnny Fox threatening her kids might remind her that she loved Teddy.

Nellie shot Cissy a poisonous look. 'It'll have to be the sofa, Jasper. We're stuffed to the gills,' Nellie said sharply, though she wanted to cry with relief at the thought of having him here.

'Oh, but if Jasper stays, then he'll know . . .' Donny trailed off.

Nellie sighed. 'All right, Jasper, the game's up. We are 'avin' a little gatherin' to celebrate your birthday. Everyone'll be 'ere. But maybe we should do it next weekend?'

'But it won't be Jasper's birthday then,' Donny whined.

'Well, now, we can't have that, can we?' Jasper's eyes flicked to Nellie and he shook his head slightly. 'I can't wait. And it don't matter that it's not a surprise. The fact that you arranged it is surprise enough.'

Delighted, Donny went on to tell Jasper every detail of the plan, while Jasper did his best to look enthusiastic. But Nellie wasn't fooled. She could tell that his nerves were stretched as tightly as hers at the thought of what the next day might bring.

When the all-clear sounded, Jasper put a hand on her arm, indicating he wanted her to stay.

They waited as everyone gathered their things and went upstairs.

'What the hell's goin' on?' she asked as soon as Cissy had shut the door with a snap.

Jasper sighed. 'No more than I told you earlier – we've just got to go on as normal so as not to give the game away.'

'It's a bit late for that,' she shrilled. 'So now what are we expected to do?'

The door opened and Cissy burst in. 'There's someone upstairs to see you. And you two owe me an explanation. You can't keep me in the dark like this.'

Nellie and Jasper exchanged a panicked glance.

'Are the kids upstairs?' Jasper asked urgently.

Cissy nodded.

'You two, stay here.'

Then, taking the gun out of his holster, Jasper went upstairs.

# Chapter 49



*Abbots Cliff House*

Marge closed the kitchen door and leaned against it. She had no idea where the address Rodney had given her was, and it was a long walk to Folkestone in the pitch black, so it was probably foolhardy to go now. Then again, though it seemed so unlikely, if there was even the smallest chance that her sister was alive . . .

'You hidin' from someone?' Mrs Benson, the inevitable cigarette hanging from her mouth, was stirring a pot at the stove.

'You know Folkestone, don't you, Mrs B?'

'Like the back of me hand, love. Born and bred.'

She went over and handed her the paper. 'Do you know where these places are?'

Mrs Benson held the paper away from her face, squinting. 'Why's a nice girl like you askin' after The Rose Rooms? I can tell you one thing for sure, you won't find no English roses in there.' She cackled.

'But you know where it is?' Marge was trying to keep the impatience from her voice. Mrs Benson reminded her of Nellie Castle, and if there was one thing she knew about these sorts of characters, it was that if you pushed too hard, they'd resist just for the hell of it.

'Everyone knows where it is, love. Calls itself a *gentlemen's* club, but it's nothin' more than a good old-fashioned knockin' shop.' She took a last drag of her cigarette and stubbed it out on a saucer.

'Would you be able to draw me a map?' If the woman Rodney saw was Katy, then she didn't want to think about what she'd been doing just to survive.

'Don't the Navy pay you well enough?' She grinned. 'Well, you wouldn't be the first to want to earn a little extra on the side.'

Marge laughed despite herself. 'And maybe I wouldn't have been the only one, eh?'

'Ask me no questions and I'll tell you no lies. Right, so let's see. The Rose Rooms is easy enough on the High Street off Tontine Street. Trinity Gardens is off Sandgate Road. There's lots of boardin' houses along there. Bit of a walk from 'ere, though.'

'I don't care.'

Mrs Benson regarded her shrewdly. 'You really need to find this girl?'

Marge nodded, swallowing back the lump in her throat. She refused to think about how she'd feel if this was a wild goose chase.

Mrs Benson nodded, took a pen from her apron pocket and ripped a piece of paper out of a grease-stained notebook. Then she sat down at the table and started to draw a map.

When she'd finished, she held it out to her. Marge went to take it, but Mrs Benson snatched it back. 'You can't walk there tonight.'

'I'll wait till first light,' Marge lied.

'I weren't born yesterday, love. Come with me.' She went out of a door on the other side of the kitchen that led into a small, dimly lit hallway with stairs down to the basement flat.

The flat had a tiny entrance hall, most of which was taken up with a large object leaning against the wall and covered with a sheet. Mrs Benson pulled it off like a magician. Underneath was a small motorbike. A licence plate sat over its front wheel, and a brown leather satchel was strapped to the back. The panel had black and white checks with the word 'Excelsior' written in white on a black background. Marge gasped. 'A utility?' she asked.

Mrs Benson stroked the black leather saddle proudly. 'It were my Benny's. Loved his motorbikes, he did. Never ridden it meself, but I couldn't just leave it when I come 'ere or he'd've haunted me for the rest of me days.' She looked up at her. 'You can borrow it if you like?'

Marge drew in a breath. 'I haven't ridden one of these for years. My dad had one. He taught me and my sister to ride it.'

Mrs Benson dug around in the satchel and pulled out a bicycle lamp. 'You'll be needin' this. An' it's got a full tank. Benny filled up at the start of the war. Knew there'd be rationin'. Then 'e went and got hisself killed in London, so it were a waste of money in the end.'

'Oh, Mrs B!' Marge threw her arms around the woman's thin shoulders. 'Thank you!'

Mrs Benson shrugged her off. 'Calm down, love. I ain't won the war or anythin'!' But she was smiling. 'Hang on, there's a few other bits you'll need.' She opened a cupboard door and pulled out a heavy leather jacket. 'Benny always wore this. An' there's some gloves in the pocket.'

Marge took the jacket and put it on. It was a little big, but it was wonderfully warm. 'I honestly think I love you, Mrs B.'

Mrs Benson tutted as she turned out the lights, then opened the front door. 'Drive safe, love. And bring this back to me in one piece.'

Marge wheeled the bike out of the door, then leant over and kissed her cheek. 'I promise.'

After Mrs Benson closed the door, Marge carried the bike up the area steps. Then hitching her skirt up her thighs, she swung her leg over the saddle. With the jacket buttoned and just about covering her stocking tops, she stamped down on the kick starter lever. The engine spluttered into life and she sped down the drive, the gravel crunching under the wheels.

It was an exhilarating ride down the hill to Folkestone. The wind was at her back, and she felt as though she were flying – just like Ellen the Light Princess. All the worries and stresses of the day melted away at the sheer exhilaration of the ride. She'd forgotten the joy these bikes could bring. If she and Katy had argued about anything, it was about who got first go on the bike. She laughed at the memory of two fiery redheads going at it hammer and tongs, until their mother had banned them from riding for a month. After Katy had disappeared, her father had got rid of the bike, probably because it evoked too many memories of his lost daughter.

Once she approached the town, though, things became a little trickier, and she had to stop to examine the map. With only the dim bicycle lamp to guide her, she puttered slowly along until she came to Sandgate Road. Getting off, she pushed the bike the rest of the way. She had been buoyed by adrenaline on the journey, but as soon as she turned into Trinity Gardens, the doubts set in. She was grasping at straws. Katy's house had taken a direct hit, so there was no way it could be her. She was just setting herself up for more grief and disappointment.

But what if it was her? Would Katy be happy to see her? Or would she hate her for all these years of estrangement? But thinking about it, Marge wasn't sure how *she'd* feel. All these years, her family had grieved and wondered. Katy could have at least sent them a letter to let them know she was alive.

*Stop it, Marge!* She took out a cigarette and lit it, drawing the smoke deep into her lungs. *Everything was going to be all right.* If it wasn't Katy, she'd be no worse off than she was already. And if it was . . . it would be a miracle.

After finishing her cigarette, she made her way slowly up the street, counting the houses until she came to number forty-seven. She stood at the bottom of the front steps for a while, taking deep breaths, then, squaring her shoulders, she walked up and knocked on the door. She could hear voices and footsteps on the other side, but no one came to answer.

She knocked again, this time more impatiently.

'Someone get the bleedin' door,' a harsh voice called. It didn't sound like Katy, but then it had been so long since she'd heard her voice that she wasn't sure she remembered it at all.

The door opened, and a head peered round. 'Yeah?'

'I was wondering if Ellen was here?' Marge asked, her voice trembling slightly.

'Why?' It was frustrating to not be able to see the woman's face.

'I'm her sister,' Marge said, fingers crossed, praying she was right.

'She ain't mentioned ya, but come in.' The woman stepped back, and Marge followed her through the blackout curtain and shut the door.

The woman appraised her, then grinned. 'Well, you ain't lyin' about bein' her sister. You twins?'

Marge's heart started to thump unsteadily. Could it be possible? Tears rose in her eyes, and she blinked them back, trying to find her voice.

'You all right, love?' The woman was heavily made-up and wore high platform shoes and a tight blue dress that showed off her ample curves.

Marge nodded. 'Yes . . . Sorry.' She wiped at her eyes. 'I just haven't seen her in so long.'

The woman eyed her uniform. 'Disagree on what helpin' the war effort meant, did ya?'

Marge managed a smile. 'Something like that. Can you tell me which room she's in?'

'Up there, turn left, second door on the right.'

Marge nodded her thanks and went upstairs. A shabby blue carpet ran the full length of the long corridor, on either side of which were white doors. Laughter was coming from behind the first door, but there was no noise coming from the door that might be Katy's. After a moment's hesitation, she tapped on it.

There was a rustling, then a voice on the other side said, 'Who is it?'

# Chapter 50

*Falmouth*

Hunched against the persistent drizzle, Bert walked towards the town with his head down and his hands in his pockets. In forty-eight hours he might be dead and he would never see Dot or his family again. He would never be able to make amends to Jimmy for the things he'd said to him – he'd never even know if his brother was alive or dead. Nor would he know whether this sacrifice he and his comrades were about to make would mean anything in the long run. Hatred might still win, and his Dot might find herself living under occupation. The thought chilled him even more than that of his own death.

He'd succeeded in his quest to be in the first boat with Commander Stephens, but he wasn't sure it would make a difference. Colonel Newman called the plan 'audacious', but Bert thought 'foolish and deadly' would be more accurate.

Reaching the town, he went into the post office and dictated a telegram. It was all he could do for her. He'd sworn to Dot that he would never lie to her, and he hated the idea that the last message she received from him might contain a lie, but what else could he do?

*

Much later, after he and the men had eaten, they were called to their final briefing. The plan was complex and had many moving parts, and though they'd spent the last weeks memorising it, once again they were taken through it in minute detail. This was their last chance to ensure everyone understood exactly what their role was.

By the end of the briefing, Bert's stomach was roiling. He put a hand on his chest, feeling his heart thumping fast against his palm. He didn't know if he could do this. Oh God . . .

He glanced around the room at the other men. Their expressions were focused, hard, intent. Bert closed his eyes and took a long breath, forcing himself to calm down. He couldn't afford to panic. These men depended on him, just as he depended on them, and he wouldn't let any of them down.

Commander Stephens clapped his hands. 'Good work today, men.' He looked around the room, making eye contact with each of them. 'I want you kitted up and ready at eleven p.m. sharp. Now, you all know this is a dangerous mission, so before I send you off for some rest, there's one more task to complete.' He walked around the room, handing out writing paper and envelopes.

Bert looked around in confusion.

'For your final letter, mate,' the man next to him said. 'You know, in case . . .'

Swallowing back the nausea, Bert picked up his pen.

# Chapter 51

*Castle's Café*

Cissy looked round at Nellie, her eyes wide. 'Another bleedin' gun!' she squeaked. 'This place is startin' to feel like the Wild West!'

'Be quiet, Ciss!' she hissed. She would not let Jasper walk alone into danger, so as soon as his footsteps reached the top of the stairs, she crept up, heart in her mouth. She paused at the top and listened, relaxing slightly when she didn't hear Johnny Fox's voice.

She pushed open the door and tiptoed through the kitchen to peer through the hatch.

Jasper was sitting at a table with a man she vaguely recognised. A hat sat on the table beside him, and his dark curly hair gleamed beneath the bulb. He was wearing a thick coat, and considering his calm demeanour, Nellie figured it was safe to come out.

'What's goin' on?' she asked.

Jasper's head turned sharply, and he beckoned her in.

Cissy followed close behind and they both stared at the man as though he were an exhibit in a museum. 'Who are you?' Nellie asked bluntly.

The man stood up and held out his hand. 'Peter Holmes,' he said politely. 'We had the pleasure of meeting a year or so ago when I, uh, searched your friend Hester Erskine's room.' Despite his posh words, the accent was pure Liverpudlian.

Nellie blanched. No wonder he seemed familiar. 'She weren't no friend of mine. But why are you 'ere?'

'We're here for your protection,' he replied.

Nellie's eyes widened. The boy was whippet thin and with his dark-framed glasses and smooth skin, he couldn't be more than twenty. 'They're sendin' children to protect us?'

'Nellie!' Jasper stood. 'Mr Holmes will be staying here tonight. He's been sent by . . .' He looked at the young man, a question in his eyes.

But whoever he was working for, Peter Holmes wasn't telling. 'Like I said, I'm here to keep you safe.'

'About bloody time!' Cissy squeaked.

'My cousin, Cissy Ford,' Nellie said in answer to his silent question.

'Sit down. The situation is looking serious. And thanks to Mr Cane's intelligence earlier, it was decided that someone should keep watch tonight. We have men in support outside as well.'

'In the cold?' Cissy said. 'Can I take them some tea?'

'Not necessary. They're used to difficult conditions. But we believe the gang will try to take their, um, goods away tonight. And we need to catch them red-handed.'

'You can stay down 'ere then. I don't want you scarin' the kids.'

'Understood. Now, if you wouldn't mind making me a brew, that'd be lovely. Mr Cane says he'll keep watch upstairs, so you'll be perfectly safe.'

'Safe? Your lot are the reason they've got the willies in the first place!' Nellie snapped. 'You know if you don't want to be noticed, skulkin' in hats and long coats ain't the way to do it.'

'Nellie, enough. At least somethin's bein' done now,' Jasper interjected wearily.

'All right, then, perhaps you might explain how the hell Johnny Fox's whole scam is even possible?' She gave the boy a challenging glare.

'You've looked in the boxes, then?' He shook his head. 'This is a problem that started in the Blitz. A printing factory that was used by the government to print ration books was bombed and some of the presses were removed, along with all sorts of supplies – ink, paper, that sort of thing. And we've been searching for them ever since. Because someone with expertise has been putting that equipment to good use.'

Suddenly the back door flew open. Peter Holmes and Jasper leapt to their feet, reaching for their firearms, while Nellie spun round and stared in astonishment as Mr Wainwright puffed into the kitchen.

'Algie!' Cissy squealed, running towards him and throwing her arms around him. They were almost the same height, though Mr Wainwright was considerably wider.

'Cissy!' He pulled back and held her face in his hands. 'Jasper told me a few home truths today.'

Jasper had come to stand by the door, his smile wide. 'Looks like the troops are all here.'

Mr Wainwright pulled a hankie from his coat pocket and mopped his face. Nellie suppressed a laugh despite the situation; the man probably hadn't moved this fast since he was a youth.

Peter Holmes came forward. 'We're grateful for your assistance, Mr Wainwright, but it might be better if you go home now.'

Mr Wainwright clamped an arm around Cissy's waist. 'I'm going nowhere.' He looked at her and smiled.

'Oh, Algie.' Cissy leant forward and pressed her lips to his.

'Don't know where you'll sleep,' Nellie remarked. 'Jasper's got the sofa. And don't get no funny ideas about sleepin' with Ciss! She shares with Lily and Elodie these days.'

'You sound just like your mum.' Cissy giggled.

'I assure you, Mrs Castle, I'm not here to sleep. I'll keep watch with Jasper.'

'I'll feel so much better knowin' you're watchin' over me, Algie,' Cissy simpered.

'God give me strength,' Nellie exclaimed. She raked her eyes over the portly man, wondering what possible use he could be in this situation. He had many talents, but she'd be willing to bet that being a bodyguard wasn't one of them. 'Well, you sit up if you want to, *Algie*, but I need to go to bed. As for you, Mr Holmes, my daughter Lily's due back from the hospital soon, so don't go wavin' your gun at the poor girl.' She turned and stomped upstairs.

When she reached the top of the stairs, she could hear Marianne singing to Teddy and felt a flutter of hope. Usually Donny was the one singing by his cot each night. Had the thought of the danger he and Donny could have been in this afternoon softened her? Only time would tell, but it felt like a step in the right direction. She should never have let that situation carry on as long as it had. As soon as this sorry mess was over, she'd sit down with both Marianne and Lily and make them talk to her.

As she walked past the sitting room door, her eyes went – as they so often did – to a patch of wall beside the armchair. It was covered with cheerful wallpaper now, but to her it would always be stained with blood.

It was a reminder that Jasper, Peter Holmes and Mr Wainwright were all very well, but when push came to shove, the only person she really trusted to protect her family was herself.

# Chapter 52

Ellen was lying on the bed waiting for her client. Her makeup was done, and she was dressed in a satin nightdress and her faithful green silk dressing gown. She'd sent a message to the Rose Rooms earlier apologising for running out the night before and saying that she had a stomach bug. It would at least mean she could return; it was a lucrative place to work.

But then, did she have to do it anymore? There was plenty of work around for a woman these days, although she doubted there were any jobs that paid as well as the club, even once they'd taken their cut. But maybe she should get a job in a factory; change the way she lived.

She thought again about the man last night. She was pretty sure he was a boy she'd been at school with; he'd been studious and quiet, so she'd paid no attention to him. But now look at him: a naval officer, while she was just a common-or-garden whore. Would they have been friends if she'd given him the time of day?

Rodney Castle. The name came back to her all of a sudden. Brother of Marge's friend Marianne. She should have gone to the café that day. But she'd been a coward. Just as she'd been a coward all her life. Hiding away, living her sordid life rather than trying to find a way to make it up to her family and face down her demons. How long would she allow shame and guilt to rule her life? At some point, she'd have to find a way out because she was getting too old for this game, and she needed to change.

A knock at the door startled her and she checked her appearance in the mirror. 'Who is it?' she called in as seductive a voice as she could be bothered with.

The reply made the breath leave her body. Had her thoughts conjured her? Was someone playing a joke? Pulling her robe tightly around her with trembling hands, she walked slowly to the door.

When she opened it, she froze, the blood rushing in her ears. It was like looking in a mirror, except the woman in front of her was wearing a uniform, her hair windblown and her cheeks flushed. For a long moment, neither moved. But then Marge broke the spell.

'Katy! My God! It *is* you!' She threw her arms around her and squeezed her tightly. 'I thought you were dead!' she sobbed. 'I've been looking for you and looking for you, but I was told you'd died in an air raid.'

No one had called her Katy since the day she'd arrived in London sixteen years before; she'd forced herself to forget that hopeful, starry-eyed schoolgirl had ever existed.

Tentatively, she put her arms around her sister. They were the same height and their cheeks pressed together, Marge's wet with tears, her own dry and hot.

'Where the hell have you been?' Marge pulled away and glared at her. 'Why did you never come home?'

Although her tone was angry, Katy could hear Marge's sadness, and guilt and shame – her constant companions – flooded through her. To avoid answering, she pulled her sister in tighter, revelling in the feel of her. Even after so many years she felt familiar. They'd been little more than children when she'd left – though she'd thought she was a woman of the world – and it felt like a miracle to hold her again.

Marge let go of her suddenly and pushed her into the room, kicking the door shut behind her. Her eyes were tear-washed, but she looked suddenly furious. 'Don't you think I deserve some answers?'

Her sister's temper was unchanged then. No one had ever been able to shout at her like Marge. She started to laugh. Partly from sheer joy, partly because she just didn't know what else to do.

'You think this is funny? I've grieved for you for bloody years, Katy! You ruined our lives! Mum's, Dad's, mine. They died not knowing whether you were alive or dead. And I was left all alone. I needed you.' The tears came again, and Marge slumped onto the bed. 'Did you never think about us at all?'

The laughter left Katy abruptly. She didn't know what she could say to her. Nothing would ever change what had happened. The pain would never go.

'I-I . . . I thought of you all the time.'

'Then why didn't you come home? Mum prayed for you every single bloody day, and she didn't even believe in God. She even went to see Bertha Bancroft – remember her? Barmy Bertha, who runs the spiritualist church?'

Katy nodded uncertainly. 'What did she say?' she whispered.

'She said she couldn't contact you, so you must be alive. Maybe she knows more than we ever gave her credit for. Cos here you are.' Marge eyed her critically. 'You're too bloody thin. What the hell have you been doing to yourself?'

Katy let out a little laugh. 'You know there's a war on. We're all too bloody thin.'

But Marge didn't return her smile. 'What happened, love?' she asked softly. 'What happened to you after you ran off to be with that man.' She spat out those final words.

Katy sat down beside her and took her hand. 'You'll be pleased to know you were right about him. He told me to meet him in London. Said he didn't want anyone to see us leave together.' She stared into the distance. 'So I went. And I waited and waited and he never came.'

'Why didn't you just come home?'

Katy sat back and wiped her eyes. 'How could I? I'd ruined everything. I was unmarried and pregnant, and I'd walked out. How could I come back?'

'You were pregnant?' Marge breathed. 'You could have talked to me. We would have found a way. Mum and Dad would never have abandoned you and their grandchild.'

Katy bit her lip and looked away. 'There is no grandchild,' she whispered. 'He died. I did come back. I saw you walking with a friend. You looked so happy, and . . . I figured you were all better off without me.'

'Oh, love!' Marge pulled her into her arms and Katy laid her head on her sister's chest and wept; huge, gulping sobs that shook her body. And all the while, Marge kept her arms around her, rocking her back and forth as though she were still a child. And in that moment, Katy felt as if she were fifteen again. Betrayed, grief-stricken and homesick. How she'd needed her mother and sister when her little boy was born. She'd called him Victor, after their father, but he'd lived for only an hour and been buried in a pauper's grave.

'It's all right,' Marge whispered against her ear. 'Cry it all out, my darling. I'm here now, and I'm going to take care of you. And the first thing we're going to do is get you out of this place and somewhere safe.'

Katy sat up and wiped her eyes. 'You have to leave. I'm expecting someone.'

'I don't care if you're expecting the Pope, I'm not leaving you here.'

Katy felt a spark of anger. 'I have a job to do. Your mate Rodney lost me money last night.'

Marge's eyes went flinty. 'You don't have to do this anymore, Katy. I will look after you. We'll find you another job.' Her eyes raked over her. 'Anyway, your makeup's running and you look like hell. The man'll run a mile.'

Katy hurried over to the mirror and started to dab at her cheeks with a piece of cotton wool. 'I don't need my baby sister telling me what to do. I've been looking after myself for the last sixteen years.'

'Not very well, by the look of you. Or going by where Rodney saw you.'

'Don't get all sniffy about what I've done to survive, Marge!'

'I'm not! All I'm saying is you can do better.'

Katy rounded on her. 'Do bloody better? You've not changed, have you? You always thought you knew best. And look at you now! With your fancy uniform, doing your bit like the good girl you always were. Well, I'm doing my bit too!'

'By sleeping with men who don't give *that* for you!?' Marge snapped her fingers.

'I don't give a fig for them either!'

Marge's shoulders relaxed and her voice softened. 'Don't pretend you want to keep doing this. Come back with me.'

She held a hand out to her. 'Come back with me and we'll work something out.'

Marge's abrupt shift in tone took the fight out of Katy. She felt raw and vulnerable, and she longed to sink into her sister's embrace again.

'Please?' Sensing her weakness, Marge pushed home her advantage. 'I'll help you with money, and I bet someone in Dover would take you in.'

'Like who? Bertha Bancroft?'

Marge's lips twitched. 'Why not? You're proof of her powers. She could wheel you out every Sunday.'

Katy shook her head. 'This is all I know.' She glanced around the shabby room. 'I won't fit in there anymore. As soon as people find out what I've been doing, they'll run me out of town.'

'Rubbish. Dover is full of misfits and loonies. You'll fit right in. Anyway, who's gonna tell them? You can just make up some story. Come on.' She went over to the wardrobe, threw open the door and took out the emerald green dress Katy had been wearing the night before and held it up to herself. 'Nice colour, love, but really?' She pulled out another similar dress, this one in blue, and wrinkled her nose. 'You won't be needing these anymore.'

Suddenly Katy was too exhausted to protest. Marge had always been good at taking control, and it felt so nice to have someone else make her decisions.

'Put these on.' Marge threw a pair of blue trousers and a brown jersey at her.

While Katy obediently got dressed, Marge found her cardboard suitcase and packed it with the few clothes she had. Then she swept the toiletries and makeup off the dresser on top of that, emptied her underwear drawer, and shut the lid.

'Where are we going?'

'I'm staying in a big house up on the cliffs. Motorbike's outside.'

Katy felt a stirring of excitement. Was this really it? She and her sister were going to go riding off into the sunset together. 'What sort?' she asked.

Marge grinned. 'Excalibur Utility. Just like Dad's. And no, you can't drive.' She marched to the door and opened it. A man stood there, his hand raised to knock. Middle-aged and portly, he was wearing a suit and tie, and had a white moustache, stained yellow with nicotine.

'Ellen?' he said, taking in Marge's uniform. 'Are we playing dress-up tonight?' He smiled, running a tongue over his lips.

'We're not playing anything. Get out.' Marge pushed him in the chest.

He frowned, while Katy flattened herself against the wall, hoping he wouldn't notice her.

'Hang on, you're not Ellen. Where is she?'

'Ellen doesn't exist. And I said get out.' Marge pushed him more forcefully. 'And don't ever come back, you pervert!'

A door opened along the corridor and a girl poked her head out. 'Keep it down, love.'

Marge advanced on the man as he retreated, his cheeks bright red. 'I mean it. Leave, and don't bother to return. If you do, I'll tell your wife where you get to on a Saturday night!'

Katy peeped around the door, feeling nothing but relief as the man turned and ran down the stairs. Although she'd have to stay away from Woolies from now on.

Marge came back into the room. 'Ugh. Nothing you say will convince me that you'd rather be jumping into bed with *that* than hopping on a motorbike with me. Now come on, let's go.'

Katy laughed, and for the first time in a long time, it felt real. 'Wait one moment.' She went to the corner and wrenched up the floorboard where she kept the tin containing her meagre savings. Holding it up, she rattled it. 'I can pay my own way.'

Marge rolled her eyes, then hesitated a moment. She shut the door.

'I need to tell you something before we go,' she said softly. 'Where we're going . . . Tom Bennett's my superior officer.'

Katy felt sick. She should have known this was too good to be true. 'I saw him the other day. I was going to confront him, but . . . I got scared.'

Marge nodded. 'I swore that I would get back at him for what he did to you. How do you feel about confronting him with me by your side?'

Katy shook her head. 'What's the point? What's done is done.'

'The point is, the man's disgusting. You were bloody fourteen when he seduced you!'

Katy thought about the way he'd eyed up those schoolgirls in the street, the lust in his eyes, and the way he'd manipulated her, and sighed. 'I think it's best I stay here then.'

Outside in the hallway a shriek of laughter made them jump, it was accompanied by the low rumble of a male voice. The door next to Katy's opened and soon the bedsprings started to squeak, the headboard thumping against the thin wall.

Marge looked at her and raised an eyebrow. 'I can see why you'd hate to leave.'

Katy's smiled, but then she sobered. 'How can I stay in the same place as him? Won't you get in trouble?'

Marge shrugged. 'Maybe. But I have a plan.' Then she grinned wickedly. 'And once I've got you safe, we will bring that man down.' She held out her hand, and Katy took it, feeling a weight lift off her chest.

The future was still uncertain, but for the first time in years she felt a little burst of hope in her chest.

# Chapter 53

*Casualty Hospital*

The telegram was sitting in her pigeonhole when Dot went for her break, and she stared at it for a long time before picking it up. If the worst had happened, she wasn't sure whether it was better to know now or allow herself a few more hours of blissful ignorance.

But there would be no peace until she knew what it said, so she took it to the garden where she and Bert used to meet to go over the sporting fixtures for the week. This was the place where their friendship had grown and where her love for him had blossomed and taken root. Bert had later confessed it was the place he fell in love with her too.

Outside, she barely noticed the cold wind that whipped through the branches of the trees, nor the vegetable patch and the abandoned Nissen hut at the bottom of the garden.

Sitting down on the top step that led down to the garden, she ripped open the envelope. The message was brief.

*Whatever you hear, keep the faith and I will find a way to come back to you. I promise.*
*Bert xx*

Dot stared at it transfixed trying to work out what he meant. There were two possible explanations: the first was that Bert was about to embark on something dangerous. The other was that he'd run away from the Commandos – her heart leapt with hope at the thought. But reason soon came rushing back. He would never do that. Not when he was so hell-bent on proving himself to everyone.

She ran her finger over the words, wishing she could sense his mood when he'd dictated this through the paper. Though she cherished any communication from him, she almost wished he hadn't sent it. Because now she'd be unable to think of anything else.

Holding the paper against her chest, she looked up into the grey sky. 'God, please spread over Bert your shelter of peace, and let him rise again. God, please spread over Bert your shelter of peace, and let him rise again.' It was the prayer of protection her mother used to whisper to her and her brothers each night.

Over and over again she said it, barely noticing the tears that soaked her cheeks. Finally, she buried her head in her lap, wiping her face on her skirt, and whispered a final plea. 'Please, just come home safe.'

She longed to talk to Lily, but her friend had enough to worry about. She couldn't forget the scene she'd witnessed with Colonel Mason. It was frustrating to watch her suffer and be unable to do a thing about it.

It worried her to see Lily looking so defeated, and she knew that the colonel wasn't the only reason for it. The lack of contact from Charlie was also making her feel insecure and uncertain. But no matter what Lily believed, Dot could remember the way they had been together, their luminous happiness . . .

There was no way Charlie had abandoned her. Had she told Lily this though?

She realised with shame that she hadn't. It was past time that she put their friendship back on an even keel. And to do that she had to talk to her properly. About Bert, about Charlie, and about the colonel.

Lily slumped wearily at a table in the canteen. She was still reeling from her encounter with Colonel Mason and his unwelcome letter. Why did men just not *listen* when a woman said no. She put her head in her hands, contemplating the murky surface of her tea. It was grey and greasy, and with her stomach tight with anxiety, the thought of even one tiny sip of it made her feel sick.

'Are you all right?'

Lily looked up to see Dot. She sat up straighter and plastered a smile on her face. 'Course.'

Dot eyed her sceptically. 'I'm not blind, love.' When Lily didn't answer, she carried on. 'Don't forget, I *know* what's happening with the colonel. You can't keep this to yourself for much longer.'

Lily's sighed and nodded. 'You're right. Especially as he'll soon be mobile, and I don't like to think what he'll do then.'

Dot's lips thinned. 'He won't do anything, cos I'm going to talk to Matron. This has gone on long enough.'

'No.' Lily reached over and grabbed Dot's wrist. 'Please don't say anything. This sort of thing goes on all the time. Soon he'll be gone, and we can all relax.'

'Or I can take over his care. No way he'll fancy me.' Dot smiled.

Lily shook her head. She wouldn't wish the colonel on her worst enemy, let alone one of her closest friends. 'I think he'd

go for anything with a pulse, to be honest. But today I got this.'
She pulled the crumpled letter from her pocket and passed it
to Dot.

Dot read it and threw it on the table. '"One day, when I am
strong again, you and I will meet, and then we shall see . . . Perhaps then your fiancé might not seem quite so attractive." Is he
serious? Compared to Charlie he's a . . . a . . . toad!'

Lily nodded in agreement.

'I can't believe any man could be so blind,' Dot fumed.
'Especially as he's so bloody old!'

'Even if I never saw Charlie again, I would never go out with
a man like him,' Lily agreed. Dot was firing her up, and the
anger felt good.

'Charlie will write, you know.' Dot put a comforting hand
on her arm. 'He's mad about you. If you could just have seen
what I saw when you two were together. You both *glowed*
with love.'

'It doesn't matter! Charlie can go to hell, and so can Mason.
You're right, Dot! If I intend to study to become a doctor one
day, I can't let a stupid *man* intimidate me!'

'What are you going to do?' Dot squealed as Lily pushed
back her chair.

'I'm going to put him in his place!' Lily stood up and
marched out of the canteen, heart pumping, breath coming in
short bursts. Mason wasn't the first man to give her unwanted
attention, and she'd never allowed it to get to her like this
before. She refused to let him do this to her anymore.

She entered the officers' ward and stalked up to the colonel's
bed. He looked up at her in surprise as she drew the curtains
round the bed.

'Nurse Castle.' He smiled smugly. 'Do we require privacy?'

She stood at the side of his bed. 'Not in the way you hope, Colonel. I just wanted to let you know that I'm afraid I won't be able to care for you anymore, so I came to say goodbye.' She smiled sweetly. 'And if you ever approach me again, or write to me, or try to touch me, I will make sure you're in plaster for the rest of your nasty little life.' She picked up the jug of water on his bedside table. 'In the meantime, perhaps this will cool your passions a little.' She poured it into his lap.

Before he had a chance to recover from the shock, Lily threw the curtains back and walked away. Out of the corner of her eye, she noticed one of the other men wink at her, and she grinned back.

She knew there'd be hell to pay with Matron, but she didn't care. As for Charlie . . . she just had to trust in his love. In the meantime, she would work hard and study hard. There was more to life than men, after all.

# Chapter 54

*Abbots Cliff House*

After Marge had left, Rodney reluctantly joined the others in the drawing room. Someone handed him a cup of tea, and he sat down on one of the tatty old sofas, his eyes on the door as he waited for Marge to reappear.

The cushion beside him dipped and a familiar Yardley perfume wafted over him. Though he knew it couldn't be Marge, he still felt a little surge of hope. But it was Becky, the dark-haired woman who'd paired with Marge when they'd demonstrated how to play the game that morning. His shoulders slumped. He shouldn't have let her leave; he knew what she was like once the bit was between her teeth. He leant forward and placed the cup and saucer on the table in front of them.

'Lieutenant Castle, are you all right?' Becky asked.

He turned and smiled. 'Apologies, I have somewhere I need to be.'

She put a hand on her arm. 'If you're looking for Marge then she'll be here soon. She just needs a bit of time alone.'

'I'm not looking for Third Officer Atkinson.'

But the woman just smiled knowingly. 'How do you know her? Bit of a coincidence, the two of you turning up here together. It must be fate.'

A braying laugh suddenly filled the room and they both looked over at Tom Bennett, who stood with a tumbler of whisky in one hand, a cigarette in the other. He frowned. Commander Worthing hadn't been wrong about the man. There was something very off about him.

'Lieutenant Castle?'

He looked back at the woman. 'Is Marge all right, do you think?' he asked.

She shrugged. 'If you don't mind me being blunt, you upset her today. And after what she told us about what Captain Bennett did to her sister, it's no wonder that she's been off since she came here.'

Rodney raised his eyebrows. 'What did he do to her sister?'

'That's for Marge to tell you. But the man's a menace to all women.' Her lip curled as she glared at the captain.

Oblivious to it, the captain gave another loud guffaw of laughter and Becky wrinkled her nose. 'He's not fit to wear the uniform.'

From the little he'd seen of Bennett, and considering Worthing's warning, Rodney had to agree. He looked over at him. From a distance he was still a handsome man, but when you saw him up close, the broken veins in his cheeks and the red nose betrayed exactly what he was: a drunkard well past his prime.

He watched as Emily went up to the captain holding a bottle. She was exceptionally pretty with her blonde hair and big brown eyes – all the men had noticed her, though they'd all tried to pretend they hadn't. She refilled the men's glasses and as she turned away, he saw Captain Bennett's hand reach out and stroke her buttocks. The girl flinched away and glared over her shoulder at him.

'What the—' Rodney stood up, disgust rising within him. 'Captain!' he called. 'May I have a word, sir?' He walked over to him and saluted.

Captain Bennett nodded pleasantly. 'How may I help, Lieutenant?'

Rodney led him over towards the window, then bending his head low, he said, 'I feel it's only fair to warn you that if I see you lay your hands on any of the women again, I will be forced to report you.'

Captain Bennett rocked back on his feet. 'Have you gone mad, Castle? May I remind you that I am your superior, and if I choose I could have you out of here and demoted so fast you won't even have time to shit.'

He could see exactly why Marge hated him, but had she had to put up with his unwanted advances too? A cold anger started inside him at the thought of this man touching her. 'I should warn you, *sir*, that I was asked to keep my eye on you and report any unseemly behaviour. And I assure you, I will have no hesitation in doing so. Furthermore, I will be talking to each of the women before we leave to find out exactly what their experience with you has been. Sir.'

Then he turned and left the room. He couldn't sit here and play nice with this lot anymore. Especially as he had a horrible feeling that Marge's non-appearance could only mean one thing: she'd gone to Folkestone. But it was over an hour's walk and in the pitch black, anything could happen. She could be run over, she could be attacked, she could even now be lying in a ditch with a broken ankle. Christ, where the hell was she?

She'd left him to go into the kitchen, so he'd start his search there. Knocking on the door briefly, he went inside. Mrs Benson was standing at the stove mashing potatoes. There was an unpleasant smell of boiled cabbage in the air, and a large pie of some sort sat on the kitchen table, the pastry pale and sunk in the middle. It made him suddenly long for the café, and Marianne's crisp pastry.

The woman turned her head. 'Dinner will be ready in a jiffy. So be a love an' tell that lot to get their arses into the dinin' room.' She turned back to her task.

Rodney was taken aback. She reminded him a lot of his mother, and he felt another surprising pang of homesickness. 'Have you seen Third Officer Atkinson?' he asked. 'The red-haired one?'

She looked at him sharply. 'Nope,' she said, then turned back to the potatoes.

Rodney could tell she was lying. 'Did she, by any chance, ask you to help her with some directions?'

Mrs Benson didn't even look at him this time.

'I'm worried she's gone to Folkestone. It's a long walk, she doesn't know the town that well, and she could get into trouble.'

The woman dropped the masher into the pan and turned. 'She's fine. Lent her my Benny's bike. She were 'appy as a lark ridin' off on that. Now, if you could get everyone into the dinin' room, the sooner I can get this lot on the table, the sooner I can clear off to bed.'

Rodney wanted to groan with frustration. She'd gone riding a bloody motorbike to Folkestone in the pitch black? If anything, this made him more worried, but realising he'd get no more out of the woman, he left to do as he was told.

The meal was as unappetising as it had smelt, and as soon as it was finished, Rodney excused himself and went outside where he began to pace up and down the driveway, his ears straining for the sound of a motorbike engine.

It felt like hours before he heard a faint putt-putt and he jogged to the end of the drive and looked down the track to the main road, holding his breath in anticipation. Finally, the noise grew louder, and he saw the faint light of a bicycle lamp coming towards him.

Soon the bike turned into the driveway, and if the driver noticed him, they didn't slow down until they stopped by the house. Rodney crept forward, squinting to try to see if it was Marge. And then he heard her voice and he let out a sigh of relief.

'Marge!' he called, hurrying over. 'Where the hell have you been? I told you to wait until tomorrow! You could have been killed!'

He could smell her now: cigarettes and Yardley, and he reached out to touch her.

'Christ, Rodney. Did anyone ever tell you not to creep up on women in the dark?'

He could see the dim shape of her, and he grabbed what he hoped was her arm. 'I mean it, dammit! I said to wait!'

'Katy, love, you remember Rodney?' Her tone was dry. 'He seems to be under the impression that he's our father.' She shook his arm away and Rodney turned his head to see someone else standing there. 'It really was you, Katy?' he asked softly.

'Long time no see, Rodney,' Katy responded.

'It really was her. Now if you could just sod off, we need to find her somewhere to stay out of sight of that evil bastard.' He could hear her footsteps heading for the steps that led down to the basement door. She tapped on it, and it opened, but before they could disappear inside, he leapt down and pushed into the tiny hallway.

'For God's sake!' Marge muttered.

'What evil bastard?' he asked.

The door shut behind him, and Mrs Benson turned on the light. Rodney stared between Marge and Katy in astonishment. When he'd seen Katy before, she'd been wearing a lot of makeup and a tight dress. The woman in front of him had black streaks of mascara down her cheeks and in the harsh light of the bulb he could see she was paler and thinner than Marge. But the hair . . .

'Katy,' he breathed. 'I'm sorry I didn't recognise you last night.'

The woman looked at him and smiled sadly. 'Seeing as you'd probably forgotten I existed, I don't blame you.'

Shame flooded through him. It was the truth. After ten years away, he'd not thought once about Marge's sister.

'Right then, mister,' Mrs Benson said briskly. 'This has nothing to do with you, so git.' She turned out the light and opened her front door. And Rodney had no choice but to walk back out into the cold.

# Chapter 55

After she'd shut the door, Mrs Benson turned to Marge and Katy, and grinned. 'Well, anyone with half a brain can see that you two are related. So, what's the plan?'

'I'm going to take her to Dover tomorrow. But . . .'

Mrs Benson smiled knowingly. 'She needs somewhere to hide tonight?'

Katy's eyes flicked to Marge. 'I don't want to put you out. I don't know why I came, really.'

'You came because you've got me now. You don't need to do that stuff anymore.'

Mrs Benson regarded her seriously. 'She's right you know, love. It ain't no life. You got a chance to get out, then I say, take it.'

Marge looked at the housekeeper in surprise. 'You sound like you speak from experience, Mrs B.'

Mrs Benson winked. 'We've all got our secrets, love. So, if you need to kip here, I can offer you the sofa.'

Katy nodded gratefully. 'Thank you so much.' She turned to Marge. 'But just so you know, sis, I'm perfectly capable of running my own life after this.'

'Cos you've done such a great job so far,' Marge responded irritably, then instantly regretted it.

Katy's eyes glittered. 'Don't you go all holier than thou! Just thank your lucky stars you've never been in my position!'

Marge put her hand on Katy's shoulder. 'I'm sorry, that was uncalled for.'

'Yes, it was. You can't control me, Marge.'

Marge looked away guiltily. Maybe she was being a tiny bit controlling, but she was terrified of losing her again. If she had her way, she'd never let Katy out of her sight again.

Mrs Benson tutted. 'Sisters! Can't live with 'em, can't live without 'em. Now, let's get you a cuppa and then I'll sort out some blankets and a towel. And if you're hungry, I've got some steak and kidney left over from dinner. Thought they'd gobble the lot but seems they weren't keen.' She cackled. 'Can't imagine why.'

Marge raised her eyebrows. 'Do you make it horrible deliberately?' she asked.

'Like I said, we all got our secrets.' She laughed and disappeared through the door into her flat.

Marge turned to Katy and took her hands. 'You promise you won't run off?'

Katy nodded. 'Where would I go? You've basically taken my life away.'

'That wasn't a life, love. That was existence.' But she was worried. She was pretending there'd be no trouble finding Katy somewhere to live, but Dover was stuffed with servicemen and women, every available spare room taken. As for the café, with the new baby, the place was full as well. Mr Wainwright might help, but she couldn't see Katy wanting to stay there . . .

'You don't have to find me somewhere to live, you know. I've got a bit of money. I can go back to London.'

'No!'

'Did you hear me earlier! It's *my* life, Marge!' Katy stamped her foot.

Mrs Benson poked her head out of the door. 'Gawd's sake, you two. Enough. I'll look after 'er tonight. Meantime, you better get back to that lot. The captain's been askin' for ya.'

Katy paled and looked towards her. 'What'll you say?' she whispered. 'You won't . . .'

Marge pulled her into a hug. 'That man will never go near you again. I'll see you tomorrow, love, all right? You, me and Reenie will go to Dover together. You remember my mate, Reenie?'

Katy frowned. 'Curly blonde hair?' she asked. 'A sister called June? She was a right cow.'

'That's the one. June died years ago, though.' She gave her one last squeeze. 'I love you, Katy. I never stopped loving you.'

Her sister squeezed her back, her shoulders shaking.

Dropping her arms reluctantly, Marge went upstairs to the kitchen. The evening had been a whirlwind, and she was finding it difficult to take it all in. When she'd woken that morning, she'd been alone in the world with a gaping hole in her heart. But now . . . She wiped her eyes. It was a miracle, and suddenly she felt as light as Princess Ellen herself, ready to float off into the sky.

She opened the kitchen door and was surprised to find Rodney sitting at the table. He stood and held out his arms to her, and she felt no hesitation in running into them. He clasped her tightly, holding her head against his shoulder as she sobbed into it, soaking the thick wool.

'What did Captain Bennett do to Katy?' he murmured against her hair. 'Becky mentioned something.'

Marge sighed. 'He seduced her when she was fourteen, got her pregnant, then abandoned her.'

'Why did you never tell me?' he asked

Marge shook her head. 'My parents didn't know the details, but they never told anyone she'd run away. It was as if they couldn't admit that she was gone, so they invented a life for her – a life they hoped she was living. But it couldn't have been further from the truth.'

The door burst open and they jumped away from each other. Becky stood there with a knowing look on her face. 'Captain Bennett was asking for you, so I told him you had the squits.' She grinned. 'That shut him up. As for you' – she pointed at Rodney – 'whatever you said to Captain Bennett it's put the wind up him. He's been sitting on his own with a whisky bottle since dinner.' She grinned. 'And may I suggest, if you two want a bit of privacy, maybe find a room.' She smirked and left.

Marge shuffled awkwardly. 'I'm exhausted and I need to go to bed. Questions will have to wait till tomorrow. Come back to Dover with me and Katy tomorrow?'

'Wherever you go, Marge, I'll follow. Forever.'

She stared into his eyes. 'You've said something similar to me before, Rod. And you lied.'

He shook his head. 'The only lie I told you was when I said I didn't feel anything for you but desire.' He looked at her intently.

Marge averted her gaze. It was everything she'd ever wanted to hear, but her heart was too sore and her head too full of the events of the past few hours.

He put his arms around her again. 'I understand if you don't trust me. But I swear I'll prove myself to you. And I'll keep on proving it for the rest of my life if you'll let me.'

She pulled away. 'I can't think about all this now, Rod. I've just found my sister. I thought I was alone, and I'm not.' She felt the hot sting of tears at the back of her throat again. She wasn't sure whether they were happy or sad – maybe both.

'I know, love. I know.' His voice was so tender that she buried her head in his chest again.

They stood for a long time in silence, before he said quietly, 'I've let you down, Marge. I will never forgive myself. But I'm never going to let you down again. So I need you to tell me everything you know about Captain Bennett.'

Marge wiped her eyes and stepped away. 'What do you want to know?'

'If you and Katy are in trouble, you must know I'll do anything I can to help.'

Marge hesitated. But Rodney was looking at her with such tenderness and warmth and the thought of leaning on someone when she'd felt so alone for so long was irresistible. 'Not here. Let's go out.'

She opened the kitchen door and after looking both ways to ensure no one was in the entrance hall, she grabbed a couple of coats from the hook by the door. Beckoning him to follow, she stepped outside.

Before they went any further, they shrugged on the coats, and Rodney took her hand. The weight and warmth of it was comforting. He'd always had the power to make her feel safe. Even when she hated him, something about his wide shoulders and perfectly pressed uniform made her feel that she could always lean on him.

But, of course, she couldn't, no matter what he said. He was just a man; no one had the power to keep her safe except herself. And she mustn't forget it.

At the end of the drive, by silent agreement, they turned right towards the sound mirror. Above them the sky was bright with stars and a half-moon hung over the sea, its reflection shimmering in the water.

'Thought you might like to tell me how this thing works,' Marge said, when they reached the huge structure. She sat down on the lip of the concrete, and Rodney sat beside her.

'I'd rather you tell me everything about Captain Bennett,' he said. He put his arm around her, drawing her close against his shoulder and brushed a kiss over her hair.

It reminded her of how she'd imagined Rodney sitting beside her when she first came here – and how she'd decided to give him another chance. She turned towards him. 'It was the summer I turned thirteen and Katy was fourteen,' she began.

When she'd finished, Rodney drew in a deep breath. 'That bastard,' he muttered. 'Commander Worthing warned me about him, and tonight I saw him feel up Emily's bottom.'

Marge stiffened. 'I knew he'd go for her! He likes them young. But what can we do? How can I prove any of this? Unfortunately, feeling up a woman is not going to get a man sacked. If it did, there'd be no one left to fight this bloody war.'

'It can't be that bad,' Rodney said.

'Can't be—? You've got to be joking, Rod! Do you never speak to your sisters? And there's *nothing* we can do about it! In fact, men think they're doing us a favour! We're expected to be *flattered*!' She stood up. 'And that's why the captain thinks this sort of behaviour is his *right*! Seducing schoolgirls, feeling up any woman who comes within reach, we're all fair game for him. Katy was fourteen when they met! It's not even legal, but no one would care! In fact, they'd probably blame her, call her a whore and say she was asking for it!' Marge wanted to scream at the injustice of it all. Her sister had lived a life pandering to men like Bennett because that's all she thought she could do after he'd warped her when she was so young.

'Like I said, Commander Worthing told me to keep my eye on him, so clearly someone wants to do something.'

Marge stared out towards the sea, allowing the beauty of the moonlight rippling across the water to calm her. 'How can we get proof, though?' She thought for a while. 'You know, when he met me at Dover station, he said he'd just picked some stuff up. I saw a torchlight bobbing along the cliff path on my first night as well. Do you think he was coming here?'

'I almost forgot! I saw him coming out of the hut carrying a box. I was going to come back to have a look, but something distracted me.' He nudged her shoulder.

'He told us it contained top secret equipment,' Marge said. 'But I think he's lying.'

'Well, there's only one way to find out.' Rodney pulled out his torch and went to examine the hut. Then, handing the torch to Marge, he took a penknife from his pocket and started to fiddle with it.

'Such a good Boy Scout,' Marge said. 'Always prepared.'

He turned and flashed her a smile, and Marge's heart stopped. She'd promised herself that she'd give him one more chance, but who was she kidding? Rodney would have as many chances as he needed. She'd probably still be giving him chances when they were in their eighties. She was well and truly stuffed.

The lock clicked and Rodney opened the door.

Marge followed him inside, shining the torch around the small space. A few boxes were piled against a wall, and she knelt to open one.

Pulling the flaps apart, she shone the torch on the contents. 'I might have known it,' she said. 'Dirty magazines. Is this enough to get him sacked?'

Rodney had opened another, smaller box and he let out whistle. 'I don't know about those ones, but these will.'

She stepped over to him and looked down. 'Oh my God . . .' She felt sick. The box was full of pictures of young girls and boys mostly naked and in suggestive poses. Some of them couldn't have been more than ten, others looked a little older, their bodies just budding into adulthood.

Rodney closed the box. 'Let's not touch anymore. I'm going to phone Worthing.'

'That filthy bastard! I hope he rots in hell,' she muttered as they stepped out of the hut.

'I can't promise that, but I can promise they'll have to find you a new commanding officer.'

He shut the door and turned her towards him, lifting her chin with a finger. 'Whatever it takes, love, we'll see that he pays for what he did to Katy, and no doubt to a whole host of other young girls – and boys, if those pictures are anything to go by.'

Then his lips came down on hers, and all the fear and loneliness seemed to melt away. Even the evidence of the captain's perversions seemed to disappear as Marge allowed herself to give in to the love that had never gone away.

They were breathless when they pulled apart. 'I'm sorry. After what we've just seen . . .' Rodney murmured.

Marge put a finger to his lips. 'This is *nothing* like that.'

He touched his forehead to hers. 'I know,' he whispered. 'This is love. Tell me you feel it too.'

Marge nodded. 'Rodney, after you've made that phone call . . . you know what Becky said?'

'Which bit?' But she could hear the tautness in his voice; he knew exactly what she was referring to.

'That we should find a room . . .' She left it hanging for a moment, and when he still didn't speak, she said, 'I believe you might have just the place.'

'Are you sure, love?' he whispered.

'Oh yes. I'm very sure. We've waited far too long, and we might not get another chance.'

They kissed again, but briefly this time. Then Rodney grabbed her hand, and they jogged back to the house.

# Chapter 56

*Castle's Café*

Sometime in the middle of the night, Nellie woke with a start, her stomach in knots. She'd fallen asleep fully dressed, sitting up against the pillows, the gun on her lap.

Outside, it was eerily quiet, and Nellie couldn't help thinking it was the calm before the storm. She reached for her glass of water and took a few gulps trying to soothe the dryness in her throat.

She could hear Jasper moving about in the sitting room and the low murmur of voices. Switching on her bedside lamp, she saw that it was 3.30 a.m. She got up and checked her appearance in the mirror. She hadn't put her curlers in, so her hair was flat and lifeless, and more grey than chestnut. When had that happened? Her eyes looked no better. She pulled her skin back, smoothing the wrinkles. These last few years had aged her. It was all downhill from here.

She opened the drawer of her dressing table and took out a small parcel tied with a blue ribbon. She'd thought long and hard about this present, and in truth she couldn't afford it, but she'd wanted to make a gesture. She and Jasper hadn't got back to the closeness they'd shared that drunken night in the

Oak before they went to London for the trial. But things had changed. They'd both made mistakes – granted, hers were far greater than his – but maybe it was time to try to heal some of those old wounds. She looked back up at her image – her pale, wrinkled face, her grey hair, her tired eyes. Would he really still want her? She wasn't the woman he'd fallen in love with all those years ago. But then, he wasn't the same man either. Love tricked you into seeing only the face you first knew. And when she looked at Jasper, she still saw the blond giant with the kind eyes and wide smile. The man she should have chosen. She sighed heavily. She'd made so many mistakes in her life, but perhaps that was the biggest of all.

She put the package back in the drawer and shut it. She'd give it to him when this was over. In the meantime, they'd been told to carry on as normal, and in a few hours, they would have to start preparing for the party. Ordinarily, the thought of having her friends and neighbours here, the whole place bustling with excitement, would have delighted her. But with this threat hanging over them, all she felt was dread.

She picked up the gun. It weighed heavily in her hand, the metal glinting menacingly in the lamplight. Would she really be able to use it? She closed her eyes, fighting the memories of that snowy December day; Donald screaming at her, the loud report, the shock as she stared at the blooming stain on the wall . . .

She shuddered and put it in her pocket. Jasper and Mr Wainwright were just outside the door, and that ludicrously young man was downstairs, but she still needed to be prepared.

She went out into the sitting room. Jasper was on the sofa, his white hair standing around his head like a lion's mane, his eyes bloodshot. Mr Wainwright was on one of the dining room chairs, his glasses on the table beside him, making his face look strangely vulnerable.

'Mornin', everyone. Is Lily home?' Nellie asked.

Jasper nodded. 'Came in at midnight. I explained what was goin' on, and she just nodded and went to bed. Is she all right? She looked . . . strange.'

Nellie shrugged. 'Cissy said someone's been botherin' her at work. Once this is over, I'll winkle it out one way or another. Anything happenin' down there?'

'Ain't been a peep all night. It's almost eerie how quiet it is.'

'I'll make us some tea.' She went into the small kitchen across the hall, taking comfort from the familiar ritual. Before taking the tray into the sitting room, she crept downstairs to the café. A torch beam came on. 'Cup of tea?' she whispered. Peter Holmes's eyes were alert behind his glasses. Oh, to be young, she thought as she put the cup and saucer on the table beside his gun and walkie-talkie.

He nodded his thanks, then gestured for her to leave.

Upstairs, she handed out the tea then sat in her armchair, listening to the carriage clock on the mantelpiece tick the seconds away.

Outside, the silence persisted. Not even the tweet of an early bird, or a gust of wind. It made Nellie nervous. Dover was a noisy place: if it wasn't the gulls, it was the wind, if not the wind, it was the traffic. But this morning, it felt like they might be the only people alive on earth.

Jasper sat up straighter suddenly, reaching for his gun. Nellie's stomach flipped. 'What?' she asked, her voice unintentionally loud.

He put his finger to his lips.

Her gaze flew to Mr Wainwright, who was frowning in concentration.

And then she heard it too.

A click. Jasper rose and turned off the lights, and they waited in the darkness, their ears straining.

Another click.

She could sense, rather than hear, Jasper moving into the hallway. Mr Wainwright stood and followed him. Nellie, however, felt frozen in her chair, the gun weighing heavily in her pocket.

Upstairs she heard Teddy start to cry and she held her breath as she listened to Marianne's voice murmuring to him. Don't come downstairs, she thought desperately.

But she knew it was only a matter of time.

She heard the basement door squeak downstairs, and stuffed her fist into her mouth to stop herself from yelping in alarm. The tension in the room was so thick, it was suffocating.

And then Teddy let out a scream so loud it could wake the dead. He had a strong pair of lungs on him, and he was putting them to good use at exactly the wrong time.

Suddenly a gunshot rang out downstairs, followed by the crash of a chair falling over. Was that young man lying dead on her café floor?

Jasper moved quickly after that, hurrying down the stairs before Nellie could tell him to stop.

And then all hell broke loose.

# Chapter 57

*Abbots Cliff House*

Through the open curtains, Marge stared out of the window. The stars glistened like frost as the moon made its slow progress across the navy sky.

Beside her in the narrow single bed, Rodney lay on his stomach, one arm thrown across her, his nose buried in her hair, effectively trapping her in place. Not that she wanted to be anywhere else.

For the first time in years, Marge felt that she was exactly where she was meant to be. The night had been impossibly perfect, and she didn't want sleep to bring an end to it. She made a mental inventory of her blessings: the heat of Rodney's arm slung casually across her chest. The prickle of his hairy leg entwined with hers. His breath, calm and even, whispering over her skin. And downstairs, even more miraculous still, her sister . . .

And watching over all of it, a sky so vast and beautiful that she almost believed in God.

She clasped Rodney's hand where it lay on her chest. Soon, the realities of war would come crashing back, but right here, right now, life was perfect. She sighed contentedly.

As soon as they'd got back to the house, Rodney had called his commander at the castle and been told the Royal Marine Police would be with them the next morning. She could hardly believe it had been so easy. She'd go down early to make sure Katy could witness Thomas Bennett get his comeuppance. And then they'd go back to Dover.

The only sadness was that her parents weren't alive to see this day. So she whispered it out loud, hoping that somewhere in the infinite blue, they'd hear her. 'Mum, Dad. Katy's home.'

They were words she'd never thought she'd say. Words that, just yesterday, had seemed utterly impossible.

Rodney stirred beside her, releasing her hair, and she turned onto her side, away from the window, and pulled him to her. He raised his head sleepily, and she pressed her lips to his, relishing the curve of his smile.

'Can we do it again?' she whispered.

Rodney needed no further encouragement, as he rolled on top of her, deepening their kiss.

Before she succumbed completely to her desire, Marge sent one final thought into the sky. *I'm in love with a naval officer, Mum. Like mother, like daughter.*

'It's time, darling.' Rodney's lips were against her ear, and her eyes blinked open. The curtains were shut, the bedside light on, and his beautiful blue eyes were gentle as they gazed into hers.

She stretched her arms above her head. 'Time for one more?' she asked hopefully.

Rodney chuckled. 'If only.'

She could feel his hardness pressed against her leg and she reached her hand down to clasp it. But he jumped away. 'We can't. They'll be here soon. We need to get dressed.'

'You're nothing but a tease.' She threw a pillow at him and lay back, one hand over her eyes, her body thrumming with pleasure.

'Come on, lazybones. You need to get back to your room before anyone knows you spent the night here.'

Somewhere in the house she heard a clock strike five. And just like Cinderella at midnight, the magic of the night evaporated. Soon the RMPs would be here, but what about her and Rod? Did those chimes spell the end for them too?

She sat up and pushed the hair away from her eyes, making a show of looking for her clothes, which were scattered across the floor. Knickers and stockings by the bed, brassiere just beyond that, her skirt, her blouse, her jacket. Like stepping stones leading to the door, away from Rodney.

He seemed to sense her uncertainty, and pulled her round to face him, cupping her face in his hands. 'This is just the beginning, Marge . . . If you still want me?'

'What do you think?' she murmured.

He stared into her eyes. 'Tonight has been perfect, love. But I hope you know that I want so much more than this. I want all of you.' He stroked her hair. 'I want your thoughts.' His fingers drifted to her lips. 'I want your words.' They drifted lower, settling over her left breast. 'I want your heart.'

Marge's breath hitched in her throat, her eyes clouding with tears. 'You've always had them, Rod,' she whispered. 'You just couldn't see it.'

'I see it now. Every glorious inch, every beautiful freckle. Every gasp, every breath. I love you. Always have, always will.'

Her body tingled with happiness, and she wanted nothing more than to stay in this moment. But time was ticking on, and they needed to see this through. 'Once this is over, we'll talk more.'

He laughed, and it sounded different to her. More certain, less restrained. She'd always thought of him as controlled. But he'd proven to be the opposite last night. What must it have taken for him to stay so tightly coiled all his life? She smiled with satisfaction. Now she knew how to make him lose control, she intended to ensure she employed her weapon as frequently as she could.

Jumping off the bed, she gathered her clothes and got dressed. 'Later then,' she said with a wink.

She opened the door cautiously, but everything was silent, so blowing one last kiss at Rodney, she tiptoed to her room, where she grabbed her washbag and towel, and went to wash the night away.

When she returned, Emily had put the light on. 'And where did you get to last night, you little minx?' She grinned slyly.

Marge touched her nose. 'Ask me no questions and I'll tell you no lies.'

Maria sat up. 'Ugh. Look at her, glowing like a bollard. It doesn't take a genius to work out what's put the colour in those cheeks. I take it he knows what he's doing.'

'Oh, he knows *exactly* what he's doing.' She laughed throatily. 'Now, chop-chop, girls. There are shenanigans afoot, and I don't want you to miss the fun!'

'What?'

'Be quick! Gather in the hall in thirty minutes!'

Then she left, running lightly down the stairs and through the kitchen to the basement flat. She burst into the small sitting room where Katy was just a dark shape under some blankets on the sofa.

'Wakey, wakey, rise and shine!' she trilled, turning on the lights.

Katy emerged from her cocoon, blinking in the sudden glare. 'Go away!'

Her eyes were puffy and red, and Marge felt a twinge of guilt. She should have stayed with Katy last night; she should have held her sister while she cried. She dropped down to her knees in front of her and grabbed her shoulders. 'Are you all right, love? I'm sorry I left you.'

'I'm fine. I just don't like bloody mornings. I'm a night owl. You've got to be in my job.'

'Not your job anymore, Katy,' she growled.

'Not your decision, Marge,' Katy responded shortly. 'You sweep in, drag me away from my life, tell me where to stay, what to do . . . What do you expect from me? You want me to fall on my knees in gratitude?'

'No! I just want you to be happy again.'

'Well, it's not going to happen overnight, is it?' Her sister's voice was sharp as vinegar.

Marge sat back on her heels, wondering how best to handle her. Stupidly, she'd expected Katy to be all smiles this morning, excited to start a new life, happy to be reunited with her. But it seemed the opposite was true.

'Well, I'm sorry to have inconvenienced you. How could I have been so stupid as to make you leave your wonderful life!' The words were out before she could stop herself.

'Oh, sod off, Marge.' Katy pulled the blankets over her head.

'I'm sorry. I'm sorry, Katy. But listen. Bennett's about to get his comeuppance and I thought you might want to see it?'

Katy lowered the blanked and peeked over the top at her. 'What?'

Marge nodded. 'Me and Rod . . .' She hesitated, wondering how her sister would feel about this. The memory of what she'd seen in that box came back to her. All those children with empty, haunted eyes. Horrible, disgusting images that she'd never forget.

'Tell me. I won't bloody break!'

So she did. When she'd finished, Katy lay back with a sigh. 'He used to take pictures of me, you know. I thought it was romantic. He'd pose me in all sorts of ways. Once he made me lie in a nightdress in the sea with flowers in my hair. It was a very thin nightdress.' She grimaced. 'I wonder what he did with them.'

Any residual glow from her night with Rodney disappeared. Had he sold pictures of her sister to other men? It seemed more than likely. Marge swallowed back the nausea.

'Well, now he's going to get punished for what he's done. And you need to see it.'

Katy shuddered. 'I don't think I can.'

'You bloody well will do this, Katy! I want you to tell everyone what that man did to you!'

'You want me to expose myself in front of a bunch of strangers! Do you know what you're asking?'

Marge had never considered it like that. How could she have been so blind? This was her sister's story, something raw and painful, and she had no right to expect this of her.

'God, no. I'm sorry, love. No, you don't have to see him if you don't want to. And I won't say a word about you. I promise.' She clasped her sister's shoulders, shaking her slightly. 'You can hide in the kitchen, peek through the window as they take him away. At least see that.'

Katy nodded, her eyes flashing. 'Oh, I'll be watching. And I hope they lock him up and throw away the key.'

Marge breathed a sigh of relief at her fierce expression. This was the sister she remembered. The one with spirit and courage. Whatever happened in the future, whatever path Katy decided to take, she could at least live on her own terms – whether that was in Dover or London. Or anywhere else she fancied.

Katy was right. She had no right to dictate to her. As long as they knew they had each other, that was really all that mattered.

# Chapter 58

*Castle's Café*

The building shook as the front door crashed open downstairs. Gunshots rang out and all Nellie could think about was Jasper running into danger. Upstairs, Teddy's wails grew louder, and Donny burst out of his room, his eyes wild with fear.

'Gran?' he said, his voice trembling.

But Nellie couldn't stop to comfort him, she was too intent on getting to Jasper.

'Jesus, Mum!' Lily was standing on the stairs. 'What's going on?'

Marianne stood behind her, Teddy screaming in her arms, his face bright red. And behind her was Cissy.

'Nellie! Algie! Are you there?' Cissy's high-pitched voice rivalled Teddy's increasingly frantic wails.

'I'm scared!' Donny cried, tears welling in his eyes.

'All of you, get back upstairs!' Mr Wainwright ordered. He put his arm around Donny and urged him towards the stairs. Lily grabbed him, holding him close.

Marianne seemed frozen in place, the only movement Teddy arching his back against her tight grip, his screams escalating.

'Cissy!' Mr Wainwright snapped. 'Get them upstairs. You too, Mrs Castle.'

But Nellie ignored him. Putting her hand in her pocket, she moved to the stairs and breathed a sigh of relief as she saw Jasper's tall figure at the bottom, his back pressed against the wall as he tried to remain hidden.

She watched in horror as he pointed his gun into the kitchen and fired. There was another yell and Jasper hopped back as a bullet slammed into the plaster beside him.

'Get back!' someone shouted.

Nellie ran down the last few steps and grabbed Jasper's collar, pulling hard.

'Do as he says, Jasper. I can't lose you!' She wasn't sure he'd heard what she said, but he retreated a few steps, panting heavily.

Another shout went up. 'They're fucking getting away!'

Figures rushed past the stairs and, she assumed, out of the back door. And suddenly everything went quiet.

'Get back upstairs,' Nellie whispered. 'Look after the others.' In the dim light, Jasper's eyes were glassy with shock. Her heart went out to him. She knew he'd never wanted to fire a gun in anger again. Nor had she. But if she had to she would.

She put her hand in her pocket, clutching the gun, and crept into the kitchen.

It was empty, although a groan from behind her suggested someone was lying injured, but they'd have to wait.

The basement door was hanging off its hinges, and the back door swung open. More shouts and shots came from outside. She dithered for a moment, but the urge to see what was happening was too strong.

From the light shining from the kitchen, she could see a car at the back gate and men crouched around it, pointing guns at it. For a moment she was disorientated. It was years since she'd seen light spilling out of a building, and she was distracted by the sight.

But then the car's engine revved, the men around it shouted for whoever was in the car to stay where they were, and she pulled the door shut, plunging the yard into darkness once more.

With the number of men and guns around, she let go of her own and crept round the side of the yard, keeping close to the wall. When she reached the gate, she switched on her torch, counting on everyone being too distracted to notice her. In the dim light, she could see two figures inside the car. The man in the driving seat's head brushed the roof of the car. Johnny Fox.

There was another shot, and one of the men fell back. Suddenly, unnoticed by everyone but her, a figure crawled through the gate. Nellie pointed the light at it, her heart beating a mad tattoo against her chest.

'Hell's bells!' she gasped.

Lou Carter, wearing her hat and long coat, glanced up at her and winked.

'What the hell is goin' on?' Nellie hissed, bending down and grabbing Lou's hat. Throwing it aside, she grabbed her hair and pulled her face up. 'I thought you'd scarpered.'

Lou grinned. 'I were goin' to. But I couldn't leave me mate in 'ot water, could I?'

The engine revved again and Lou cackled. 'They can rev as much as they like, they ain't goin' anywhere.' She reached into her coat pocket and pulled out a knife. 'Slashed all them tyres to pieces while they was busy lookin' elsewhere.'

A scuffle by the car drew their attention, and in the wobbly light from her torch, Nellie saw Johnny Fox and Francis being wrenched from the car. Someone else opened the boot and started to unload the boxes. Dumping one on the ground, he opened it and pulled out a handful of ration books. He shook them in Johnny's face. 'Take a long breath of this fresh air, mate, cos it's the last you'll be having for a while.'

Johnny Fox sneered at him, but it was sheer bravado. Francis, on the other hand, was snivelling. 'Th-this isn't my fault,' he stuttered. 'He threatened me and my family. I had no choice.'

'Yeah, yeah. You're innocent as a newborn. Save it for the courts.' He wrenched the man's arm and manhandled him back into the café, followed closely by Johnny, whose face was set like stone.

Nellie shivered. She prayed he never got out of prison, because that was the sort of man who held a grudge, and he'd be back here the moment he was let out.

'Ration books?' Lou said, aghast. 'Bloody hell.'

Nellie turned to her. 'Don't tell me you didn't know about their forgin' business.'

Lou tutted. 'I got me fingers in a lot of pies, it's true. I ain't averse to dirty mags – sold a load to a Navy bloke the other week, as it happens – dirty bugger wasn't 'appy when I told 'im I didn't do kiddie stuff.' She shuddered. 'See, I'm a lot of things, Nell. I smuggle tobacco, bit of petrol, bits and bobs like that. Stuff that'll make me a quick profit. But I've got me morals. I don't mess with kiddie stuff, an' I don't do forgery. Ration books! I thought it were impossible to forge the buggers.' She shook her head. 'That's cheatin' the people, that is.'

Nellie didn't bother to tell her that selling black market goods was just as bad, if on a smaller scale. After all, hadn't she benefited herself on occasion. 'I think they sell them,' Nellie remarked. 'So somewhere around there's rich folks with lots of ration books, each registered to a different shop. Mr Wainwright reckons they're worth 'undreds of thousands of pounds.'

Lou whistled. 'You don't say . . . You reckon they missed any?' she asked hopefully.

'Thought you didn't like to cheat people.'

'Well, course not. But just one box of them would take me out of the game for good. Which would mean I'd actually be doin' less cheatin' in the long run. Still, maybe we'll get a reward for helpin' to catch them, eh?' She took out the knife and kissed it. 'Great piece of kit this.'

Nellie started to laugh. 'Bleedin' heck, Lou, you don't 'alf have some balls!'

Lou grinned. 'Does that mean we can be mates again?'

Nellie linked her arm through the other woman's. 'One thing at a time, love. One thing at a time.'

They walked back into the café to find Lily kneeling beside Peter Holmes. To her shame, Nellie had almost forgotten about him, but now she was relieved to see he was alive. Lily was tying a bandage around his upper arm while Cissy, Jasper and Mr Wainwright looked on.

'Will he be all right, love?' Nellie asked.

'Don't worry, Mrs Castle, it's just a scratch,' the man said, though his voice was a little wobbly.

'He'll need to go the hospital, but he'll be fine,' Lily said.

Nellie would have investigated further, but at that moment, Cissy let out a screech.

'What the hell is she doin' here!'

Everyone turned to look at Lou, who shrugged. 'Oh, don't mind me, Ciss. I only saved your bloody bacon by slicin' the blokes' tyres. You can thank me later.'

A cold breeze gusted in and Nellie looked over to the window. 'Oh, for the love of God! They've only gone and cut open the winder.'

The blackout curtains had been torn down, and once again light spilled into the street, the plastic window flapping in the wind.

'I hope there's no bombers out there, Mr Holmes, cos the square's lit up like Christmas. Oh, and I expect your lot to pay for that damage.'

The advantage of having no curtains or window was that she was able to watch as Johnny and Francis were loaded into a car and driven away.

An arm came round her shoulder, and she looked up at Jasper and smiled. 'Happy birthday, love.'

Jasper started to laugh. 'This was all for me? You shouldn't have.'

'What in the name of God's goin' on 'ere?' Ethel Turner, her hair in curlers, a pair of slippers on her feet and a coat hastily thrown around her nightdress, poked her head through the window.

It was only then that Nellie noticed all the other figures in the square. Unsurprising really, given the commotion.

'Anyone fancy a cuppa?' she called. 'You'll need to wrap up though. And if anyone's got any boards they can put over that, you'll get a free meal.' She grinned at the astonished faces lined up along the window frame.

'Well, you never liked this thing, anyway, Nell,' Phyllis Perkins said, flicking the plastic.

'Don't just stand there. Come in, come in!' She gestured towards the door.

The bell above the door rang merrily as her neighbours made their way into the café, most in their nightclothes, although a few who had been returning from fire watching or a nightshift were dressed.

'Mum!' Lily's voice was taut with annoyance. 'It's the middle of the night.'

Nellie glanced at the clock. 'It's five o'clock, love. May as well start the party early.'

'Excuse me!' An ARP warden was peering through the window. 'This is goin' to get you fined, Mrs C.'

Nellie waved her hand at Peter. 'Speak to the ministry.'

'Joe, mate! You gotta be off duty now,' Jasper said jovially. 'Come in and join the party.'

'This 'ere is a breach of all regulations. I can't just let it go.'

Nellie went over and turned out the lights. She felt almost hysterical with relief. They could fine her till the cows came home, and she wouldn't give a stuff. 'Cissy, go get the candles.'

'It's still too much light!'

'Oh, shut your mouth, Joe. Come in and stop bein' such a busybody!' Phyllis said. Beside her, her grandson Freddie's cheeks were pink with excitement.

Nellie's heart swelled. 'Go see Donny, Fred. 'E'll tell you all about it.'

Freddie zoomed past her and went upstairs.

She looked around. Brian Turner was now arguing with Joe, as were Mr Gallacher and Graham Jones from the shoe shop on Cannon Street.

Everyone else was making themselves at home at the tables, and the room rang with laughter. Meanwhile, Lily got Peter Holmes to his feet and guided him upstairs.

Jasper put his arm around her again. 'When it comes to surprise parties, Nell, you really go all out.'

Nellie laughed. 'Anythin' for you, Jasper.'

Then her eyes caught Cissy's. Her cousin was standing by the counter, a smile of relief on her face. She was wearing a long white flannel nightdress printed with yellow daisies, her hair in curlers under a pink net.

Nellie put her hand up to her head and cursed. She'd forgotten about her bloody hair.

'You couldn't get me a hat, could you, Ciss. Me hair's an absolute mess.'

Cissy shook her head at her. 'I swear to God, Nellie Castle, you will be the death of all of us one of these days.'

'But not today, Ciss. Not today.'

Lou sidled up. 'So, am I included in this party, or what?'

Jasper stiffened beside Nellie. She knew he had a few choice words for Lou, but now wasn't the time. Adrenaline was still flowing through her veins, and she felt almost euphoric. She didn't want to spoil that feeling with a row.

'Course you are,' she said, before Jasper could say a word. 'We're all mates 'ere.'

She looked around at the faces, now lit by candlelight. Joe, she noticed, had taken off his helmet and joined the Turners at their table. The door opened just then and Adelaide Frost came in – fully dressed of course!

Nellie braced herself for a lecture, but the woman surprised her when she clapped her hands and said, 'Behold, how good and how pleasant it is for brethren to dwell together in unity!'

Nellie raised an empty teacup. 'Amen to that, Adelaide. Amen to that!'

# Chapter 59


*Abbots Cliff House*

Marge was on tenterhooks as they all gathered in the drawing room waiting for breakfast to be served. They had been told the RMPs would be here at six, but the sky was pink and already the first rays of a winter sun were shooting across the sea. If they didn't arrive soon, they'd have to start the day as normal.

'I heard you had a spot of . . . uh . . . stomach trouble last night, Atkinson.' She jumped as Captain Bennett came up to her. He looked calm and unruffled, though his red-rimmed eyes betrayed the bottle of whisky he'd apparently sunk the night before.

'Apologies for not being here, sir. I was taken ill quite unexpectedly.'

He bent towards her. 'I know you're lying. I went to find you in your room, and there was no sign of you. Don't think your misdemeanour will go unreported. Your days here are numbered, girl.' The mintiness of his toothpaste couldn't disguise the stale alcohol on his breath.

Marge wrinkled her nose. She wanted nothing more than to turn that warning back on him, but she couldn't risk him running away. 'You went into the women's dormitory, sir?'

She opened her eyes wide. 'I am so very grateful for your concern, sir.'

She was conscious of the other officers watching them curiously.

'Don't get smart with me,' he hissed, before turning away.

'Yes, you were missed last night, Atkinson,' Captain Fry said. 'Pretty redheads are few and far between in our line of work, what?' He grinned around at the other men, who laughed dutifully.

The door opened and Mrs Benson stuck her head round. 'Breakfast's about to be served in the dinin' room!' she grunted.

'Where are they?' Marge whispered to Rodney as everyone started to leave the room

'They'll be here. Don't worry.' He put a hand on her arm and smiled reassuringly into her eyes.

'Oh, I see how it is.' They hadn't noticed that Captain Bennett was still there. 'You, sir' – he pointed at Rodney – 'are a hypocrite. And you are a whore.' His lips twisted as he pointed at Marge. 'I shall be reporting you both.' He turned on his heel and left the room.

Heat flooded Marge's cheeks. 'I won't let him get away with that,' she muttered, making a move to follow him.

Rodney held her back. 'Let him go, Marge. Only a few more minutes. Where's Katy?'

'In the kitchen. She doesn't want to face him.'

He nodded. 'I don't blame her.'

'I want to strangle him.' She held her hands up, squeezing an imaginary neck.

'I know, love. As do I. But you have to control yourself.'

'Urgh.' She shrugged him off. But then she smiled slowly. 'I always hated your control, Rod. But now I know you're not as controlled as you make out.' She ran a hand down his chest. 'How do you manage it?'

His breath hitched. 'Only you can make me lose it. Only you, love.' He glanced quickly at the door to check it was shut, then dropped a quick kiss on her lips. 'Later.' He breathed the word against her mouth, then he straightened his jacket and sauntered to the door, leaving Marge tingling with frustration and lust.

Emily poked her head around the door. 'You look like the cat that got the cream.' She winked. 'That man is glorious. If you ever grow sick of him, chuck him in my direction will you.' She shivered. 'All that protective manliness has really got me going.'

Marge laughed. 'Not a chance, love. He's all mine.'

Linking her arm through the younger woman's, they walked out of the door. Mrs Benson was crossing the hallway pushing a hostess trolly containing various covered dishes.

'Sausage à la fag ash today, Mrs B?' Marge laughed.

'My speciality, love.' She cackled as she continued through to the dining room.

'You go on, Emily. I'm just popping to the loo.'

Once Emily had disappeared, Marge put her head round the kitchen door. Katy, wearing the same slacks and jumper as the night before, was sitting at the table, biting her nails. Marge's heart melted. Katy's nail-biting had driven their mother to distraction. And now it reminded her that for all her hard edges, she was still the same girl.

'Fingers out!' she said sharply.

Katy jumped and put her hands rigidly by her side, then laughed. 'I promise I don't do it normally,' she said with a sad smile. 'I broke the habit eventually. When are they coming?'

'Soon, love. Just sit tight.'

Marge went back into the dining room and sat down at the table. She put a piece of soggy toast on her plate, but she had no appetite. She glanced up at Rodney, but he was speaking to one of the other men, studiously ignoring Captain Bennett, who was glaring at him.

And then, finally, there was a loud banging on the door. While everyone else stopped talking, Marge and Rodney leapt to their feet, almost colliding as they tried to get out of the door.

'Third Officer Atkinson, Lieutenant Castle, if you don't mind.' Captain Bennett threw his napkin onto the table and stood up. 'I am the commanding officer here, so I will open the door.'

They stood aside to let him through. On the opposite side of the hall, the kitchen door opened and Katy stood there, her eyes fixed on Bennett.

Marge gasped in surprise. There was a determined set to her sister's mouth and a gleam of malice in her eye. Had she changed her mind?

Bennett stopped mid-stride and stared at her. Then he looked at Marge. Then back at Katy. 'What the hell is going on? Who is this woman?'

'Oh, I think you know,' Marge said.

Captain Bennett moved towards Katy, who stood her ground, arms folded tightly, her eyes narrowed. 'You don't scare me anymore, Tom. I wasn't sure I could face you, but then ... Well, I couldn't miss this.' She looked over at Marge and smiled tightly.

'What nonsense is this? This is *your* doing, isn't it, Atkinson?' His head whipped round to look at her and Marge was gratified to see the panic in his eyes.

'I believe it was *your* doing, sir.' Her eyes flew to Katy's, and she raised her eyebrows in silent question.

Katy nodded.

'You don't have to do this, Katy,' Marge said.

'I do. I've been thinking a lot about what you said. And a lot about my life. I've spent too long being scared. Too long hiding, too long pandering to men. It ends here.' Her gaze switched to Bennett.

'Wh-what is she talking about?' Bennett blustered.

Behind him, Rodney had opened the door. A man in a navy blue uniform came in first and Rodney saluted. 'Commander Worthing, sir.'

The man nodded and stood aside as four royal marine policemen entered. Dressed in the khaki uniform of the marines, they glanced at Worthing who indicated Bennett. 'This is the man, gentlemen. Arrest him.'

Captain Bennett blustered. 'How dare you, sir!'

'Silence, Bennett!' he snapped. Then he turned to Rodney. 'The evidence?'

'This way, sir.' He went outside, followed by Worthing, who glanced over his shoulder at the policemen. 'Hold him until I return.'

Then he was gone.

'I say,' Captain Fry stuttered. 'What on earth is going on?'

Marge looked at Katy who stepped forward. Though she was pale, she looked resolute. 'You might recognise me, gentlemen.'

They looked at her in bemusement.

'I believe you came to the Rose Rooms the other night. I was there at the bar. Green satin dress, high heels.'

The men stared at her, mouths dropping open.

The girls came to stand beside Marge. 'Is that your *sister*?' Maria whispered. 'I thought you said she was dead?'

'I thought she was,' Marge said. 'But shh. Listen.'

'Perhaps you'd like to know how I ended up there?' Her eyes raked over them. 'Or would that make you uncomfortable? I presume you have wives, mothers, daughters, sisters . . . All respectable women, brought up under the protection of their menfolk.' She smiled thinly. 'How lucky for them.'

Captain Bennett was standing stiffly in the grasp of the policemen, his Adam's apple bobbing as he swallowed convulsively.

'Tom, here, has a lovely wife and daughter. Did you know? I imagine his daughter is about my age. Maybe a bit younger. Unfortunately for me, my path crossed with this man's when I was fourteen. Such a funny age for a girl. I was a child, but I thought I was an adult. Tom liked me *very* much. So much, in fact, that he made me all sorts of promises. Didn't you, love?' She walked up to him. 'Goodness, I thought I was the luckiest girl in the world. Even though I knew you were married . . . But then I fell pregnant.'

The men stared at Bennett in shock. 'I say, Bennett. Is this true?'

Bennett didn't answer.

'Yes, it's true. He said we should run away to London. He gave me the money, said he'd meet me there. Can you guess what happened, gentlemen?'

There was a dead silence in the hallway. Mrs Benson had opened the kitchen door and was leaning against it, smoking, an inscrutable look on her face.

'That's right, he never turned up. There I was, fifteen by then, pregnant, too ashamed to go home. What's a girl to do?'

The men looked deeply uncomfortable.

'In the end, I let another load of filthy bastards carry on where Tom had left off. Oh, they loved me with my child's face and my swollen belly. Such a naughty combination, don't you think? But at least this time they paid me.' She walked over and spat in Tom Bennett's face. 'Your son died,' she said. Then she turned and walked back into the kitchen.

Marge hurried after her.

Katy was standing by the door, her face in her hands, her shoulders shaking. Marge put her arms around her and held her close. 'You were magnificent,' she whispered.

'I don't feel magnificent,' Katy sobbed. 'I feel ashamed. I feel dirty. I wish . . . Oh, I wish I'd never met him.'

'I know, love. I know.' Helpless to do anything else, Marge tightened her arms around her sister.

Outside, she could hear a man's voice. 'Is this true, Bennett? Good God, man! My daughter is fourteen! She wears knee socks and bows in her hair. Hanging is too good for men like you.'

The kitchen door opened, and Mrs B and the other girls came in. 'Oh my God, is that true?' Emily cried. She marched over and pulled Katy out of Marge's arms. 'You poor thing, you've been through absolute hell. But look at you now! Triumphant! A phoenix rising from the ashes! The look on his face!' She started to laugh.

Katy stared at her for a moment. 'You don't think it's my fault?'

Becky patted her shoulder. 'Don't be so bloody stupid! This is all his doing. And you did what you had to do. Until we've been there, who are we to judge?'

These girls, Marge thought proudly. Captain Roberts really knew how to pick a good team!

'Right then. That's done. Another cup of tea, anyone?' Mrs B filled the kettle and put it on the stove.

Rodney popped his head round the door. 'Do you want to see him taken away?' he asked Katy with a grin.

'Why's he being arrested?' Maria asked as they crowded back into the hall.

Commander Worthing came in, his expression grim. 'Captain Bennett is a disgrace to the Navy. He has been selling child pornography to a newsagent in town.'

'What?' Captain Fry fell back. 'Kiddie porn. By God, man, you are nothing more than filth.' He walked up to him and slapped him round the face. 'I hope we never see your face again, Bennett. May you rot in hell!'

A couple of RMPs were carrying boxes out to the car and the group watched as Bennett was manhandled out of the door.

Commander Worthing turned to them. 'Good job, everyone. Course is over for the day and I'm heading back to Dover. Can I give anyone a lift?'

Marge glanced at Rodney and nodded. 'We're waiting for my friend, then if you could take four of us, that would be wonderful.' She looked over at the other women. 'Do you mind, girls?'

'Go, for God's sake.' Becky flapped her hands at her. 'But what are we to do about a commanding officer?'

'I will take over just until someone else can be found,' Worthing said. 'Roberts has agreed. I'll be back tomorrow.'

They stood on the doorstep and watched as Bennett was thrust into the back of a car. His shoulders were hunched in defeat, and the sight was glorious to Marge. There was nothing like giving someone their just deserts to put a girl in the mood for some dancing.

A figure coming up the drive on a bicycle caught her eyes. 'Reenie!' She waved as her friend wobbled closer. She was dressed in a pair of khaki slacks, bicycle clips around the hems, her blonde curls covered with a red-spotted scarf.

'What on earth is going on?' Reenie puffed as she got off the bike.

Marge pulled her into a hug. 'Long story! We'll tell you later.'

Reenie disentangled herself and gazed around her in astonishment. 'Rodney?' She grinned and looked between them. But then her eyes fell on Katy, and she frowned. 'K-Katy? Oh my goodness, Katy!' She flew over and hugged her. 'How *are* you? It's been bloody years since we saw you. Are you moving back? How's your husband? Have you left Ireland?'

Katy looked at Marge in bemusement.

'Yes, sadly her husband died and now she's come home.' She grinned at her sister, who smiled uncertainly back.

Finally, she understood why her parents had lied all those years. It wasn't shame, it wasn't denial. It was so that when Katy did return, no one would ever question what she'd been doing.

# Chapter 60

*Pearson's Garage*

It might be Sunday, but news of what had happened at the café had already reached the garage, and Edie felt the familiar ache of longing in her chest. She wanted to go back there to check everyone was well. But at the same time, staying away had become a matter of principle. She was softening ever so slightly, but the thought of her mother still made her want to weep with anger.

Still, she had other things to look forward to today. She'd spent the previous evening and this morning cleaning, and now the little flat was spotless. She looked around the sitting room, with satisfaction. Even her mother would approve.

She batted the thought away impatiently. She didn't care what her mother thought of anything anymore, least of all her housekeeping skills. But she did care what Bill thought, and he'd be here in just a few hours. Her heart skipped with a mixture of anxiety and happiness. She wasn't the same girl he'd left all those months ago after their wedding night. She was a mother, with the soft stomach and stretch marks to show for it. And the bags under the eyes, she thought ruefully, examining her face in the mirror above the fireplace.

She could hear grunting coming from the bedroom and went in. Vivvy was clutching her feet, staring at them as though they were the most wondrous things she'd ever seen. Edie smiled. She estimated she had two minutes to make a cup of tea before her daughter made her presence felt.

Returning to the kitchen she put the kettle on and spooned some leaves into the pot. What would it be like to see Bill again? Would he have changed as much as she had? Would he find her boring now? Well, she'd soon find out. And though her nerves were taut, she couldn't wait to see him.

Reaching into her pocket, she pulled out his last letter and read it again. Her worries were unfounded. Bill loved her and she loved him. And when he returned from war, they would make some brothers and sisters for Vivvy. Just as long as they didn't make any tonight. She shivered in happy anticipation at the thought of the night ahead.

A faint cry came to her, and she hurried back to her bedroom. Vivvy's eyes were open, her hair spun gold around her head, her little mouth opening and closing as she looked for milk. Edie's heart tweaked. How could such a perfect creature have come from her?

'Hey, my little darling.' Edie sat on the bed and picked up her daughter, wrinkling her nose at the sharp tang of urine. 'Change first, my love. Then milk time.'

By the time she'd finished, Vivien was yelling at the top of her lungs, her tiny fists flailing, her cheeks cherry red.

'All right, all right,' Edie soothed, picking up the bottle and putting the teat in her mouth. Like magic the cries stopped, replaced by those little gurgles and gulps that Edie loved so much.

She stared down at her face, marvelling again at her beauty. While she'd been pregnant, she'd loathed the thought of this child, thinking it would remind her of Greg, the Canadian pilot who'd fathered her, and who'd turned out to be a nasty piece of work. But the opposite was true. Her heart had expanded so far that it ached sometimes.

'Edie, telegram for you!' Mr Pearson's urgent voice floated towards her, and suddenly all her contentment drained away.

He knocked on the door and came in, his expression fearful. He'd lost more weight, what little hair he'd had was gone, and dark puffy circles sat beneath his eyes. His usual expression of kind warmth was now replaced with one of stark fear – an expression that she imagined was reflected in her own face.

For a moment, they stared at each other, Mr Pearson holding the telegram towards her, his hand shaking. It was clear from his face that this was not the good sort of telegram. This was the sort that delivered heartbreak and despair.

Edie's grip on Vivien had tightened instinctively and Vivvy spat the teat out and arched her back, letting out a squeal of protest.

But Edie barely noticed. All her attention was focused on that envelope. She looked between it and the man who had become like a father to her. 'I can't,' she whispered.

Mr Pearson's shoulders sagged, and he came to sit beside her on the bed. 'I don't think I can either, love,' he muttered.

He put the telegram on his pyjama-clad knee, and they sat looking at it, the tension building, until finally he snatched it up and tore it open.

Edie watched his face, and the breath caught in her throat as his complexion went even paler. Wordlessly, he handed it to her.

But she didn't need to read it. She knew. If he'd just been missing, then wouldn't Mr P have talked about not giving up hope? While there's no body there's hope, he'd say. Because that was his way: he looked for the best in every situation and every person.

But he said none of that.

Nausea rose to her throat. 'Please don't say it,' she whispered. 'Please don't say it. He's meant to be here in a few hours. He's on a train. He must be . . . He promised. He wanted to meet Vivvy . . . He promised.' She eyed the telegram fearfully. She'd known this moment could come. The survival rate of pilots was shocking and something she'd tried not to think about.

'Oh, love.' Mr Pearson pulled Edie into his arms, and they clung together, her tears soaking into his shoulder, his wetting her hair, while Vivvy, trapped between them, screamed louder – as though she knew that at the tender age of just five months, she'd already lost two fathers.

Edie pulled away and held the baby against her shoulder, rocking back and forth as she patted her back. 'What'll we do?' she asked shakily.

Mr P shrugged. 'What can we do? We'll carry on. You've got a home here for life. You and Vivvy are all I've got left . . .'

Edie's heart contracted. She didn't want to carry on. She wanted to run away and hide. Pretend this had never happened. That her strong, handsome husband would be coming back to her. It was the only reason she'd been able to keep going.

Vivien's cries quietened, and Edie cradled her in her arms, staring down at her rosy little face. Before Bill had left, she'd promised she would continue to help his uncle run the garage, so that when he came home, they could take over the business together. That had been the plan. But what now? Mr Pearson wasn't getting any younger and he wasn't well. Sooner or later he'd have to lay down his tools. How would she be able to carry on alone with Vivvy to care for?

At least they had Louis. The French boy who'd arrived in Dover with Elodie and Colin all those months ago had filled in for her while she'd been in London at the trial, and he was proving to be a quick learner and an able mechanic. But it wasn't enough.

Mr P started to cough and she grabbed the glass of water from her bedside table and tried to give it to him.

He shook his head and reached into his pyjama pocket for his handkerchief, wiping his mouth.

'I think you should see Dr Palmer again,' she said.

'It's just a virus. Should go in time.' Taking the glass, he drained the water and stood up, his shoulders stooped. 'The only thing to do when life looks bleak is to keep busy. But you stay up here with Vivvy for a bit, love.' He rested his hand briefly on Vivien's silky blonde head. 'She'll need you more than ever now.'

When he'd gone, Edie stroked her daughter's hair, pressing a kiss to her cheek. How could Bill be dead? They'd only just begun to explore each other. Now she'd never know what their life might have been like. Or if he really would have loved Vivien as much as he said he would.

Knowing Bill, he would have kept that promise and loved her with all his heart. At the thought of the endless years in front of her, working at the garage with no Bill and nothing to look forward to, the tears started to fall again.

She had her little girl, but what sort of a life would it be? She got up and walked to the window. The shadow of the castle fell across the forecourt. She'd always loved that place, but suddenly its crenelated towers and battlements felt oppressive, and its violent history weighed down on her.

She kissed Vivvy's head. 'Don't worry, my love,' she whispered. 'Mummy will always be here for you.' It was a promise she wasn't sure she could keep, but it was all she had to offer her daughter right now.

# Chapter 61

With a rare Sunday off, Dot lay in bed, wondering what to do. Lily had invited her to Jasper's party, and she was tempted. It would at least take her mind off Bert and that telegram he'd sent, which she spent every spare moment puzzling over.

Was he safe? Was he in this country? The Commandos, that's all she knew. It was nothing to go on, and there was no one to ask.

She would go, she decided. She loved Jasper and she loved Lily, who needed her support right now. She would set aside her animosity against Nellie and maybe try to enjoy herself.

She threw back the covers and dressed carefully in her best skirt and blouse. Her hair had grown recently, and the dark curls were getting out of hand. But Bert said he liked them, so she had decided not to cut it again until he was back with her.

Going downstairs, she saw the landlady had left the newspapers on the hall table. A large headline ran across the top: 'Most Daring Feat of the War! An Epic of British Courage! German Defences Defied'.

Curious, she picked it up and as she read any thoughts of attending the party disappeared:

The raid on St Nazaire will go down to history as an epic of British courage. The most daring and in many ways the most important of combined operational attacks on the enemy so far undertaken has met with splendid success, but the cost has not been light. Many of the Commando troops who forced home the attack fought on until they were either casualties or taken prisoner; but they completed one of the finest aggressive operations we have engaged in since the war started.

Dot's eyes kept going back to the words 'fought on until they were either casualties or taken prisoner'. Is this what Bert had been recruited for? She stumbled up to her room and scrabbled around in her drawer for the telegram.

*Whatever you hear, keep the faith and I will find a way*
*to come back to you. I promise.*
*Bert xx*

Her tears dripped onto the paper, smudging the ink. He must have been with the operation. He'd known how dangerous it was, he'd known she'd think the worst. And he'd sent her this small scrap of hope, which she would cling to until she got news.
Because her husband was a man who kept his promises.

# Chapter 62

In the end, Commander Worthing had been persuaded to have some breakfast before they left, which, Marge noticed, was perfectly cooked. The other men crowded in as well, puffed up with indignation at the captain's crimes.

Marge stood quietly by the wall watching them, a much-needed cigarette in her hand. She was pretty certain that every one of these men would be back at the Rose Rooms, or some-where similar, the moment they got the chance, consciences clear. She blew smoke out on a sigh. Plus ça change.

Rodney came to stand beside her. 'Well, that went pretty well, don't you think?'

She shrugged. 'It gets one dirty pervert off the street, I suppose.'

Katy was safe, Bennett had got what he deserved, so why did she feel so flat?

'You can't change the world, you know,' Rodney said.

She glanced up at him. 'It should never have happened. Katy's lived a lifetime of grief, I lost my sister, my parents lost their daughter . . .' She sighed deeply. 'It all feels so pointless.'

'When this war is over, Marge, you can start a crusade to help women like Katy. I can't think of anyone better. But for now, be happy with this victory.' He smiled gently at her. 'And you know, I'll help you . . .' He hesitated a moment. 'If you want me to?'

She nudged his shoulder. 'I'll always want you, Rodney.'

His face lit up. 'You mean it?'

'Yes, I mean it. Do you?'

'Oh yes. I'd go with you to the ends of the earth . . .'

Marge's breath caught. She'd said that to him once, and from the gleam in his eye he remembered it too.

'You remember that day?' she murmured.

'Of course. Every moment with you is unforgettable.'

'Oy, lovebirds,' Mrs B called. 'The commander's ready to leave.'

'At last!' Rodney smiled ruefully. 'Let's go and see what trouble my family have got themselves into while we've been gone.'

She laughed. 'For once, I'm pretty sure we'll be the ones with a tale to tell.'

The other officers retreated into the drawing room until transport could be arranged, but Marge had no wish to say goodbye to them. All men were the same as far as she could tell. Rodney put an arm around her, and she leaned into him.

Apart from her Rodders, of course.

After kisses for the girls, and a strong hug for Mrs B, the four of them piled into the car. Rodney sat in the front with the commander, while the three women sat in the back, hands clasped.

It didn't take long to get to Market Square but as they pulled up by the café, Rodney cursed. Two men were busily boarding up the café's window – the one that was meant to be bomb- and shell-proof. Briefly Marge's eyes met Rodney's in the rear-view mirror.

'I should have known. The Castles are unmatched when it comes to drama,' she muttered.

But Rodney was already out of the car and hurrying into the café before she could even open her door. It was a sharp reminder that not everything had changed. He would always be at the beck and call of his family, whether she liked it or not. But at least it was love that drove him, and if they ever had a family of their own, she knew she would always be able to count on him. Just as he could count on her.

It was gone ten o'clock and the impromptu pyjama party was still going strong. Earlier in the morning, Donny and Fred had been sent to fetch Mavis and Derek from the Royal Oak, and Ethel and Phyllis had left briefly to collect the supplies they'd been saving for Jasper's birthday.

Now, Don and Fred were handing round sandwiches, hastily made by Elodie, and Teddy was sitting on Adelaide Frost's knee, clapping his hands in delight as Cissy, still in her daisy-print nightdress, played 'When the Saints go Marching In' at Adelaide's request. Muriel Palmer – appropriately dressed, of course – sat with her, while Dr Palmer sat with the men.

Mr Wainwright stood beside Cissy, his eyes never leaving her face, his pudgy cheeks flushed with excitement while his foot tapped out the beat.

Marianne was in the kitchen, chopping vegetables for a quick soup, and the kitchen was heady with the scent of the bread rolls she'd made. And, in pride of place, was Jasper's birthday cake. Marianne had piped little horseshoes on it – a nod to Jasper's forge – and made a cupcake into the shape of a helmet, which she'd covered with black icing, piping a white W on the front of it.

Nellie took it all in, her heart full. She'd taken five minutes to go upstairs and change into a green rose-patterned dress.

Her hair was beyond redemption, so she'd plonked her orange turban on, and swiped some of Cissy's bright red lipstick over her lips. No one else seemed bothered that they were still in their nightclothes; if anything, it added to the celebratory atmosphere.

Jasper was sitting with a group of men – and Lou – holding forth on the events of the evening. Lily sat with Ethel, Mavis and Phyllis. Mavis had already cracked open a bottle of champagne and the strained look that had been hovering in Nellie's daughter's eyes recently had dissipated.

This wasn't quite how she'd envisaged today, but it would do. All she needed now were her other children. If they could walk through that door, she would never ask for anything again. She sent a silent plea to Edie. 'Please come back, love. Please.'

The door burst open and Rodney strode in, his eyes frantic, then puzzled, as he looked around.

Nellie started to laugh. It wasn't Edie, but she was grateful all the same.

'Mum!' His gaze landed on her. 'What's happened? Why are you all in your pyjamas?'

The room erupted into laughter. But then the door opened again, and Ethel let out a shriek of joy. 'Reenie!' She got up and barrelled towards her, her nightdress flying out behind her, the net over her curlers slightly askew.

'Aunt Ethel? Why aren't you dressed?' But Reenie's words were muffled as her aunt clasped her to her shoulder.

Behind her came Marge, who stood beside Rodney and took his hand. About bloody time, too, Nellie thought with an inward smile. And behind her . . . Nellie's breath caught. She looked between Marge and Katy. How many years had it been since she'd seen those two redheads together? She'd always suspected something wasn't quite right about the story old Captain and Mrs Atkinson had spread around, but what did it matter? She was back where she belonged.

She bustled forward. 'Katy? Oh, love, it's so good to see you again!' She took her hands and smiled up at her. It did a woman's heart good to welcome back one of their own.

'Katy!' Hearing the commotion, Marianne had come into the café. She hurried over and threw her arms around her. Katy's cheeks were wet with tears. 'Hello, Mrs C,' she said. 'Marianne.' Then she looked around at everyone else.

'Welcome home, Katy,' Adelaide Frost said with a smile. 'Glory be! A daughter has returned to us.'

'What is all this?' Rodney cast his eyes over the group, his hand still gripping Marge's.

'It's Jasper's birthday. We thought we'd have a party.' Nellie grinned.

'What happened to the window?'

Nellie waved her hand dismissively. 'A friend decided to help me get rid. But no more questions, Rod. Get some food and have some fun.'

The window was completely boarded up now and the two men who'd done it came inside. 'Boss says we should be able to fit a new winder next week. No charge.'

Nellie smiled. Peter Holmes had left promising to make sure the repairs were carried out quickly and free of charge. She was sure there were easier ways to get a free window, but she'd take what she could get.

Jasper looked over to her and smiled, and suddenly she wanted to be in his arms. But would he welcome it?

She turned to her cousin. 'Ciss, play "My Bonnie Lies Over the Ocean".' It was the song she'd kissed Jasper to last year, and she hoped it would bring back those memories for him.

Cissy smiled knowingly and started to play.

Jasper excused himself and came over. 'How are you feelin', love?'

Nellie shrugged. 'Not too bad, all things considered.' She hesitated a moment. 'I've got somethin' for you, if you want to come with me.'

Jasper nodded and followed her up the stairs, the sound of joyful singing muffling their footsteps.

While Jasper sat in his usual chair by the fireplace, she went into her bedroom and retrieved the package.

'It's just a small thing,' she lied, handing it to him.

She watched nervously as Jasper pulled the paper apart, revealing a small box with gold letters. Opening it, he plucked the silver ring out of its cushioned bed. He looked up at her, eyebrows raised.

'A ring, Nellie? What's this all about?'

Nellie flushed. 'It's not a proposal, Jasper.' Or was it?

He was silent for a moment, and Nellie felt a flicker of uncertainty. She'd known it was a mistake! A ring of all things! Of course he'd get the wrong end of the stick.

Jasper held it up to the light. Around the outside, in cursive script, was his name and date of birth. 'It's really lovely, Nellie. I ain't never had a ring.' He slipped it onto the fourth finger of his right hand, and she was gratified to see it fit perfectly. She'd ordered the largest size, but even then she hadn't been sure.

'Thank you, love,' he said gruffly.

When he didn't seem inclined to say more, she slapped her hands on the arms of the chair and stood up. 'Right, then. We should, er . . . get back to it.'

Through the floor, they could hear their friends and neighbours singing. 'So bring back my Bonnie to me.'

If only she could bring those feelings back in him, she thought. This had been a horrible, embarrassing mistake.

Jasper stood too and took her hands. 'You, Nellie Castle, are the most infuriatin' and obstinate woman I've ever met. But somehow, no matter what, you worm your way right back in . . .' He stopped and looked away.

Nellie held her breath as she watched his face. This was a good sign, wasn't it?

'Oh, who am I foolin'! No matter what you do, I can never get rid of yer.' He thumped his chest. 'Cos you live right here, Nell. An' I can't see that'll ever change.'

Tears sprang to her eyes, even as her lips curved into a smile. That was love, though, wasn't it? It hurt you and delighted you in equal measure.

As the last bars of the song faded away, and cheers and whistles erupted downstairs, Nellie reached up, took Jasper's face in her hands and kissed him.

# Acknowledgements

I am lucky to have so many people who support me – both professionally and personally. As always, a huge thank you to my agent, Teresa Chris, who is endlessly encouraging and supportive. Thank you for everything.

To my editor Claire Johnson-Creek and the team at Bonnier. I deliver late every single year, and every year you pull it out of the bag. I owe you both my apologies and my thanks.

To my wonderful mother and brilliant sister, Ali. I dedicated this one to you, Ali, because you are fabulous: always patient and kind despite me wailing down the phone at you.

To Tanita and Natacha. Two inspiring creatives whom I love unreservedly and forever.

To the three most important people in the world: Maddie, Sim and Olly. Still making me laugh. Still making my heart burst with love and pride.

To the Minuty who are always up for fun and laughter.

And finally to my colleagues at The Novelry. Never have I worked with such a talented and inspiring bunch of people. I've learned so much from all of you – authors and editors alike. Not least the art of persevering when it seems impossible that the book will ever be finished.

# Author's Note

Thank you everyone for reading *Secrets at the Dover Café*. As many of you will know, I try to use real events that happened in the war, and try as far as possible to keep to the actual timeline of events.

I am sorry to admit that for this book, I have played a bit fast and loose with the timings. I have already explained about The Game in the front of the book, but the raid on St Nazaire didn't take place until March 1942. I won't go into details about it, but suffice to say, it is a legendary and fascinating story that marked one of the early turning points in the war. The casualties, however, were horrific. The sacrifice of everyone who fought in this war breaks my heart.

I should also say that the forgery storyline is completely made up. It came to me when I read a tiny little piece in an old newspaper about boxes of stolen ration books being discovered in the basement of someone's house. The estimated value for them was about £100,000. Which is about £5 million in today's money.

Then I read about one of the factories that printed ration books being bombed in the Blitz, and I put these two events together and Johnny Fox and his dastardly forging business was born.

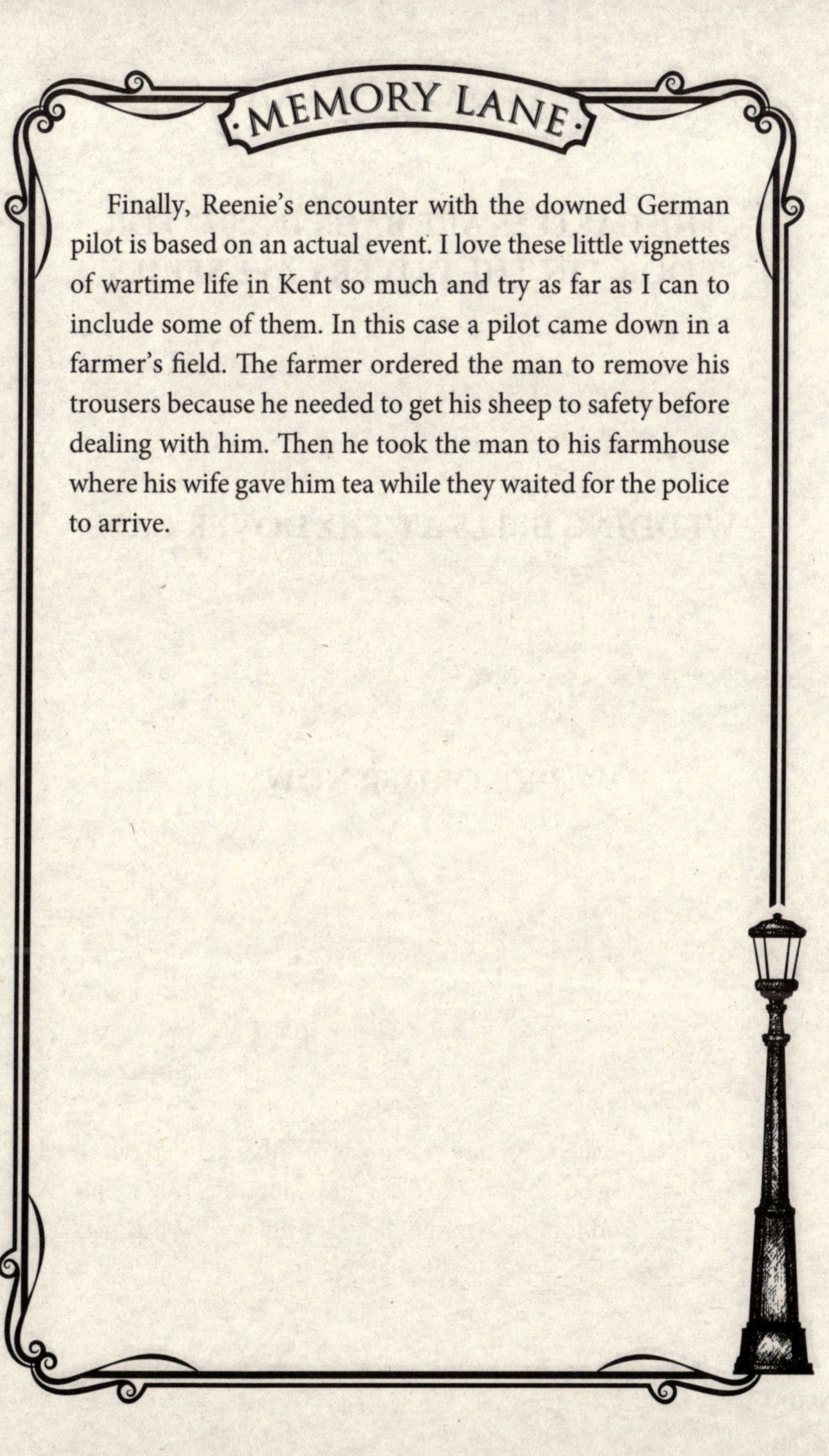



Finally, Reenie's encounter with the downed German pilot is based on an actual event. I love these little vignettes of wartime life in Kent so much and try as far as I can to include some of them. In this case a pilot came down in a farmer's field. The farmer ordered the man to remove his trousers because he needed to get his sheep to safety before dealing with him. Then he took the man to his farmhouse where his wife gave him tea while they waited for the police to arrive.

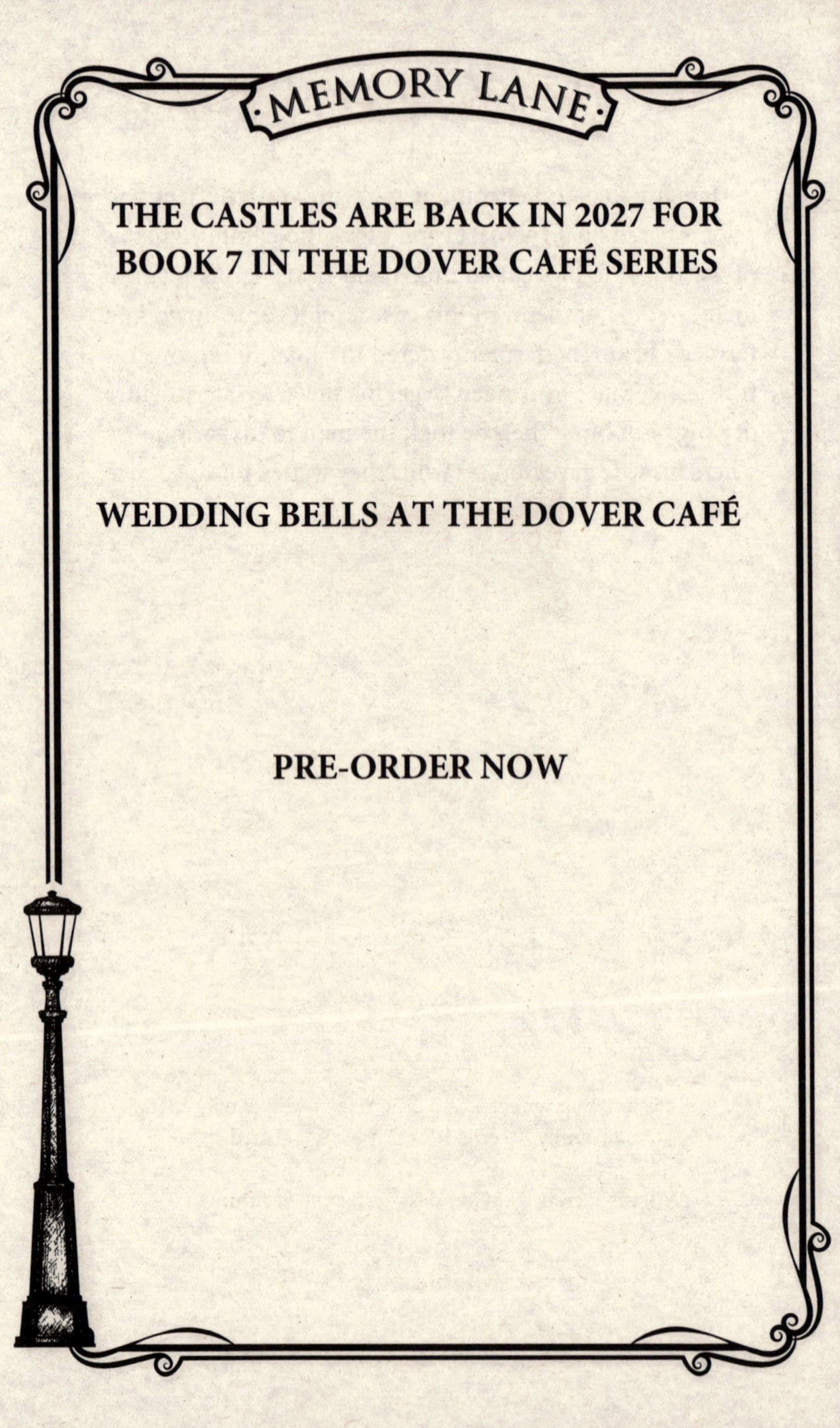

· MEMORY LANE ·

THE CASTLES ARE BACK IN 2027 FOR
BOOK 7 IN THE DOVER CAFÉ SERIES

WEDDING BELLS AT THE DOVER CAFÉ

PRE-ORDER NOW

**_Dover, 1940_**

With the Battle of Britain raging overhead and German guns firing across the Channel, the people of Dover suddenly find themselves on the front line. But despite the danger, Nellie Castle is determined to keep the café open, no matter what.

For Nellie's daughter, Lily, it is an exciting time as she starts her nursing career. The work is demanding, but with romance on the horizon, she still finds time to enjoy herself. That is until a prisoner escapes from the hospital and everything she holds dear – including her freedom – is put at risk.

Meanwhile there are strange goings-on at the café: rumours are circulating and long-buried secrets are surfacing. Secrets that could tear the Castle family apart once and for all . . .

**Available now**

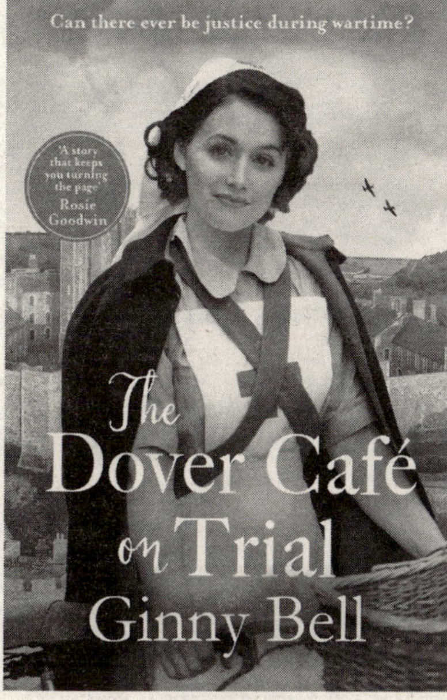


**Dover, May, 1941**

It's been a difficult few months for Nellie Castle, but at last the café is getting back on its feet. And with Marianne's baby due soon, there is much to look forward to.

Meanwhile, Bert Castle is recovering from the injuries he sustained during an enemy attack. And though he is plagued with nightmares, at least one good thing has come out of the incident: his friendship with nurse Dot Calloway.

But when Nellie, Bert and his sister Edie are summoned to give evidence at the trial of the woman who who shot Nellie's best friend, Gladys, they soon realise that Susan Blake will not be the only one on trial . . .

**Available now**

**Loved this book?**
**Join the Memory Lane Community**

A welcoming home for all readers who love
heart-warming tales of family, romance and
history.

Sign up to our newsletter via the QR code
below for book recommendations, giveaways,
deals and behind-the-scenes writing moments
from your favourite authors.

https://geni.us/memory-lane

Or you can also join the conversation in the
Memory Lane Facebook Group.